WHAT OTH

Vanessa Rasanen's honest portrayal of Christians struggling with doubt, painful pasts, and unresolved sin is a breath of fresh air. She truthfully and realistically chronicles the ups and downs of the baptized life as the assaults of sin, the world, and the devil threaten Meg's faith and her marriage to Charlie. Set against the backdrop of military deployment, Vanessa's story touches on hard realities and the ways in which God's Word brings healing. With humor and honesty, she creates winsome and real characters while addressing deep theological truths. Grab a cup of tea (or Meg's favorite beverage: coffee), curl up, and enjoy!

—Elizabeth Ahlman, Author of *Demystifying the Proverbs 31 Woman*

Rasanen pulls you into the lives of her characters with such a gritty realism that their hopes and fears, pains and triumphs become your own. Her beautiful storytelling will certainly touch hearts.

—Sarah Baughman, Author of *A Flame in the Darkness*

I really loved Soldier On, because it describes the very real struggle many Christians have with the Old Adam. Mrs. Rasanen does a phenomenal job portraying life as one on pilgrimage, wandering in a broken world, waiting for our King's return.

—Chloe Fisk, 13-year-old avid reader and daughter of author Rev. Jonathan Fisk

This gripping story will reshape prayers for military families. It explores anxieties and doubts that Christians can feel, especially after months of lost control and uncertainty. Vanessa Rasanen is a needed voice in contemporary Christian novels, as she combines realism with God's mercy and the gifts of the church, in particular by recognizing pain after prayer and doubt within faith. This is an enjoyable, satisfying, and cathartic book with a surprising number of laughs.

—Mary J. Moerbe, Deaconess and Author

Far more than a fictional emittance born from obvious familiarity, Vanessa Rasanen tells an important story, one that artfully captures and then sets the reader at the edge of a human darkness that many know but few understand. And yet, even as she does this, there is hope. The light of Christ and the Gospel of His hard-fought fight for our forgiveness is the constant wellspring for new life that streams throughout. Rasanen knows this Gospel well, and she takes great care to reveal its power for muscling through fear, regret, despair, and doubt—and not just any doubt, but rather the most dreadful kind—the kind that teeters at the cliff of unbelief. *Soldier On* is high drama stationed at the foot of the cross. It will serve any reader's heart very well.

—Reverend Christopher I. Thoma

Vanessa beautifully articulates the raw (and often ugly) emotions military families experience during deployment. Meg and Piper feel like close friends, now—solidarity sisters who know how to turn you to Christ and remind you of His grace, peace, and forgiveness when you feel alone, undeserving, and desperate for hope in seemingly insurmountable circumstances.

—Courtney Woodruff, mil spouse blogger, freelance writer, and web content strategist

SOLDIER ON

HEARTS ON GUARD BOOK 1

VANESSA RASANEN

To
Michelle
Vanessa Rasanen

ISBN 978-1-7327652-0-7

Crab Apple Books
P.O. Box 21034
Cheyenne, WY 82003
crabapplebooks.com

For my husband,
who daily teaches me
what it means
to serve.

In memory of
Captain Bruce Hays,
killed in action
September 17, 2008
Afghanistan

1

Meg Winters gnawed on the tip of her thumbnail, her petite frame huddling over the yellow paper as she reread the items. Tapping her pen at each line, she paused only to tuck her hair behind her ear each time it fell loose against the page.

For the past week she had been building this list, adding words whenever she passed the counter. The meticulous and careful undertaking had become a rushed chore in these final days, which was evidenced by the gradual shift in her writing as the pristine script gave way to a more haphazard hand with sporadic cursive letters popping up throughout the printed words.

"Okay, I think that's everything," she said, straightening up and stretching out the stiffness in her neck.

Charlie came up behind her, his hand settling on her hip as he glanced over her shoulder. He reviewed her work and nodded, but his blank expression gave no indication of his approval. His chin, square and strong, still showed the two-day start of his beard, a stark contrast to the rest of his hair that had been trimmed into a short crop that morning.

She would miss his beard, even the prickly growing-in stage

that poked her nose when he kissed her. Tomorrow it would be gone.

"What's this one, here?" His finger stopped about five lines down at a particularly messy scrawl of words.

"Don't let the plants die. Pretty self-explanatory, I think." She pulled the edge of her mouth into a half-smile, hoping he would appreciate her attempt at adding humor to the tedious and somber task at hand.

"You could've just written *water plants.*" He raised an eyebrow at her. His gray eyes always seemed to flash when he made that expression.

She poked him in the ribs with her elbow. "I think the drowned bush out front would beg to differ." His first, and probably last, gardening failure had given her only one chance to return all the teasing he dished out, and she had every intention of doing just that for as long as she could.

"That bush isn't dead." Charlie shrugged. She narrowed her eyes at him, wondering how he could possibly defend that sad mound of twisted brown beside their porch. "It's resting."

"It's a bush, not a bear. It can't hibernate!" She tried to match the seriousness on his face but failed.

"Says you."

"Maybe I'll just take out all the flowers and replace them with bamboo. That stuff is unkillable, right, plant whisperer?"

"That's Mr. Plant Whisperer to you. And you mean like your bamboo over there?" Charlie leaned back and pointed to a blue-and-white porcelain pot that contained the dry remains of a once flourishing pair of bamboo stalks. Meg had bought it on a whim last summer in hopes of adding some low-maintenance greenery to the kitchen window. To her dismay, the green had only lasted a few months, and for the last week she had been meaning to give it a proper memorial service before pitching it in the trash.

"Touché." She directed his attention back to her list. "But what about the rest? Did I miss anything?"

He obliged, dropping the matter of dead plants, and reviewed the paper again. "Okay, I know you can mow the lawn—assuming it doesn't die."

"Har, har, har."

"We've gone over all the regular house maintenance, and you've changed the oil in the Jeep plenty of times. But this?" He pointed to another line. "I wish I could be here to see you tackle that again. Remember the last time you did it on your own?"

She crinkled her brow at him, but she knew the twitch at the corner of her mouth betrayed her offense for the show it was. Despite her resolve to defend her honor, she couldn't deny this any more than the dead bamboo mocking her in the corner. "We can't all be expert mattress flippers, you know."

Charlie wrapped his arms around her waist, planting a kiss on her forehead before tickling her freckled cheek with his whiskers. "I love you. Even if you kill every plant and somehow manage to trap yourself under the bed."

"I'm just being a good wife and helping you feel needed around here." She shrugged and gave him a smile before pulling him closer and laying her head on his chest. She breathed in the scent of his shirt. It had not gone unnoticed that he had chosen to wear his expensive cologne every day that week. She buried her head in him, wanting to get lost there—in his smell and all the memories that came with it. First dates. First kisses. Vacations and proposals.

She mumbled, not caring if he could hear or not, "I'm not ready."

Pulling her tighter, he kissed her hair. Every muscle ached to remain there nestled against him, but so much was left to be done. Her shoulders slumped. As if reading her thoughts, Charlie took the initiative, and with quick hands he released his wife and gave her sides a gentle squeeze until she fell into him in a fit of giggles, snorts, and "no mores."

Meg ran her hand along the smooth edge of the dining room table. She couldn't say what type of wood it was, who had made it, or whether the wood—with all its knots and nooks and cracks—had once been a barn or a bridge or something else. She only knew she loved it. She'd spotted it at an antique shop along a two-lane highway on one of their weekend trips to the mountains and had swooned. Over a table. Ridiculous, perhaps, but there was something about the history in its veins and the spots that were worn smooth, not by machine or sandpaper but by life.

She hadn't insisted on buying it and had done her best not to let her growing attachment to it show. This little antique shop couldn't ship such an item, and there had been no way to fit such a large piece into the back of or onto the top of their Jeep. Yet there it sat the morning of their first anniversary, nestled into their dining room, as if it had found its true home among their mismatched chairs, its grooves and lines pairing nicely with those in the floor.

But nothing here felt like home anymore. Paper, envelopes, and folders were strewn across the dining room table. She leaned into Charlie, seated beside her, as close as their chairs would allow. While he shoveled through the mounds of paperwork, she got lost in the view outside the picture window and the pine trees beyond it that circled the house, guarding it.

Guarding it from what? Wind? People? Life? That was laughable.

Charlie cleared his throat, pulling her away from the scene outside. He raised a thick stack of pages, the staple barely holding it all together, and a large manila envelope marked "POA."

Snatching it from him, she mumbled, "Like it does any good anyway." Not bothering to tuck the pages inside first, she dropped it all onto the edge of the table with a thud.

He sighed. "You know it's better to have it—even if people don't know how it works—than to not have it..."

"...when I really need it," she said, finishing his sentence. "Yeah, I guess. You'd think such a standard legal document wouldn't be so difficult for some people. I still can't believe the bank wouldn't let me close that account."

Charlie ignored her complaints and handed her another set of pages. "I put the contact info for both the FRG and the unit on the top sheet, along with names and numbers of some offices you might need—finance, JAG, DEERS, Tricare. I know you can google 'em but figured it was best to have it all in one place. The next page has plumbers, mechanics—"

Meg interrupted him with an annoyed huff through clenched teeth. "I've done this before, Charlie. Remember? I know I kill all the plants, but I'm not clueless. I'm not some dumb blonde bimbo you dated back in the day. I can find a stupid mechanic when the car breaks down, and I know how to deal with DFAS when your pay gets screwed up—as it probably will." She stood up from her chair and growled with frustration when its legs caught on the carpet, hindering her dramatic departure.

Charlie lowered the papers and let his chin fall. "Wait," he started.

She braced herself for his rebuke for overreacting. Over the past week it had become routine, both of them losing their cool over minor infractions. Five days ago the number of dirty dishes in the sink had led to an argument. Then it had been the stack of clean laundry left unfolded on the bed. Yesterday had found them stewing in a mutual silent treatment after Meg stubbed her toe on a pair of Charlie's boots only to throw them right into his shins when he came around the corner to investigate her screams.

But now when his gaze met hers, she did not find the resentment she expected.

"I know you know, Meg." He sighed again. "I should've done this all earlier and not put it off till now. I'm just trying to make this easier for you while I'm gone, but I don't think you're clueless. I know you can take care of yourself. Just—"

Meg's groan cut him off, but her anger had fled as quickly as it had come on. Her shoulders slumped, and her face dropped, her eyes tearing up. "I hate this. I feel like a crazy person. We've been planning and preparing for months, and I'm done. Done!"

Charlie grabbed her hand as he pushed his chair back. She let him settle her onto his lap. "I just want to get it over with already!" Leaning his forehead against hers, he kissed the tip of her nose. No list of contacts, no legal documents, and no number of checklists could really ease the situation. No amount of preparation, no matter how logical or reasonable, could guarantee she would not struggle during his absence.

Meg wrapped herself around him, pulling her legs up onto his. Should they be praying instead of merely sitting? What did other couples do the day before? What had she done leading up to previous deployments? Even if her mind hadn't already tucked away all those memories, they wouldn't have done her any good. She was a different person now. They both were.

There would be no ceremony today. No speeches. No crowds or news cameras. Those had all been reserved for the official farewell sixty-eight days ago—not that Meg would ever let Charlie know she had been counting. She couldn't have helped it anyway. For sixty-one days, after all the speeches and pictures, she had waited at home while he had trained four states away. For the past seven days he had been home with her—one final taste of normalcy.

But this was day sixty-eight, and it wasn't normal.

I can't do this again. I can't. I won't.

I have to.

Her mind raced. She shook her head at the night sky, or what she could see of it over the tops of the trees. Dawn was still a couple of hours away at least. Even the birds hadn't started their morning songs. Elbows on her knees, she wrung her hands, unable to keep still due to her shaken nerves.

The last time had nearly broken her, and she wasn't even the one over there fighting and facing the enemy. Lips pursed, she struggled against the dread rising in her gut. She had known what she was getting into when she married him, hadn't she? People always reminded her of that, as if that truth made the danger and the worry and the separation any easier to endure. People were idiots.

So was she.

She shouldn't be here, sitting on the front step, her soul screaming into the heavens for help and peace. She should be inside, nestled beside him, soaking up every last second with him.

What if he didn't come back this time? What if this was it? A tear slid down her cheek. *God, please. Bring him home. Protect him. Protect—*

A hand on her shoulder interrupted her prayer, and she settled into it, every muscle relaxing under his touch. "I know you're a morning person an' all, but, babe, three a.m. is a little early even for you," Charlie said, his voice hinting at what little sleep he had gotten.

She turned to face him and opened her mouth to explain, but she had no words as she lost herself in the stormy ocean of his eyes glinting in the light of the lamppost beside their walkway. Her hand itched to touch him, to run her fingers over his hair—that familiar color of wet sand with the same texture of the beach where they'd honeymooned in Puerto Rico.

When would she stop reacting to him as if she were a clumsy teen who had just gotten asked to prom by the star quarterback?

She could almost smell the ocean when she looked at him, nearly hear the roll of gentle waves mixing with his laughter. Almost. The smell of pine trees and coffee engulfed her, pulled her back to reality. They didn't carry their usual comfort this morning, only reminded her of where she was and what was about to happen.

She gave him a shrug before turning back to the view in front of their house, her gaze trailing the stone pathway he'd laid last summer to the gravel driveway, which wound down the hill before disappearing into the trees. She expected him to say something, tease her in his usual way, but instead he settled in beside her in silence.

How he could be so calm was beyond her understanding. Except it wasn't.

This was Charlie, the epitome of cool under pressure. Nothing ever seemed to get to him. It was what made him so good at his job, or he was good at hiding his feelings. She chuckled at the thought.

"What's so funny?" Charlie turned to her, a half-smile creeping across his face.

"Just thinking about how cool you are," she said, her eyes searching his for any hint that he shared—or at least sensed—the worry she couldn't shake.

"That's not funny at all. That's just fact," he said.

"Well, you know me. I'm not the funny one."

He nodded. "This is true. I hoped your humor would start to improve under my tutelage."

"Maybe you're just a bad teacher," she said, her brows raised.

She waited for some witty response to meet her challenge, but his mouth closed, his eyes softening as they swept over her. She grabbed his hand and raised it to her cheek, and their gazes locked. A sob threatened to rise out of her. Her lip quivered, but his thumb swept over it to ease away her pain and fear. His hand slid along her neck and brushed her hair behind her as he pulled her into the familiar spot under his shoulder. Her spot.

"It will all be okay," he said, but his voice lacked his usual confidence. He seemed as worried and nervous as she felt.

"How do you know?" she whispered, the tears brimming. She anticipated his response, confident and comforting, wise and trusting. When he remained silent, she stole a glance up at him. The calm was gone, replaced by a tension in his jaw and a storm brewing in his eyes.

If her rock of a husband was crumbling—even a bit—she knew she was right. She couldn't do this again.

Yet she had to. She had no choice.

Get it together, man.

Charlie forced his face under the water streaming down from the showerhead. It was too hot, but he ignored it. Maybe it could wash away the uncertainty and dread he felt invading every part of him.

She needed him to be strong, and he couldn't bear the thought of failing her. They'd lived this life for so long, but this time was different. The last time had wrecked her, as it would have done to anyone under the circumstances. But she had survived, thrived even. She had been dragged through hell and had come back stronger than ever.

He ran his hands over his face and through his hair. Yes, she would be okay. They would be fine. He would do everything in his power to make that happen.

God, keep her. Please.

He stepped out of the shower and reached for his towel, but the bathroom door inched open. Her head peeked around it. He caught her eyes trail down his body before rising to meet his gaze.

"Like what you see?" He grinned at her as he continued to towel off.

"You know it." A smile burst across her face before she giggled.

That smile. That sound. She was his whole world, his everything. After all these years, she still had such an effect on him, turning his insides into mush, threatening to break every inch of his resolve. No woman had ever messed him up the way she did, though plenty had tried.

Every morning he expected to wake and find his attraction had faded. Wasn't that what happened to old married couples? Didn't they stop feeling that yearning after a while? Yet, here she was, in one of his T-shirts, no makeup, her eyes still showing the signs of her sleepless and tear-filled night, and he could barely breathe. His heart thumped inside his chest as he willed his legs to stay rooted in place.

They had places to be after all.

"You know," he said, stealing a glance at the clock on the wall, "we have some time..." He winked, waiting for her to throw something at him or otherwise turn down his ridiculous attempt to entice her back into bed.

"Well, coffee is ready, and I was just about to make breakfast." Her gaze fell to the floor, her hand still on the door. Of course she wouldn't indulge him; they didn't actually have that much extra time before they needed to head out.

He turned around to hang the towel back on his hook, but before he could reach for his clothes, her hands were on his back, her fingers tracing the scars from his reckless youth. He wanted to turn, to take her up in his arms and love her with every part of him, but he waited, let himself melt under her touch, afraid any movement might scare her away.

Her lips grazed the spot between his shoulder blades, as they had so many times before, and he felt the warmth of her body inching closer to his. His eyes closed. Man, he'd miss this. Miss her.

When he finally faced her, he expected to see the sadness that had settled in her face for the past week that she had tried to cover up with smiles and bad jokes. But her eyes held none of that fear or worry, only passion.

I don't deserve this woman!

Lord knew he had made mistakes, even with her. Especially with her. But here he was, with the wife of his dreams, and he wasn't going to take her for granted. He saw her bite her bottom lip ever so slightly, and with that, he had her off the ground and into their bed, their lips meeting with an urgency, a desperation that only came when a separation loomed.

They had time. For this, for love, they would make time.

The familiar sound of ripping Velcro and rustling fabric echoed from their bedroom as Meg stepped out of the shower. She cringed and was glad her view was blocked by the bathroom door. She had already made the mistake of stealing a glance at him earlier when he was shaving. That razor. She hated the thing. Each stroke of its blades against his face felt like a slap to her own, a painful reminder that he was leaving and that when she looked in the mirror again this evening, she'd be alone. No, she didn't dare watch him don his uniform and risk undoing all the morning's efforts to pull herself together.

The day's outfit, tossed on the edge of the tub, had been selected weeks prior, though she had hidden that fact from Charlie, not wanting him to know how preoccupied she was with each detail. It was nothing special really—some faded jeans that had finally, after so many years, been worn and laundered enough to be deemed perfectly broken in, paired with a simple dark brown T-shirt, soft and fitted. They might have seemed like afterthought articles to all who saw her that day, but they were Charlie's favorites—and hers—carrying memories of their past adventures, joys, and even heartaches. Years ago, Charlie had noted, probably only in passing, how the shade of this shirt brought out tinges of orange and auburn in her normally green eyes, almost as if by magic. That comment had stuck with her all this time.

Her makeup she kept simple, more due to time than anything else, as the shower had taken longer than expected. It was her hair she wanted to focus on this morning anyway. With her towel back on its hook, she stood staring at the wet and stringy mess of waves atop her head and made a face at her reflection, eyes wild and tongue out. Perhaps a bit of silliness would make this all easier to handle. But the angst in her heart wouldn't be placated, no matter her efforts, and she resigned herself to simply getting through this day, angst and all—preferably without her hair looking like a bird's nest.

With her dryer and curling iron at the ready, she went to work primping, combing, curling, bouncing, fluffing, and nearly burning herself several times along the way. The whole endeavor took twice as long as she had hoped, but she had achieved the perfect "last image" for her husband to carry with him on the plane. Her hair now neatly fell in perfectly smoothed, yet still soft, curls around her face and shoulders. She smiled at her reflection as if to reassure the woman on the other side of the glass that all would work out and be okay. She nearly believed it.

From the hallway she snuck a glance into the kitchen. At the stove with his back to her, Charlie stood perfectly straight and confident as though the bacon and eggs he cooked demanded such a stance. On light feet, she stepped across the hallway and into the living room, careful to avoid the spots on the old floor that creaked with the slightest bit of weight. His bag sat beside the front door, and from the front pouch she pulled out his worn copy of *Luther's Small Catechism*.

Had she planned this better, she would have chosen an appropriate page, the perfect placement, but there had been no time for that now. Using her best super-spy moves, she checked over her shoulder before stuffing the envelope inside the front cover and returning the book. The zipper gave her away, with its teeth sliding together more loudly than she had hoped, and she winced. Some secret agent she turned out to be.

"Babe? Breakfast is ready." She jumped at the sound of his voice, sure she was caught red-handed, but she turned to find he was still in the kitchen. With a sigh, she stood and smoothed her shirt down. A peek at herself in the entryway mirror confirmed she had been successful in her covert op without disrupting a single curl.

"Babe?" he called again.

"Hey." She turned the corner and pulled her chair out from the table. Her plate smiled back at her with two fried eggs for eyes and a bacon smile. She smiled back, thankful for her husband's attempt to make their last morning together more bearable.

Charlie gave her cheek a kiss before sitting at his own spot.

"You look nice today," he said with an easy smile. His words were simple but loving and genuine, more than she needed to make the morning's primping worthwhile.

"Thanks. You too. You always did look good in uniform." Meg shoved a bacon slice in her mouth. "How'd you sleep?"

Charlie looked up from his coffee with a quizzical look.

"Oh, right. Three a.m. My bad. At least I made it up to you this morning, eh?"

"True enough. Consider your debt paid in full."

They finished their meal in silence, cleaned their dishes, cleared the table, and wiped down the counters—their last moments of daily life together spent with an unease that plagued the air around them but not between them. Their usual jabs and teases were soon traded for a tender brush of an arm and the calming stroke of a thumb against a back of a hand while fingers lay intertwined. Though the minutes seemed to crawl, dragging out the inevitable, the hours raced by, and soon it was time to go.

The drive to the armory took forever. Meg agonized at each red light, sure the city had plotted against her, planning this as some special torture to prolong her pain, but it didn't compare to the pangs in her gut upon pulling into the parking lot. It was soon full of families bidding their loved ones goodbye. Tearful mothers hugged their uniformed sons while fathers looked on. Children clung to their daddies with noses buried against freshly shaved faces. Wives held babies or grasped pregnant bellies while husbands reached out to caress them for a final time.

Then Charlie moved, and everyone else disappeared from Meg's view.

For all her talk about wanting to get it over with, Meg couldn't budge, her limbs weighed down by fear and worry. Sixty-eight days she had counted. Three months they had planned and anticipated. But now she wasn't ready. Charlie came around to open her door, and she forced her reluctant muscles to work.

With the door to the Jeep hanging open, she flung her arms around his neck and held tight. She could neither speak nor look at him. She could only hold him. Charlie held her head in his hands, his fingers getting lost in her hair, and he kissed her forehead again and again.

"I love you, Meg. You've got this." He moved her head to look into her eyes, but she kept them hidden behind clenched lids as tears began to pool at the corners. "Look at me, babe."

When she finally opened her eyes, she found him beaming at her with such strength—almost a hint of excitement—that she felt her confidence growing in turn. She breathed deeply.

"I love you." It wasn't enough, but her mind blanked on what else to say. Everything that came to mind felt wrong and out of place for such an occasion, but the silence made her anxiety worse.

"I'm doing this all wrong, Charlie!" Her eyes grew wide with panic. "I'm ruining this because I have no idea what to say. I don't know how to say goodbye! When you look back at this moment, you'll only remember your crazy wife fumbling over her words like an idiot…"

He cupped her chin in both hands and smiled down at her. "Meg, that's how I'll always remember you—regardless of how today went. It's part of your charm. Plus, I don't think there's a right way to do any of this."

"But there's a *wrong* way! And I've already broken the rule." Meg frowned at him, sure he'd caught her mistake in her rambling.

"What rule is that exactly?"

"I said *goodbye*! You're not supposed to say goodbye. You're supposed to say, 'See you later' or something, you know, less permanent than goodbye. Goodbye is bad. They all say so!" Her nerves took over and made her rambling worse, but she couldn't keep the words from falling out freely.

"They who? Screw 'they'! *They* aren't us, Meg. I don't care if you say goodbye or see ya or *ciao* or whatever. As long as the words don't come with a divorce notice or death certificate, I know it's not permanent. It's fine."

"Charlie! You can't say the D-words," Meg playfully scolded, her nerves beginning to relax.

He smiled at her. "D-words? What about donut? Or dingo? Can I say dinglehopper?"

"Shush! They'll hear you." Meg had to fight the giggles now as Charlie looked around suspiciously.

"Good thing I'm not afraid of a little…danger," he joked.

"You're such a doofus," Meg teased him, thankful for the lighthearted turn in their conversation, no matter how temporary.

Charlie kissed her nose. "One last thing." He pulled his wedding band from his finger and strung it onto the chain around her neck, letting it fall against the silver crucifix she always wore. "Hold this for me until I get back."

"As always," she said. The carefree moment was gone, but so were her tears. She stole a glance around to find the crowd thinning as soldiers entered the armory and families left to establish new routines without them. Charlie would be running late if they lingered much longer.

"I love you. So much," she whispered and threw herself into his arms again, the anticipation of emptiness and loneliness pushing her to hold him as tightly as possible.

Charlie loosened her arms from his neck and began to turn, but Meg resisted. She grabbed him once more to bring his lips to hers for one last kiss—a kiss that, to the outside world, would have seemed ordinary and routine, certainly not Hollywood romance worthy. Yet the kiss carried with it every word of love they failed to voice, every worry they shared, and every bit of hope they clung to.

When he pulled away once more, she could do nothing but drop her arms in surrender and watch her husband—this man who made her waffles on the weekends and held her hand in the pew each week—walk away.

2

SWEAT POOLED under Meg's hands as she gripped the steering wheel. She had at least managed to get herself back into the Jeep, but moving any farther had proven impossible. How long had she sat? Hours? She should move, but her muscles wouldn't listen. Frozen, she could do nothing more than stare out the windshield.

All intentions of handling this goodbye with poise had failed. Any grace she had mustered seemed to have vanished with Charlie's final wave from the armory door. Had he noticed? She cringed, hoping he hadn't seen her body buckle with that last look over his shoulder. She had contained it, managed a smile and a wave, blown a kiss—all while the weight of the emotions of the past months crashed into her like waves against rocky shores…or military helicopters against foreign mountainsides.

Why are you thinking of that? Don't!

Fear coursed through every part of her, from her toes to the tips of her fingers. Even her ears felt prickly and on edge, if that were possible. Her chest rose and fell with a sigh, and she stretched her fingers far and wide before wrapping them back around the worn leather, finger by finger, in an attempt to push the tension away.

The tears hadn't started yet, but they would arrive in their own time. There was no controlling them, as if any of this was within her control. She couldn't simply will these months to be easy or stress-free any more than she could will Charlie to come home safely.

Thy will be done.

"All of this is God's will, on earth as it is in heaven. He will provide. He will comfort. Through all the ups and downs, even if the downs dominate, the Lord will hear your prayers and forgive your sins. The world will tell you you're alone, Meg, but God's Word says otherwise: 'I will not leave you or forsake you.' The Lord said those words to Joshua, but they hold true for each of us as well."

The words of her pastor rang in her ears, and she nodded to no one.

Even sitting by herself in an empty parking lot, she was far from alone. Time would dim the memories and eventually steal them completely, but even when she forgot the smell of Charlie's neck in the morning or the feel of his kisses on her forehead or the warmth of his arms around her, God's promises for her in Christ would remain, as they had all these years.

It was time to rest in those promises and trust His will would be done.

Move, Meg. You can't mope around for the next year.

She stiffened and straightened her shoulders. Goodbyes were over. She had to keep going. Her to-do list said as much. That last item, added in the sharp and confident angles of Charlie's hand, had stood out from her own smooth yet carefree strokes.

Stay busy. Have fun.

Did sitting in the armory parking lot for hours count as busy or fun? Not likely. She winced thinking about the look Charlie would have given her if he were here. But with another stretch, her neck cracking as she rolled out the kinks, she backed the Jeep out of the lot.

The turn toward home lay ahead, but the quiet of their hallways and the glaring void he had left made it the last place she wanted to be. Without risking a glance down that road, sure the mere sight of it would bring tears, she drove past.

The worn sign of Finn O'Connor's Pub crept over the hill on the left. Home away from home. Yet she couldn't go there either. Matt was working. Though he was their favorite bartender—friendly, but not too chatty—and he always remembered her usual without giving her grief for being such a creature of habit, the pressure to make small talk or answer questions, even with someone as nice as Matt, weighed heavier than that suffocating silence at home. So she drove farther into town.

The Jeep ambled along, as if directing itself, carrying her along for the journey. She passed their favorite taco place and the local sandwich shop. Though her stomach rumbled, reminding her she still required food to survive, nothing sounded appetizing save one option.

She spotted an empty spot right in front of the little coffee shop. God certainly provided.

Thanks be to God for coffee. And convenient parking.

But any gratitude she'd felt washed away with the opening of the shop door. The tension returned, hitting her gut first before settling in her shoulders. The small room buzzed with too much energy and commotion for a weekday.

Teens chattered in the corner, their banter mixing with the whirr of the espresso machine. A man dressed unseasonably in skinny jeans and a flannel shirt talked loudly into his phone, as if his beard—a bit pretentious and not as nice as Charlie's—could muffle his words. A lady stood a few feet from the counter, staring up at the menu as her voice squeaked out a number of questions to the barista, who showed an amazing level of patience.

"What's a macchiato exactly? I've never heard of that. What about a mocha?"

Meg crossed her arms tightly against her chest.

"Is your chocolate syrup made with real sugar? It is? Oh, I can't have real sugar. Let's go with a…."

A groan rumbled in Meg's throat, echoing in her chest.

"Wait, it's four dollars for a medium?"

She shifted her weight to the other foot. Her teeth clenched.

You shouldn't get so annoyed all the time.

Her bad attitude had earned her plenty of lectures growing up. Though she knew there was some wisdom in those words, she didn't want wisdom right now.

She wanted coffee.

"I guess I'll just have a small cappuccino. What do you mean 'dry' or 'wet'? It's coffee, isn't it? I thought coffee was always wet."

That woman's voice, how it pierced Meg to her core. Digging her toes into the hardwood floor, she swallowed the sigh. No point in letting her agitation show. There was no one here to notice. Or care.

If she had gone home, she could be enjoying her sweet caffeine without this headache from the incessant noise of coffee shop novices. She turned on her heel and dropped her hands to grab the car keys. The shop across town had a drive-thru.

But as she turned to go, two couples entered, blocking her escape. They chatted with eyes wide and smiles even wider. Something about a camping trip, plans to raft and hike. She dropped her eyes to the floor. Maybe she could sneak past them, mutter an "excuse me." But her gaze fell on their clasped hands. Her chest tightened, burned. She should push past them, break their hands apart so they'd be empty like hers.

But her mom's voice echoed in her mind once more. *"Maybe when you're older, you'll calm down a bit."*

With a shake of her head, she shooed her mom's voice away, the last voice she needed or wanted to hear. Still, she sighed at her silent tantrum, leaning her head back and letting her posture collapse. *Grow up, girl.*

Turning back to face the counter, she clamped her eyes shut, wishing she could shut out the voices behind her. She wanted to be like them, with her husband's hand in hers, instead of alone and angry at everyone. Even the smug hipster didn't deserve her disdain.

"How can I help you?"

Meg looked up to see the barista smiling, his eyebrow ring glinting under the lamp above the counter. She stepped forward and swallowed, pushing the threatening tears back down. She would be an easier customer than the last lady. The last thing this guy needed was to have her falling to pieces on that counter.

She smiled, hoping it appeared more genuine than it felt.

"Large mocha, please."

"Whipped cream?"

"Extra...please?"

Having paid, she found a spot in the corner to wait away from the teens, couples, and Mrs. Screechy. Maybe distancing herself from them would calm her nerves and ease the annoyance. She pulled her phone out of her pocket, shifting between email, news, and social media. It was better to be a zombie staring at a glowing screen than to assume the fetal position with fingers shoved in her ears while singing la-la-la-la-la above the racket.

Wouldn't that be a sight.

"Large mocha, extra whip." The barista's voice caused her head to snap up. She pushed her way through the crowd and reached for her cup.

"Thanks, kiddo," he said with a grin.

She bristled at the word, especially from someone who looked barely older than herself. The urge to kick him in the shins rose in her chest. She should slam her coffee down, outline every moment in her past that made her far from being a kid. But she couldn't. For one, the counter protected his legs from her rage. She'd also hate to waste a perfectly good cup of coffee.

She forced her mouth into a tight smile before offering a polite, albeit terse, "Thank you."

Back in the Jeep, cradling the hot cup in both hands, Meg decided being at home alone maybe wasn't so terrible after all.

Meg opened the door that Saturday morning expecting a deliveryman or a neighbor kid who had lost his ball over her fence yet again. She didn't mind the kid at all, or the frequent interruptions, but how he hadn't learned to control his kicks or throws after the millionth time of having to ring her doorbell was beyond her.

It was no clumsy kid that day, though, but a man in faded cargo shorts and a black T-shirt, his hair a bit shaggy but still showing a hint of the military fade. From the length of his beard she guessed he'd been on leave for a few weeks at least. She almost didn't recognize him until he raised his left eyebrow at her. How often had she laughed at that expression, even if only to keep herself from acknowledging how attractive it made him?

"Hey, so..." he said.

"Oh!" She realized she was staring, shocked by the sight of him, her mouth hanging open like an idiot.

She flung the door open. "How are you, Charlie? Come in!"

He let out a chuckle but didn't move.

What was he laughing at? Hadn't she said the right name? She looked down. One hand dropped to her worn blue pants while the other reached up to the nest of craziness on top of her head. She swallowed hard and felt the warmth spread across her face.

Why was she embarrassed? This was Winters. He had certainly seen her in much worse states.

She tossed him a nod and relaxed her stance.

"Dude, it's Saturday. This is how I look on Saturdays." She eyed him, wondering if her attempt at being laid-back and cool had failed as miserably as she expected, but his nod and gentle smile gave no indication either way.

She opened the door wider and stepped out of the way so he could enter. "Come on in."

So many questions flitted through her head as he passed by, but he interrupted them, his arms lifting her off the ground a few inches. The shock of his hug—so familiar and comforting— nudged the questions away, and she melted into him, thankful their friendship hadn't changed after all this time.

"It's been too long," he said. Had he read her mind? He set her back down on the ground and glanced around the house.

"Whose fault is that?" She mimicked his raised eyebrow and smirked.

He raised his hands in defense. "I take full responsibility."

"As you should. So what brings you to town?" She didn't give him a chance to respond. "Wait! How did you know where I was living? I don't think we've talked since I moved here."

"I have my methods." He flashed a coy smile while raising that eyebrow again. Did he know how that look affected her?

"Fine, don't tell me." She frowned at her feet, but her mock irritation gave way to a light laugh.

"If you must know, it was your mom."

She snapped her head up. Her smile faded. "What?"

"I'm surprised to find you here actually. She said it'd been nearly as long since she'd last talked to you. Wasn't sure if the address was still correct."

Her face warmed again. Stupid embarrassment. She rushed to change the subject. "Still haven't said why you're in town."

"Like you gave me a chance to answer?" Another smile. Another eyebrow.

She stuck her tongue out and squinted at him.

He ignored her. "Looking to move here actually. Or somewhere nearby."

"Oh? Finally get out?" Why did she sound so excited by that possibility? His career was of no concern of hers, was it? They hadn't even spoken in over a year.

He settled himself onto the couch. "Sort of. My enlistment was up. Got tired of all the movin'. But you know me. Switched to the guard unit here."

"Oh, Air Guard?" She shot him a smile as she plopped down beside him, tucking one leg up underneath her and pulling the other to her chest, resting her chin on her knee.

"Army Guard. I said I got tired of moving, not working." Why she had kept the silly military rivalry alive after all these years she couldn't explain. Second nature, she guessed. "Seem to be good guys. I get all the fun of the Army while getting to settle down a bit. Even managed to snag an AGR job. So that's pretty nice."

Something in his tone said he didn't quite believe his own words, but she could be misreading him. She was out of practice on that front, after all.

She nodded but remained silent.

"How've you been? It's been a while since..." His voice trailed off, and his eyes lowered. As if she could have forgotten the last time they'd been together. Had he really forgotten?

"It's okay, Charlie." She lowered her knee, crossing her legs beneath her and folding her hands in her lap. "I'm doing pretty good. Going with the flow. Hanging in there. It is what it is."

His chest puffed slightly as he let out a small laugh. "How many clichés was that?"

Eyes narrowed, she threw a pillow at him.

"Shut up."

Charlie blinked the sleep from his eyes and shifted his weight in the stiff leather of the seat. His elbow slid on the cold metal of the armrest, but it didn't meet Meg's slender arm as he expected. He glanced down. Her bag sat in the seat beside him, her sunglasses tucked into the outer pocket.

"Meg?" His voice came out barely above a whisper.

He tried again, more loudly. "Meg!"

His eyes darted around the gate area, but he couldn't find her brown shirt for the crowd bustling around. A sick feeling landed in his stomach and then bubbled up until he could feel it in his throat. It wasn't like her to get up and leave. Even if he had been sleeping soundly, she would have woken him up to keep him from worrying.

"Final boarding call for flight 1112." The announcement echoed over the PA system. "Final boarding call. Flight 1112. Gate 32C."

He choked down the fear. This was their flight. They weren't on it, and Meg was gone. No one seemed to notice when he leapt from his seat and began spinning in frantic circles, searching for his wife. His mind sped through every possibility. She had lost track of time. She had slipped and hit her head. She'd been abducted.

Anything could have happened.

He reached a sweaty palm into his pocket for his phone but stopped short. The fabric against his hand was all wrong. He looked down, but he didn't see the khaki shorts and T-shirt he had put on this morning. Why was he wearing ACUs and boots?

His eyes widened.

"Meg!?" He spun around in a final search for her, but the

crowd was gone. Every seat was empty, save one. A few rows ahead of him, a soldier sat with eyes on the ground. His desert camo was caked in dried blood and sand. It covered most of the man's torso, including the name tape. But Charlie didn't need to see it to know it was Haas.

The soldier lifted his head so his blue eyes met Charlie's. Despite the old blood smeared down his chin and neck, no wounds were visible. He seemed fine, healthy, alive. But that wasn't possible. Haas had died years ago. Charlie had watched it happen.

He shook his head and clamped his eyes shut, determined to make the apparition disappear. When he opened them, he expected Haas to be gone, but he still sat there, staring back at him.

The corner of his mouth pulled up into a half-smile, and he gave Charlie a subtle nod and said, "Hey, Winters. You ready?"

Charlie's eyes flashed open as the jolt of fear shot through his body. The first breaths brought no relief. It was as if he'd taken a slam to the chest and had had all the air knocked from his lungs. He leaned forward, elbows to knees, and dug them in as hard as he could, focusing on the sharp ache that resulted. That ache meant he was awake now. He hoped he was, at least. He ran his hands across his head, but nothing helped shake off the weight of the dream.

The back of a hand struck his arm, and he jumped away from the contact, half-expecting it to be Haas grabbing him. Josh Murphy, a shorter guy in his mid-twenties with tattoos crowding both arms, faced Charlie with a look of amusement and confusion.

"You okay?" he asked.

"Yeah. Why?" Charlie tried to play it cool, though he felt far from it.

"Well, you nearly fell out of your chair when you woke up." Murphy stifled a laugh.

Charlie's mind ran through any number of comebacks he could use, but all he had was the desire to avoid all conversation, even witty banter. He shrugged before pointing to the gear at his feet. "Watch my stuff?"

Murphy nodded while putting his headphones back on.

Charlie found the restroom at the end of the gate area. He didn't bother to check the mirror, sure he looked like a ragged mess, and instead bent over the sink. The splash of cold water against his face couldn't clear his head or drive out the sick feeling from his gut, but it at least helped wake him up from the fogginess of the nightmare.

He'd left home so many times, deployed more times than most of the guys in this unit. But this time was different. All the confidence and excitement he had felt during past tours was gone, replaced by dread and worry. The image of Haas flooded his mind with painful memories. He steadied himself against the sink.

You failed your friend. Failed his family and his wife.

He sucked in air, desperate to drive away the panic, but the sting of the commercial air freshener in his throat only made it worse. He stared into the basin and watched the water drip from his nose and chin before it trailed into the drain. His hands gripped the edge of the counter, yet the room wouldn't be steadied. His head continued to spin.

He clenched his eyes shut again. If he was going to make it through this deployment, he couldn't be this much of a wreck from a stupid dream. He needed to pull himself together —and fast.

God is our refuge and strength, a very present help in trouble.

He filled his chest again with a deep breath, thankful the chemicals in the air had begun to dissipate.

Therefore we will not fear, though the earth gives way...

The earth might give way, and his past might haunt him,

but he had been trained for this. And where his training lacked, he'd trust in God.

He lifted his head and faced his reflection. He half expected to see Haas's face—blood and all—instead of his own, but the clean-shaven man he saw was himself. Yet it wasn't. Not fully. The reflection showed only one side of him—the soldier—and with his wedding band left at home, he had no outward sign that he was anything more. His face in the glass seemed to beckon him to unload that duty to home and wife, to drop it as easily as he had removed his ring.

Then he could rightly focus on the deployment, the mission, and the team without any burden of caring for or worrying about Meg.

He shook his head. As if his vocations were mutually exclusive. They weren't like hats to be removed before putting on another. No, he had to figure out how to serve in both roles without either suffering.

No pressure.

3

Charlie shifted against the pack behind him, trying to work the kinks out of his back and relieve the tension from between his shoulders from the long flights in cramped seats. The terminal's floor—whose thin carpeting provided no amount of cushioning to his travel-weary legs—afforded him no comfort to get any rest, let alone sleep.

He glanced over at the soldier sitting against a metal column a few feet away, head leaned back and to the side as he dozed, and then to the others sitting in chairs and chatting excitedly. But he didn't hear what they were saying.

He picked up the MP3 player and pushed to the next song, hoping for something more upbeat, louder, able to drown out the noise of the animated conversation and the occasional snores of the sleeping soldier. How the guy could sleep, he had no idea.

After years of gunfire, helicopters, and the din of heavy machinery, he was grateful if he could snag a handful of hours at a time. Even under the ideal conditions in his own bed with his wife beside him, that sleep was still restless, uneasy. And he'd left those luxuries behind, trading them in for sand and mortar fire.

And snoring men.

Cracking his knuckles—as if he could snap away the restlessness that plagued every joint and muscle—his gaze fell to the groove where his ring had been. He'd worn that band for nearly two years, taking it off only for training. He liked his fingers and wanted to keep them. Thankfully Meg agreed and kept the band safe for him while he was gone.

Meg.

How was she doing? Had she made it home from the armory?

She probably sat in the parking lot for a while. He couldn't blame her if she had, could he? This deployment would be harder for her than last time. It would be for him. His first one since Iraq. Since Haas.

The restlessness in his bones gave way to a weight that settled over his sternum. Who was he kidding? That weight, that pressure bearing down on him, was nothing new. He'd carried it from the moment they'd said, "I do." Or perhaps before that. Since the day she'd accepted his proposal.

It now bubbled to the surface, forcing him to acknowledge it, like a petulant child pulling at his shirt hem.

She's your responsibility. Her life. Her faith. That's yours.

How often had he wondered if he was fulfilling that duty—if he was measuring up to all she expected, to all God demanded of him? He could have listened harder. Prayed more. Loved her better.

I'm barely a decent husband at home. How am I going to do it from the other side of the world?

He had wrestled the same doubts for the past year, ever since the deployment orders had come in. Meg could reassure him over and over again, but she didn't understand the pressure, the self-sacrifice, the worry. Did she?

"It's a weighty burden we carry as husbands," Pastor Feld had instructed over a beer a few months back. "We're to love our wives as Christ loves the church. That's putting her first, doing all for her. Perhaps easier for you with your military training, but we struggle daily against our sinful nature that urges us to be selfish, to ignore those duties. It makes us irritated by the needs of others and pushes us to be served rather than to serve. For that? There's repentance. Forgiveness in Christ, always."

"But how can I help her...especially after I leave?"

"You'll be limited, sure, but your call to love and care for her doesn't disappear with the miles traveled. Study God's Word together if possible. Pray for her and with her, as often as you can."

Lord, help her.

It wasn't much, but it was enough. The Lord promised to hear even the most awkward of prayers, or even the shortest. *Thanks be to God for that.* All he had these days was awkward and haphazard, it seemed.

The weight on his chest remained, prayer or not. He'd left her behind, something he had sworn he would never do after he'd returned to her doorstep years ago. He had left her once. Now he'd done it again.

Not that you had a choice.

She at least wasn't alone this time. Her best friend, Piper Woods, had insisted on scheduling weekly dinners to pass the months more quickly, and if anyone could break through Meg's stubbornness, it was Piper. She understood the benefits of laughter paired with a bottle of wine.

Immanuel Lutheran Church had become their family during the last few years too, with the older congregants taking turns hosting them for holiday meals. Meg had agreed to continue that tradition this year, but knowing her, without him there to drag her along, she'd find some excuse not to attend.

"Yo! Dude!" A voice snapped him out of his thoughts, and a boot struck his foot. "Let's go!"

He looked up at Aaron Woods, who was towering over him, long limbs loaded down with gear. His face drooped, but it wasn't from sadness—it was as though his muscles couldn't be bothered to move. But then his jaw tensed, ever so slightly, and his chin pushed out.

Charlie's eyes darted around the now empty terminal, and he scrambled to his feet with a mumbled expletive. Stowing his headphones into a pocket, he hauled the pack onto his back and chased after his buddy, who was already heading toward the double doors. With rifle in hand, he hurried to catch up.

Charlie fell in line behind his team as they walked across the tarmac toward their chartered flight, but his mind wasn't on this flight or the distant deserts that awaited them. Looking to his right, he could almost see Meg in the fading sunlight walking beside him, with the same goofy grin that had spread across her face on their last vacation.

Meg poked Charlie in the ribs with her elbow, trying not to disturb the balding man sitting to her other side.

"Where are we going? You can't possibly keep it a secret forever!" she said.

He draped his arm over her shoulder and flashed her a devilish grin. "Have you forgotten who you married?"

With an eyebrow lifted, he lowered his lips to hers. She leaned into him, her guard lowered for only a second before she pushed away from him with a scowl.

"But you know I hate surprises!"

It seemed to take every ounce of her control to keep her eyes narrowed and brow furrowed, but when he turned his own mouth into a mocking frown and squinted at her, she broke into a fit of giggling.

"Gotcha!" He laughed with pride. "So, any guesses?"

She lifted her hand to her chin, her thumbnail sliding between her teeth as she thought. He chuckled at the strained look of concentration on her face, but she ignored him.

"Well, we're currently headed west..."

"Uh-huh."

"But...that doesn't mean we'll continue heading west." Her shoulders dropped as the corners of her mouth fell into a frown.

"Don't hurt yourself, babe."

She swatted his arm and threw her hand in the air. "Whatever. I give up. I'll figure it out when we get there."

She slumped in her seat, defeated. Wrapping his arm around her shoulders again, he lifted her chin, pulling her eyes to meet his.

"I sure hope so." He gave her a sympathetic nod before pressing his lips to hers, stopping any possible protest.

He blinked, the memories vanishing as he climbed aboard and settled into his seat beside Woods. Resting the butt of his rifle on the floor between his boots, he made some smart remark to the guys behind him before falling silent. Just another soldier heading to war. Again.

Meg's phone buzzed under her pillow. She rolled over with a groan, her eyes hidden beneath her folded arms. Though she had made the effort to turn in early every evening during the last week, she still woke each morning with a restless ache. She had no explanation for her poor sleep, since her dreams fled with the sound of the alarm, but explanation or no, the fact remained—she was tired.

Sliding her arms to the pillow above her head, she forced her eyelids open, bracing herself for the morning sunlight that would be pouring in. But the room was still dim, gray. She turned her head to the window with a huffed breath. Wisps of pinks and creams were creeping across the sky outside, but not enough to signal a decent hour of the day.

Her phone buzzed again. Whoever was texting her now had some nerve. Didn't they know the time? She fumbled for the device, already forming her response as she unplugged it from its cord.

`4:00 a.m. – MORTGAGE PAYMENT DUE`

It wasn't a text at all, but a calendar reminder. She'd need to double check all those reminders to ensure they were set for a more reasonable time. Like noon. But she'd do that later.

She tossed the phone to the foot of the bed and lay back down, rolling onto her side and pulling her legs, knees bent, up in front of her. The other side of the bed lay pristine, covers undisturbed. Only the pillow showed any hint of use, but his head hadn't laid there in several days. The ache hit again, this time in her chest and not from her exhaustion.

She let her arm wander across the invisible boundary and into the cold that was his side of the bed. Her eyes closed. Tears gathered in the corners. If she could fall back asleep, she could leave behind this emptiness and see him in memories or dreams.

Pulling his pillow down into her arms, she buried her face in his scent, but no sleep came, or any refreshing memory of him. Instead her chest caved in on itself, the weight of his absence crushing her and the pain choking her until she could do nothing more than let the sobs have their way. She had no prayers. Only sobs mixed with the occasional groan sounded into his pillow.

Then as quickly as her fit had come on, it ended. Her tears ceased, her pulse calmed, and she once again lay still, silent. She sighed, certain it was an answer to a prayer she hadn't been able to utter.

Thanks be to God for the Holy Spirit, my Helper.

Sleep no longer appealed, and instead her stomach growled at the thought of fresh coffee, bacon, and fried eggs. Charlie would have rolled over and pulled the covers over his head begging for more sleep, but Meg could never wait once bacon was on her mind. She hopped up from the bed, hastily threw the covers back into place, and bounded down the hallway to fulfill her cravings.

Over breakfast she perused the day's Bible study with pen in hand, ready to jot down any questions or notes that arose. She read through the psalm and then hummed her way through the hymn excerpt. She grimaced at the wrong note she hit but recovered, realizing no one was around to hear. It had, at least, been somewhat of a joyful noise. Maybe?

A bite of egg sent runny yolk dripping onto the table, narrowly missing the pages and steering her focus off track. Charlie's copy of the study wasn't likely to get coffee rings or bacon grease stains like hers would. He probably missed bacon. Could you ship bacon overseas?

Her mind went to work contemplating plans for transporting the meat to him without it spoiling or being detected by bomb-sniffing dogs. Those dogs must be properly trained to ignore such distractions, even a distraction that delicious, but she had no idea how to send meat safely, and she refused to risk the possibility of wasting it. This wasn't turkey bacon, after all.

How can they call it that anyway? It's an abomination. Not bacon.

She picked up her pencil and wrote: *Bacon shipping to APO.* If anyone could send it to him, the internet would find them.

With her bacon shipment plan settled for the time being, she pushed away her empty plate and vowed to get back on track and finish the study for the morning. The Old Testament reading was lengthy, and she stumbled through it, getting hung up with the unfamiliar names in each line.

The names distracted her so much that by the end of it, she had no clue what she had just read; she couldn't pronounce most of it. She scribbled another note in the margin.

Phonetic spellings of Bible names.

She grabbed the Bible again, flipping ahead to the epistle reading in Galatians, but a word caught her eye on a random page. She stopped.

Peace.

She read the line and then the whole paragraph. She'd heard this section of John 14 preached every year on Pentecost, and she knew it well—Jesus reminding His disciples of His pending departure, promising them they wouldn't be alone. They would have a Helper. They would have peace.

Her lips tightened. How eerily appropriate for her situation. Her husband had left, but the Holy Spirit had brought her peace.

Peace I leave with you; my peace I give to you. Not as the world gives do I give to you.

Meg shook her head and chided herself. *Don't be ridiculous, Meg.* Pastor Feld had spoken a few weeks earlier about not using the Bible as a Ouija board, as if you could open it to any page and find some secret hidden message just for you at just the right time. It was only a coincidence. Nothing more.

How Charlie would have poked fun at her for this, probably picking up their Bible and asking it a question as you would a magic eight ball or rubbing it like a genie's lamp. The thought of his probable teasing pushed a smile across her face, but the sight of his empty chair beside her undid it.

The tears crept up again. The emptiness beside her seemed deafening, demanding her attention now, and it pushed aside all the peace and comfort she'd found less than an hour ago.

She slammed her Bible shut. Leaving her dishes on the table, she jumped up and headed to the front door, ignoring when her papers scattered to the floor in her hurry. She was still in her ratty pajamas, but she grabbed her running shoes anyway. The morning sun was inching up from the horizon, keeping the day's heat from fully hitting yet, but any discomfort from running in these clothes had to be better than the sight of that blasted chair with its mocking void.

Rounding the last corner of their driveway, the regret set in. With each stride, the wide legs of her pajama pants caught on each other, slowing her down and threatening to trip her every few feet. Even with the pine trees towering over her, the sun was heating the air quickly. Sooner than she'd anticipated, sweat ran around her hairline and down her neck.

She fought to ignore it all, focusing instead on the earthy scent of the pine needles in the air and the steady beat of her feet against the gravel road—as steady as it could be with these pants. Her breathing mixed with the sound of the crunching rocks, and she forced it to drown out everything else in her head.

Though her thoughts calmed somewhat and the tension in her limbs began to ease, that perfect peace from earlier in the morning was gone. Had it been real, or had she imagined it? She scolded herself for thinking she could ever be free from missing Charlie. How naive of her to believe that peace was lasting.

Life was hard. That was a fact. Her husband had left. Half of herself was missing, and he might not return.

She skidded to a stop in the middle of the road. Hunched over her knees and breathing hard, she struggled against the fear. The war had shown no signs of slowing. Even with the typical winter lull in fighting approaching—when the enemy would hole up in the mountains—she had no guarantee, no comfort.

With all the determination she could find, she pushed the thoughts away. A frustrated growl exploded from her chest as she turned around and started for home. What she wouldn't give for a decent breeze, but the air remained still, heavy.

All the calm she'd started to find in the run unraveled. Her anxiety crept back up, the growing tingling in her chest acting as fuel to the fire inside. She'd let herself get worked up. Let Charlie leave. Let the military take him away. It was what the Army did, wasn't it? Tore apart families. Wrecked homes. Ruined lives.

She shook her head. *You don't believe that.*

Adrenaline pushed her through each mile toward home until she stormed through the front door, not bothering to stretch or grab water. There was no fatigue in her muscles, only a bitter ache, an edge.

Meg grabbed her phone. She should text Piper, ask for help. That's what army wives were supposed to do, right? She swept the sweat off her forehead, the battle in her head raging on. Piper didn't need her problems, didn't need to hear Meg whine about some stupid chair and being lonely.

She lifted the phone to throw it across the room, but it buzzed, and she looked at the text.

I'm on my way over. I have wine.

How had Piper known? Another coincidence or divine intervention? Either way, Meg would take it.

Great. See you soon.

With her reply sent, Meg crumpled onto the floor. Her running shoes were still on, and her hair was still streaked with sweat and matted against her temples. She should shower, but she couldn't move.

She sat and waited. Help was on the way.

With wine.

4

CHARLIE TOOK a sip from the cardboard cup as he stepped into the tent, escaping the afternoon heat that refused to be quelled by the breeze that had picked up after lunch. *Dry heat my ass.* The hot coffee wasn't helping either, but he wasn't about to waste it. He raised the cup to his mouth again, the faint hint of burnt wood hitting his nose as he choked down another sip. Still bad.

Glancing over the rim, he spotted his gear still sitting next to Woods in the corner, with the other four guys scattered about the small area. He stepped over Jack Baker's long legs and dropped to the floor beside his pack. Knees bent, he leaned forward against them, rounding his back to stretch out the kinks that had formed between his shoulders from the long days of travel.

Terry Martin sat a few feet away, reading a book that showed as much wear as the soldier holding it. Its corners were bent and ragged, and the faded cover left the title illegible. Beside him, Brandon Carter wore his standard grin and shuffled a deck of playing cards a few times before sliding them back into their sleeve as Murphy slumped back, stewing over his apparent loss to the younger soldier.

The guy really needed to work on those "Go Fish" skills. As Charlie readied to throw the jab at his buddy, Woods's voice cut in. "I hate this." His chin, tucked to his chest, turned to the side as he stretched his neck, sending a crack loud enough that caused everyone, even those who hadn't heard his words, to turn toward him.

Charlie relaxed his posture and lowered the cup to his lap. "Hurry up and wait. The Army way. But Kyrgyzstan isn't that bad, is it?"

"It ain't Disney World," Murphy said, a half-smile briefly flashing before his frown returned, as if it had just now dawned on him where he was…and where he couldn't be.

Baker sat up, his cap—which Charlie had assumed he'd been sleeping under—falling off his face. His honey-colored eyes flashed at Murphy. "Seriously? Disney? What are you, five?"

"I'll have you know it's the happiest place on earth." Murphy lifted his chin at Baker.

Charlie couldn't resist jumping in. "If you're a toddler, maybe."

Patting his palm to his chest, Murphy said, "Or young at heart."

"Still a bit sketchy, man," Baker said.

"I know you are, but what am I?" Murphy leaned back against the wall with a smirk.

Baker's hands flew up. "That doesn't even make sense." He looked around for support, but no one noticed—ignoring them as if they were a couple having an embarrassing spat in public—except Charlie, who watched them lob insults back and forth. They really were like an old married couple.

"You two should really kiss and make up," Charlie said with a nod. He shot them the look of an elder imparting wisdom on a younger generation—which he kind of was. Not that this wisdom was much help.

Murphy ignored him. He pushed his sleeves up, revealing the intricate patchwork of ink spreading over his forearms as he leaned his elbows against his knees, his fingers steepled at his chin, eyes on Baker.

He didn't get far in his lecture—something about rides for teens and the park's attractions for the over-five crowd—before Woods slammed his knuckles into the cement floor.

"Will you two shut up about Disney?" His expression hardened, the muscle along his jaw twitching as he glared at Baker and then Murphy and back again.

The guys froze. Martin and Carter raised their heads but remained still, as if any movement or sound would direct Woods's rage at them next.

Charlie risked leaning forward to grab his attention. He pulled his expression into a silent question. *You okay?*

But Woods slumped back and appeared to return to his nap, not bothering to answer Charlie. Not even an eye roll. That was new.

"Who invited Grumpy?" Murphy tossed his head in Woods's direction. Woods didn't move.

Baker chuckled and pointed back to Murphy. "I blame Dopey."

"Don't look at me! I'd prefer Snow White over this guy."

Woods still hadn't budged. Charlie raised a brow at the two soldiers. "Don't poke the bear. He bites."

"Like your mom," Woods added, peering down his nose at Murphy with a hard stare, no hint of jest or mirth that should have accompanied the taunt.

"Dude. You're so lame."

"Not what your mom said." That effectively shut down the conversation as they all shared a laugh—except Murphy.

As the laughter died down, giving way to silence, Charlie

dropped his forehead against his arms, which were propped up on his knees. He could almost see the frayed ends of his nerves.

They had so little information about this tour, only a vague idea of what they'd be doing, how they'd be serving. It sabotaged any attempt to find peace or calm. But he closed his eyes regardless, hopeful for any rest he could snag while they waited.

Carter's young voice startled him. "I like Disney."

Seriously?

"Thank you!" Murphy sat back up, his words mixing with the collective groan from Baker, Woods, and maybe even Martin, but Charlie couldn't be sure, as the guy had buried himself in his reading.

Charlie dropped his head back into his palms and shook his head. "Dude, why? Why would you do that, Carter?" he asked. This kid, together with Murphy, would be the death of him this deployment.

But Carter said, "What? I mean, the princesses are pretty hot, right? Especially the redhead." Murphy raised his hands toward Baker and then to Carter, encouraging him to see the kid's point, but Baker only frowned.

"The ginger? With the fins?" Charlie asked.

"How do you even know that, Winters?" Woods laughed, his sour mood lifting a touch.

Murphy waved a hand at Carter. "We should totally go once we get back. You in?"

Carter nodded. "Yeah. Can I bring Molly?"

"I guess. But I'm not letting her cramp my style."

"What style?" Baker laughed.

Carter turned to him, excitement painted across his face. "You should come too, man! Bring the wife. It'll be fun!"

Baker shook his head. "I think I'll hold off on Disney until we have kids, which may be sooner than later if Jen has her way."

Martin cleared his throat, but his voice still came out gruff. "I'm getting too damn old for this." His lips pressed together under his graying mustache.

"For babysitting these yahoos?" Woods asked, waving a hand at the younger soldiers, but Martin only huffed out a small laugh.

"You're down to, what, a year left, aren't you?" Charlie asked as he downed the last of his now cold coffee. It didn't taste any better, and he couldn't stifle the grimace on his face.

"Yup. I'll be done and out about three months after we get home."

"Promise to write, won't ya?" Woods asked.

The older soldier grinned. "Hey, you're not rid of me yet. Might still need me on this tour." His eyes betrayed him though. His typically carefree demeanor had disappeared. He seemed more tired, more ragged.

"Well, you are pretty damn old," Woods said.

Martin smiled again, but it was Murphy who jumped in, his palm back to patting his chest. "Hey, age ain't nothing but a number, baby."

Baker lowered his brow. "Says the grown man who'd rather spend his free time with other people's kids…and a bunch of people dressed up as talking animals."

"Seriously, shut up about Disney World!" Woods's glare bounced between the pair again, daring them to keep arguing.

"Aren't those called fuzzies?" Baker asked, with no sign he'd heard the reprimand.

"No. Furries…I think." With that, Murphy began recounting some past adventure involving someone in a panda suit, a missing beer, and a stolen car—stolen by the panda, not Murphy. Charlie couldn't keep up. *Not that I want to.*

Martin, who seemed as eager to ignore this rabbit hole Murphy and Baker were treading down, continued. "Old or not, I just need to know you're willing to drag me out of danger if needed."

"Then could you lay off the donuts?" Carter laughed at his own cleverness. He glanced from face to face, but a wave of eye rolls and groans greeted him, even from Murphy, who had paused long enough in his own rambling to catch the joke.

Charlie chucked his empty coffee cup at the kid, a hollow thunk sounding where it hit him squarely on the forehead before falling into his lap. "Lesson one, Carter: don't laugh at your own jokes."

But the snub couldn't break Carter's smile, his blue eyes still shining.

Woods's monotone chimed in. "Lesson two: tell better jokes."

Another laugh. Even Carter joined in at his own expense. He didn't seem to mind the teasing and appeared to relish it even. Didn't he have three older sisters? It wasn't the same, of course. Not like this hodge-podge of guys tied together by a common duty.

The kid's attitude, the way he rolled with the punches and the jabs, added to the team's rapport. They might give him a lot of grief, but the whole team loved him like a little brother. This was why Charlie stayed in, re-upped even. Family. Camaraderie.

Maybe it was why Woods had too, despite all the signs he hated this life.

"At least this beats sitting in briefings with the LT," Murphy said, changing the subject. "I mean, seriously, anyone else feel like they were enduring some sort of ancient Chinese torture?"

"I think they teach that at ROTC," Charlie said, glancing down at his watch. No time for another coffee, which might be a good thing.

Murphy smirked. "Yeah, classes like Dull and Lifeless Public Speaking maybe."

"Woods would get an A in that class for sure," Baker said. He straightened, drawing his face down into a deep frown. But Woods didn't seem to notice the mockery on display, leaving Baker pouting over his failure to rile the guy up.

"Yeah, but not for what he did in class." Charlie's loud laugh filled the room.

Carter shot him a glance. "Dude, don't laugh at your own jokes!"

"Nope." Charlie held up a finger. "There's an amendment to the aforementioned rule. You can laugh at your own jokes if they're hilarious."

Woods added, "Or if you're Winters and *think* you're hilarious."

Another round of hearty laughter escaped from Charlie, and Woods pointed his thumb at him with a shrug as if to say, "See?"

The sound of approaching boots thumping on the cement broke through their chatter. The lieutenant colonel loomed over them. "Okay, all. Our flight to Kabul is scheduled for an hour. Grab your gear. Line up." He turned to inform the rest of the unit but tossed over his shoulder a final command. "And don't be late!"

"That means you, Winters." Woods nodded to him as they all stood up in unison.

Charlie flashed him the finger before reaching down to gather up his stuff.

"Hey, I get it now!" Carter said, hauling his pack onto his shoulders and grabbing his rifle. He stepped between Charlie and Woods, who gave him confused looks. Though he was a good ten years younger and twenty pounds lighter than each of them, he matched them for height and easily looked them in the eyes. "You know. Why you guys are friends. Woods makes us hurry up...Winters makes us wait."

Charlie turned to Woods, noting his buddy saw the truth in

the kid's observation. They nodded in unison. *The kid has a point.*

"Plus," Carter said, raising his hands to gesture between the two, "your names kinda go together. Winters...Woods... Wintery Woods."

"And..." Charlie drew out the word for effect. "There it is."

"Keep trying, Carter. One day you might be as funny as this guy here." Woods patted Charlie on the chest before giving the younger soldier a slap upside the head and walking off with his gear in hand.

Charlie gestured to himself with both hands and smirked. "What can I say? I'm kind of a big deal." A wide smile beamed across his face, and with a sympathetic nod to the kid, he hurried after his friend.

Behind him, the laughs of the rest of the guys continued, the occasional jab made at Carter's expense mixed with a word of encouragement.

Charlie called over his shoulder at Carter, who was still standing there with that goofy grin plastered on his face. "Come on, kid. The Afghans are waiting."

Meg still sat on the floor in the entryway, not having moved since Piper's text. Had it been one hour? Maybe two? The angle of the sun peering through the front door—and the pain in her lower back—hinted at the latter. Why wasn't Piper here yet? She'd said she was on her way. Maybe she'd missed the turn onto the driveway. Again.

Meg's mind wandered from memory to memory, helped along by the pictures on the wall beside her. Too bad she couldn't really escape to those better times.

If only.

The phone rang to life in her hand, and she jumped. Few

people called her these days, and the only one she wanted to hear from was likely still traveling. The number on the screen was unfamiliar, but even the local area code couldn't squelch her hope, however irrational it was, that perhaps Charlie had found a way to call her early.

She lifted it to her ear. "Hello?"

"Hi. Meg? It's Karen from the FRG. How are you?" The voice sounded cheery enough, but it still disappointed. Meg winced. *Why'd you get your hopes up? You know better.*

"I'm all right." She cringed again. Why did her voice always have that edge when these volunteers called? *Be nice.* Meg searched for the grace she wanted to offer, but the heightened emotions from the morning kept it out of reach.

"Have you heard from Matt yet?" Karen's slight Southern accent, though unusual for the area and likely a remnant of the woman's childhood, added warmth to each word.

Bless your heart. Meg seethed at the mention of the wrong soldier's name. *I don't know, Karen, why don't you ask Matt's wife?* She clenched her teeth and swallowed hard to push the snark back. The woman didn't deserve her poor attitude today—or any day, for that matter.

"No." Meg dropped her head into her hand and massaged her temple with her thumb. Her response had still come out sharper than intended. Poor Karen was likely overworked and tired, having probably made several calls already that day. *It was an honest mistake. Let it slide.*

"That's not unusual," Karen continued in her singsong way, seemingly unfazed by Meg's curtness and unaware of her mistake with his name. "It'll take time for them to arrive in-country. Then they'll have to get to their assigned FOB and get settled."

Meg silenced a sigh, glad Karen couldn't see the way her face contorted as she rattled off more information and tips on how to cope and what to expect during the days ahead. *I know all this.*

Her mind wandered to Charlie. Had he gotten to Kabul yet? Would he be able to call then, or would she have to wait? Where would he end up? Some eastern province, maybe. Not that she knew any of their names anyway.

Her mind refocused only to find the line silent, the chatter ended. What had the lady asked her? Or had she already hung up? Meg's eyes darted around the room, as if she could somehow find the answer in front of her, but she still didn't say anything.

The voice sounded on the other end, with a new chill to its tone. "Well, I'll let you go."

Meg slumped, her face falling. This woman wasn't the enemy. This woman hadn't meant to say the wrong name. This woman simply wanted to help.

"I'm so sorry, Karen. It's been a bit of a rough day."

"It's okay, Meg. I understand. Again, I mean it, I'm always available by phone and email if you need anything. You can even text me anytime."

With a quick thanks, and after goodbyes had been exchanged, Meg hung up. She'd need to try harder the next time the FRG called. But how could she pull that off? Especially if they continued to get Charlie's name wrong? She could always borrow Karen's friendly lilt to sweeten her responses and hide any irritation.

She snorted, knowing she'd never be able to pull off that sweet drawl.

At least Karen's call had her laughing. That was a plus, right?

Stepping onto the covered porch, Piper shifted the bottles of wine under one arm and raised a hand to the doorbell, ignoring the cobwebs that had formed along it and across the house's siding. She waited, listening for footsteps from within as she reached a hand to the knot of blonde hair at her neck to ensure it was still in place.

At least the roof overhead provided some respite from the midday sun. She looked back over her shoulder and down the gravel driveway to the tree line where storm clouds could be seen brewing beyond their boughs.

A good summer storm would be a nice change of pace from the recent dry heat—assuming she didn't have to walk or drive in it.

Don't stay too long then.

The door pulled open, and Piper burst into laughter, nearly dropping the bottles of wine as she threw her head back. "Girl, you look like a hot mess." She motioned the merlot toward Meg's hair as she stepped inside.

"I feel like it too." Meg chuckled. That was a good sign. She hadn't expected laughter, even in such a small dose.

"I figured as much. It's why I came prepared." Piper drifted into the kitchen, setting the bottles on the counter as she retrieved the corkscrew from the drawer by the sink. She stopped at the sight of the papers strewn across the floor, her mouth falling open as she turned to Meg, who held two glasses.

"There appear to be signs of a struggle." She shot her friend a curious look, angling her head toward the mess at the table.

Meg's shoulders slumped, but she didn't respond, instead busying herself with filling each glass nearly to the top.

Piper accepted the glass Meg proffered. "I was going to ask how you were, but you've already answered that." She dropped her gaze to the full glass and back up to Meg, whose eyes flitted from one corner of the room to another as she took a sip.

Without a word, she motioned Piper to follow her into the living room. *That's not a good sign.* She grimaced, hoping she'd know what to say to this seasoned Army wife. *What can I offer her? She's the experienced one here, not me.*

They settled onto the couch, each of them pulling their legs up under them. Piper waited, taking in her friend's appearance —the mess of hair, the ratty pajamas with a fresh coat of dust up to the knees. Expected, sure, but still worrisome.

"I feel like a moron for falling apart so early." Meg's voice came out quiet. If Piper hadn't caught her glance, she would have assumed she was speaking to herself.

Piper offered a warm smile and tucked her chin to her chest, her shoulders dropping an inch. "Yeah, but really, hon, have you and Charlie ever been apart for more than a couple weeks?"

Meg stuck her tongue out at her. "Hey. The guys were just gone for two months, remember?"

"Oh, right." Piper tried again. "But, really, you guys are practically one person."

"Attached at the hip, I know," Meg mumbled into her glass.

Piper scrunched up her nose. "It's kinda disgusting. In a cute way, of course."

"Uh-huh. Right."

"So is work going as well as…all this?" Piper gestured to Meg's haphazard appearance.

Meg shrugged. "Beauty of freelance work. I can turn down editing jobs whenever I need to."

"Probably for the best. Not sure clients are ready for deployment-Meg just yet."

Meg relaxed and lifted her chin, the hint of a smile appearing at the corners of her mouth as she changed the subject. "So how are you doing? Not as desperate for wine as I am?" She motioned to the untouched glass in Piper's hands as she set her own, now empty, on the end table.

Piper swallowed hard and settled back against the couch cushion, still holding the glass. Unfolding her legs, she stretched them out before her, resting her feet on the ottoman and crossing her ankles. "Don't let my extreme coolness fool you. It's been a tough week."

Meg cocked her head to the side, her eyes searching, prying. Piper waited, hoping Meg didn't notice the tension in her jaw.

"Wait. Are you...?" The corners of her mouth rose into a smirk. But Meg didn't say the word, and Piper wouldn't let her. It was still so new, so weird to hear aloud.

She rested a hand on her belly. "Well, this sure isn't from all the beer I'm not drinking."

Did Meg flinch? Piper couldn't be sure. It had been so slight. She'd probably imagined it. A wide smile burst across Meg's face, giving way to a high-pitched squeal, startling Piper. She'd definitely imagined the discomfort.

Before she could recover, the questions rushed at her in a flood of rambling words and flying hands. "When are you due? How far along are you? How are you feeling? What does Aaron think? Wait...have you told him? Does he know?"

Meg took a breath, but only a short one.

"How did I not know?"

Piper snorted and lowered her head. Setting the glass down on the floor, she raised her hands. "Woah. Slow down, killer. I can't even think that fast!"

Meg rolled her eyes as Piper's expression pinched, exaggerating the concentration it took to form her answers. "March fifth. Sixteen weeks right now. Good, still a bit tired. Pukeyness is thankfully over. Um, yeah, Aaron's happy. Nervous, of course. Yes, I've told him, and I'm pretty sure that means he knows. And you? Maybe you're not observant."

Meg beamed at her. "This is awesome! I'm so happy for you guys!"

"If I'd have known you'd be this excited, I would have saved the money and not brought the wine." Piper nodded to the glass behind Meg.

"Eh, I don't know. Love babies, but wine is appreciated too. Oh!" She threw her hands up, flailing as if she couldn't quite decide what she was doing. "Here. Give me your glass. Can I get you some water? Chocolate? Pickles with ice cream?"

"Oooo. Tempting. I'll just take some water though."

Meg rushed off to the kitchen for the water, and Piper called after her. "So what about you and Charlie? Any babies planned? Or…expected?"

She immediately regretted the question as Meg rounded the corner and returned to the couch. She dropped her eyes to her lap. Why had she pushed? You never asked women that. *But we're close friends, right? Isn't that allowed between best friends?*

Meg paused and swallowed. "Someday, maybe. God willing." Though Meg showed no sign of irritation, an awkward cloud had descended. *Way to go, genius.* Piper gnawed on her bottom lip, not sure where to go in the conversation now. Stupid pregnancy brain was making words so…hard.

But Meg spoke first, her cheeriness returning as she unleashed another torrent of questions. "So are you guys finding out the gender? Have you started thinking of names? I hear Meg's a good name, you know. Oh! Can I throw you a baby shower? Though I guess we don't have many friends in the area, do we? No bother. We can still have a party. Is it too early to go shopping? For the baby…not the party."

Piper slumped in her seat, feigning exhaustion and fatigue. "Man, how does Charlie put up with your rambling?"

"Oh, you know you love me. Plus, I'm pretty sure he has excellent selective hearing."

"Probably helps that you put out too."

Meg groaned. "I hope you clean your mouth out before you ever kiss that baby."

"Oh, lighten up. You guys are married. Pretty sure everyone knows you *do it*." Piper exaggerated the last two words and pulled her expression into the silliest contortion she could imagine. A fit of giggles exploded from Meg. Exactly her intention.

For the next few hours, the giggles continued, mixed with the occasional belly laugh and even a few snorts. Piper had gotten so lost in the conversation that she hadn't noticed the room darkening with the invading storm clouds. The wind picked up, slamming against the house with a sudden ferocity. Then the rain started, beating against the windows like a jackhammer.

She'd have to drive home in this. Hopefully it wouldn't hail. She hadn't thought to bring an umbrella in from the car. *Like an umbrella would help against hail.*

Piper glanced over to find that Meg had grown quiet too, though she wasn't watching the storm outside. In fact, her friend seemed oblivious, her expression blank as her gaze settled a few feet in front of her on nothing in particular.

Piper waved her hand in her line of sight. "You okay?"

Meg's head snapped up. Though her eyes met Piper's, her gaze remained distant, foggy. Piper raised an eyebrow at her, waiting for her to answer.

"Yeah. Of course." The corner of her mouth pulled up, but her gaze remained vacant, her thoughts lost somewhere Piper couldn't follow.

Piper snatched up the glasses and carried them to the kitchen. She looked out the window above the sink. It wasn't that bad, just some sideways rain and a bit of lightning. She grimaced and swallowed. Driving in sheets of rain when you were in town was one thing. It was quite another when you were winding around trees on gravel.

She called over her shoulder, pushing her voice to be heard over the din of the storm, "I should probably get going."

"You sure?" Meg asked from the door to the kitchen, giving a chuckle when Piper jumped. When had she followed her in here?

"Yeah. I need to stop at the store on my way home. Those pickles and ice cream sound delicious now, and I'm sadly out of both."

"Sounds good. Well, not the pickles and ice cream. That sounds awful." She motioned to the sink and the glasses Piper still held. "But really, you don't need to clean up. I can do that."

"I'm pregnant, Meg, not dying. I can put a few glasses by the sink."

"Fair enough. Well, if you need anything—even if it's a midnight run for watermelon and anchovies—call me. We Army wives stick together."

At the door, Piper turned. She raised a finger and shot Meg a stern look. "And don't even think about ditching me next week for dinner. I don't want to have to come over here and drag you out of your house."

Meg shuffled her feet, shoving her hands into the pockets of her sweatshirt. "I won't. Maybe."

"I'm gonna hold you to that."

"To the maybe? That's weird."

"You know what I mean." She opened the door and wrapped Meg in a hug. "I left the other bottle of wine on your counter, but promise me you'll get yourself some actual food for dinner."

Piper stepped out onto the porch, the air now cooled by the rain that was still falling. It had quieted enough that she could hear Meg's deep sigh. "Yes, Mom."

Bracing herself to step out into the storm, she called over her shoulder. "See? I'm good at this parenting thing already."

"Says the lady who forgot an umbrella..."

Touché.

5

CHARLIE'S UNIT had arrived in Kabul after a short flight, the shortest leg of their trip. The temporary lodging, a large tent lined with cots and cooled by a large air conditioner at one end, left little in the way of privacy, but sleep had thankfully come easily for him. Not that it helped. He still woke weary, as if he hadn't rested at all.

The earplugs Meg had insisted he pack blocked out enough of the noise around him, but the constant, vivid dreams had kept him from getting the rest he had needed. He'd woken with a thick fog clouding his mind, erasing the images. He'd spent all night running or fighting, but from what, he had no idea.

Feeling on edge was bad enough. Not knowing why was torture.

They had some time to relax before in-processing began, and while the rest of the team spent it working out or chatting, he attempted to catch a nap. The sporadic bursts of laughter several cots away made it impossible though, and with a sigh, he rolled over and pulled a small red book out of his pack.

It had been years since he'd had to memorize the sections of this book for confirmation. But he had plenty of months ahead of him to relearn them. Lying back into his pillow, he opened to the Ten Commandments and read through the first in his head. He closed the book, his thumb marking his place in the pages, and with eyes closed, he repeated the words in a barely audible whisper.

"You shall have no other gods. We should fear, love, and trust in God above all things."

As he picked the catechism back up to read through the second commandment, something stuck the palm of his left hand. He pulled a small envelope out, and a rush of warmth filled his chest. Its carefully tucked flap and the sharpness of the stationery's fold seemed inconsistent with the quirkiness of Meg's hand on the monogrammed paper—a perfect display of the paradox that was his wife.

Charlie,

You haven't left yet, but I already miss you terribly. I want you to focus on whatever mission you're given and not worry about me... too much. I love you. Never forget that.

You are mine. I am yours. Always.

Be strong, and let your heart take courage, all you who wait for the Lord. (Psalm 31:24)

Your wife,

Meg

A clearing throat spooked him. Woods stood at the foot of the cot looking more annoyed than normal.

"Winters. Man, we gotta go."

He looked around. When had they all left? He put Meg's note back into his catechism and pushed to his feet, dropping the book onto the floor.

"Seriously. We can't be the last losers showing up…again."

"I don't know what you mean. I'm never late. It's everyone

else who's so early." Charlie's laugh only grew louder at the sight of Woods's slumped shoulders.

"Next time, I'm leaving you behind."

Charlie pulled his chin back, letting his mouth fall open. "You'd leave a brother behind? What kind of soldier are you?"

Woods turned and stormed off. *Apparently a soldier with no sense of humor.*

He caught back up to him at the door to the briefing room. Tables ran the length of the room, which was already packed with their unit and another from some other state. He and Woods settled into their chairs in the back corner beside Carter, who slid a cup of coffee to him. He'd need that for this mid-afternoon briefing. He sniffed it. Burnt.

Tastes like freedom. How many times had Haas said that during their tours?

He forced himself to focus on the major's droning, but he couldn't keep from glancing at the assembled soldiers, watching the yawns spread around the room. Most remained hidden politely behind arms. Others weren't quite as tactful and came out loud and obnoxious, earning them a throat clearing from the commander. At least the major seemed as eager as the men to get through this briefing, which saved them from any further reprimand for their disrespect.

A few minutes later, though, Charlie noticed Carter doze off next to him and kicked his boot under the table, jolting him awake in time for the major's conclusion. He didn't want the kid to be the one soldier called out. Carter nodded his thanks. The guys shuffled out of the building, agreeing an early dinner at the chow hall would be better than having to go back out later.

The dining facility was nearly empty, but the guys still crowded at the end of one table, their elbows close enough to knock into each other as they ate.

Charlie looked up between bites. "Anyone else get the feeling this tour is going to drag?"

"Drag like that damn briefing," Murphy said, taking a sip of his V8 juice—the safest source of vegetables over here.

Martin leaned his elbows on the table, his head down as he spoke. "Not the most exciting missions I've been assigned."

"Would be nice if it even pertained to our MOS though." Charlie looked around at the guys.

"Welcome to the guard, dude." Murphy raised his chin and smirked. "That's how we roll—or how they roll us."

"It's how the Army rolls." Woods kept his eyes fixed on the food on his plate. He swore through a bite of food.

Carter elbowed Woods's arm. "Why are you such a downer?"

"Daddy issues probably," Murphy said, egging Woods on, and Charlie shook his head. Would the guy ever learn?

"More like mom issues…" Woods lifted his head and turned to Murphy, his eyes blank, face stern. "Your mom."

Everyone laughed…except Murphy. He threw his burger onto his plate. "Always with my mom. Not cool!"

"We all think she's pretty cool, dude." It was Carter this time who had the guys laughing harder.

"Y'all have girlfriends and wives—so lay off my mom." Murphy returned to his food, pulling his head down like a turtle retreating into its shell.

Charlie couldn't resist. "Lay off? Or *on*?"

"I hate you." Murphy shot him a stern look from the side, though he didn't look up or make a move to leave.

As more laughter ensued, the conversation continued with a mix of insults, mom-jokes, and random stories. Even Murphy couldn't refrain from joining in. But Charlie's focus shifted away from his buddies to the phone call he had waited nearly a week to make. The quivering in his stomach crawled up under his sternum, which left him confused. It was just a phone call.

Not even the most nerve-wracking one he'd ever made. But hopefully it'd be less embarrassing than *that* particular call.

Charlie's hand rested on his phone. Though he'd picked it up several times to call, he hadn't found the guts to do it. You can go to war and face the enemy, but you can't call a girl? *His thoughts mocked him. This wasn't just any girl though. This was Meg, and this wasn't his usual call.*

For months they had talked and laughed over pots of coffee and pitchers of beer, falling back into their roles as friends easily enough. He hadn't intended this though, nor could he even pinpoint when the change had happened. He simply knew it had, and he had to do something.

Taking a deep breath, he dialed again. The seconds between rings dragged, quickening his pulse. He rehearsed the words in his head, but each ring broke his train of thought. He had started to pull the phone away from his ear when her voice sounded.

"Hey, Charlie!" Her voice came out labored and short. "Sorry! I was in the shower and heard the phone. Nearly killed myself running with wet feet! I'm such a klutz!"

His rehearsed speech faltered at the mention of showers and wet feet. Come on! Pull it together, man! But the image in his head wouldn't budge.

"You there?" she asked, her voice returning to normal.

"Yeah. Sorry, I'm here." He stumbled over the words.

"So what's up? You want to come over? I had plans to order a pizza." Her casual invite caught him off guard. He could accept, forget his original plan. He steeled himself against the temptation.

"Actually, I wondered if you wanted to go to a movie tonight."

"Sure! What time?" she asked quickly. "I can meet ya over there and..." Her standard giddiness poured out with every word as she rambled into the phone. "Oh! Want me to pick up some burritos on the way? You've gotta love the big girly purses. They're perfect for sneaking in dinner."

His head dropped, and he pinched the bridge of his nose, closing his eyes. She had to make this more difficult than it needed to be.

"What if I came and picked you up? We could have dinner at the pub and then go to the movie."

There. It was asked, put out there for the world to hear. He held his breath and waited.

"But it doesn't make sense for you to drive over here. My house isn't on the way to the pub."

He drew in a deep breath and counted to ten.

"Meg, I am asking you out on a date," he said, mouthing each syllable with slow precision to avoid any further confusion and hopefully end this torture so he could either get ready to pick her up or retreat in shame and humiliation.

Silence. Was it really that hard to decide? Maybe he'd screwed up. Maybe it was too soon for her. Maybe she didn't like him. He waited until he thought the anxiety would break him in two.

"I know." She paused. "I just wanted to make you squirm a little. Pick me up at six?"

It was rare for Meg to fool him, but he hadn't minded.

"Should we leave him here?" Charlie heard Murphy say with a laugh. But it was Carter's hand waving at him that snapped him back to the present.

"Hey, you comin'?" The guys had all stood from the table and now stared at him like he had fallen asleep with his eyes open.

"Huh? Oh, yeah," he said. "Think I'm gonna find a phone actually."

Woods turned to him and motioned to the door. "Good idea. I need to give Murphy's mom a call."

Murphy went rigid, his nostrils flaring. He flipped the bird in their direction. Woods didn't seem to notice, but Charlie laughed heartily. Murphy was a pretty good sport, but eventually the guy had to realize it was his negative reactions that kept the jokes coming his way. If he didn't learn to shrug it off, the deployment—and every drill back home—was going to be rough for him.

The team split up as they left the chow hall, with most of the guys heading back to the PX or the tent. Woods and Charlie walked along in silence. Their friendship probably seemed odd to most, with Woods's glass-half-empty worldview being the opposite of Charlie's carefree attitude, but they had become fast friends over mutual frustration with the unit and its often-illogical processes.

Both had transferred in around the same time, though Woods had moved from a different state's national guard, rather than from active duty. His curmudgeonly demeanor hadn't made him many close friends, though no one actually disliked him. Charlie appreciated his ability to hang out without the need for mindless chit-chat. There were certainly worse people he could be stuck with when all he really wanted was to be left alone.

They entered the building to find a few chairs sitting empty outside the phone room. A movie played on a TV on the opposite wall. One phone was available.

Woods gestured to the phone. "Go ahead, man. I know you're anxious to call her."

"You sure?"

His buddy pulled his sleeve back to check his watch, and he laughed. "Yeah. I'm sure. Piper'd kill me if I called her this early."

Charlie glanced at the time. Barely past four a.m. at home. Sunday. She'd be up. Probably reading over a cup of coffee before taking a run before church.

Giving Woods a nod, he headed to the phone. He punched her number in, glad he'd memorized it all those years ago. Each ring seemed to go on for minutes. Each pause brought a new wave of anxiety. She could be in the shower or on her morning run. He checked his watch, calculating the time difference in his head. She should be around, but then again, a million things could keep her from answering, or perhaps he'd remembered the wrong number.

On the fifth ring, he lowered the receiver, his heart dropping into his stomach.

"Hello?" Her voice came, muffled by his hand. He lifted the phone again, the unease in his chest calmed by the sound. How sweet it was.

"Hey, babe. How ya doin'?" He winced. The words seemed so ordinary, so boring, as if he had called from the grocery store to ask about an item on the list. But he sat there, miles away, speaking to his wife for the first time in a week, and this was all he had.

"I'm good! Man, I miss you a ton! How is it over there?" Meg hadn't seemed to notice his mundane greeting.

"Oh, same ol' same ol'. We arrived this morning."

"What time is it for you anyway?"

"Six…ish. Sunday night. Just had dinner with the guys."

"Wait. You're ten and a *half* hours ahead? I completely forgot about the half-hour time difference. Why is that anyway? I thought all time zones were on the hour."

Her rambling was a welcome sound, that way she chattered on without a care. He could see her nose scrunching up like it always did when she found something odd, curious, or annoying.

"There's this thing. You might have heard of it. It's called the in-ter-net." He hoped the playfulness of his words translated over the phone.

"Har, har, har. Okay, smart guy. I'll look it up after church, because obviously you don't know the answer either." He could hear her smile in every word.

He softened his tone. "You ready for church? Nervous?"

"Yeah. A bit. I know I shouldn't be. It's church. I need to be there, but still, I hate going without you."

"I'm sure it will be okay. Maybe sit with Annie? I'm sure her kids will provide good distraction."

"That's a good idea. I don't want to deal with all the questions from everyone. Where is Charlie? How's he doing? When does he get back? It's obnoxious!"

"Aww, you hate talking about me so much. That's sweet." He heard her scoff into the phone. "Babe, they aren't trying to bother you when they ask questions. They're only trying to care for you."

She groaned. "I know. I just…I don't like it, is all. Why do I get so pissy?"

"Do you really want me to answer that?"

She stifled a chuckle. No doubt she was fighting against a smile, her face twitching to hold onto the bitterness he was poking holes in.

"Yeah, yeah, yeah. Okay. I'll try not to snap at the old ladies when they ask about you."

"Good." The image of his wife taking on the ladies of the church had him shaking his head. The line went quiet. Silence usually wasn't a big deal for them; it was comfortable, without the stumbling to fill dead space with whatever chatter they could muster. But here...here every quiet minute was one wasted.

Before he could fret any longer over what to say, her words came. "Any idea what you're going to be doing over there? No specifics, I know, but you weren't really sure before you left."

"Not really. We're still being briefed. We'll be here for a bit before heading out to camp, but looks like it'll be pretty low-key." He tried to hide his disappointment, but it clung to each syllable. "Just filling in as needed. Lot of driving probably."

"That sucks. You'd think they'd put you to better use with all they've spent on training you."

"Well, somebody's gotta do it, right?"

"Hopefully it's not as boring as it sounds. Should at least be more exciting than your usual commute." She let out a hearty laugh, no doubt accompanied by that goofy grin and the wild eyes she always had when trying to convince others to laugh with her.

"Meg, that was sad. I think your jokes are actually getting worse." Though she said nothing, he knew she smiled.

More silence.

"Piper's pregnant," Meg said, her voice coming out steadily, albeit more softly than usual.

That was news. His mind raced ahead of his mouth. This wasn't the average "so-and-so got a new car" or "the neighbors down the street painted their house the ugliest shade of purple" type of news. There was a shade of pain to his wife's words. This warranted a more thoughtful response, but she interrupted him before he could determine what to say.

"Did Aaron tell you?"

"No, he hasn't said anything, but you know how he is." He ran a hand along his jaw. This was rather big news to hide, even for Woods. "How's she doing?"

"Good. Only mild morning sickness thankfully. Already easing up for her too, which is awesome." Charlie frowned. To anyone else, her answer would have sounded like that of a loving friend, but he recognized the dry edge in her voice.

"And you? How are you, babe?"

Another deep breath came through the phone before she spoke. "I don't know. Happy for her—for them—of course."

"But...?"

"But you know. It stings a bit."

"Or a lot?"

"Yeah. A lot. And I hate it. I don't want to be jealous or bitter, but..." Her voice melted into a low groan.

"I bet she'd understand though."

"I guess, but I can't ever tell her that."

"But she's—" He stopped short, cutting off his plan to tell her Piper would want her to be open, honest. But could Meg open up, even to her best friend? *Meg is so much like Woods. But cuter.* "I mean, she's lucky to have you there."

Meg remained quiet. He wanted to reach out and hold her, to offer the comfort that words couldn't quite accomplish, but words were all he had, and those were now failing him. Failing her.

He couldn't give her a child any more than he could hold her in his arms right now, but he could still be the husband God had called him to be. He had to be, or at least he had to try.

"Meg. Babe. I'm sorry. I know it sucks, this whole balancing joy and pain thing. I wish I could be there, but..." He could hear her sniffing back tears. "Just remember, our Lord is with you. Always. He knows the ache you feel, the pain you carry. That we carry. You aren't carrying this alone, ever. I know it can seem that way at times—"

"It just hurts so much." Meg choked through her sobs. "I feel so...so broken."

"I know. It's not how it's supposed to be. Our bodies aren't supposed to be broken, but that's the sting of sin in the world." He paused to collect his thoughts. *God, help me out here!* He knew what to say, if he could only get it out the right way.

"We may not ever have children in this life, but we still have a loving God who cares for us daily, provides us with all we need, hears our strained prayers—even when we scream at him in anger. And he rescues us from this world of sin, protects us from evil and the devil, and wraps us in his grace. We may not have kids, babe, but we have Christ—crucified and raised for us and our salvation."

Meg drew in a long breath before responding, her voice still strained by the tears that lingered. She uttered the words "Thanks be to God," but they sounded devoid of any comfort.

Give her a break, please? She could use one!

He looked back out into the hallway to see the chairs filling up as others finished dinner. He turned back to the phone and dropped his forehead against his closed fist. "Babe, I gotta go. Time's up, and people are waiting. Once I get to Foster, I'll try to get internet set up so we can chat more often."

"Sounds good. I'm running late for church now anyway. And now I look awful with red eyes and…" She groaned again.

"Have a good time at church. And try not to run away too quickly when it's over."

Another breath seemed to clear the last of her tears away. "I love you. Sleep well."

"Love you too."

He found Woods waiting for him back in the hallway. Without a word, they started back, passing Humvees and tents along the way, but they remained blurred in his periphery, his focus stuck on the conversation replaying in this head.

"Feel better?" Woods asked.

The corner of Charlie's mouth pulled back slightly. He could crack a joke, ask how Murphy's mom was doing, maybe call him out on the news he was hiding. Woods had to know their wives would talk, but maybe he had his reasons for not mentioning it.

They squeezed past guys chatting and laughing loudly at the front of the tent. As he stepped over to his own cot, he was grateful Woods left him to go see what Martin was up to at the far end. He lay down with his boots still on, but he struggled to relax and settle into this new life so far from home.

He should pray—for her, for him, for the team, for everything—but his mind drew a blank, as it had on the phone. Staring at the ceiling of the tent, he remembered Pastor Feld's suggestion to pray as scripture taught, especially when other words didn't come. He closed his eyes, picturing her face and that giddy grin he had heard in her voice before their conversation had turned to more difficult topics.

Ignoring the sounds around him, he sent the prayer to God.

Our Father, who art in Heaven, hallowed be thy name. Thy kingdom come. Thy will be done on earth as it is in Heaven...

6

Meg's heels tapped against the pavement of the church parking lot. Though this building was her second home and the people within were her second family, her heart thumped wildly. There would be questions, so many questions, from all the sweet old ladies and the older gentlemen whose arms they held. She'd have to smile, nod, and provide the standard non-answers to questions of where Charlie was, when he'd be home, and what he was doing.

They meant well, of course, but each question and hand on her shoulder provided little comfort. Reminders of the absence of his hand in hers.

With a deep breath, she opened the doors and stepped into the narthex. The large entryway bustled with people who were grabbing bulletins, shaking hands, and chatting politely with one another. A young couple stood in front of her, hands clasped together. She pushed back against the tension rising in her throat.

She hadn't met them yet but knew they'd been married at the church a few months earlier. Charlie had insisted they invite them over for beers as a welcome-to-church-and-town gesture, but deployment preparation had forced the invitation to be delayed and subsequently forgotten. Charlie would want her to pick up the slack while he was gone, but she could barely stand the sight of them here. How could she welcome them into her home to flaunt their togetherness?

Meg's internal debate over when and how to invite strangers over for beer, without knowing if they even liked beer, was interrupted by the sudden and tight squeeze of arms around her shoulders. She should have escaped to the pews when she had a chance.

The familiar wave of Mrs. Goetz's perfume—a rich gardenia scent—hit Meg's nose. It was too much like her mom's. She cringed. As if she didn't already dread talking to people as it was—even Mrs. Goetz, the sweet, self-proclaimed matriarch of the congregation who had taken it upon herself to act as a surrogate mother to both Meg and Charlie upon discovering they had no family in town. And just like family, she had that habit of sticking her foot in her mouth and making things awkward.

Though Meg adored this kind woman, as one adores an aunt who pinches your cheeks every Christmas, she still tensed under the unsolicited hug, eager to run away. From her and from that perfume. But there was no good way to do that without hurting her feelings, so she relented and forced herself to relax under the mother hen's wing.

"How you holding up, sweetie? Charlie left already, right?" She looked Meg kindly in the face. Meg tried to return the smile.

"I'm fine, thank you. He left this week."

She looked down at her feet as she spoke. Talking about his absence made it that much harder to ignore. She should be handling this deployment better.

What's wrong with you? It's only week one. You're fine. It'll get easier. It's week one. You shouldn't be falling apart so soon.

The inner debate didn't help her feel any less crazy. *There really is something wrong with you.*

"Well, if you need anything, anything at all, you let me know. Mike and I are happy to have you over anytime." Mrs. Goetz released Meg's shoulders and gave her hands a final squeeze before walking away.

Meg scanned the room. The crowd thinned as folks entered the set of double doors to the left and found their seats in the pews. She attempted to avoid eye contact with some of the more intrusive congregants, but a wave of a hand caught her attention.

Annie Feld motioned her over. On her hip was propped two-year-old David, his head resting on his mom's shoulder, thumb in his mouth. By the look of his collar—folded the wrong way and stuck inside his shirt—his mismatched socks, and his shoes, which were on the wrong feet, it must have been a hectic morning in the Feld home.

"Meg! Glad you made it," Annie said. "Do you want to sit with us?"

"Yes, please." Her posture relaxed.

"Lydia has been dying to see you all week." Her pastor's wife gave a slight nod over her shoulder, and a little girl of five years old peeked around her mom's leg. Upon seeing Meg though, all timidity vanished, replaced by a bright smile and beaming eyes framed by a mess of blonde hair that had probably once been smoothed down and fixed in the barrette that now hung askew.

"Mrs. Winters!" Lydia ran up and hugged both of Meg's legs, nearly sending her toppling over from the impact. Meg laughed and leaned down to pick her up.

"Hi, Lyd! How are you? Did you help your mommy get everyone ready this morning?" Meg asked, not having to fake the cheeriness in her voice.

"I did! I put David's shoes on. He didn't want my help, and

he tried to bite me. See?" She turned and pointed to her shoulder where two small teeth marks still showed.

Meg widened her eyes. "Ow! That must have hurt!"

"It's okay. I didn't cry. I'm a big girl," she said with pride.

"Except you bit him back," a small voice said. Meg glanced around Lydia to see the oldest of the Feld kids, Matthew, standing there smirking, his hands in his pockets. Meg hid her chuckle and put on her best stern face for the little girl, who shrugged at her.

"What? I learned it from Mom!" She pointed accusingly at her mother.

Annie threw her head back before looking back down at her daughter. "I was pretending! It was a game! And even if it wasn't, Lydia, you are not the mama, and it's not your place to discipline your brother."

Lydia again shrugged off the reprimand and went back to smiling at Meg as they walked into the sanctuary. She pulled strands of Meg's wavy hair up and twisted them around, insisting, "I make your hair pretty."

Even if Lydia made her hair into a nasty nest of knots, Meg would have no complaints, thankful for this sweet distraction from the uneasiness that was still nestled inside her chest, albeit quieter now.

They settled into their seats. Lydia knelt on the pew, still playing with Meg's hair, throwing the ends in the air and giggling as they fell about her shoulders. Matthew sat on Meg's other side, his serious expression displaying as much ten-year-old maturity as it could. He marked each of the hymns listed in the bulletin before smoothing the pages open to service setting three and looking to the altar with patience. Annie dropped beside her eldest and quickly pulled off the toddler's shoes, quickly switching them onto the correct feet before the service began.

After Pastor Feld's greeting to the congregation, Lydia

insisted Meg hold her through the sharing of God's Peace. The chatty five-year-old helped to keep any awkward questions at bay and instead brought delightful smiles from all who could see her. As Lydia hummed along with the opening hymn, watching Meg's lips move through the verses, Meg regretted having ever dreaded being in the pew that morning.

"In the name of the Father and of the Son and of the Holy Spirit," Pastor Feld said after returning to the chancel steps. Meg made the sign of the cross and beamed as Lydia did her best to mimic the movement.

Throughout the Divine Service, Lydia and David took turns being held by Meg and their mother, who both worked to pay attention to God's Word amidst the commotion. It was Matthew who had the most difficulty ignoring the antics of his siblings though, and he eventually escaped their constant climbing over him by retreating to the far end of the pew.

During the sermon, Annie and Meg managed to avert disaster and calm a sudden meltdown from the younger children with an emergency pack of fruit snacks and some crayons. With new tools in hand, Lydia went to work coloring in the children's bulletin all while her lips recited the words of the Nicene Creed along with the congregation and her head bobbed its way through the offering music. As Meg stood for the prayers of the church, she glanced down at the girl's work to see a few stick people taking shape under a yellow sun and blue sky.

Meg struggled to listen to her pastor as he spoke. After all these years, though, she knew prayers would be lifted for all people, the government, families who were celebrating, and perhaps those traveling or moving. Despite all her effort to join in the prayers, her mind wandered, only being brought back to focus by Pastor's repeated "Lord, in your mercy" and her responsive "Hear our prayer." With guilt rising over not actually praying, she clenched her teeth and concentrated on each of Pastor's words.

"... for the Scott family as they mourn the passing of their beloved father this past week. May the Holy Spirit comfort them in this time of grief. Lord, in your mercy..."

There, she heard that one.

"Hear our prayer," she said.

"... for Charlie Winters currently serving in Afghanistan, that he would be strengthened by God's Word, be granted courage in the Holy Spirit against all foes, and be brought home safely to his wife, Meg. Lord, in your mercy..."

This time she could only whisper her response—"Hear our prayer"—due to the tears that had sprung up from hearing Charlie's name. She kept her eyes clamped shut to block out the faces of those she assumed must be turned toward her. If anyone had not known he had left, they did now.

She failed to hear any more of the prayers, and with her head a mess of guilt for dreading her church's loving support, and anxiety over how to graciously deal with that support, she nearly missed the final "Amen." She wanted to cry, but she wanted to cry alone, away from all these witnesses. But she couldn't run, not when little Lydia pulled on her arm and asked if she could stand with her at the Lord's Supper.

Kneeling at the railing with the little girl leaning against her shoulder, Meg tried to clear her head to focus on what was about to be given to her. Every muscle wanted to get up and run in the opposite direction, to hightail it out of the building to be alone. It was that very desire to leave that kept her rooted to the rail—though not wanting to create a scene helped as well—as she knew it was her sinful nature, and not God, who insisted she leave.

But God was who she needed, in blood and flesh.

Pastor Feld stopped before her. "Meg, the true body of Christ, given for you."

She ate and closed her eyes. What did others think of or pray while partaking in communion? She should be praying rather than wondering about it, but before she could pray, the elder stopped with the chalice.

"The true blood of Christ, shed for you."

She sipped and bowed her head. Maybe if she looked like she was praying, a prayer would come to her. But all she could think of was *thank you.*

Meg opened the restroom door. Dark. Empty. Perfect. She flipped on the lights and headed to a middle stall, shutting herself inside. She didn't actually need to be in there, but it was one of the few places where she could compose herself in privacy without questions or prying eyes. The broom closet would have been more suspicious, raising more questions.

This shouldn't be this hard. These weren't strangers. These were people who cared for her and Charlie, who had welcomed them in with such warmth it had always felt like coming home.

Yet without Charlie, this home away from home felt less… something. She wasn't really sure what the word was. It wasn't less welcoming or less friendly. It wasn't that his absence had changed any of the people, but it had changed something. It was that empty seat beside her. Always that blasted empty seat, whether in the pew or at the dining table. It ate away at her, a constant reminder that he was gone and would be for a while.

She dropped her head to her hands, her elbows propped up on her knees as she sat. Church wasn't a place to go only when life was going well. This was where God Himself came to meet her—with or without Charlie—in His Word and Sacrament, to give of Himself all that she needed. And she needed that whether she was alone or not. Whether she was sad or not. Whether she was able to focus or not.

She knew all of this, yet that sinful nature within her fought tooth and nail against it, countering each bit of truth with the temptation to run. Escape.

The bathroom door squeaked open, and two sets of heels clicked across the tile.

"I just feel so bad for the poor girl, you know?"

Meg didn't recognize the woman who spoke. She held her breath, hoping her suspicions weren't true. They couldn't really be speaking about her.

"Oh, I know. Bless her heart. I've been praying for her every night since they shared the news he was leaving. I just can't imagine," another unrecognizable voice responded, and Meg thought she really should make more of an effort to get to know the congregation, though not specifically for the purpose of restroom eavesdropping.

"I've been praying for him as well. I mean, not just for his safety—that's a given—but for his faith. I don't understand how one can be a soldier, to go over there and fight and possibly kill people, and still be a Christian."

Meg's jaw tightened. Her pulse raced.

"Uh-huh. I had the same thought. Doesn't make sense, does it? Been meaning to ask Pastor about that. It seems that job is so at odds with faith in Christ. I do hope..." There was another squeak, and the door opened again. The women left, taking their conversation with them.

Meg clenched both fists. What nerve they had. These old birds didn't even know Charlie, didn't even know he had been a Lutheran his whole life and had been raised in the confessions, not just with the cultural title alone.

Meg breathed deeply to regain her composure. She would have to leave the restroom eventually and walk amongst all these people enjoying their coffee and donuts with no way of knowing who it was who had questioned her husband's faith.

Charlie would insist she hold it together, to forgive them

and let it go. She could picture him walking into the fellowship hall with a smile on his face, acting like nothing had happened, like he hadn't heard someone doubt his faith. She could be like that. She could mimic his confidence. She could extend forgiveness to them for their words and maybe even thank them for their prayers—in her head, of course. She didn't trust her tongue quite yet. It had a way of pushing through any filter and saying the regrettable.

She washed her hands and stepped out into the hall, looking for Annie and the kids and the hopefully empty seat they had saved for her. Lydia waved excitedly to her and then pointed to the table where a cup of coffee and a maple donut waited.

"I picked that donut special for you, Mrs. Winters!" The little girl beamed up at her.

"Thanks, sweetie," Meg responded as she sat down.

"And I didn't even lick it. Promise!"

"I appreciate that. More than you know."

The little girl pointed to a brightly colored drawing on the table. "Look at the picture I drew for you!" On one side was a group of stick figures, each with one arm held up. She spotted Princess Lydia immediately, with her mess of hair, pink scribble of a dress, and yellow crown atop her head.

"There's me! And David and Matthew and Mommy and Daddy. And here's you!"

"Who's that?" Meg asked, pointing to the lone stick figure on the opposite side.

"That's your husband, silly. Don't you recognize him?"

"Oh, how embarrassing of me. It's just been so long since I've seen him, I forgot he looked like that. Is that a sword in his hand?"

"Duh. He needs a sword if he's going to war. Like King Peter in Narnia."

Meg nodded in understanding now.

Lydia continued chattering. "Except King Peter was a boy,

and Mr. Winters is old. But that's okay. He's not tooooo old. He can still fight pretty good."

Meg wrapped her up in a tight hug and whispered, "It's a perfect picture."

"It's yours! You have to take it."

"For me? Really? Are you sure?"

"Uh-huh. That's why I drew it. Mommy said you needed something to cheer you up."

"What if we sent it to Mr. Winters? He could use some cheering up too. You think?"

Lydia's mouth dropped open, her eyes growing wider and wider. She didn't speak, but she bounced up and down as only little kids could.

"I'm still waiting on his address, but as soon as I have it, we will sit down together and get it all ready to send to him."

Lydia stopped jumping, her shoulders drooping, no doubt in response to the delay in their fun adventure, but she soon added, "We should send him cookies too. My dad likes cookies. I bet Mr. Winters does too."

"Especially chocolate chip," Meg said, giving the girl another hug. She took a sip of her coffee and looked around the still-crowded hall.

This was family—her family—and what family didn't have a bit of drama?

7

Charlie hunched his shoulders as he stepped out of the small building that served as Camp Foster's dining facility. The fall air was crisper than expected, but it was still early, the sun starting to creep over the mountains that loomed closer here than they had back in Kabul. Soon, snow would be capping the peaks.

Even after several months of being here, he couldn't shake the familiarity the scenery held, so similar to the foothills of home. It was almost comforting, though it was an eerie sort of comfort.

Though he preferred video chats, they weren't conducive to the others' sleep, even with the plywood partitions between their rooms in the B-hut. They were better than the temporary tents back in Kabul but still not the most soundproof. While they'd all taken the opportunity to sleep in this morning—a well-deserved rest after being out in the field for five days—he had pushed himself to get a quick run in before the afternoon heat made it unbearable.

The camp was still quiet as he made the short walk to the comm building. All four phones were available, and a female soldier had her laptop connected to an internet jack in the corner, her fingers tapping quickly at the keys. If she noticed Charlie enter and sit at one of the phones, she didn't give any sign. He kicked himself for not thinking to bring the computer here, but that wouldn't have helped him much on his run. He'd remember it next time. Maybe.

He picked up the receiver and dialed. He'd barely uttered his "hello" when Meg launched into a recap of the week's happenings.

"This week was awful! I mean, I expected all this to happen months ago after you first left home, so I guess I was just due —" She paused, probably taking a sip of wine or beer or something, before continuing. "So, a few days ago I got some weird, nasty twenty-four-hour bug or something. I had a fever and was beyond tired. Completely out of it. But stuff still needed to get done. I had no clean dishes at that point, so I had to run the dishwasher, but in my loopy state, I must have put the wrong kind of detergent in."

"Uh-oh. That doesn't sound good."

"Yeah, not so much. Went to take a nap and woke up to find our entire kitchen swimming in bubbles. Crazy bubbles. The Feld kids would have loved it. Maybe even Matthew."

"Did you get it all cleaned up?"

"After a bit. I had to look up online how to get bubbles out of a dishwasher. Oil, apparently. So that was easy. But then I found out a bunch of water had somehow run into the basement and flooded part of it. Thankfully not near any of our boxes—just a few of the plastic bins, which were easy enough to dry off. I thought we had a shop-vac, but I couldn't find it."

"It's in the garage."

"What? I looked in there! Crap. Well, I bought another one. Went to the store. In the snow. Looking all sick and gross. They probably thought I was nuts."

"Or they thought you were sick," Charlie said, trying not to laugh at the image in his head: his wife trudging through the store, huffy, puffy, and undoubtedly still cute.

"Yeah, yeah, okay. Anyway, so you have a new shop-vac. Or I can return it. Whichever."

"Well, I'm glad you got all that sorted out. And that the bug only lasted a day. And at least it was all handled before your birthday, right?"

"Definitely. But the Muellers insisted on a cake after church. And singing. In front of everyone, Charlie! It was awful." Her words streamed together, as if she wanted to get through the reliving of the public embarrassment as quickly as possible.

"The horror!" Charlie feigned disgust. "How dare they want to celebrate your birthday? Such nerve. At least they didn't blab your real age or anything."

"Like I care who knows how old I am. I don't think that matters until at least forty, and I'm not even thirty yet. But at least the cake was chocolate, so that was good."

"And the rest of the week? Went okay?"

"Yup. The flowers you sent came a day early, and Piper let me pick the restaurant for our weekly dinner. Such a blessing, because I know she probably wanted to take me to that Mexican place where they make you put on the giant sombrero and force you to stand up while a bunch of strangers sing some stupid song to you that they don't know the words to."

"All you needed was to get lice from some communal hat, right?" His laugh came out louder than intended given the joke wasn't that funny, but he ignored it and continued. "Did you get your birthday present? I ordered it a few weeks ago, but I haven't checked my email yet. Not sure when it was set to arrive. I don't even know if it's shipped yet actually."

"You mean the flowers weren't my present?"

"Yes, because when I can't be there in person to honor the

day you were born, I'm only going to send you a present that dies within a week."

"Hey! I like flowers. At least when they die it's not completely my fault." She laughed. "But on the bright side, the delayed package means an extended birthday for me. Woo-hoo!"

"Still, would have been nice for it to arrive on time. Let me know when it does?"

"I will. So, anything exciting happen? You know, that you can tell me about?"

Charlie thought back to this week's mission. Boring. Pointless. Why was he even here?

"Well, I did see a monkey riding a motorcycle. That was kind of cool."

"Wait, what? Like, by itself?"

"Yeah, a small monkey-sized motorcycle. He had a little helmet and some leather chaps."

"Really?"

"No, of course not."

She groaned. "I fall for your crap every time."

"Every. Single. Time." He smiled. Her reactions made the jokes so much more fun. "But no, there really was a monkey. He was riding on the back of an Afghan's bike. I'll have to send you the picture I got when I'm back in my room."

"I bet Lydia would love to see that. I'll have to show it to her on Sunday."

"She'll probably be begging her mom and dad for a pet monkey then. They might tell us to find a new church if we keep giving their daughter new things to ask for."

"Hey! That trip to the pet store was a great idea! How was I to know a little five-year-old would insist on owning every animal she saw?"

"And continue to insist for weeks? I don't know. Maybe

because it's a pet store? Where you buy pets? Pretty sure Lydia understands how stores work by now."

"Yeah, but I thought it'd be like going to a zoo…only smaller. And with price tags."

Charlie could sense her frown over the phone and pictured her mouth scrunched up. Since she only ever made that face when she was mildly perturbed, he didn't feel too bad for finding it so cute. He never wanted to find her real distress attractive, but then again, it would take a lot for her to be anything but.

"Well, I hate to cut this short," he said, "but I want to try and get caught up on the Bible study before the guys wake up and it gets too noisy to focus."

"Good idea. That reminds me though, I might have sent you a lot of emails this week. So maybe put off reading those until you get caught up. I know you're so easily distracted and all."

"Will do. And we on for a video chat tonight? I mean, in the morning? Your morning?" Charlie asked.

"Yeah, do you have a time in mind so I can be sure to be up and showered first?"

"Sure you can't video chat from the shower?" he asked.

"Not so much. No."

"Then I guess I'll settle for seven."

Back in his room, Charlie stifled a yawn behind his hand. The words on the pages in front of him had long since blurred. Everyone was still asleep, or at least quiet, yet his focus still managed to derail—and due to nothing in particular either, which frustrated him all the more. He dropped the papers to the desk and made one last effort to regroup, rubbing both palms over his face and forcing the sleep and boredom from his eyes. He looked at the clock next to his cot. It was still early, but the others would be up soon.

Above his desk, a children's bulletin from church was pinned onto the plywood, with uneven lettering across the top: "FOR Winters." Meg's accompanying letter had explained the sword he held in the picture. Along the bottom, in Meg's own hand, were written the words of Psalm 27:3.

> *Though an army encamp against me, my heart shall not fear; though war arise against me, yet I will be confident.*

She had intended it for comfort, and perhaps she thought more was happening here that he simply couldn't talk about. But the verse only reminded him of the lack of war rising around him and the boredom that loomed, not just over him, but the rest of the team too. He should be grateful for it, for the ease, for the relative peace they'd found so far even with the sporadic mortar fire aimed at the camp.

But there was that twitch, that itch for battle that couldn't be scratched here at this camp with this mission. *Just do the job and suck it up. It needs to be done by someone. And you're it.*

"It's called duty for a reason..." he muttered to himself, recalling Woods's words from their last convoy.

Next to the drawing, Meg's face smiled at him from a framed picture, his favorite picture. The photo, taken years earlier before he had ever dared think of her as more than a close friend, seemed like any other, with no notable scenery or situation to set it apart. But it captured much more than her goofy smile. He couldn't even remember when it had been taken or where, but that smile, her eyes, they held every kind word and warm hug mixed with all her awkward and silly moments, with a hint of the fiery spunk he adored...even when it was directed at him.

And now that smile told him to get back to work. She'd be

expecting a response to her daily emails about the study. With new determination, he straightened in his chair and leaned forward against the desk. He picked up the papers again and read through the psalm.

The LORD is my light and my salvation;
whom shall I fear?
The LORD is the stronghold of my life;
of whom shall I be afraid?
When evildoers assail me
to eat up my flesh,
my adversaries and foes,
it is they who stumble and fall.
Though an army encamp against me,
my heart shall not fear;
though war arise against me,
yet I will be confident.

There it was again. Just a coincidence, but still, he stopped. He had tried for the last month to see the bright side of the slow pace of this tour, but all he found was disappointment. All his training, all his experience, was wasted driving a convoy back and forth, back and forth. Nothing ever happened. Even with the pain of past buddies lost in other deployments, he hated being taken away from home to do what amounted to so little.

The sound of the guys stirring in the adjacent rooms broke Charlie's moodiness and pushed him to finish the readings before anyone could interrupt. He read through the remainder of the psalm, saying it aloud as a prayer to God, and then skimmed over the hymn. Without Meg with him to hum the tune, he had no hope of reading the music, and this was a hymn he wasn't familiar with. He opened his travel Bible to Isaiah 55 and then to Ephesians 5:15.

Before he could finish with the reading from Matthew, his door shook under someone's fist.

Without a word, he darted to the corner and reached into one of the boxes Meg had sent earlier in the month. He couldn't use the rubber snake anymore. The guys had caught on after finding it in their boots or on their pillows. He needed something new, and Meg had come through for him with her latest care package.

Slipping the mask over his head, he snuck across the room as someone pushed the door open and poked a head in.

"Hey, Winters?" It was Carter. The younger soldier stepped a foot inside. "Winters?" he asked again. Charlie stood as still as he could, lying in wait behind the door. Carter's head scanned the room. As his eyes turned to the corner behind the door, Charlie jumped.

"Holy—what the…!" Carter leapt back. "I hate you, Winters! What the hell is that?"

Charlie burst out laughing. "It's a crying baby face." He took the mask off and tossed it onto his cot. "Don't you know a baby when you see one?"

"Well, yeah, but…dude. That baby's just creepy. You're such a jerk." Carter shuddered, but his frown soon turned into an awkward, embarrassed smile.

"And you're just so easy."

"Your mom's easy."

"You mean Murphy's mom..."

"Screw you!" Murphy's voice sounded from the other side of the plywood wall.

"Do you kiss your mom with that mouth?" Charlie shouted back.

"If he doesn't, I would," Carter said with a nod. "She's hot."

They heard a groan from Murphy's room, and the two laughed harder.

"Anyway, we were all headin' to breakfast." Carter

composed himself and motioned to the door in invitation for Charlie to join them.

"I grabbed a bite before calling Meg," he said.

Woods appeared in the doorway with Martin. "Man, you're making the rest of us look bad with all these phone calls."

"Not my fault you guys can't step it up."

"I already ate too," Martin said and then changed the subject. "You up for killin' zombies?"

"Sure. Not gonna get a taste of combat anywhere else, are we?" He stood to follow the guys out, but he stopped at the sight of Woods lingering in the hallway behind the others, like he was going to retreat back into his room.

"Yo, Martin, I'll meet you there!" he called before turning back to Woods. "You okay, man?"

Woods's head snapped up. His hand pulled at the back of his neck. He gave a tight smile and shrugged.

Charlie chuckled. "Yeah, that's convincing."

Woods didn't say anything. Didn't move. Just stared at the wall ahead of him, his head leaning to one side as if weighed down by something. He wasn't tense or on edge; that manifested differently—jaw tight, fists clenched. Neither described the guy in front of him. It was almost as if he'd given up. Surrendered.

To what though? The guy had it all: Piper, the baby—which he still hadn't mentioned to Charlie at all. Not that he cared. He had long since given up expecting his friend to make any kind of announcement, even for something as big as a kid.

Don't read too much into it. He's fine.

Charlie ran a hand across his mouth and chin. Aaron was a grown man. Whatever was bugging him, he'd handle it.

But that was the opposite of what he'd been told to do in all the briefings they'd been subjected to year in and year out. A good soldier looked out for his teammates, made sure they were healthy, ready.

He should talk to him, check in. But how? It wasn't like they could go grab a beer.

"You should go, man." Woods nodded toward the door.

"Nah. If I ever show up on time, they'll start expecting that." Though he smiled, he felt a familiar pang of regret. He couldn't expect his friend to open up to him when all he ever did was brush things off with a joke and a laugh. He had no chance of helping him—helping anyone—if he couldn't show them he was good for more than goofy one-liners.

He could take the easy route again and ignore it, assume Aaron had everything under control and that it was all in his head, his imagination getting away from him.

Laugh it up. Run away. Like you always do.

He clenched his jaw. Not this time. This time he'd do it right. He'd help. If he could figure out how.

"Hey, come on, dude. Let's go grab a coffee." If beer was out, coffee was the next best option, even the sludge they served here.

"Thanks, man, but I'm just gonna head back to my room."

"You sure?" He gestured to the door.

"Yeah. I'll catch ya later." Before Charlie could say more, Woods had turned and was halfway down the hallway, his long stride aiding in his fast getaway.

Finding himself in the hallway alone, Charlie let a curse fall from his lips. What was he doing here? The disappointment of this tour and the lack of fulfillment he found in the day-to-day was bad enough. But now he was failing his team, his friend. All he was good for was a laugh.

Maybe that wasn't a bad thing. Laughter could still serve his neighbor.

Maybe.

Raindrops pinged the windshield as Meg pulled into the parking lot behind Finn O'Connor's pub and cut the engine. Not seeing Piper's sedan, she considered waiting outside, but the disappearing warmth within the Jeep encouraged her to head in and grab a seat and perhaps a beer. She slid her coat on and headed out into the rain, her shoulders hunched to protect her from the cold drops. The heat and familiar sounds of the pub greeted her, and with a wave to the hostess, she strolled to her usual stool at the bar, draping her now wet jacket over the back.

"Hey, Meg!"

Matt dropped a coaster in front of her, his tattoos peeking out from under his rolled-up shirt sleeves, though not enough to identify what they depicted. With his height and muscular build, he could be intimidating, but his warm demeanor and easy smile made that nearly impossible.

"Hey. You're looking…different." She smirked at him and waved a hand to where his beard, once full and a bit scraggly, was now trimmed close to his face.

"Thanks? I think?"

"I mean, good…different. Different in a good way." She winced. *So…awkward.*

He chuckled before running a hand over his chin. "Rachel insisted I finally tame the beast a bit. Said I was probably scaring away customers."

"Your wife's a smart cookie. Though I don't think customers care. They just want beer, right?"

"That's what I told her. Thinking of shaving it all off though. I don't want to look like one of those skinny-jean hipster guys."

"Shush. You don't want to offend your customers." Meg nodded to a guy with perfectly coiffed hair and thick-rimmed glasses at the other end of the bar, and Matt laughed. See, she could be funny. If only Charlie were here to witness it.

She leaned forward and lowered her voice to a whisper. "Is he wearing a bow tie?"

Matt met her whisper and added a grimace. "I think so."

"Yeah, you've got nothing to be afraid of. You could never look like that." She settled against the back of the stool.

"Thanks. Anyway, you look like you're doing well. It's been a while since you've been in though. I was starting to worry."

"Totally not my choice, I swear. Piper keeps pushing me to branch out and *try new things*." She paired the last three words with a smirk and an exaggerated use of air quotes to emphasize her annoyance.

"Whatever," Piper's voice said from behind her. "It's for your own good, silly."

She pulled Meg into a side hug before angling her body onto the stool, with a hand guarding her belly—her baby—from hitting the bar. "Hey, Matt. Oh, love the new look!"

"Thanks." Matt set a coaster and a glass of water in front of her. "I hear it's different...in a good way." He shot a wink at Meg.

"Think you forgot something." Meg raised her brow at him, her best impression of Charlie. Maybe she could get another laugh.

He gave a slight shrug. "Nope. I never forget a thing."

From below the bar he produced a small plate of sliced limes and set them beside Piper's water.

"I was going to grab your usual, Meg, but I wondered if you might want to *try something new*?"

His mocking air quotes with the last three words caused Piper to chuckle into her water glass. So Meg knew what she liked. What was so bad about that? Snapping the menu closed, she tossed it onto the bar with a huff. "I'll have the seasonal draft," she said.

Keeping his eyes on the tap as he poured Meg's pint, he

directed the question over his shoulder. "So how are the guys doing?"

Piper answered for them. "So far, so good, I think. Right, Meg?"

Matt moved to set the pint on the bar, but Meg reached for it instead. She took a long sip. No point in wasting time letting it sit on the counter.

"They sound pretty bored," Meg added with a nod, cradling the glass in both hands.

Matt leaned back against the sink behind him. "That can't be all bad, right?"

Though Piper nodded, Meg sat, watching the bubbles rise in the deep browns of her drink. "You were in before, right, Matt?" she asked, her eyes still on her beer.

"Yeah. Army. Six years. Been out a few."

"Miss it?" Meg tried to keep the question casual. She looked up.

"Sometimes. Why do you ask?"

"Just curious." She didn't have to look at Piper to know her friend was giving her *the look*—of accusation, of suspicion. She was used to it. You got used to it when you kept secrets.

"I'll leave you guys to chat then. Let me know if you need anything."

Meg's eyes followed Matt as he headed to the other side of the bar where an older gentleman had taken a seat next to the hipster. He seemed happy with civilian life. Fulfilled. Content.

Maybe Charlie could too. Someday. He'd worn the uniform for as long as she'd known him. She could never ask him to quit. It was as much a part of him as the scar on his left elbow or the birthmark on his wrist. She cringed, hating how selfish she felt for wanting him home, wanting him to leave behind the military and everything he loved.

Everything she hated.

You don't hate it...not all of it anyway.

Despite the irritating quirks of military life and the unique challenges that came with the national guard, it really wasn't bad. Plus, he looked good in a uniform. And he loved it. She couldn't really hate anything that was so much a part of him, could she? But the least they could do was use him properly. As much as she wanted him home, she hated when he was bored.

Maybe he's just not telling you everything.

Of course, he couldn't tell her everything, but it didn't take a genius to hear the disappointment in his voice or see it in his face. He had been trained for so much more, to do more. And they had him driving? What was the point?

He's filling a need though.

True, maybe the need right now was a driver, but still, she couldn't shake her fear. Was he content? Would he be content when he came home? Or would this deployment—with all its mundanity—be the tipping point that pushed him back to active duty? And could she handle that if it did?

"How are you holding up?" Piper's voice cut into her thoughts, and she turned to face her friend.

"Pretty good so far. Just..." *Don't divulge too much. She won't understand.* "...miss Charlie is all."

"Do you guys talk a lot?" Piper asked.

The dreaded question. Few guys called as often as Charlie did—phoning twice a day when he wasn't on a mission. That didn't include the countless emails and instant messages they exchanged either.

"I guess." She hid her face behind her beer, wishing she could disappear into the glass.

"Aaron's not much of a talker." Piper showed no sign of frustration or irritation. It was merely a fact.

"You don't say." Meg laughed, hoping they could get off the topic soon, but she couldn't think of any way to divert the conversation.

"Honestly, I don't even know what you guys find to talk about that often."

"Random stuff, I guess. You know Charlie always has a story to tell or something, some joke or prank I don't get. But it's nice to hear each other's voice."

"I shouldn't be surprised. Even distance can't faze your sappiness." Piper pretended to gag, but it soon morphed into an actual fit of coughing that refused to be calmed by her gulps of water. "Darn pregnancy gag reflex."

There was Meg's out, the path away from having to talk about herself and Charlie. "How is pregnant life anyhow? Any new cravings?"

"Not really. Nachos. And strawberries."

"Not together, I hope."

Piper only offered a sly smile.

"Ew!"

"Hey, you're the one who asked. Don't blame me."

With a laugh, Meg sat back in her seat and ran a hand through her hair, her fingers getting stuck briefly where the waves had tangled in the wind and rain that still raged outside. Her mood shifted as abruptly as the conversation had.

The chatter of the other patrons at the bar, the laughter from the dining room behind her, and the clinking of glasses and plates all around began to grate on her. She clenched her teeth, fighting the tugging at her limbs and the tightening in her chest that pushed her to leave. To escape. She was spent. She had done her socializing for the day, and she couldn't give any more. Would Piper understand if she ducked out early? Even before eating?

You can't leave. She needs you.

Meg stole a glance at her friend, who was playing with the last two limes on the plate. All the laughter and joy had washed away, replaced by a quiet unease. How had she missed this—the obvious signs of loneliness and worry playing across her expression, stealing the fun from her eyes?

Piper was alone too. It was her first deployment, her first time sending a husband off to war. That's what kept Meg coming to these dinners, enduring new menus, and forcing herself to branch out. She didn't agree to these outings for herself. She would have been content, happy even, to stay at home and order a pizza.

Serve your friend. Get over yourself and stay.

Though she couldn't push the discomfort aside, like a coat she could remove and sling over the back of the stool, she could ignore it.

And she would. For Piper.

8

MEG WRAPPED the blanket around her shoulders as she settled back into the dining room chair. The rain—unusual for this late in the fall—had left her so chilled, nothing seemed to undo it—not the blanket, not the fire, not the cup of tea in her hands.

She flipped open her laptop and checked her watch. Nine thirty. It was nearly her bedtime, and there was no point in staying up when she was alone. But she needed to see him, not just hear him, and he'd thankfully agreed to oblige, waiting until the others had gotten up and left for breakfast.

He should call soon. She took a sip of her coffee, burning her tongue on the still-hot beverage. She let out a curse as the screen dinged with his incoming call.

She answered, pressing the *accept* button on the screen. She smiled.

"Hey, babe!" Charlie said.

Man, he looked good. Even without the beard.

"Hey. How's it going? Sleep okay?"

"So-so. As well as I can when I have four different alarm clocks going off through the night."

"What? Why'd you set so many?"

"I didn't." He gave a small laugh and ran a hand over his face, rubbing the sleep from his eyes.

"More pranks?" She smirked at him. He nodded. "Who?"

"Carter. Maybe Murphy too. It was a strong retaliatory effort."

"So I take it the mask worked then?" She'd been an accessory to his antics, unable to say no to those eyes and that smile.

"The first time? Yeah. You should have seen Carter's face. Totally got him." Charlie laughed. "Though, he got me back later."

"With the alarm clocks."

"Oh, no. That was for this last time. The first time it was the standard bucket of cold water in the shower trick," Charlie said with a shrug.

"A classic." Meg nodded, not that she knew anything about pranks. Boys were so weird. "Wait, so what'd you do this last time? Do I even want to know?"

His smile spread—larger than normal. That couldn't be good. As his smile gave way to laughter, she forced a smile back, bracing herself for what was coming.

Sure enough, his laughter grew louder. His eyes closed as he threw his head back, reliving some mischief he would divulge eventually. He started to explain a few times, but each attempt derailed into a set of hysterics complete with hearty belly laughs and chuckles so strong that all sound was stifled.

She had witnessed this many times before. All she could do was sit and wait for him to compose himself enough to share the epic tale of hilarity. But after a minute or so of watching him double over, clutching his stomach while his eyes teared up, her patience started to give.

"And....?" she said, nudging him along.

He calmed himself down as much as he could. "So, the other day..." His fits of laughter had subsided long enough to get full words out. *He's really lucky he's cute.*

"Carter gets a care package from his girlfriend for his birthday. He was so excited. Apparently she had promised some great surprise for him."

"What did he hope it would be?" Meg hoped questions might keep the laughs under control, but it had the opposite effect. He pursed his lips and clamped his eyes shut again in an effort to keep from busting up again. "What? What was it?" Meg asked again with caution, not sure she wanted to know what had him laughing this hard.

Charlie steadied himself with a sigh. "Whew. Okay. So, he thought maybe it'd be some zombie movie or a Will Ferrell movie or something." He leaned closer to the camera like he was about to reveal some deep secret.

"But?"

"No one knows what she was thinking, because she sent him some chick flick, *Walking to Remember* or something." His eyebrow raised, and his eyes lit up with a childlike excitement Meg couldn't understand, at least not in this context.

"*A Walk to Remember*?"

"Yeah, something like that."

"So a girl sends her boyfriend a girly movie, and that's why you're laughing like a hyena?" Meg rolled her eyes with an exaggerated sigh.

"Oh, that's not why I'm laughing. He couldn't bring himself to tell her he didn't like it, and he knew she was going to ask him about it. Apparently it's one of her favorite movies."

"Yet she's never made him watch it before?" She raised an eyebrow at him. "Maybe his girlfriend's playing a little prank of her own."

His eyes lit up her screen, making him look more like a kid on Christmas than a grown man serving his country. "Man, that would make this so much better! If he watched it and didn't have to, oh, that would be great. But anyway, so he's watching this movie, and Woods and I walk into his room, find him sitting on the floor, crying like a baby. So Woods and I sit down on either side of him, just sitting and watching the movie with him."

"What part of the movie?" Meg asked, now curious what had moved Carter to tears.

"I don't know. Some chick was in a hospital, and there was talking. I wasn't really paying attention. Does it matter?" Of course he hadn't paid attention. He hadn't even been able to remember the name of the movie.

"Guess not. But…wait, was that the funny part of the story? There's more, right?" What was she doing encouraging him to continue? She braced herself for the fits of laughter to overtake him again, but they must have passed.

He leaned back, his brow furrowed as he shook his head.

"How would that be the funny part? Yeah, there's more. So, we're sitting there, and Carter glances at Woods, who's staring at the screen looking bored, then looks at me real quick. And I'm wearing that mask. Freaked the crap out of him. He practically jumped into Woods's lap."

His head leaned back with another roar of laughs, not noticing she hadn't joined in. She couldn't stop the smile from forming on her lips. As boring as the deployment had been so far, she was grateful it hadn't kept him from having fun. She had to admit—though never to him, of course—some part of her loved this side of him, however obnoxious his fits were.

"And Woods then—"

"Oh, it's not over?" She looked around the room, pretending to look for an escape.

"Oh, shush. So Woods wraps his arms around him and says, 'There, there, I've got you.'"

She leaned her head to the side, eying this strange creature who was her husband. His eyes were closed again, his head shaking back and forth as he continued to laugh. So, so weird. She'd never understand this part of him, but did she need to?

She cleared her throat to get his attention. "I guess I had to be there."

"Probably. Maybe." He shrugged and flashed her a smile. "Or you're dead inside. Still, it was awesome. And now we'll have plenty to give him crap over for weeks."

"Sounds like fun. I bet Murphy will be happy to have the heat off his mom finally."

Charlie shook his head. "Nope. Not a chance. Aaron's not gonna let that one die down anytime soon. Not with how riled up it makes Murphy. He can handle it though."

"Do you guys do any actual work over there?"

"I'll have you know all these jokes take quite a bit of work and planning."

"I'm sure."

Their conversation hit a natural pause, a comfortable silence with Charlie still smiling that dorky grin at her. No way could she top his story. Her mind blanked, the long day wearing on her. She looked down at her hands and twisted her wedding band around her finger, causing the dining room light to dance off the stones.

"Remember Prague?" Charlie's tone had shifted, all the mirth and hilarity from the last ten minutes gone.

Meg snapped her head up, her gaze catching his. Pursing her lips, she pulled her chin back. "You mean where you abandoned me?"

"I did not! You left me!" His arms raised in defense, countered by a glint in his eyes that showed a smile that had bypassed his lips.

"Nuh-uh. No way! One minute we were looking around for our hotel, turning around in circles, and then suddenly you were gone!"

She had stood in the center of that neighborhood over three years ago, staring at a useless map that didn't even show that area of the city. Confused. Lost. Not knowing the language. And when she had looked up, she had found herself alone to boot. She had been so mad at him, and all the guilt trips she had unleashed after finding him had ruined the rest of the day.

"Why would you even bring that up?" she asked. "It wasn't exactly my most shining moment."

"That wasn't what I was talking about, doofus. Don't you remember the bridge?"

She snapped her mouth shut. Of course she remembered the bridge, how she had stood there letting her crappy mood and stubborn pouting keep her from enjoying a perfectly good sunset. Did he remember the bridge? Or was he thinking of a different bridge? He couldn't possibly have some sentimental memory from that stupid day when she'd completely and utterly failed to forgive him and let it go.

She nodded to him, her confusion scrunching her nose and shooting a look of disdain across her expression.

His gaze softened before dropping to his hands. "That's when I realized we could overcome anything." He paused to rub a hand across his neck before looking at her again. "Arguments, disagreements, misunderstandings, even your crappy attitudes—none of it could undo us. I just knew. I knew I wanted to marry you."

Deployments had this power—over both soldier and spouse. The separation upped the sentimentality, pushing people to voice things that never quite fit into conversations back home. But she hadn't expected it. Not now, after his ridiculous story.

But he looked at her with such love and admiration that her eyes welled up with tears. Her lip quivered just enough that he couldn't have missed it. "Way to make me cry." She wiped the moisture from her cheek with the back of a hand.

"Well..." Charlie disappeared from the screen for a moment, and from off-camera he asked, "Would this help?"

When he reappeared, he was wearing the crying baby mask, and it was Meg who couldn't control her laughter.

That man. He really was lucky he was cute.

The headphones did little to block out the noise from the guys chatting in the hallway. Though their words were muddled, Charlie could identify Murphy's cocky tone, the pause when someone quieter—Martin, perhaps—responded, and the quick words of Carter mixing in. Had it been music playing in his ears, he could have better ignored the bursts of laughter and the swells in volume as they shared jokes and stories, but he needed a half hour to get caught up on everything Pastor Feld had sent him in his last email.

Charlie,

Things have been pretty busy here, which is no surprise for this time of year. I'm sure Meg has told you how hard the kids are working on their Christmas program, and we're so thankful she agreed to help out again. All the kids love her. I'm hoping we'll be able to record it and share it with you, though you may have to settle for a poor-quality video from someone's phone if we have any more mishaps with our equipment. Seems like something's always breaking or falling apart.

Attached is the bulletin from this last week's service and the mp3 for the sermon. Hopefully sending the file to you directly will help with the streaming issues you were having last time.

If you have any questions on the readings or anything, let me know. Advent is a busy season, but I will make time to respond.

Know that we are praying for your continued safety, and I pray God's Word would continue to sustain you through all the trials—even if it's the burden of feeling idle.

God's Peace to you,
Pastor Feld

The recording of the service did work much better than the streaming. He'd be sure to thank Pastor for sending it. As he listened to the sermon, he smiled at the intermittent laugh or cry of a baby that broke through, thankful for those noises that made it feel like he was sitting back in the pew beside his wife rather than in a room made from plywood with the crude humor of friends echoing behind him.

Around the ten-minute mark, a loud cry came from the recording, the unmistakable voice of the pastor's own daughter as she yelled out, "Mrs. Winters, I went potty!" Meg would have turned a bright red with embarrassment as she shushed the young girl. Even Pastor Feld struggled to stifle a laugh and not let the interruption derail his preaching.

As the sermon neared its conclusion, another voice interrupted, this time from behind him.

"Hey, you have a minute?"

Charlie placed the headphones on the desk and turned to find Woods standing in the doorway, his hands shoved in his pockets. There was an edge in Woods's voice again, but it was so subtle that Charlie nearly gave up believing it was real.

Each time he had decided to confront Woods, to see what was going on and offer some help, the guy had delivered his trademark wit, perfectly-timed and with enough of a smile to change Charlie's mind.

You're imagining it. He's fine.

But if he wasn't...

Seeing Woods in his door now brought the concern back, and he closed his laptop before standing.

"Sure. What's up?" He offered the desk chair to his friend, opting to sit on the cot.

Woods took a step in but stopped. He turned to leave. "Forget it. It's nothing."

"Dude, wait. You can't do that." Charlie rose again and took a step forward, his eyes searching for any sign of what might be troubling his friend. But the guy was impossible to read, even after years of friendship.

"Think I can, and I just did." Woods's voice remained flat, emotionless, but he didn't make another move to leave.

"C'mon. Something's up," Charlie pushed, but Woods looked at his feet. "Look, you don't have to talk about it. I won't make you, but it's obviously big enough that you brought it up."

"It's nothing," he repeated with a shrug.

"Yeah, I can see that." Charlie gave a small laugh—anything to break through the tension Woods had brought with him.

A minute passed in silence. Neither man moved. Both stared at the floor.

Charlie treaded lightly. "How about a prayer then? If you don't want to talk."

Woods looked up and met his gaze, his eyes narrowed. "You know I'm not into those pre-written prayers you use. They're so...dry."

Charlie let out a laugh. "That's rich, man. Do you need a mirror?"

But his friend didn't smile.

"C'mon. Humor me then."

Woods sighed but took the few steps to the desk chair and sat down without a word. Charlie reached for his Bible and opened to the Psalms as he sat on the edge of his cot. He turned to a page whose corner had been bent and smoothed out again too many times.

He cleared his throat and read:

"Incline your ear, O Lord, and answer me, for I am poor and needy. Preserve my life, for I am godly; save your servant, who trusts in you — you are my God. Be gracious to me, O

Lord, for to you do I cry all the day. Gladden the soul of your servant, for to you, O Lord, do I lift up my soul. For you, O Lord, are good and forgiving, abounding in steadfast love to all who call upon you. Give ear, O Lord, to my prayer; listen to my plea for grace. In the day of my trouble I call upon you, for you answer me."

Charlie stopped. He closed the Bible, keeping his thumb secure between the pages he had read. He whispered an "Amen" and heard his friend repeat the word even more quietly. The men sat in silence for a brief minute before Woods posed a question.

"You pray the Psalms?" His curiosity seemed genuine. His tone no longer carrying the opposition he'd shown earlier.

"All the time. I mean, that's what they are—prayers from the psalmists to God. And they cover every emotion—despair, worry, fear? And joy."

Woods sat still. He didn't fidget or budge. He didn't even seem to breathe, but Charlie could see his friend turning this over in his mind. He waited, hoping the guy could let go of whatever was nagging at him, even if he never voiced it.

He opened the Bible again and flipped back several pages.

"Cast your burden on the Lord, and he will sustain you; he will never permit the righteous to be moved."

Woods shifted a bit in his chair but still said nothing.

Keep trying. This is what he needs to hear.

Charlie moved the pages to the Gospel of Matthew.

"Come to me, all who labor and are heavy laden, and I will give you rest. Take my yoke upon you, and learn from me, for I am gentle and lowly in heart, and you will find rest for your souls. For my yoke is easy and my burden is light."

Charlie began to lose heart as he looked at his friend. There was no sign on Woods's face that the words were helping or having any effect at all.

Woods leaned forward. Placing his elbows on his knees, he

rubbed his hands over his head before looking up at Charlie. This silence wasn't their standard. There was no comfort there, no ease, only the weight of Woods's hidden burden.

He could pray. He needed to pray, even if only silently.

Lord, help him. Even if that help isn't from me. Give him peace.

After a few minutes, Woods sighed. "I…" He shook his head and clamped his mouth shut again. He wouldn't budge.

Charlie formed his words with care. "You really don't have to tell me. I'm not going to push you to talk, because whatever it is, it's obviously weighing on you. A lot. But remember, Christ knows what you're facing. You're not alone. Ever."

Woods nodded slowly.

"Thanks."

He stood, and in two long strides he was at the door. He turned to face Charlie before leaving. "What…what do you do when you try to give your crap over to Christ but that rest He promises doesn't seem to… I never feel it lifted or removed."

"Well, we know a couple things," Charlie answered. He set his Bible back onto the desk and settled back into his heels, putting his hands in his pockets to keep the conversation casual and relaxed. "First, God gives us a peace that's not necessarily what we expect—that whole 'not as the world gives peace' thing. Doesn't always feel the way we want it to, I guess. But then we know life in this fallen world is gonna blow. It's going to be hard and suck a lot of the time, and that means the peace and the rest Christ offers may not actually come while we're here."

Charlie sighed, not sure if any of what he was saying helped at all, but he had one last point to make. He looked up at his friend, and with confidence he proclaimed, "But we have assurance of an eternal peace in Christ crucified. And knowing what He's done for us? And the life we have in Him? That brings us some peace regardless of what we face now. We know he'll come again, so right now we wait. But we wait with hope."

Woods's shoulders slumped slightly, and his face remained unmoved as he digested the words. Just as Charlie was ready to admit failure, Woods lifted his eyes and gave a half-smile.

"You ever think about being a pastor?"

Charlie scoffed at the suggestion, but the corners of his mouth lifted slightly. "Dude, I'm far from qualified for that."

"I dunno. You say that, but...anyway, thanks again, man." With a final nod, Woods turned to leave.

"Anytime," Charlie said as he followed Woods into the hallway and watched him squeeze past the other guys before disappearing into his own room. He ignored the questioning looks from Murphy, Carter, and the others. Woods had given no sign that the conversation had helped, but that was no surprise. The guy could be a spy for how well he guarded and controlled his emotions.

Charlie returned to his room and settled onto his cot, hands behind his head. He stared at the ceiling, thinking. Had those been the best psalms to pray? What if he had given his friend the wrong scripture for whatever plagued him?

The questions nagged at him. But Isaiah 55 came to mind and eased his worry. God's Word was never empty. It would accomplish whatever God intended.

Charlie couldn't, however, push away the fact that his friend still battled something. The guy might never open up, but that was okay. Charlie could help shoulder the burden without details.

God knew what plagued Woods. That was enough.

Charlie walked out of the B-hut to find the guys had strung up Christmas lights along one side of the building. The evening air had cooled enough to warrant heavier jackets, but it was still warmer than the Decembers back home. Someone had brought their iPod out to play the comforting sounds of Christmas songs. Several of the guys had Santa hats, while others donned reindeer antlers, and everyone was laughing and singing.

For a moment, Charlie forgot he wasn't back home enjoying a holiday unit party. If only. At least they'd omitted the mistletoe from the decor. That would have been awkward, to say the least.

"You bring 'em?" Carter called excitedly over the music and ran to meet him.

Charlie lifted the box. "Of course. But what makes you think I'm sharing with you?"

"Ah, man. Please? Don't make me beg." The kid jutted out his lip, his eyes drooping into such a sad expression that Charlie couldn't help but chuckle as he lifted the lid.

"Well, she did send a double batch this time, so I guess I can let you have one."

"One's enough for me!" Carter beamed and snatched a cupcake. He shoved the whole thing in his mouth and downed it in one bite. Closing his eyes, he nodded in appreciation. "So good. Your wife rocks. Seriously."

"That she does." Charlie made the rounds through the crowd, offering the cupcakes to the rest of the guys with a nod of his head toward the box.

Murphy peered at the baked goods with suspicion before picking one up. "What's she put in them anyway? They can't be that amazing. They don't even have frosting. What's the point of a cupcake without frosting?"

"You don't have to have one," Charlie said.

Baker ran up, his Santa hat falling into his face as he spoke. "I'll take his! They shouldn't be wasted on someone who can't fully appreciate their awesomeness."

Murphy turned to block Baker from grabbing the cupcake from his hand.

"How did you not know about these yet, man?" Carter

asked. "She's sent him several boxes already the past few months. Hell, she sent me a batch for my birthday back in October!"

"Winters must not love me as much," Murphy answered, still holding the cupcake.

From a chair beside the wall, Martin pointed his cigar toward Murphy. "I can't imagine why. I mean, you're just so lovable."

"I am!" Murphy took another look at the cupcake, sniffed it, wrinkled his nose at its strong scent, and then plopped the whole thing into his mouth.

Carter's eyebrows raised in anticipation, waiting for his reaction. Everyone seemed to be holding their breath. Murphy closed his eyes and choked it down through a fit of coughs.

"Holy…what the hell are in those? They're so sweet!"

"And strong!" Carter added with an excited nod.

"Are you even old enough to eat these, Carter?" Murphy questioned, still trying to recover from the shock of the booze he'd consumed unknowingly.

"I don't know what you're talking about, Murphy. Alcohol is strictly prohibited," Charlie said, fighting back a smile.

"Yeah. Well, you could've at least warned me."

"Where's the fun in that? Anyone see Woods around? He loves these things."

Carter reached for another cupcake from the box. "I think he's still in his room. Is he okay? He seems a bit…I don't know, off?"

"Tired of this pointless tour maybe? Not sure," Charlie said.

It wasn't a complete lie. He didn't actually have any answers, but discussing his friend's situation so publicly wasn't an option. He'd already said too much by acknowledging the guy was off at all, that Carter's concern was warranted. But Carter seemed satisfied with the half-truth, and he turned to Baker to talk about some movie or TV show.

Charlie grabbed the nearly empty box of cupcakes and started to head back into the building. With his hand on the door, he stopped. Woods couldn't have missed all the noise and music from the party out here. If he hadn't joined them already, there was a good reason for it.

Charlie slid the box under a folding chair beside Martin. He shook a finger at Carter as he settled into the seat.

"Don't touch these, Carter. I'm watchin' you."

Carter laughed. "Roger that, bro. I think two's my limit anyway."

Martin handed him a cigar. On a normal occasion, smoking was out of the question, but it was Christmas, and Martin's excitement over his wife sending the cigars was too much for Charlie to even consider declining.

Under the twinkling lights he let himself relax, reveling in the sound of laughter. The guys belted out Christmas carols through the cigar smoke—off-key and with the wrong words half the time but still with all the joy the season invoked.

The absence of Woods cut through the mirth though. Charlie had done everything he could for him. He had to believe that.

Trust the Lord. He's got this.

I sure hope that's true.

9

Meg's sigh came out in a mist of white, swirling with the snow before it disappeared. She wiped the back of her hand across her brow. It seemed wrong to be sweating so much in below-zero temperatures.

Despite having woken up early that morning to spend an hour and a half shoveling the sidewalk and driveway, the snow had continued through the children's Christmas program, covering the entire area in another four inches of wet flurries by the time she arrived home for lunch.

She returned to shoveling, her frustration driving her to keep digging and tossing. She hated this part of deployment. The loneliness of deployment was doable. The cold side of their bed and the empty seat beside her had become manageable, but dealing with the mounds of snow pushed her to a new, though admittedly silly, edge.

Stupid snow. She loathed snow. Actually, she liked the thought of snow, maybe even the sight of it. Driving and walking in it wasn't all that terrible either. But the digging. The shoveling. The tossing it about was another.

And here she'd had to do it twice in one day.

Her nose hurt. Her ears throbbed. Her face stung. Her hair, though it hadn't been wet, had somehow frozen and become strands of wavy icicles escaping wildly from under her cap. Each shovel load thrown to the side drained more energy, and the bitter wind knocked her joyful attitude down further with each gust that blew snow back onto the driveway and into her face.

Meg was about to toss the shovel into a growing drift in the front yard when a small SUV pulled into her driveway, easily navigating its wheels through the snow she hadn't yet cleared. An older woman in a full-length wool coat stepped out into the wind. Her shoulders hunched as high as they could reach to further protect her from the cold, as if the soft green scarf tucked around her neck had been made of thin lace rather than alpaca wool. To her chest she clutched a round tin, and despite the wind whipping the snow up between the two women, Meg easily recognized the bright greens and purples of the woman's oversized purse bouncing against her legs as she shuffled across the driveway.

"Mrs. Goetz! You didn't need to come all the way out here. Especially in all this snow."

Meg dropped her shovel to the ground and rushed to the woman's side. "Watch for ice. I've nearly slipped a million—"

Before she could finish her warning, her own boot met a slick spot, and her leg gave out from under her. Her arms flew up from her sides in an effort to catch her balance, but it was too late. She landed with a hard thud on the driveway.

"Oh!" Elizabeth Goetz transferred her tin to one arm and offered her other to Meg. "Here, sweetie, let me help you up."

"Thank you. Have I ever told you I hate snow?"

Meg, with the help of Mrs. Goetz, steadied herself, not bothering to brush any of the snow off her clothes, accepting that either the wind would blow it right back or she was going to fall again.

"Are you sure you're okay?" The woman smiled at her warmly, her eyes showing genuine concern.

"I'm fine. A bit cold and tired," she answered. "And cranky. Would you like some coffee? I have a whole pot brewed. It should still be hot."

"Coffee sounds perfect."

With their coats hung up and boots dripping in the entryway, the women made their way to the kitchen. Meg attempted to smooth down her thawing hair, but she soon gave up. There was no point. She was at least glad she had tidied up the other day, as her mom had always instructed: *"We want the house to be visitor-ready, especially during the holidays. You never know when someone might drop in."*

"Here, Meg. You sit and rest. I'm sure I can find a mug or two and get us settled." Elizabeth set the tin on the counter before busying herself with opening a random cupboard and then another. An excuse to snoop? *Don't be ridiculous.*

"Thanks again, Mrs. Goetz. The mugs are in the corner cabinet. To the right. No, the other one." Meg pointed to the correct cupboard and settled her weary self into a stool at the counter, convinced now the sweet woman really was snooping.

"Oh, please, Meg, call me Elizabeth. I was meaning to tell you earlier how much I love your earrings. Are they new?" She set a steaming mug in front of Meg and carried her own around the counter to pull up the other stool.

Meg gave a polite smile, and her hand instinctively reached up to the antique bronze hanging from her ear. "Charlie got them for me for my birthday a couple months back."

"The design is so unique. Luther rose jewelry is so hard to come by. I must not know where to look."

"I think Pastor Feld recommended the shop. You could always ask him. But you didn't come all this way to chat about earrings, did you? I mean, it's fine if you did, obviously, but—"

Elizabeth gave a slight laugh and cut off Meg's rambling.

"Of course not, silly. Mike and I couldn't bear the thought of you spending your holiday out here all by your lonesome. Plus, our women's group did a cookie exchange this past week, and there's no way I can eat all of these cookies by myself. I told you Mike is having to watch his sugar intake right now, right? Well, that means I can't exactly have them around the house. I'm not even sure why I agreed to participate in the exchange this year, but I didn't want all the questions from the ladies if I declined for the first time in over a decade."

"I do like cookies." Meg smiled again, this time with less effort. Cookies could always lighten a mood and brighten the spirits. She moved to open the tin so she could investigate the goodies. The snow might have been a miserable part of the season, but the sweet treats more than made up for it.

"I was going to give them to Pastor Feld's family," Elizabeth said between sips of coffee. "But Annie insisted the kids didn't need any more sweets this year. So here I am, bringing them out to you."

Of course. How silly of her to think she had been the primary recipient. She swallowed the snarky remark forming at the back of her throat. These were cookies, whether intended for her or not. And cookies that required no baking or dish washing weren't the type to turn down. She snagged what looked like a snickerdoodle and took a bite.

"Well, I'm happy to save the Felds from a sugar-induced frenzy. These are delicious."

"The Christmas program was wonderful this year too. We are so glad you and Charlie joined the church and that you've jumped right into helping with all the kids. They seem to adore you."

This was a dangerous shift in topics, and Meg took another bite of her cookie, hoping it might ease the tension that seemed to be rising. Though maybe it was all in her head. *Best construction, Meg. You don't know that she's going to go there.*

"They are great kiddos, and we had such a good turnout this year. Thanks be to God we didn't have that flu outbreak like we did last time."

"I'd almost forgotten about that! And we only had one wardrobe malfunction this year, which really is a blessing. The ladies in my group are still giggling over the oversized angel gowns that led to the great pileup of 2002. And who could forget the year little Matthew Feld decided the shepherds should have superhero powers to help them guard their sheep and toppled the Christmas tree over when he displayed those for the crowd. Of course, that was before you guys moved here."

Meg stifled a giggle. She couldn't fathom Matthew being a ball of energy like his little sister. She had heard of the various past Christmas program mishaps when she volunteered to help out, but they were still too hard to believe. Surely they'd been blown out of proportion over the years, exaggerated for effect.

"It's a shame you and Charlie have waited to have kids yourselves. You'd be wonderful parents." Elizabeth looked Meg in the eye as she spoke. There was an edge to her words, or maybe Meg's dread had invented it.

"Yes, it is a shame the Lord hasn't blessed us with our own children." Meg forced a smile while alarms rang in her head, signaling the danger she was quickly approaching. This was bad. Nothing good could come from this turn in the conversation.

"Oh! You've been trying?"

Meg ignored the question, quickly taking a too-large bite of a gingerbread man. If Elizabeth noted the stalling tactic, she didn't let it show as she continued.

"Too bad you didn't meet Charlie earlier. After all, everyone knows the prime time for childbearing is your twenties, and now you've passed that." The lady's shoulders slumped, and her brow furrowed, as if it were up to her to devise a plan for her younger sister in Christ to remedy any fertility issues so she could start her family.

"I actually met Charlie ten years ago. But we were only friends back then," Meg said. She could feel her cheeks flush with color. She'd been so eager to get off the subject of children no matter what path she had to take to do so, and now she'd taken the worst possible detour.

"Really? I didn't know. What took you guys so long? I mean, you seem so smitten now. I can't believe you didn't have an inkling of love earlier."

Meg fidgeted in her stool. What was she doing? *Back off, lady.* She clenched her hands around the mug, ignoring the heat that threatened to burn her hands. Any pain from the coffee was better than this conversation.

When she didn't answer, Elizabeth shrugged. "Well, whatever kept you two apart all those years...it's just too bad, is all."

Meg breathed deeply through clenched teeth. She blinked slowly. She couldn't fault Mrs. Goetz for making an honest conclusion with such limited information, but the sting of her words remained. She felt the truth rising up in her chest, threatening to expose her and her past, to lay it all out there on the counter among the coffee mugs and Christmas cookies.

She dropped a hand to her lap and balled it into a fist, squeezing as hard as she could before releasing. Another deep breath forced the feelings back down, where they settled uncomfortably in her stomach, leaving a trail of anxiety tingling through her torso.

It wouldn't help. Talking only brought more pain—and questions. Questions Meg didn't want to answer. Ever. Especially not to this rude old lady who had the nerve to bring her second-hand cookies paired with judgy stares. She downed the last of the coffee, regretting she hadn't thought to bring out the Irish cream.

Meg stood to retrieve the carafe. "Would you like some

more coffee?" She hoped her guest didn't notice the tightening of her jaw as she offered to refill their mugs. *Please let her decline.* Certainly with the accumulating snow outside she'd need to head home to make dinner for her husband or deliver more re-gifted items to other unwitting families.

"Yes, please. I can't seem to warm up with all this wind these days," Elizabeth said.

Meg gave the cheeriest smile she could muster as she poured, leaning her hips against the counter. No need to return to her seat and further encourage the woman to stay any longer than necessary. At least the weather seemed a safe enough topic. "It does seem a lot colder this year, but on the bright side, everyone loves a white Christmas, right?"

"I certainly do. I've always loved having snow for the holiday. I wonder if there was snow when Jesus was born. Do you think?"

"Well, scripture doesn't say anything about snow, does it? And I don't know anything about the climate of that part of the world." Cradling the mug in one hand, she ran her fingers through her hair, working through the tangled mess more out of nerves than necessity.

"The nativity looks so much more serene with a bit of snow around it. Not like this snow, of course."

Meg chuckled. "Can you imagine the nativity scene with this wind and those snow drifts?"

"Oh, man, baby Jesus would have needed more than a bit of swaddling cloth, wouldn't He? But I guess if God was going to become man, He could control the weather a bit so He didn't get frostbite, right?"

"I suppose."

They paused to take sips from their freshly warmed mugs.

"What are your plans for Christmas, Meg? Going to see your family at all?"

Meg swallowed hard. Were there any safe topics to discuss

with people? Charlie always wondered why she wasn't more social, more outgoing. This was why.

"No. It'll just be me, a cozy fire, and a good book, I think." The image made her smile, but when she looked up, she saw Elizabeth frowning at her.

"That's a shame. Doesn't your family live nearby? I thought I heard they were fairly close by."

She hadn't heard that from Meg, that was for sure. So that meant people were talking, though they probably didn't see anything wrong with discussing her family. Most people loved their family. Meg wasn't most people though.

"About two hours away," she said dryly, careful not to offer more information than was necessary.

"That's so close. You could certainly make that trip, even in this snow. That Jeep of yours would have no problems, I'm sure of it." Elizabeth lit up at this prospect, now seeming to take it upon herself to ensure she wouldn't be lonely for the holiday, never mind how Meg felt about it.

Meg faltered, unsure what to say and afraid that this disastrous conversation would take another uncomfortable turn. She watched as her guest traced the edge of her mug with a thumb. "Well, Mrs. Goetz…"

"Elizabeth. Please, call me Elizabeth."

"Elizabeth. Sorry. I do hate to cut this short." She cringed at the lie, but this was safer than risking the too-honest approach and hurting the poor woman. "But that driveway isn't going to shovel itself, and I really should get back to it before it gets too late in the day."

"Of course, sweetie, of course. The sun does seem to disappear quite quickly these days, doesn't it?" She stood and took their mugs to the sink.

"Thank you for the cookies though. They were a lovely surprise." Meg forced each word to sound as polite as possible while leading the way to the door.

Elizabeth bundled up to head back into the wind and snow but stopped, no doubt noting Meg had made no move to do the same.

"Aren't you going back out?"

And risk having this chat drag on in the snow and wind? No thank you.

"Oh, I will in a bit." The short answer had to suffice. This visit was draining Meg more quickly than she had anticipated.

"Of course. Well, if you need anything at all, Mike and I are always around. You know, now that our own children have all grown and moved so far away, we love having the chance to be here for you and Charlie."

Meg reached for the door slowly, not wanting Elizabeth to know how eager she was to boot her out of it. "Thank you again. So much. I do appreciate it." Her words came out sharper than planned, but Elizabeth didn't seem to notice.

"Perhaps I can come back tomorrow to bring you some supper. I can't imagine you'll be whipping up a whole meal just for yourself."

Meg pulled open the door. She wanted to lie and say she had plans, but she tried to give this woman the benefit of a doubt. She was only trying to help, after all. Meg should let her.

"Yes, thank you. That would be wonderful. And please be careful walking on the driveway, Mrs.…Elizabeth."

Meg meant the warning to be genuine, but she couldn't ignore the thought that—after the last hour of tortuous conversation—it would be just desserts for the older woman to slip a bit and tumble into a snow drift.

Oh, stop. The woman braved ugly weather to bring you cookies.

Yet she couldn't completely refrain from smiling at the possibility that the lady could end up trapped in a snowbank. Just a little one.

"Merry Christmas, Meg!" Elizabeth called back with a wave as she carefully traversed the sidewalk. Returning the wave,

Meg watched to ensure she made it to her vehicle safely, although she wasn't exactly dressed to run out and help if her guest did happen to slip.

Once the SUV had backed out of the driveway and Meg's home was once again quiet, she got to work lighting a fire in the fireplace. The crackling of the wood calmed her heart, exactly what she needed after that awkward exchange.

She pushed the couch up a few feet closer and piled the throw pillows and blankets onto the floor between it and the fireplace like she and Charlie often did on winter nights. Though the snow continued to pile up in the driveway and the sun hadn't even begun to set, Meg settled under the blankets, her toes warming up by the fire and the tin of cookies resting in her lap.

It had been months since the emptiness of the house had bothered her, months since the loneliness had troubled her. All that time spent settling into her new routine had been undone in one afternoon by a single visit from a well-meaning neighbor. She clenched her teeth, angry she was letting it eat at her to such an extent.

She wanted to curl up against Charlie's chest and tell him everything she hadn't had the guts to say to Mrs. Goetz. Well, not everything. Some things you could only say to God. Regardless, he wasn't there and wouldn't be calling for another few hours. No matter how hard she fought, and even with a tin full of chocolate and sweets for company, she couldn't keep herself from falling apart. For the first time that winter, with Charlie's wedding band clutched in her palm, she felt her tears fall as freely and wildly as the snow outside.

She hated snow.

10

Piper shifted on the couch, pulling the quilt up over her lap. Finding a comfortable position was impossible these days. At least Meg had agreed to come over, saving her from waddling through the snow.

She laid a hand on her belly, trying to support herself as she moved a leg out from under her so she could stretch it out in front. A sharp kick jabbed from beneath.

Would she ever get used to that? It was so odd. Aaron would never feel it, at least not this time around. Maybe he'd get to share the experience with the next kid.

If there is a next kid. Whoever said pregnancy was fun was out of their mind!

"You still planning to force me to celebrate New Year's?" Meg walked into the room and handed Piper her water bottle, freshly filled.

"I have to. I promised Charlie I wouldn't let you mope around."

"What he doesn't know won't kill him, you know. Can't we stay in?"

She flashed Meg a disapproving scowl. "What's the fun in that?"

"Plenty of fun, I'll have you know. I bring the fun wherever I go."

Piper couldn't stifle the laugh. She waved a hand at her friend. "Uh-huh. And how many days in a row have you worn that sweatshirt?"

Meg huffed and threw a pillow at her, but Piper dodged it—as well as she could with this bowling ball of a baby sitting in her lap. The pillow grazed her shoulder and fell to the floor.

She prepared to give Meg a firm lecture on how it wasn't proper to abuse pregnant women. The Lord knew she was beat up enough from this boy's strong legs. The buzz of her phone on the table stayed her tongue. She reached for it but didn't get very far before Meg rushed to retrieve it for her.

"Thanks," she said, taking the phone and answering the call. "Hello?"

"Hey, it's me." *Aaron.* She glanced at her watch. Why wasn't he asleep?

She looked up, but Meg—the ever-observant friend that she was—had already stood up and was walking into the kitchen, likely to get more coffee and give Piper some privacy.

"What's up? Shouldn't you be sleeping?"

"Just missed you is all." Her mind mulled over each syllable, tossing it about as she hunted for some hidden meaning she was sure was there. The guy had to be so secretive, so cryptic. Why couldn't he just call to say he missed her? He might do that, right?

These pregnancy hormones must have been making her edgier if she was being cynical about such a sentimental expression from her husband.

"I miss you too. How are things going over there? Did you guys have a good Christmas?" She pushed aside her doubt. He was fine, happy.

"It was okay."

Silence.

Charlie and Meg did this twice a day? How in the world?

She tried again. "Did you get the package I sent?"

"Yeah. Thanks. It was the highlight of the week actually."

Running a hand over her forehead, she smoothed the hair away from her face before resting her chin in her palm, fingers across her lips. She shook her head. She had nothing. Nothing to say to him. What kind of couple were they that they couldn't even have a normal, casual conservation?

Because a call from Afghanistan was the definition of normal, right?

"I'm struggling, Piper." His voice came out weak, strained—like he'd had to drag the words out, fighting them to release the grip they had on his heart.

Her breath caught. Her heart sped up. "Struggling? How? There anything I can do?"

"I dunno." His breath released into the receiver, sending a whooshing sound into her ear. "Nervous, I guess."

"About what?" That was a dumb question. He was in a war zone, riding around in convoys on dangerous roads, and she was asking him why he was nervous?

He paused. *Talk to me.* But he couldn't, not really. She knew from the news—which she wasn't supposed to be reading—that things had been dicey over there lately.

Convoys getting ambushed. Suicide bombers attacking bases. Helicopters going down.

But that wasn't happening to him, was it? They were bored. No, Charlie was bored. The other guys were bored. But Aaron…

"I'm not like the rest of these guys," he said, as if he'd read her mind. "They go out on these missions all gung-ho, ready for a fight—hoping for it even—and all I can think is they're insane."

"Oh, babe. I'm sorry." She had to offer him more than that, but what did she know about war and the military? He'd kept his Army life so separate, hidden in the back bedroom closet. She had needed a crash course in everything from LESs to POAs when the deployment came up.

And up until last summer she hadn't even known what MOS stood for, let alone what his MOS even was. Even now she couldn't remember exactly what it was. All she knew was he wasn't using his training over there.

"What if I don't…make it home?" His voice came out a whisper.

"Don't say that," she snapped, the words bursting out of her before she could think. "Don't even worry about that."

But shouldn't they? Shouldn't they have prepared for the possibility? The worst-case scenario? He'd drawn up a will, but she had refused to be a part of it, insisting instead that she would read it only if the time came and not a moment sooner.

He breathed again but didn't say anything more.

She dropped her head back and pointed her face toward the ceiling, eyes closed.

Lord, help him! Give him the strength he needs. Because I've got none.

"I don't know what to tell you, Aaron. I just don't. I'm no help." Her shoulders slumped under her defeat. Meg—who couldn't even try a new thing off the menu without freaking out—somehow managed to support her husband across the distance with such ease. *You're stronger than this!*

"I don't know what I expect you to say or do," Aaron said. "Just needed you to know."

"I…" A nudge of a leg—or was it an arm this time?—to her elbow stopped her mid-sentence. "I wish you were here. You're missing out on so much—the baby's kicks, his hiccups…"

She cringed. Those weren't the words of encouragement he needed. Quite the opposite actually.

"I'm sorry. That wasn't fair of me. I shouldn't say all those things." She fisted a hand and pressed it to her lips. If only she could snag all those words and shove them back inside.

Like putting toothpaste back in the tube. Impossible.

"It's okay, Piper. It's all true, right? I am missing it, and it sucks. But what can I do?" Exhaustion seeped through the words, hinting at the depth of the sadness and regret that must plague him. How long had felt this way? Yet he had gone all these months without mentioning it.

This was classic Aaron. No, this was classic Aaron times ten. Maybe a hundred. Others might assume he kept himself guarded for selfish reasons, not trusting anyone to see the real him. Nothing was further from the truth. The man cared, more than he ever let on, about those around him, bearing his cross alone, insisting everyone walk beside him as he trudged along under the weight. Piper understood…to an extent.

But she found none of that understanding now with her nerves shot to hell with the lack of sleep, the sharp pains in her ribs from the constant kicks and jabs, and the aches in her back from her loosened ligaments carrying the extra weight.

Don't unload that on him. Pull that tongue back, Piper!

She drew in a deep breath, biting back the harsher words she felt scratching to get out. "Just stay alive so you can meet this baby of yours." She'd meant it to come out softer, more lighthearted, but the sharpness had cut through, tainting each word.

"As you wish." There was no smile in his voice, but the fear and sadness he carried couldn't completely mask his love.

They might not be like other couples, attached at the hip and sickeningly cute, but this was them, with their own brand of marriage and love, however odd it might seem to the outside world.

"I love you. Always." She choked back tears. *Darn hormones!* Crying was not her thing, but at least no one was here to see it.

"And forever." He paused, another breath coming through the phone. "I'll call you in a few, okay?"

"I'll be here. Bye, love."

With his muttered goodbye, she tossed the phone beside her lap. Wiping the tears away with frantic hands, she sniffled. Meg couldn't see her like this, a blubbering pregnant lady.

This was nothing. She could handle this. Control it. Stifle it.

Like she'd done before.

Piper watched as the trees crept by her window. So beautiful, serene. All this time she'd lived an hour away and had never ventured out here.

A squeeze on her hand pulled her gaze around.

"Don't be so nervous, silly," Aaron said, shooting her a wink. The sun, barely peeking over the trees, highlighted the swirls of caramel that ran through his coffee-colored eyes.

She raised her brow. "Calmer than you are."

"Uh-huh. Sure. Is that why your hands are shaking?"

"I'm just cold."

He laughed. "I could pull over. Warm you up?"

She poked him in the ribs, and his elbow dropped to protect himself. "We can't be late. I don't want them to hate me right off the bat."

He laughed again. "Winters would understand. The guy's always late."

"And his wife? What's her name again? Amber? Allison?"

"Close." He glanced out of the corner of his eyes. "It's Meg."

"How is that close?"

Aaron didn't answer. The crunch of the gravel under the tires ceased, and he cut the engine. Piper looked out the window again.

The house nestled among the trees didn't resemble the others they'd passed along the way. Those had seemed so out of place, forced into a habitat that didn't want or need them. But this house—rustic and simple, well-kept and homey—seemed to grow from its surroundings, as if the trees and hills themselves had created it.

Piper kept her gaze on the house, her eyes trailing across the stone path and the porch that ran along the front, trying to imagine the couple that lived here among the pines.

"What if she doesn't like me? What if we don't have anything in common?"

"How could she not love you? You're amazing."

She turned to look at him, wringing her hands in an effort to steady them.

"What's really wrong, Piper?"

His eyes locked onto hers, sending her heart into flutters. This man—from the moment they'd met, he'd gotten her, understood her, as if they'd known each other their whole lives and not only a handful of months.

"I—I don't know. I'm not an Army wife, you know?"

"Well, they're not all like what you see on TV."

"What if we have nothing in common?" She turned back to the house. Who would choose to live in such seclusion? It had taken a good half hour to get here from town. What a hassle.

"Well..." He paused. "You're both married to awesome guys, so..."

Her head snapped around, sure she hadn't heard him right. She opened her mouth, but no sound came out.

Aaron's head tilted slightly, one corner of his lips pulling back. "That is, if you say yes."

Piper blinked. Her stomach tensed. It refused to heed her calls to settle, instead flipping once, twice. She was going to be sick.

He waited. Patient. Calm. No sign of worry or anxiety crossing his expression. She blinked again, feeling her gaze drawn into the richness of his eyes.

"Will you marry me, Piper?"

She ignored the tears that threatened to spill over and down her cheeks, not caring if he saw them or how weak they made her look. Her heart raced up into her throat, pushing her answer out with its pounding.

"Yes, of course. Of course I will!"

The Aaron in that car was not the same one who had called. Had it only been two years ago? But that guy—the one who'd teased her with his winks and his half-smiles—seemed to have disappeared with the deployment, like he'd left that side of him at home, tucked away for safekeeping.

A clearing of a throat drew her gaze up to meet Meg's eyes, peeking around the corner of the kitchen. If Meg had heard the conversation or witnessed her tears, she hid it well.

"I ordered us a pizza for dinner. It'll be here in thirty. Can I get you some tea or pickle juice or something?"

"Tea would be great. Thanks."

For all the grief she gave Meg for her silly and stubborn ways, Piper could not have wished for a better friend. She smiled to herself. Just this once she'd let Meg have her way and they'd stay in for New Year's. It was the least she could do for the friend who understood. Who was there but didn't pry. Who was close but not intrusive.

Such friends were one in a million.

The metal chair creaked under Charlie as he shifted his weight. He slid the playing cards across the table and bent the edge of them up, revealing enough to assess the hand he'd been dealt. He could work with this.

Without lifting his chin, he glanced around the table from man to man. To his left, Murphy huffed and tucked his cards back under the deck, folding his hand as soon as he looked at them. On Charlie's right, Martin held his cards close to his chest, his expression calm while his leg bounced under the table. Woods, his forearms resting on the table's edge, fanned out the cards and shifted one or two around before gathering them back up and laying them down.

That left Carter.

The kid squirmed across from Charlie, avoiding his stares and those of the guys around them. He rearranged his cards. Back. Forth. Back again. He glanced at the pile before him. The ante wasn't much—a candy cane leftover from Christmas. Charlie shook his head. It shouldn't take that much thinking.

Carter straightened and lifted his chin. Pulling the cards from his hand, he laid them down beside Murphy. "Four."

Martin hid a snort behind a hand. Woods muttered something inaudible.

"No," Murphy said. "You don't take four. You fold."

"But what if I don't want to fold? What if I want four cards?" Carter said, becoming taller in his seat.

"Then you're a dumbass." Murphy rolled his eyes but dealt the kid the four requested cards. Carter rearranged his hand, his eyes lighting up.

Charlie chuckled. "You've got some mad bluffing skills there, kid."

Carter shrugged.

"How many, Woods?" Murphy asked.

"Two," Woods said, not looking up. He tossed his rejected cards onto the table.

Martin held up two fingers when Murphy glanced at him.

Charlie said, "Just one. Thanks."

Finished dealing, Murphy turned back to Carter. "You're opening the bets. Guessing you won't be folding with that stupid grin on your face."

Carter perused the items he had to toss in the pot and pursed his lips as he considered each.

"This game is going to take forever! C'mon, kid. Bet already." Murphy seemed more on edge than usual, but no one commented or acknowledged it. The same tension had settled into Charlie, and he assumed the others felt it too. Leave it to the lieutenant colonel to ignore all concerns about tomorrow's route.

"All right, all right." Carter moved a homemade chocolate chip cookie into the center.

"Fold." Woods dropped his cards and leaned back in his chair, arms behind his head.

"I see your cookie," Martin started, dropping one of his own onto the top of the pile, "and raise you a rum ball."

Charlie glanced from the pot, to Martin, to Carter, and back to his cards. "Call. A cupcake matches the rum ball, I assume."

"Yeah, I think so." Murphy nodded. "You call, Carter?"

Carter leaned forward and put one of his own cupcakes in to match Charlie's raise. "Yup." He laid his cards on the table and beamed. "Full house. Jacks over sixes."

"Lucky bastard," Murphy said, ignoring Carter's gloating grin.

Charlie tossed his own cards face up. "Beats my straight."

"And my three kings," Martin said as Carter reached for his winnings. "Good job. He steal all your luck, Murphy?"

"Yeah, must have."

Martin gathered up the cards and shuffled several times. As he started to deal out the next hand, Carter spoke up, his head down. "I think I'm going to propose to Molly."

"What?" Murphy's face contorted into a mix of confusion and disgust. "Why would you do that?"

"Congrats, kid." Martin smiled.

"Another one bites the dust," Murphy muttered, his eyes focusing on the cards in his hands as he rearranged them to his liking.

"Don't listen to him. He's just bitter and alone," Charlie said.

"So very alone," Woods added, not looking up from his own hand.

"He's not alone," Carter said with a shake of his head. "I mean, he's still got his mom."

Charlie's laugh filled the room, and even Woods cracked a

smile. Murphy's jaw tightened for a second but then relaxed. "You guys need some new jokes."

"So..." Charlie nodded at Carter. "How you going to ask her?"

"Well, I have the ring all picked out. Just need to order it. Was thinking of sending it directly to her with a note. I think the store has one of those gift note option things." Carter looked at Charlie, his expression full of youthful innocence. Or was that stupidity?

"Really?" Charlie raised a brow.

Carter smiled his boyish grin and nodded excitedly. "No."

Charlie burst into another boom of laughter but said nothing.

"Good one," Martin said.

"I was actually wondering how you guys asked your wives. You know, get some ideas," Carter said.

"All you gotta do, kid, is hand her the ring and ask," Martin said.

"But in person," Woods added. "Always in person."

"What do you think, Winters? How'd you ask Meg?" Carter asked.

"Like Martin said. Simple works best. Get too elaborate and you risk pieces falling out of place. Keep it simple, and the only thing you really risk is misreading her feelings for you and having her say no," Charlie explained.

He looked down at his hand where his wedding band had been months before. The tan line that once marked its absence had disappeared, and now his hand looked as innocent and unhitched as Murphy's.

"But when and where? Does that matter?"

Woods shrugged. "Yes and no. I wouldn't ask her while she's washing the dishes or something."

"But that could work still. I dunno," Charlie said. "Maybe

avoid saying, 'Babe, I want you to clean up after me for the rest of my life.' That might not go over so well."

"Also don't ask her when she's watching *The Bachelorette* or whatever show she's into. You want her full attention if possible," Martin said.

"And make sure you know her style," Charlie said. "You know, ring-wise. Don't get her yellow gold if all her other jewelry is white gold. And get the right size if you can. Might have to be sneaky about that, which might be a challenge for you."

"Should I be writing this down?" Carter smiled, avoiding a glance at Murphy, who was sulking to his right. "But really, how'd you guys ask? When? Where? What'd you say?"

"I asked her at dinner one night," Martin answered. "Pretty sure I said, 'Wanna get married?' She didn't expect me to have a ring with that half-assed delivery though, so that was her surprise. After she shrugged and said, 'Sure,' I got down on a knee and opened the box for her. Thirty-some years ago now."

"I asked in the car. Gave her the ring later," Woods said, his voice flat and matter-of-fact. "Seemed to work just fine."

Charlie leaned back in his chair. "Meg and I were camping when I asked. Figured everything else had gone wrong that day so either she'd say no and it'd be the worst day ever or she'd say yes and it'd make up for it."

"And she said yes, obviously," Carter said.

"Not immediately."

"What? How long did you wait?"

"Not long. Ten minutes or so? But even one is brutal after asking that. It was hell. But I kinda expected her to need time to think."

"Why? You that mediocre in the sack?" Murphy asked.

Charlie smiled at his buddy. "That wasn't exactly a measure she could use at that point."

"Oh, right. The Christian thing. I forgot." Murphy rolled his eyes.

"But wait. Why'd you expect to wait?" Carter asked.

"I knew her, is all," Charlie answered. "Whose turn is it anyway?"

"Still moody, I see." Charlie raised his eyebrow and gave his wife a goofy grin over their video chat, but his silliness only elicited a slight smile from her.

"The snow won't stop," she complained. "I don't remember any winter being quite this bad."

"Probably because I usually do all the shoveling."

"Have I told you lately how much I miss you?"

Charlie watched her smile grow, but he hadn't missed the slight fidget in her chair and the twitch in her eyebrow at the mention of snow. She was withholding something about the past week. It wasn't merely the wind and cold that had dampened her spirits, but he didn't push. He didn't need to.

The visit from Mrs. Goetz the other day had notably irked his wife, and though she hadn't provided any details of their conversation, he knew it must not have gone well. And if Meg—this woman who had always been open and forthright with him—had decided to withhold it, it was likely for his own benefit.

He couldn't exactly be irritated with her secrets anyway, since he had been keeping his own, not telling her about the mortars and alarms or the worries he'd had concerning Aaron over the last few weeks. She didn't need that worry, but she wasn't dumb either. She had to have noticed the edge in his voice and the extra weariness in his face after nights with less sleep than usual. He was as sure of her perceptiveness as he was sure she wasn't just pissed off by the weather.

"Don't forget, Meg. Plus seven." His expression became more serious.

She nodded. "I remember."

Months ago, before he had left, they had picked a date they could both remember, a number they could use—by indicating how many days to add to or subtract from that date—to communicate when he'd be out on missions or otherwise unable to contact her.

"Crap, Charlie. I'm running late to pick up the Feld kids. It's their anniversary—Pastor's, not the kids'—and I offered to give them the day to celebrate alone. I hate to cut this short, but I really gotta go."

"No problem, babe. Try to have fun, okay?"

"Yeah, yeah. I love you, hon. Be safe." She smiled at him.

"Always. Love you too."

Charlie closed his laptop and leaned back in his chair. Meg's moodiness, even if not related to him, wore him down, but there was little he could do but pray things would settle down for her.

He shooed away the curious thoughts about what Mrs. Goetz must have said to tick Meg off to this point. If it were truly serious, wouldn't she have said something? Maybe. Maybe not. That went against all the guidance the Army gave spouses.

At least she was still getting out of the house, and time with the Feld kids always brightened her mood. He grabbed his notepad and scribbled a reminder to send Pastor an email of congratulations.

"No. Absolutely not. That's ridiculous." Carter's voice sounded from behind the wall. Charlie reached for his headphones to give his friend privacy but stopped at Carter's next words. "C'mon, babe. You don't mean that. Don't say that, please."

He cringed. This couldn't be good. He could listen so he

could offer help or advice later, but that wasn't right. He wouldn't appreciate others eavesdropping on a difficult call, and he couldn't do that to Carter.

With headphones in, he switched on the latest sermon from Pastor Feld. It couldn't hurt to hear God's Word preached again, especially before tomorrow's mission. But he couldn't focus on his pastor's words, not when he had one friend possibly facing heartache ten feet away and another still noticeably battling some inner demon down the hallway.

He couldn't help them out of their problems. He couldn't take their places, no matter how much he wished he could, but he could pray for them.

In the name of the Father, and of the Son, and of the Holy Spirit. Amen. I thank you, my heavenly father, for the blessing of good friends and neighbors to serve daily. Help me to be the friend I am called to be—through whatever they are facing—and to share Your Holy Word so that they may be comforted and find solace in Your Son, crucified, died, buried, and raised for their sins and mine. I don't know the faith of their hearts, but You do. If it is your will, may they hear Your Word and believe. In Jesus' name, I pray. Amen.

It was a more structured prayer than his usual haphazard variety, but Pastor Feld had been helping to guide him in how to pray for the past month. Even if the prayers were inaudible to others, it brought comfort, reminded him of being at home in the pew with Meg and reciting the liturgy with his church family.

He reached for the Bible sitting next to his computer, wondering if there was a particular psalm he could find to pray for his friends, but a knock at his door interrupted his search. He turned and saw Carter standing there with his head down.

"So I'm guessing you heard all that." The young soldier shuffled his feet slightly before looking up at Charlie.

"Actually, no." He lifted his headphones in explanation. "I

was catching up on last week's sermon from back home. What's up?"

Carter didn't answer. He stretched his shoulders out and shifted uncomfortably. Charlie waited. He needed to say something, but what could he do to help a guy get through a bad breakup—and over the phone, no less? That was at least better than a *Dear John* letter though.

"Well..." Carter started. He cleared his throat and breathed deeply.

"Wanna sit?" Charlie shifted to indicate he'd give up his chair if needed.

"Nah. I just needed to ask you a question."

"Anything you need." He cringed and then laughed. "Well, almost anything."

"How do you look in a tux?"

Charlie froze. That wasn't the question he had expected, though he wasn't sure what he had expected exactly. "Wait. What?"

"Want to be my best man?" Carter's nervousness faded, and he raised his eyebrow at his friend, a mocking look in his eye.

Charlie's laugh echoed in his room. "Yeah, man, of course. Does that mean it's official and all? She said yes? You asked?"

"Well, not in that order, but yeah. Looks like October third. She's gotta check with her pastor first, but pretty sure that'll be the date."

"I completely thought she was dumping you!" Charlie blurted out.

Carter pulled his face back and dropped his chin. "And I thought you said you didn't hear anything."

"No, I said I didn't hear it all. Heard you arguing and grabbed the headphones. Big difference, but a bit confusing in the end. So what happened exactly?"

"Nothing really. She had a crappy day fighting with her parents. They're worried she's making a mistake waiting for me. Think I'm not serious about taking care of her and all. She said she was going to move out and stop talking to them, but I can't have her ruining their relationship over this. So I figured go big or go home, right?"

"Good move. Sometimes you've gotta ignore all the advice and just go with it. I'm glad it worked out."

"Thanks, you know, for not listening…and for the best man thing. But don't be late to the wedding. Molly will kill you."

11

THE CONVOY WAS SET to leave earlier than usual, and Charlie lamented not having the time to get his run in. Even a quick sprint around the camp would have helped calm his nerves and work out the kinks in his restless muscles from the repeated nights of sleeplessness. For weeks following Christmas, mortar attacks and alarms had blared each night, as if the enemy was ringing in the new year with their own brand of fireworks. Then suddenly it had all stopped, and last night had been quiet…eerily so.

That unnerving feeling continued as Charlie stepped out of the briefing. Grey clouds hung low, and the air, though still on the cooler side, felt heavy and stifling. He looked down at the envelope in his hand, thankful he at least had enough time to get it mailed off to Meg. The guys all laughed at him for this ritual, not that he cared. *Let them scoff.*

"What? Talking twice a day every day isn't enough for you?" Murphy asked.

"Should I be sending letters too?" Carter looked from face to face.

Woods said, "Nah. That's how Winters avoids Meg finding out about his mistress. No internet trail that way."

Charlie nodded.

Regardless of what they thought, he'd continue to send the cards and letters prior to every mission. He and Meg talked often enough, sure, but in this age of email and video chatting, the nostalgic side of him reveled in the thought of sending his wife something tangible, something she could hold and feel.

His writing was nothing special or romantic; he could usually only muster a simple *I love you* or a bit of scripture. This time, though, he'd managed to share a bit more, about his worries over the mission—in generalities only, of course—and the excitement of Carter's engagement, with a request to tentatively mark the date in October and perhaps send a box of congratulatory cupcakes to the kid.

With each bit of news he had jotted down, he'd reminisced about his grandfather doing the same in France during World War II, remembering all the letters his grandmother had saved in that old hat box on the hall closet's top shelf. Not that she had let him read any of them.

"Sorry, son, they're for my eyes only," she had always said. "Until I'm dead, of course, then I guess I can't stop anyone."

As a young kid he hadn't understood her desire for such privacy. He assumed those letters merely contained his grandpa's epic tales of battle and heroism, but he was determined to honor her wishes. When she passed away years later, he had ensured they remained unread, and despite his own mother's protests, he had managed to have the letters buried with her. He doubted there was much of anything in his own letters home to warrant similar demands from Meg to the grandchildren they dreamed of having, but that didn't dissuade him from sending them.

With the letter sent off, Charlie approached the convoy. He would be driving the third truck this time, which was fine by him. Murphy leaned against the rear door of the Humvee and after taking one last drag of his cigarette flung the butt onto the ground.

"Dude, I'm tired," he grumbled with a curse added for emphasis.

"Too quiet last night?" Charlie asked.

Murphy kicked the ground with his toe. "Yeah. Just got used to all the interruptions, and then nothing? Couldn't fall asleep 'cause I figured as soon as I drifted off, boom, I'd have to get up again."

"Huh. Weird. I slept fine—I think anyway. Just try not to fall asleep in the turret, 'kay?" Charlie opened the driver's side passenger door and threw his gear in, nodding to Baker, who was doing the same on the opposite side.

Murphy's sudden burst of laughter startled Charlie.

"It wasn't *that* funny," he said, turning sharply on his heel. But Murphy wasn't paying him any attention. He glanced up to see what had the guy doubling over in hysterics.

"Morning." Carter greeted them with a genuine smile, Woods beside him. Both guys looked more refreshed than everyone else, almost cheery even.

Murphy struggled to get the words out through his chuckles. "Yo, I think you have something on your face, Carter."

"What? You don't like it?" Carter asked, proudly rubbing his fingers over the light hairs that sparsely covered his upper lip.

"You mean, that's intentional?" Murphy asked before letting his head fall back in another howl of laughter. Charlie couldn't help but laugh behind his hand, but Carter's good mood couldn't be shaken.

"Yeah. Well, I figured since I'm gonna be a married man soon, I should look more grown up." Carter stood taller, lengthening his spine as he spoke.

"Make sure you give Molly some warning first," Charlie said.

"Exactly," Woods added with a nod, his mouth pulled into a half-smile. "It's an unwritten rule of marital life. Any desired changes to facial hair must first be submitted to your wife in writing and approved before they can be implemented."

"Really?" Carter's eyes darted among the guys for verification. Murphy opened his mouth to answer him, probably to tell him it was a load of crap and not to listen to the others, but another look at the kid had him laughing again. He turned, supporting himself against the Humvee to keep from losing his balance.

Watching Murphy fall apart with laughter, Charlie stepped forward and spoke, keeping his face and tone serious. "Oh, yeah. Everyone knows that."

"Don't listen to these idiots, kid," Martin said as he came around the front of the Humvee. "They're just jealous they can't rock the 'stache."

"Dude, yours? Maybe. But this?" Woods grabbed Carter's chin and gave it a playful shake. "I'm not jealous of this."

Martin leaned closer and squinted his eyes at the young soldier. "Oh, yeah. That's awful. Sorry, kid, but you should definitely rethink that. That's...yeah. No." Martin's words had the whole group, including Carter, sharing a laugh.

"What time is it?" Martin asked as he pulled his sleeve up to check his watch. "We need to get. Carter? Woods? We're in truck two, right?"

"Yup. You're driving. Carter's up top," Woods answered. He moved to follow the guys toward their Humvee ahead but stopped when Charlie nudged his arm with an elbow.

"You doin' okay?" Charlie asked, hoping he could keep his voice low enough the other guys didn't hear. Sure, the guy looked happier, but Charlie had to make sure.

"Yeah. I'm peachy."

Charlie eyed his friend, searching for any hint that the ease on his buddy's face was genuine. "You know I'm always around...if you need anything."

Woods gave him a wink. "You'll be the first one I call."

Charlie reached into a pocket on his thigh and pulled out a small card. Holding it out, he said, "Oh, by the way, Carter asked me a while back about that psalm I carry in the truck. I had Meg send another one for him."

"Right. I'll get it to him." Woods pocketed the verse and slapped his buddy on the shoulder. With a tap on his wrist he added, "Better get movin'."

"Yeah, I know. Always late. See ya when we get there."

Woods turned and jogged back to his vehicle, and Charlie did a final stretch before climbing into his own. He pulled an identical card from the same pocket and tucked it onto the dash. After keeping it close for so many drives, he no longer needed to read it and instead prayed it silently to himself, his eyes closed and head bowed slightly.

Blessed be the LORD, my rock,
who trains my hands for war,
and my fingers for battle;
he is my steadfast love and my fortress,
my stronghold and my deliverer,
my shield and he in whom I take refuge,
who subdues peoples under me.
Amen.

The Humvee rumbled along the narrow road, dust and rocks hitting the windshield as they were flung up by the truck in front of them. Charlie shifted his focus between the terrain around them and the road before them as he joined in the guys' conversation.

"Okay, okay," he said. "Matt Damon...was in *Saving Private Ryan* with...Tom Hanks."

"Too easy," Murphy said over the comms from his perch in the turret. "Tom Hanks. Helen Hunt. *Castaway*."

Baker and Charlie shouted "Wilson!" in unison, getting a groan from Murphy, who nudged them along. "Your turn, Baker. And don't take forever this time. Last time we had to wait a whole five minutes for you to come up with your play."

"It's called strategy," Baker said with a bite in his tone.

"Only a game, dude. No need to get all testy," Charlie said, not needing to glance over to know Baker wore a scowl.

"You're testy. Whatever... Fine. Helen Hunt in *Twister* with Bill Pullman."

"Wrong Bill, moron," Murphy corrected him with a laugh. "It's Paxton in *Twister*. Pullman's the *Spaceballs* guy."

Charlie turned to see Baker muttering something under his breath through his clenched teeth. These two would be the death of him if he didn't keep their bickering in check. He jumped in before Baker could rip into Murphy for calling him out.

"Bill Paxton was in *Tombstone*." He paused, but only for a second. Murphy would be barking at him over the time delay, but he'd get more grief if he made it too easy again. "With Billy Zane."

"Who the hell is Billy Zane?" Baker asked.

Charlie answered, "You don't really need to know, right? Murphy's turn."

"He was in that movie?" Murphy's voice sounded in their ears.

"Yeah, bit part, but he was in there."

"Okay, fine. I won't require verification. Billy Zane..." Murphy began to take his turn, but he was soon interrupted by Baker.

"No, really, who the hell is Bill Zane?"

"It's Billy. And he was the jackass villain guy in *Titanic*," Murphy said. "With...Kate Winslet."

Charlie laughed. "Picking some real manly movies today, eh, Murphy?"

"What? It's a classic," Murphy said before switching to a falsetto. "I'll never let go, Jack. I'll never let go."

Baker groaned. "That movie ruined my sophomore year of high school. Like I was the only guy named Jack."

"That's ridiculous," Charlie said. "You're not nearly as dreamy as Leo." He risked taking his eyes off the road to see Baker raising his middle finger in response.

BoooOOOoooom!

The ground shook. Charlie slammed on the brakes, bringing their truck to a stop.

The three guys looked for the Humvee they'd been following, but they could see nothing but a cloud of dust and rock hovering in the winter air.

Charlie scanned the horizon around them as rocks pinged the hood and roof. His eyes darted across boulders and bushes, searching for any sign of combatants. Baker did the same on their right. They remained quiet and focused, listening to the chatter on the comms.

Murphy's voice rang out in a string of expletives. "Do you guys see anything?" Another curse.

"Nope. It's clear," Baker said. He readied his rifle.

"Clear here." Charlie kept his voice calm, pushing aside the panic that gripped his chest. He swallowed. Hard. "Baker, you and me. Let's go. Murphy, cover us on the 240?"

"On it," Murphy answered.

They exited the truck, rifles and eyes panning across the hills that surrounded the road on either side. It was the perfect terrain for an ambush, which was not unlikely with the convoy stopped, men dismounted. They were vulnerable.

"Watch for secondary IEDs," Charlie warned.

They stepped with caution, eyes darting between the ground and the ridges above them. Despite the chill in the air, stress sent a trickle of sweat down the back of his neck, but he kept moving.

"Where's the damn medic?" Charlie glanced over his shoulder, then back to the trucks ahead of them. He opened his mouth to call for the medic, but Baker stopped him.

"Don't think he could help anyway."

He followed Baker's gaze to the mangled mess of metal. He cursed, then nodded.

The guy was right.

The first truck, stopped fifty yards ahead, must have narrowly missed the IED. Someone—Charlie couldn't tell who—manned the radio, frantically calling in the report. The commander directed the rest of the team to provide cover for Charlie and Baker as they cased the scene.

Charlie didn't hear any of the words. Just chatter. Noise.

Something moved to his left. He snapped his head toward it, his rifle lifted and ready. His eyes scanned. He could see nothing but sparse brush, dirt, and rock. A cold breeze cut through the stifling air, and a bush shifted slightly.

He watched, waited.

Nothing else moved. Squinting his eyes, he looked again, sure he had seen something move. But when everything lay still again, he released his breath, keeping the tension in his limbs as he returned his focus to the destroyed Humvee and resumed looking for any sign of life. Nothing but twisted and charred remains.

Baker's calm reserve vanished as they neared the wreckage, his words spilling out in a torrent of anger, a swear word slipping in with every other syllable. The strong language was out of character, but Charlie ignored him, letting him rant and go off as much as he needed to in that moment.

But a sharp curse from Baker snapped his head up. "What is it?" he asked.

Baker responded by doubling over, retching, and heaving.

He waited for the guy to get it out of his system. He should move, check it out firsthand so Baker didn't have to put it into words, but his boots wouldn't budge.

Baker stiffened. "Not what—who." He swallowed hard, managing to choke the bile back down. "Pretty sure...this was Carter. And that? Woods? Maybe. By the size of the boot." He coughed. "No sign of Martin."

Baker seemed to choke on the guys' names. He turned as his body heaved vomit into the dirt.

"Easy, dude. Just breathe," Charlie said, still rooted to his spot, making no effort to inch closer to him or the last remaining pieces of his friends.

"How—how are you so calm right now?" Baker spewed, spitting another glob of stomach contents onto the ground, with more curses and expletives following.

Charlie cringed at the spite thrown at him. But he could take it. He could be the proxy for his buddy's rage that he knew was intended for the enemy who had buried the explosives. The corner of his mouth moved to speak.

Say something! Anything! Baker stared at him, but he couldn't even muster a shrug or a nod.

He stiffened, letting the numbness wash over him, and turned back to the task at hand. The mechanics wouldn't arrive to retrieve the remains for a while. Until then, they had a job to do.

Charlie swallowed hard. He had to ignore the queasiness in his gut. He could be sick later, but now he had to focus on guarding his fallen buddies, though he couldn't bring himself to look at them—their limbs lying in the Afghan dirt.

The air became frigid with the setting of the sun over Camp Foster, turning Charlie's breath into a billowing cloud of steam as he exhaled. The clouds from that morning had lifted, revealing a sea of stars looming above him. He barely noticed them. With the mission canceled and the convoy returned to camp, the team had dispersed just like the clouds. To where, to do what, he neither knew nor cared.

He nudged past a few who had gathered outside their B-hut for a smoke, quickening his pace so he could avoid any talk of the blast. Not that any of them really spoke.

He stepped inside, weariness urging him to slow his pace and take it easy. He ignored the fatigue and forced himself down the hallway as quickly as his long legs would let him, sure to keep his eyes locked on his own door ten feet ahead in an attempt, albeit a hopeless one, to ignore Martin's room to the left and Carter's and Woods's beyond his own.

He flung his door open, took one step in, then another, and slammed the door closed behind him.

His breathing quickened under the heavy silence of the room. No laughter. No banter. Even if anyone had been around, there'd be none of that now. In fact, a laugh at this moment might have deserved a swift knock to the teeth—one Charlie would gladly deliver.

He lowered himself to his cot with a drawn-out exhale, as if he could push all the tension away on that breath. Every muscle in his body ached. Not like the satisfying ache after a good run. This pain left no part untouched. No bone unaffected. No nerve un-singed.

His elbows dug into his knees as he leaned forward. His head dropped to his hands. The shower had washed away the feeling of grime and death from his skin, but no amount of water or soap could remove the scene from behind his eyelids.

In the moments after the blast, he'd pushed it away, focused. During the hours that followed he'd focused all his energy on getting the team back in one piece, spending the entire drive back to Foster in silence, avoiding Baker's occasional glares as if he had been watching and waiting for the moment Charlie would finally crack.

But it hadn't happened.

Until now.

Here, with no distractions, the IED and its aftermath slammed into him. His chest swelled. His exhales rushed forward with the sound of a freight train in the back of his throat. He pulled his shaking hands away from his head. Tightening them into fists, he watched as the knuckles turned white and all feeling left them.

His rage surged. His breathing accelerated. He clenched his teeth, pushing the screams back down into his chest.

But they wouldn't be contained.

He leapt up and crossed the room in two quick strides. With jaw held tight, he slammed his fist into the plywood door, his fury blinding him from the pain of the impact. A flood of expletives rushed from his mouth. He punched the door again and again.

The wood gave in to his blows and cracked. Unsatisfying. It should be the faces of the cowards who had killed his friends, not this cheap wood. But if he were completely honest, he wanted to do more than give them a beating.

They needed to pay, to suffer. *Break the arm of the wicked and evildoer...*

They need more than an arm-breaking, God!

He dropped his fists to his sides, ignoring the blood covering his knuckles. His heart continued to pound with wrath-fueled adrenaline. His head fell forward, teeth clenching until they throbbed and ached.

With another curse he crossed the room again, this time to his desk. In a flurry, he sent papers and letters flying to the floor as he searched. Opening box after box, he threw each across the room when they didn't hold what he wanted.

His hands picked up his Bible and catechism. He paused.

These books had what he needed. He knew it. God's Word had the answer to this rage, a prayer in the Psalms to reflect all that coursed through him, the healing balm for all this pain.

Screw healing. This pain couldn't be healed, only numbed.

With a thunderous growl he turned and threw the books at the battered door.

His hunt continued with a sweep of his arm clearing his desk and then his shelf, sending papers, pictures, letters, and boxes flying through the room. He scanned the room, eyes wild, breathing labored.

There—behind the mess under his cot a box lay. He pulled it out. Two boxes fit perfectly inside. Yes. This was the one. He ripped open the first lid. Empty. He swore and tossed it aside. The second lid fell beside him, and he pulled the plastic bag from within. They were gone. Had he eaten the last one, or had he given it away? He couldn't remember.

Not that it mattered.

Carter. Martin. Woods. Gone. Dead.

Charlie's failure caved in on him. He'd failed—again—to get his brothers home to their wives. Or fiancée in Carter's case.

He'd had a job to serve his team, and he had failed. He should have been in the truck with Woods. He should have spoken up when the lieutenant colonel had switched up the assignments. He should have insisted on being in that Humvee as he had been for months. Maybe if he had been driving instead of Martin—as he was supposed to, as he always did—they would have lived, would have survived.

Too late now.

He threw the empty box against the wall, sending it flying into Meg's picture, which crashed to the floor. He made no move to retrieve it, his mind too focused on those damn cupcakes. He didn't *actually* want the cupcakes. They were delicious, sure, but he needed the sharpness of the booze they had soaked in. Even that was a poor substitution for the bottle of

Laphroaig ten-year-old cask-strength scotch he had back home for special occasions.

Or hard nights.

But the satisfying burn of that scotch couldn't undo the IED blast or bring his friends back. Nothing could bring them back now.

Still, the sharpness of the liquor in his throat would have distracted from the stabbing pain of loss in his gut and given him that peaceful numbness to help him sleep without the images of twisted metal and torn flesh. Here he was in a war-torn country watching buddies die, and he couldn't even have a drink to soothe the pain.

One drink. Hell, one cupcake soaked in rum would have sufficed, at least taken some of the edge off, but no.

His shoulders slumped, and he stepped over the mess he'd created. Ignoring it all—even the picture of Meg, glass now shattered and frame cracked from the fall—he threw himself onto his cot and buried his face in his pillow. All efforts to calm down and rest failed.

Always failing.

The images from that morning came flooding in. With another burst of cursing from his lips, he rolled over and stared at the ceiling. His curses filled the room. There, attached to the ceiling, the mask with its empty eyes and wincing face stared back at him.

"Murphy! You jackass!" he cried out, not sure if Murphy was even next door. No answer. He was alone.

It had to have been Murphy. The thought of Carter or Woods doing it before they'd left, before they'd...

He shook his head at it. He should reach up to pull it down or at least look away, but he just stared into its dark eyes. He couldn't shut his own. He ran his hands across his forehead and down along his temples, his gaze fixed on the empty eyes above him.

Carter hated that thing—or rather, he *had* hated it. Charlie would have smiled at all his past antics, but he couldn't recall any of the kid's ridiculously scared looks or that stupid grin he'd always tried to hide when he yelled at him for pulling that prank again and again. Nor could he see Woods's perfect deadpan expression that had accompanied every stunt. Or hear Martin's chiding remarks to lay off the kid and give the jokes a rest.

Every memory of every moment with those guys seemed to have vanished with the attack, erased with the clearing of the dust and rock from the air, leaving behind only that scene of death and destruction. Blood and boots and twisted metal.

For all the memories he sought to recollect, there was one he tried to avoid, a memory he wanted desperately to keep tucked away in the back corner of his mind. But as his vision blurred and his eyes dried and throbbed from being held open for so long, that memory forced its way to the surface.

When he finally closed his eyes, he no longer saw the damaged Humvee in the Afghan hills, but the image he faced was just as ghastly.

Their patrol had been an easy one. No action. Nothing out of the ordinary. They'd be home in a couple of weeks and could leave this stinking desert behind them—at least for a while. Lord knew he'd likely be back.

They were outside the gate to their outpost when the round hit.

Charlie didn't see where it came from. He only saw the soldier twenty feet ahead of him fall to the ground.

Haas.

The men shouted, but Charlie didn't hear.

As the team took positions to provide cover and return fire, Charlie ran to the front, toward the wounded, ducking and weaving around his teammates. Lee, the medic, had been walking beside Haas. At least he was close.

Together they dragged him to the safety of the wire, leaving the sound of the firefight behind them. Charlie forced himself to ignore the blood gushing from his buddy's neck.

A cheap shot. Lucky. Landing above the Kevlar. He grabbed Haas's hand, locking eyes with his friend.

Keep him conscious. Keep him here.

The medic worked feverishly. Charlie knew he should help, but he felt useless. Unable to assist. In the way. He focused where he could, on what he could do.

"You're good, Haas. It's just a scratch. Lee's fixin' you up. Hold on. You're gonna make it."

He didn't need Lee's confirmation to know he was lying. It was far from good. Haas turned his head to answer, but no words, only blood, spilled from his open mouth. His eyes focused on Charlie's face. Pleading. Begging.

Charlie nodded to him, gripping the guy's hand harder. "I know. I won't forget. I'll get it to her. Promise."

Charlie held his friend's gaze. He needed to reassure him, to give him some sort of peace, but Haas was fading, his eyes dimming.

"The Lord is my shepherd; I shall not want. He makes me lie down in green pastures..."

A ragged breath rose and fell beneath his hands.

"He leads me beside still waters. He restores my soul. He leads me in paths of righteousness for His name's sake."

Another breath. Shallower.

"Even though I walk through the valley of the shadow of death, I will fear no evil, for you are with me..."

Still.

The medic pushed to his feet and backed away.

Charlie's prayer trailed off into a whisper. Jaw clenched, he forced his eyes to stay open, locked on his best friend.

He'd made a promise.

By the grace of God, he'd keep it.

12

MEG WATCHED as Pastor Feld turned away from the altar to face the congregation and step forward. She smiled with a sigh, waiting for the sweet words of the benediction. A slight tug came at the hem of her skirt, and she looked down.

"Is it over yet?" the little voice asked, barely staying at a whisper. Lydia's body stood limp in her red sweater dress, her pigtail-adorned head hanging to the side and her arms drooping toward the floor.

Meg settled herself onto the pew so she could look the little girl in the face when she smiled again. Pointing to their pastor she said, "Watch your daddy. This is one of my favorite parts of the Divine Service."

"Because it's the end?" Lydia's eyes lit up with her question. She forgot to whisper this time.

"Shush," Annie said, reprimanding her daughter from a few feet down the pew. Meg mouthed an apology.

Pastor's voice rang out from the front as he addressed the church body: "The Lord bless you and keep you..."

"Ready to do the sign of the cross?" Meg whispered to Lydia, who nodded emphatically.

"...The Lord make His face shine upon you and be gracious to you…" Pastor continued.

"Now?" Lydia asked. Meg shook her head.

"...The Lord lift his countenance upon you…"

Meg lifted her right hand to her forehead and glanced down to ensure Lydia was following along.

"...and give you peace," Pastor Feld concluded, his hand making the same sign of the cross before his parishioners and the congregation joined the organ for the final Amens before continuing into the closing hymn.

His poor daughter, realizing she would have to wait even longer for the cookies out in the fellowship hall, slumped into the pew, her head hitting the wooden back with a thud. Her sigh came out more as a moan, but her mother ignored her and proceeded to balance David on her hip with her hymnal in the other hand. Matthew stood on the other side of his mom, dutifully singing the first stanza in his still-boyish voice, though Meg was convinced he looked more grown-up with each week that passed.

Once the brief announcements were wrapped up, Lydia took off out of the pew, leaving her mom to nod to Meg. "Do you mind?"

"Not at all!" Meg smiled and with her purse in hand went to chase down the red dress and pigtails. She caught up with her in time to see her hug her dad's leg and take off again into the crowded narthex. "Wait for me, Lydia!" The little girl didn't stop.

"Good morning, Meg." Pastor offered his hand with a greeting.

"Morning!" She smiled as she shook his hand quickly. "Great sermon today, by the way. I'd say more, but I've got a little girl to wrangle."

"Of course," he replied. "And thank you for helping with her. I know Annie appreciates it."

Meg nodded before returning to her pursuit, but she didn't need to look hard. Sure enough, Lydia had already made her way through the short line, snagged two cookies and a cupcake, and settled into her usual seat at one of the large white tables.

"What? You didn't get me a cookie?" Meg pulled up a chair and gave Lydia her saddest face.

Cookie crumbs tumbled out of the girl's mouth as she responded with a shrug. "Sorry. But there's plenty up there if you want one."

Meg chuckled and tugged on one of Lydia's pigtails. "It's all right. I didn't really need a cookie."

Annie dragged a high chair over to the table and began to buckle David into the seat while he reached for the cookies on his sister's plate. "No, mister. I'll get you your snack in a second. You must be patient."

"He's getting so big, isn't he?" Meg marveled at the toddler. "Wasn't he just born yesterday?"

"Seems like, some days. And others I'm so exhausted it feels like it's been forever!" Annie snapped the tray in place, turned, and then stopped. Her hands made erratic movements in the air, pointing this way and then that. "It's crazy how my brain can't keep anything straight sometimes. What was I doing? Cookie? Sippy cup?" She huffed with weary frustration.

"Let me help. I'll grab him a snack. You snag his sippy." Meg stood and headed to the refreshment table.

"Thanks. Really," Annie said, kneeling down to search her bag for her youngest's elusive cup of water.

Meg returned with the cookie and broke it into pieces on the tray before settling back into her chair. "C'mon, Annie. You've gotta sit down sometime."

Annie stretched her neck out and then pulled out the chair across from her friend. "Thanks again. I don't know why, but lately I've been a mess. David's waking up at night again, so I'm not sleeping enough. Sometimes I don't know how I manage this." She gestured to her young kids and then gave a sideways nod to her oldest, who was sitting at the other end of the table, engrossed in conversation with the kids from his confirmation class.

"Same way everyone else does, right? You just do," Meg said. "Plus, there's coffee."

"Yes. Coffee. Lots of coffee." Annie giggled. "And a beer now and then."

"Well, if you ever want to relax for a girl's night of beer, I'm sure Pastor would watch the kids for a few hours? Maybe?" Meg gave a warm smile. She had known Annie Feld since she and Charlie had become members a couple of years ago, but getting together outside of the church building always proved difficult for some reason. She tried not to take it personally, knowing it must be hard for a pastor's wife to befriend congregants, so she merely kept the invitation open.

"That sounds like a great idea," Annie replied. "I may just have to—"

Her words were cut short by Meg's phone buzzing loudly against the table. The women both looked at it and shared a puzzled glance, as Sunday-morning calls from anyone were pretty rare. She flipped it over to view the screen. With one look at the caller ID—*Karen, FRG*—she threw it down into her purse. Annie shot her a curious glance.

"It's nobody. They can leave a message. Church is more important anyway, right?" Meg explained.

"True. I mean, Bible study hasn't started yet, so you could call them back if you needed to."

"Nah, I'm sure it's nothing. Or sure it can wait..." Meg began to ramble but stopped when Annie let out a sharp yelp.

"What did you just say, little miss?" Annie leaned over the table and asked her daughter in the sternest of voices, her face showing she meant business.

"What? I was telling David that he's a little shit." Lydia looked confused and lifted her shoulders to her ears in an exaggerated shrug.

"We do *not* use that word, Lydia," Annie said, ignoring Meg, who was now struggling to stifle a giggle behind her hand.

"What word? Little? But he is little! It won't hurt his feelings, promise." Lydia's eyes shone with every bit of innocence. Had she been thirteen instead of five, one might have thought she was being smart with her mom, but instead her words and tone dripped with sincerity.

"No. The other word." Annie pursed her lips, unable to repeat the word. They were in church, after all.

"Oooooh. Shit?" Lydia repeated loudly, finally understanding. Sort of. "But it's in the Bible."

At this, Meg had to fully turn her face so the little girl wouldn't see her laughing. Five-year-olds needed no such encouragement, and she pressed her hand to her mouth to keep the snorts from exploding.

"It is *not*!" Annie scolded, desperate to keep her own voice low and not draw attention to her daughter's ill manners.

Now Lydia got defensive. "But it is, all the time."

Annie's was now the face showing confusion. Her mind seemed to race a mile a minute, trying to determine where Lydia would have heard that word all the time in scripture. "Where? Which stories?"

"Abel had them. David took care of them. They were at the manger with baby Jesus," Lydia explained with remarkably patient words, as if she were almost proud to be teaching her mommy something.

"Wait, were you saying *sheep*?" Annie asked, her brows furrowed.

"Yeah. What did you think I said?"

"Oh, nothing. Forget it." Annie flopped back into her chair and glanced at Meg, who had finally calmed down. "I swear."

"Mommy, we shouldn't swear." Lydia shook her head with a frown, sending Meg back into hysterics.

"I think it's time for Sunday School, sweetie," Annie noted.

"I didn't hear the bell."

"I'm sure they'll ring it soon. Why don't you go on and wait for them to start?"

"Okay! Bye, Mrs. Winters!" Lydia shoved the last bit of cookie in her mouth and then turned to tell her mom with her mouth still full, "Save my cupcake."

"I will. Now go!"

Lydia began to run off but turned suddenly with her finger pointed back at her mom. "Don't eat it! All right?"

Annie nodded at her daughter and smiled as she watched her skip off to her class. She looked back to Meg, who had picked up her phone and was listening to her voicemail. When she had set the phone back down, Annie asked, "So? Any news?"

Meg's nose scrunched up, and her mouth tightened to one side. "I dunno. I mean, she asked me to call her back. Didn't sound urgent or bad or anything. I'm sure everything's fine. They usually wait until the afternoons to call. Morning seems…weird."

"Well, if you need to go and call her back…"

"No, no. I want to stay for Bible study. Another hour won't hurt anything."

Pastor Feld approached their table, his coffee cup in one hand and his Bible in the other. He looked first to his wife and then to the plate sitting in front of her. "Oh, hey, thanks for the cupcake."

Annie gently slapped his hand away. "Nope. Not yours. Saving it for Lydia."

"Ah. Then I guess I'll just go see if there's another left. Gotta get my blood sugar back up if I'm going to be ready for Ol' Mike's questions this morning." He chuckled to himself before walking away. Mike Goetz, while typically on the quieter side, could always be relied upon to get Bible study rolling with his questions, which always started out of left field before meandering their way back to some obscure connection with the day's readings.

When Pastor Feld had first been installed as their pastor, he had fumbled around with how to respond to the unpredictable—and often absurd—topics Mike brought up. But after several years, he'd seemed to discover that sometimes the best answer was of the non-answer variety—a smile and nod, perhaps a laugh if appropriate. These were often enough to appease Mike, and the rest of the congregation seemed to appreciate his ability to speed things along so they could get to the meat of the study at hand.

With his cupcake devoured and his hands wiped clean of any crumbs, Pastor Feld stood in front of his congregation once again. "Before we dive into the lesson for today's Gospel reading, does anyone have any questions?" A hand shot up in the back, and Pastor smiled. "Yes, Mike?"

"So, this past week, Elizabeth and I were out for our evening walk—you know, now that the snow is cleared up we can get back to those. And while we're out walking..." Mike rambled on, but before Meg could hear what had happened on their walk that was worth noting in front of thirty or so of their brothers and sisters in Christ during a Bible study, her phone buzzed again.

It wasn't Karen this time but Lauren something-or-other. Meg was horrible with names, but she at least recognized this as being one of the other wives from the unit. Whose wife, though, she wasn't sure. She silenced the buzzing but then looked at Annie with a frown before whispering, "I'm going to go take this."

Annie nodded, and Meg shuffled out into the narthex, shutting the fellowship hall door behind her so as not to disturb the study.

Meg answered the phone. "Hello?"

"Meg Winters? It's Lauren...Lauren Nelson." The voice on the other end didn't sound at all familiar, and the name—though it rang a bell—brought no faces to Meg's mind. Her pause must have clued in Lauren, because she followed up with, "Lieutenant Colonel Nelson's wife?"

"Oh, hi! Sorry. I am absolutely awful with names, and I think we've only met once or twice, right?" She cringed, hoping the woman didn't take any offense to her poor memory.

But Lauren simply ignored her question and asked, "How *are* you?"

Meg frowned. What an odd way to phrase that question. Maybe it was all in her head though. She wasn't familiar with Lauren's normal tone or inflection, so this could just be the way she talked. "Um..." she started, trying to sound casual despite her intense confusion over this phone call. "...fine?"

There was a pause on the other end and then a sharp inhale before the words spilled out. "Woods was killed yesterday—along with Martin and Carter." Lauren's voice came out in a rush, hurried, like she needed to get it all out at once before her nerves blocked them.

"Wait. What?" Meg sat at the first place she could find—a small wooden chair. It was meant for young children and had been placed in the corner beside a small table with books and puzzles on it. Meg didn't realize the chair was about three sizes too small for her before she sat down, but she couldn't stand any longer.

"What...what happened? What about the others? What... I don't..." Meg couldn't finish any of her sentences, not that she even knew what she was trying to say.

"I don't know all the details yet. I'm sorry I told you like that. I thought you already knew. The FRG was supposed to call you." Lauren's apology came out in another rush of anxious words, tinged this time with embarrassment for her mistake.

Meg couldn't believe it. This wasn't the way they notified people. There was a script.

"Karen was supposed to call you, to tell you officially."

There it was. She had missed the scripted words that would have told her. Her heart pounded in her chest. She had one question, but she could barely think the words let alone say them aloud. All she could manage was his name: "Charlie?"

"I was told he's fine. The others are all okay and safe. It was just the three guys that were hit. When, how, what happened, I still am not really clear. Maybe an IED, I think. They're on comm blackout for a week, so I haven't gotten to talk to my husband yet to confirm anything."

Meg's head spun. The guys had been on a mission, a convoy. An IED made sense, but Charlie always drove with Woods. Always. If Lauren didn't have all the details, she could be wrong about Charlie too. He wasn't necessarily safe. The officers could be waiting at her door right now.

Her arms began to shake, and her breaths came quicker as tears welled up in her eyes. She rocked back and forth in the little chair, not sure what to say or even think. All she knew was panic.

"Meg? I'm sorry again. I'll let you go. Call me if you need anything, okay?" Lauren retreated into her own uneasiness. When Meg didn't respond, though, she repeated herself. "Really. Call me anytime."

Meg struggled to gather enough energy to reply, but all she could muster was a meek "Okay. Bye."

She dropped the phone into her lap, but it slid to the floor and bounced a foot or so in front of her before coming to a rest. She didn't move to retrieve it but let her eyes settle on where it had landed. Her mind raced. She couldn't focus on any of the thoughts as they sped past. The narthex faded from view. Everything around her disappeared.

She saw nothing. Heard nothing. Felt nothing.

There was only numbness and disbelief. But then her pulse quickened, and her breathing became short and shallow.

This wasn't how she was supposed to find out. There was a script—a script she knew by heart.

The dishes clanged together as Meg moved them from one side of the sink to the other. The tree behind their house still showed the gorgeous scarlets and golds in the leaves that had only half-fallen into the yard. Against the perfect blue of that morning's sky, the day seemed the epitome of fall, and she contemplated ditching her list of chores and errands so she could sit on the porch swing all day with a comfy sweater and a hot cup of coffee, watching the sparse clouds drift by on the breeze. With his homecoming happening in two weeks —give or take—the afternoon couldn't be wasted.

Her best friend from college was arriving that afternoon to help her with some of the preparations, so when the doorbell rang, she thought nothing of it. She didn't bother to look through the window before yanking the door open with a smile.

But it wasn't her friend on the porch.

The two men stood with such somber decorum in their pristinely pressed dress uniforms that Meg didn't need to hear the words to know what was coming or what had happened. But the words came nonetheless.

"Mrs. Margaret Haas," one soldier began, "the Secretary of the Army has asked me..."

She didn't need words to confirm she was the woman they had come to visit. Her knees gave way, and her heart caved in on itself. She crumpled to the floor with a mournful wail that echoed in her head so loudly she could barely hear the soldier's voice.

"...to express his deep regret that your husband, Jon Haas..."

Her hands hit the ground, fingertips digging into the hardwood of the entryway.

"...is believed to have been killed in action on November twelfth."

She rocked back and forth uncontrollably as the notification officer reached to console her. He said nothing, just let her fall apart—her heart shattering as she cried out in denial.

"Not Jon. No. Not Jon. It's not him. Not him. No..."

13

The world stopped, freezing Meg in her seat. Her muscles and joints, tense and aching from sitting too long in the too-small chair, remained still. She couldn't blink, and had it not been for the keen awareness that she was, in fact, still alive, she would have assumed she'd stopped breathing too, the air drawing in and out so shallowly that she neither felt her chest rise nor her lungs fill.

A flash of white entered her field of vision, but she didn't acknowledge it. Her purse and Bible slid to the floor beside the phone she'd dropped, where her eyes stayed fixed, wet with unfallen tears.

"Meg?" a voice said. It was accompanied by a gentle weight against her hand, but Meg couldn't discern who was speaking or reaching for her hand.

"What's happened?" Annie's head bowed low, breaking Meg's stare with the floor, though she still kept a polite distance.

Meg heard the question, but her senses seemed locked, trapped by the news that had been dropped on her. She could barely recognize the expression on her friend's face, let alone give a voice to everything swirling inside her.

Is it real? Maybe I'm dreaming. It can't possibly be real.

If she could shut her eyes, maybe convince herself it was just another vivid nightmare haunting her, a past memory creeping out of the far reaches of her mind, then the world could keep spinning and everything could go back to normal.

That's not how this works, Meg.

She swallowed the last bits of her denial and forced her eyes to close. "IED." It came out so quietly, so breathlessly, that Meg wasn't sure she'd said it aloud at all, but she heard Annie's breath catch and felt the hand pull away from her own. The air between them lay silent and still. Meg didn't look up.

"Charlie?" Annie asked.

Meg shook her head slightly. "No, he's fine—I think." She cringed, not knowing if it was a lie, a half-truth, or what. The whole thing hadn't exactly been relayed to her properly. What if the FRG hadn't gotten the right names? The volunteer had gotten his name wrong before. Maybe they had done it again.

Annie's shoulders relaxed, and her breath released. Meg remained tense, her jaw throbbing as her teeth pressed into each other. The ache in her shoulders pulsed, intensifying, and her hands, despite all her efforts to steady them, wouldn't stop shaking as she wrung them together.

"Do you need someone to drive you home?"

She shook her head again.

"Are you sure? I'm sure George Mueller wouldn't mind giving you a ride," Annie said.

Meg lifted her chin and looked at her friend. She should let others care for her, as Charlie had always urged, but sitting awkwardly in a car with an old guy, even a friendly old guy from church, didn't seem like the best way to care for herself and her nerves. And someone else needed her now. The self-care thing would have to wait.

"No. I need to... I can't..."

Annie brought her head closer, covering Meg's hand with hers once more. "I'm not sure you should drive right now."

Meg attempted a small smile. She couldn't bear for Annie to think she wasn't grateful. "I'll be okay. There's just…somewhere I need to go. Alone."

Annie's head shifted to the side, and her mouth opened to say something but closed again without uttering a sound.

"I'm fine, really." She winced as her voice quivered and cracked. *Well, that's not going to convince Annie you're fine.*

But Annie relented with a nod. She reached down to gather Meg's belongings and handed the purse to her before wrapping her in a warm hug. "If you need anything, don't hesitate to call me or my husband. We'll be there in two seconds. I promise."

"Thanks. Tell Pastor I'll call him later?"

Annie nodded again. "Of course. And please, drive carefully."

Meg pulled the corner of her mouth back as she dropped her chin slightly. Breaking through the shock that had previously held her, she turned and, with her head down, headed for the door, not realizing she'd failed to offer any goodbye.

Though the snow had melted a week earlier, the air outside remained bitter, made worse by the blasts of wind that whipped around her. She hunched her shoulders within her coat, regretting having left her scarf on the hook at home. *Stupid forecast.* She cursed the weather app on her phone for claiming a high of forty. It couldn't possibly be more than thirty-three, and that was without considering the wind chill.

Even inside the Jeep, which was considerably warmer without the frigid wind, her limbs found no relief from their tremors. Her hands shuddered so violently that she could barely turn the key in the ignition, but with a great deal of effort and determination she managed.

The Jeep roared to life, but she had forgotten the music she had been blaring that morning back when everything was fine.

Normal. Yet it hadn't been—not really. She had just not known the truth yet. She slammed the dial to "off" and dug in her pockets for her gloves, still convinced it was the cold that kept them from steadying.

Her stomach twisted into knots, made worse as she tried to swallow the dread that had crept into her throat. She didn't want to make this house call, but she had to. There were families grieving now, probably woken up to find their loved one dead, gone.

Martin. Carter. She couldn't visit their families. She didn't know them—didn't even know where they lived. But Woods...

The name brought a fresh rush of tears to the surface, and her chest quaked under the grief. His face flashed across her mind. Then Piper's. She inhaled deeply, hoping the breath would calm her nerves enough for her to do this, to be a good friend.

She kept the Jeep moving, crawling ahead at five miles under the speed limit—if not slower—using Annie's request to be careful as an excuse for stalling. *I'm not being selfish. I'm just gathering my thoughts. For Piper.*

She tried to think back to her own day of grief, not so much to bring Jon and all her own pain to the surface, but so that she could maybe find a way to comfort her friend. But all her memories beyond that initial notification remained a blur, clouded by years of trying to forget the sting of loss.

Even if she could remember what had comforted her—if anything really had—it wouldn't help her now. Grief had that obnoxious way of being different for each person who experienced it, leaving each to seek solace in their own manner.

How would Piper handle this? They'd only been friends for a couple of years—a couple of years without tragedy.

Meg could offer psalms and other scripture, but she could only remember bits and chunks, all mixed up and jumbled. Perhaps she could share the overall theme of God's steadfast love. Or maybe she could read a psalm; she did have her Bible with her after all, and there were plenty that spoke to crying out or calling out to the Lord in grief and pain. Surely she could manage to find one, even with her still-trembling fingers and frayed nerves.

Meg pulled the Jeep up to the curb. Piper's house stood unassuming. The flag on the porch whipped violently this way and that in the fierce wind, getting stuck on the column before being thrown about by another gust. The single blue star hung in the window.

Soon it would be gold.

Aside from the flags, nothing set this house apart from the others. There was no sign that this one hid a woman whose life had been ripped apart by war that morning. With no other vehicles on the block, there was no telling how long the officer and chaplain had been gone. The notification must have come early. Poor Piper had likely woken up on what she thought was a regular, normal Sunday, and instead...

Panic grabbed Meg again. She had lived through all of this herself, but she certainly didn't feel like an expert. *What do I have to offer her? Charlie, why can't you be here with me!*

With Charlie, she would have had the confidence to do this. He would have steadied her hands and her heart, filled in the awkward silences when she didn't know what to say, and calmed her rambling when she let too many words fall out. He would have made her strong, made this doable.

But he wasn't here, and she had to do this without him. Just like everything else.

Pulling out the chain at her neck, she slid his wedding band over her thumb, gripping it and the crucifix in her hands. Her chest tightened, and she choked on the sobs that threatened to burst forth. But she couldn't suppress the images that invaded her mind, the past barbecues and unit functions, these soldiers laughing over beers and hugging their loved ones—loved ones who would never see or hold them again.

Her face contorted as she lost the battle to contain the grief, and a silent scream filled her throat. She dropped her necklace and let her head fall into her hands, desperate to pull it together and be the strong one for once.

She racked her brain for scripture that could help her, but every verse she recalled was random and out of place for the situation.

Lord, help me! Please!

With a deep breath, she pushed herself to focus. Even if she couldn't remember God's Word verbatim, she knew it was written to not be afraid, to trust in the Lord and His steadfast love. After another deep breath, she looked back at the house and remembered why she was here in the first place.

She didn't need the right words or a steady hand. She just needed to be there. God had given her a neighbor to serve, a sister in Christ to love and support, and though she was far from eloquent, she'd do it all the same

A stretch of her neck and a roll of her shoulders did little to loosen the tension, but it at least gave her one last chance to settle down. She pushed the Jeep's door open, forcing it against the wind before letting it slam shut behind her. The walk to the front door couldn't have been more than twenty yards, but each step agitated the knot in her stomach, making it seem more like a quarter mile.

By the time she stepped onto the porch she felt sure she was going to throw up.

She lifted a hand and, before she could talk herself out of it, let it rap against the cold door. No sound came from the other side, though she might not be able to hear anything with the blasted wind whirling around her head. But then faint footsteps, slow and tired, made their way to the door.

Meg drew in a long breath and held it, as if she'd lose all

confidence and nerve if she dared let it go. She looked down at her feet and waited, unable to face her friend's eyes right away. The lock unlatched, and the door creaked open, slowly at first and then wider. Before she could raise her face to say hello, Piper's arms wrapped around her.

"Oh, Meg." Piper sobbed weakly into Meg's shoulder.

All anxiety fled as instinct took over, and she pulled Piper in close, placing a hand on her head, as a mom would with a hurt child. Together they rocked back and forth, both crying there on the porch, neither of them concerned with the cold or the wind.

"I'm here," she whispered. "I'm here."

Charlie blinked at the ceiling above his cot, his lids scratching across the dry surface of his eyes. Another sleepless night. Another chance at rest stolen by the memories and images that flashed across his mind. He had seen too much in his tours, and he still had four months to go in this one.

You've gotta shake this.

The war wouldn't end and the enemy wouldn't give up just because he'd lost three friends and was struggling with the grief. It was hard enough to focus on the mission and his team, but then there was Meg.

She needed him too. But how? Of course, he wanted to call her, to see how she was doing, but even after several days he had no clue what he'd say to her. At least the comm blackout gave him time.

Still, the questions plagued him. Had she been told he was fine? Had she been told anything at all? He'd heard stories of notifications getting screwed up through various channels. Maybe she was waiting to hear from him, wondering why he hadn't called after this latest mission.

No, she would have checked the news. It was what she did. It was what all the wives did, despite all the advice to the contrary. He knew they all talked, checked in with one another if one hadn't gotten a call when expected. She'd know, but would she know he was safe, that he was okay?

Am I okay?

He sat up, cradling his head in his hands. Sure, he had survived. But why? He should have been driving that truck. At the last minute the lieutenant colonel had changed the truck assignments and assigned Martin to number two, Charlie's usual. His heart pounded against his sternum, echoing in his ears. He clenched his teeth behind a fisted hand.

Why them, God? Why? It makes no sense! Why spare me?

He wasn't anything special, yet God had spared him while taking the lives of men who had so much ahead of them. Rest. Marriage. A baby.

He knew the scripture. He knew all the words—God's Word—how He worked good through all things, how His will didn't match ours, how life was full of trials and heartaches.

He knew them, sure, but those truths held no comfort.

Anger. Grief. Guilt. Those were all he had.

It should have been me!

He pushed to his feet with fists tightened. With a low growl he kicked at the closest thing to his boot. The box went flying into the flimsy wall of his room, the contents of her latest care package scattering. His breath came out rapid and ragged, catching on the tightness in his chest. A curse escaped his lips. He needed to get himself under control.

How?

His gaze landed on the book he'd thrown the other day—its spine creased down the middle and its thin pages, bent and folded, splayed across the floor and wall. He should retrieve it and dig into those words through which God promised comfort and healing.

You don't deserve comfort. Not when your friends are dead, gone, blown to pieces.

He tried to shake that voice away, but it wouldn't budge, its seeds planted and starting to take root. If he let himself find comfort and peace, especially so soon, it'd mean he didn't care they were gone. Wouldn't it?

At least he was feeling something. Anything. Numbness would be worse. Rage was better.

He pulled his eyes away from the book, not letting his gaze fall on the mess he'd created as he turned to the door. He needed out of here. He needed a distraction.

Opening the door, he slammed his right fist into the plywood, the pain a bitter reminder that he was, indeed, still alive. And only God knew why.

Charlie turned the corner into Murphy's room, which was filled with the sounds of gunfire, groaning, dying. This was a bad idea. The sounds were too real, too vivid, like the damn images in his head. But he couldn't avoid the guys forever, and he sure as hell couldn't sit in his room any longer.

Murphy and Baker stared at the screen, giving no notice to him as he stepped inside. He looked at his buddies—one, then the other—mere shells of the guys he knew. They exchanged no insults. There was no bickering, no banter, just the occasional groan of irritation when the game disappointed. The IED had cost him more than three friends.

"Murphy's bad luck bringin' you down, Baker?" Charlie asked as Baker's player died again.

The edge of Baker's lips curved up slightly. "You know it. Can't escape it!"

"I don't know what you're talkin' about." Murphy spoke plainly, his gaze unmoved and his words missing his usual playfulness.

"You want in, dude?" Baker shot a glance at Charlie, with a

nod to the other controller sitting on the desk. "We can switch. Shoot some zombies instead."

Maybe zombies would seem unrealistic enough to make this less painful. He reached for the controller and relaxed back into the seat. "Sure. As long as Murphy doesn't leave me hangin' like last time." He hoped his voice sounded as relaxed as he intended, but all he got was a roll of the eyes from Murphy.

The afternoon continued in silence, the game more comforting than expected. Maybe comforting wasn't the right word. Distracting? Yes. Comforting? That was a stretch. It was at least better than the silence that settled among the guys as they played. No one spoke of the friends whose absence weighed heavy, the empty spots around the room, or the fourth controller that was unused.

But the distraction was still minimal, incapable of erasing the images of twisted metal and torn flesh that still taunted him from the back corner of his mind where he'd tried to shove them. Someday it would all fade, but it'd never be completely gone.

He knew that much.

Some ghosts could never really be shaken.

The cabin filled with the sound of crackling and popping as Charlie threw another log onto the fire. He turned to see Meg grabbing the wine glasses from the counter before they settled onto the worn cushions of the sofa. Pulling her in close beside him, he rested his chin against her hair, the smell of her lavender shampoo mixing with the warming scent of the fire filling the room. She snuggled further into his side.

I don't deserve this woman.

But here she was. In his arms.

He gazed into the fire, but his focus locked onto the steady rhythm of her breath rising and falling beside him. Could she sense his anxiety, the questions that plagued him, the worry that somehow he'd misread all her kisses and hugs of the previous months? She had said she loved him—many times in fact. And he wanted to believe her, but still, doubt lingered.

He opened his mouth to speak, but her voice sounded first. "You think God can give us two soul mates?" It was nearly a whisper, barely audible over the popping of the wood as it burned. His mind faltered, words failing. He waited longer, unsure how to answer.

But when she turned to face him, he said the first thing that came to mind: "I hope so?"

He hadn't intended it to be a question, but the doubt had stolen all his confidence. She straightened and lifted her hand to his chin, turning him to face her. Those eyes. Green with flecks of amber. What was she thinking? He couldn't read her.

All he knew was how much he wanted to believe she was his and how much he worried that she never would be. Not really. Not fully.

"I love you," she said, a catch in her throat keeping her words restrained, hushed. He brushed her hair away from her face and tucked it behind her ear, letting his fingers trace the line of her jaw and pulling her chin closer. He leaned down to meet her lips with his own, feeling her chin quiver slightly under his fingers still resting there.

She settled back against his side and returned her gaze to the fire, her eyes glistening with the impending tears. So he hadn't imagined her being on the verge of crying. He lifted her hand in his, feeling the softness of her skin and seeing the crossed paths of their lives reflected in their fingers as they moved, weaving around each other in loving strokes. All the decisions and experiences that had brought him to this moment spun in his mind. They had this common link, the man they both missed, and he wondered if her heart could ever let go enough.

Could he share her heart with a ghost?

For months he had wrestled with that question, wondering how he could possibly compete with his friend's memory, having witnessed their love and their marriage. When he had promised his buddy all those years ago, he'd never imagined fulfilling his word would bring him to this moment. Nor did he deserve this after failing her after the funeral.

"Meg?"

"Hmmm?" She didn't move.

He stared straight ahead, focus fixed on the flames, unable to look at her and risk having all his fears manifested in her eyes. He breathed deeply. Now or never, man.

"Will you marry me?"

She froze under his arm. His heart pounded, fear keeping him still. Was that her heart racing, or was it his own tricking him? The silence crushed him as the time passed in utter agony, though it was mere seconds. Her body rose and fell with a deep breath before she pulled out of his arms, sitting up.

This was it. She was going to turn him down. He'd been an idiot to think he could replace Jon, the love of her life, her first—and last—love.

She turned to look at him, and he forced himself to meet her gaze, bracing himself for the regret and sadness sure to be in her eyes. But what he saw left him more confused. Was that a glimmer of hope and love on her face? He couldn't be sure, couldn't risk getting his own hopes up if she was going to dash them away.

Her lips curved into a smile, parted, and whispered, "Yes."

14

Meg poked her head around the office door. Pastor Feld stood at his desk gathering books and papers in-between sips from his travel mug. She waited. Maybe he wouldn't notice her, and she could turn and run. He continued to organize his Bible study materials.

He was obviously too busy, in too much of a rush to chat.

She moved to retreat, but his head lifted with a smile.

"Meg, how are you? Glad to see you this morning." His voice came out friendly enough, with just the right amount of concern to be comforting instead of smothering.

She shrugged her shoulders and sighed. "Okay. I think. Almost didn't make it actually. With all the phone calls and texts this week, I didn't know if I could stomach any more offers of casseroles or questions about whether Charlie's okay."

"Ah, yeah." He nodded. "This congregation does love to love its members to an overwhelming point."

"Overwhelming might be an understatement there, Pastor."

A single laugh escaped before he spoke again. "But it's love all the same, and remember, we serve our neighbors sometimes by allowing them to serve us."

"You do remember I'm more of an introvert than Charlie, right?" Meg smiled. The words hadn't come out as lighthearted as she had intended, instead being too on edge, too defensive.

"Speaking of Charlie, have you heard from him yet?"

"Nope. Hoping to soon. Maybe tonight. Just glad to know, officially, that he's safe."

"And your friend—Piper, right?—how is she doing?"

"As well as she can. She left for Dover pretty soon after. You know, to be there when..." She was unable to finish the sentence. "The funeral is this week, back in Kansas in Aaron's hometown. I'm feeling pretty crappy for not being there."

She looked down at her feet when she realized she'd let such language spill out in front of her pastor—and in church, no less.

But he ignored it and leaned back onto his heels with a sigh. "Well, we can't make it to every funeral, especially on such short notice and so far away. I'm sure she understands."

"I know she does. But still. Feel like I should have at least tried to be there. It's just..."

"...hard to be there?" Pastor said, finishing her sentence.

She nodded, her eyes never leaving her feet. Perhaps if she focused on lining the edge of her shoe against the pattern of the carpeted floor, the tears wouldn't spring up and embarrass her. Her chest tightened, the anxiety building beneath the surface. She had so much she wanted to ask him, but where to start?

Could he really help? He wasn't exactly a military chaplain. As far as she knew, their congregation had no other military families as members. Had he ever even been through this with a parishioner?

Pastor's eyes narrowed at her. "What's going on, Meg? What's on your mind?"

She wanted to hold it all in, to not burden this man who had so many other souls to care for, but she worried keeping it all buried would do more harm than good. This was her chance, and if she didn't take it now, she'd never find the guts to do it again.

"I'm not sure how I should be acting right now. One minute I'm fine, the next I'm such a mess you'd think my husband had been the one in that truck. And then I feel awful because *I'm* not supposed to be the emotional wreck right now. How can I be there for Piper if I'm breaking down all the time? And what if I'm crying uncontrollably and she's not? Talk about awkward. And once Charlie does call, what should I expect from him? How do I help him? What do I even say or do? I don't know."

Her shoulders slumped as she gave a heavy sigh at the end of her rambling. She hadn't meant to drown him in so many thoughts. She looked up and realized her pastor was still standing there with arms loaded down with papers and books. There was a room full of congregants waiting for Bible study to begin.

"I'm sorry. I'm going to make you late." A swear escaped her lips, and she huffed out an embarrassed and frustrated sigh. "Gah, I need to stop swearing. Sorry."

Her pastor stifled a chuckle. "I'm sure they have plenty of donuts and coffee to tide them over until I get down there, and I can handle any complaints about my lack of punctuality. But I'll keep this brief. There's no *supposed to* when it comes to grief and loss. Given your past—your own history—this is bound to bring up those memories and that pain. That's okay, and I'm sure Piper understands. Try not to overthink it. Just be a friend. Listen to her. Pray with her. Respect her needs and boundaries."

He shifted his stack of books to the other arm. His eyes seemed to be searching the wall behind her for the words she needed to hear. Maybe he didn't have any answers for her last set of questions, but his eyes met hers again as he spoke. "With

Charlie? You know your husband, but you also know that grief can affect us in ways we don't expect or anticipate. Follow his lead. Listen when he needs to talk, and let him know you're there for him. Pray with him and for—"

"So basically be his wife?" Meg interrupted, her voice timid and unsure. It sounded too simple. Yet impossible too.

He smiled back at her with a nod. "Pretty much. Remember, you both need each other right now. God's Word surpasses the distance. Remain in that together, and it'll help you both."

"Thanks." Her stomach twisted into knots around the one question she hadn't asked. It was now or never though. "I..."

She started to speak, but her voice barely made a sound.

He didn't hear her. Glancing over his shoulder at the clock above his desk, he said, "I probably should get downstairs now. Before they stage a coup over my tardiness. You joining us today?"

"Oh. No, I think I'm going to try to get some rest. I haven't been sleeping much lately," she said, backing into the hallway.

Pastor pulled a sheet off the pile in his arms and handed it to her. "Rest is a blessing in itself. Here's what we're covering today. If you have any questions, let me know. And try to make it next week."

"Sure thing. It's good for my faith, after all," she said with a nod.

"That it is. Have a blessed rest of your day. Tell Charlie hi from us when he calls." He disappeared around the corner and down the stairs.

Another swear escaped her lips through clenched teeth, and she flung open the church door, a gust of wind grabbing it from her hands. Snow whirled around her, whipping and twisting around her legs, smacking against her cheeks.

She stomped her way to the Jeep, the unasked question pulsing against her temples, nagging her. No one had told her how to be a widow—or rather, a remarried widow.

Why hadn't that been a part of premarital counseling? Why had no one told her how to grieve and how to deal with the memories?

Because everyone thought you were fine!

She had been too. No one had understood the odd sense of peace that had hit just weeks after Jon's death. Even she hadn't.

Had it even been real? Where was it now?

Meg stretched her legs out along the length of the couch, pulling her favorite blanket up over her shoulders, but the tension in her back made the position unbearable even with the couch cushions offering support. She rolled over, her face now buried into the back of the couch, and brought one knee up into her chest, then the other.

No position eased the stress that had settled between her shoulder blades, but she refused to go down the hallway to bed. Beds were not for naps, and she would never concede on that, no matter how much Charlie teased her for her stubbornness on the matter.

The need for rest hadn't been a stock excuse for skipping Bible study. She had spent the entire week surviving on minimal hours of sleep and numerous pots of coffee, but despite recognizing the need, she had resisted. Closing her eyes meant subjecting herself to images she didn't want and memories that were better kept buried.

Eventually, though, exhaustion always won, and she surrendered to the sleep and the dreams. Today was no exception.

When she opened her eyes again, Charlie was there with his bearded smile, laughing over a pint of beer, his eyebrow raising up at her as he reached for her hand across the table. She saw her hand fold into his. Something was off.

His fingers were more slender and long. His hand lacked its

usual warmth. Instead it was cold, almost clammy, and the ring on his finger wasn't right.

She looked up to ask him what had happened, but his beard was gone. His grey eyes had given way to a deep brown, and his hair had darkened slightly. But he was still Charlie. Maybe. His face still held its usual look of love and humor. She looked down at their hands, fingers intertwined, and then he spoke.

"I miss you, Megs."

Charlie didn't call her that. Ever.

She raised her eyes again, and now there was no hint of Charlie at all in the man across from her. Jon stared back at her, the dimple in his cheek appearing as he smiled, hints of freckles spreading toward his eyes of melted chocolate.

She smiled at him and hated herself for it. "I miss you too, Jon. Why'd you have to leave me?" She heard the words escape her mouth, though she didn't want to say them.

"Didn't want to, Megs. But you know God gives and He takes…in His time, not ours." With these words, he pulled both her hands into his and looked closer at the ring she now wore. "I'm sorry I left, but please don't forget me. Or us."

"But I have to, Jon. You're not coming back. You can't come back," she said, her voice quivering. She wanted to pull her hands away from his, to insist she wasn't his anymore, to tell him she had moved on, and yet his hands felt like home. He pulled the ring off her finger, the ring Charlie had given her that night in the mountains.

She wanted to protest, but she couldn't.

"This isn't right, Megs. This is the one you should be wearing." He slid a simple solitaire onto her hand, and she felt herself giving in as he leaned across the table and pulled her face to his.

"I love you, Jon. Always," she whispered before returning his kiss, letting herself melt into those familiar lips that had been hers for all those years, so long ago.

The phone buzzed loudly against the wooden coffee table, startling Meg out of her dream. She looked around the room, warmth creeping over her face, as if someone had caught her in an act of adultery.

She shook her head and squeezed her eyes shut, pushing away Jon's face—and his kiss—from her mind. It had only been a dream, but the guilt seized her all the same, twisting her stomach into uneasy knots.

Jon was gone. Dead. She had Charlie now. So why could she not get that kiss out of her mind?

The phone buzzed again. She checked the number.

Charlie.

Her heart raced. Her fingers fumbled over the keypad as she lifted the phone to her ear.

"Charlie?" She hoped her words sounded anxious from excitement and happiness instead of guilt and shame.

"Hey, babe. So nice to hear your voice." He sounded tired—and stressed—but relieved.

"You too." Her mind blanked. No, it wasn't blank. It was filled with the dream she couldn't shake. Not exactly something she wanted to tell her husband. How did you tell your husband you had just been kissing your dead ex and enjoying it? Especially after he had watched several buddies die in front of him only days ago?

"You okay?" he asked. What a stupid question. Of course she wasn't okay. She clenched her teeth. The irritation was irrational, unfounded. He was dealing with this the same as she was—more directly, perhaps, and far away from the support of his church home.

She breathed deeply, all her effort put toward avoiding snarky remarks. "I guess." It was all she could offer. She didn't want to talk about herself and her own demons. She couldn't trust herself to not say everything on her mind. But wouldn't he expect her to be thinking of Jon? Wasn't that the logical place for a gold star wife to go when facing another friend dying?

She wrestled the thoughts, and her hands balled into shaking fists. Thank goodness he couldn't see her right now. But he would know something was up if she didn't find something to say.

She took a deep breath to smooth the anxiety out of her voice. "How are you holding up?"

"Well, could be better." His words would normally have carried some tinge of sarcasm, but now they fell flat, empty, broken. He wasn't handling this well, and she had no idea how to help him. Her husband apparently could be rattled, and it had taken an IED to do it. What could she say? What could fix this?

Follow his lead. Pastor's words had seemed easy enough to follow that morning, but now that she was here on the phone listening to her grieving husband's breathing from the other side of the world, she had no idea how to do that.

"I..." She stopped. "I don't know what to say."

"Me neither. Though, guess that's my norm." Again, his words lacked the typical carefree tone. He didn't sound like Charlie. The deadpan stoicism in his words wasn't his but wasn't foreign to her either.

Jon. He sounded like Jon. She had to change the subject. She couldn't tell him about the dream, the way she wished it was Jon on the other end of the phone right now, or how she longed for him to still be alive and with her.

Quick. Think of something.

Piper. Of course. Her friend had lost a husband. Charlie had lost a friend. She berated herself for thinking she somehow had it worse than them, for letting her own grief overshadow that of those closest to her. "Piper's doing okay.

The pregnancy has at least gotten easier in the second trimester and all."

Charlie groaned into the phone. "You know, Aaron never talked about it, about the baby."

"You never mentioned it?" Meg's breathing relaxed with her question, thankful they'd managed to get back to other, safer, albeit sadder, topics. As if there were any topics that weren't plagued with death and grief.

"Babe. We're men. And Aaron is…was…" He paused, and she could picture him wincing. "…an especially quiet one. I figured he'd tell me when he was ready, like after the baby was born. But that explains it."

She shifted in her chair, thankful for this turn in the conversation, a distraction from everything she was trying to avoid. "Explains what?"

"Woods. He'd been off the past few weeks. He came to talk to me but then didn't. I didn't want to push him to speak up, figured he would eventually."

"And now it's too late." She regretted the words at once. "Crap… That's… Well, you know I'm not…not trying to make you feel bad."

"I know, babe. I know. But you're right. I lost my chance to help him. Or maybe I didn't. I don't know."

"What? What do you mean, maybe you didn't?"

"Well, it's not like we sat there in silence when he stopped by. I prayed the Psalms with him, read some of the gospel. He asked a couple questions, but about nothing specifically." Psalms. Meg wondered if the psalmists had ever prayed to God for help getting over a dead husband. She doubted it.

Charlie's voice interrupted her thoughts: "Did Piper say anything was wrong?"

"No. Everything seemed fine. I mean… Crap. He called her the other day when I was at their house, but I tried not to listen in. Left the room. When I came back, she was crying. But you know her. She's not the emotional type, so I tried to let it slide. Didn't want to embarrass her."

Charlie didn't say anything.

"Think he was worried about being a father?"

His breath hitched, and Meg knew she'd struck a nerve, because it struck hers too. Aaron would never get to be a father, would never meet his child.

"Anyway…" He sounded awkward and uncomfortable. "I need to get back to helping the team. Work still has to get done."

"Life moves on, huh?" She knew this all too well. Life moved on whether you were ready for it or not. "I love you, Charlie."

"Love you too, babe. Talk soon."

Meg was alone. Again. It never got easier, did it? This saying goodbye.

But life kept going.

After a week of propriety, handshakes and hugs, and half-smiles and quivering chins, Piper wanted life to get back to normal. Her son seemed to be in agreement, giving a gentle nudge of a limb within her belly

She pulled the car into her driveway, and her breath caught at seeing that it had been freshly shoveled after the recent snow. She should find out who had done that, maybe write them a thank you note. It was what was expected, what was proper.

Ugh. Proper.

She pulled her hair down from its ponytail, shaking it out about her shoulders before pushing the car door open. Resting a hand on her belly, she twisted and pulled herself up. Would she ever get used to this?

A kick to the ribs answered her, and she chuckled only slightly before it gave way to a sob that burst out of her before she could stop it. She'd managed the entire flight and the drive home with nothing more than a couple of tears.

She couldn't collapse here, not in the snow. She hadn't dressed properly for the weather, and the leggings she wore wouldn't protect her if she lost it.

Pushing her legs to carry herself to the house, not bothering to grab her luggage from the backseat, she fought the tears and the waves of grief they rode on.

You can break down later. Inside. Where no one's watching.

As if anyone was out here in the snow on a Sunday afternoon. As if anyone cared.

But someone did care, at least enough to clear the snow for her. She really should say thank you to whomever it was, as the cleared path eased her escape inside.

Once inside, she closed and locked the door behind her and dropped her purse onto the floor, glancing around the living area. Everything looked normal.

Her sweatshirt hung on the arm of the sofa. Her tennis shoes peeked out from under the coffee table, where she'd thrown them in her hurry to head to Dover. Her Bible was on the end table, her journal beside it.

No sign of Aaron, that he'd lived here. Nothing beyond the few pictures that peppered the walls—their wedding, a camping trip, nights out on the town.

Her knees buckled beneath her, dropping her to the floor. Her hands flew to her midsection on instinct. Holding her belly—the baby kicking against her arms—she curled protectively around him as the grief spread through her limbs, invading every muscle and nerve until it boiled over in a piercing wail.

The baby's kicks ceased. He had perhaps been startled by the scream. She raised a fisted hand to her mouth, pressing it hard against her lips to quiet the squeals and moans threatening to escape from her throat.

Her arms shook. Her legs tensed.

Help me, Jesus! Please! I need...

What did she need? She didn't know. This was new. All new. And awful.

You don't cry, Piper. You aren't a sap.

It wasn't the pep talk she wanted, but she couldn't stop the thoughts any more than she could stop the sobs. Or the pain.

She pushed her hands to her forehead, squeezing her eyes shut as her body rocked, the moans quieting to low hums in her chest.

Come, Lord. Come quickly. Give me peace!

The baby pushed against her side, stretching, and she dropped her hand to feel him moving. Gently easing the limb—or whatever body part it was—back in, the quivering of her hand eased. Her breathing slowed and deepened.

She glanced down at her belly as another limb pushed out on the other side. She slid her hand across to ease him back in again. As she sat, playing this game of nudge-the-baby, the hymn from church that morning crept its way across her mind until she was humming the tune.

She didn't remember all the words, but those she did know came to her lips.

"What a friend we have in Jesus, all our sins and griefs to bear..."

She sang them to herself, to her baby. Their baby.

I'll take care of him, Aaron. I promise.

And that promise started with prayer and Christ.

Thank you, Jesus.

15

SITTING on the edge of his cot, Charlie pushed his hands through his hair. He'd replayed the phone call in his mind so many times, but he couldn't pinpoint what he'd heard exactly.

She sounded different. He'd expected it, to a point, but not quite like that. Something nagged at him. *She's hiding something.*

But what? And why? She was reserved, quiet, sure. But she'd always been open with him. Or had she? What wasn't she telling him? What was she hiding?

He let out a curse and pushed himself to his feet. Pacing his small room, he chided himself for doubting his wife, for assuming she'd deceive him.

No, if Meg wasn't telling him something, she had her reasons. He wouldn't push, wouldn't force her to speak before she was ready.

But look how well that worked with Woods.

The thought punched him in the gut, and another curse echoed in his head. Maybe he should have pushed Woods to talk. Maybe he should have nudged him further, encouraged him to open up.

If he had known what was bothering the guy, he could have helped more, would have known what scripture he needed or what advice to give.

And now he's gone. It's too late.

He shook his head. The guilt vanished. God's Word had been shared. It was enough. It had to be enough. He couldn't keep beating himself up over that.

God would handle it, and at least Charlie knew Woods had been a man of faith. Even if he had scoffed at the way Lutherans prayed, they had shared that faith in Christ. In that, Charlie was sure.

But what about Meg? He stared at her picture, tacked back up on the wall, its edges smoothed out from where they'd gotten bent during his tantrum.

It had been taken in Hawaii, when life had seemed easier. They'd been married over a year at that point, somewhat settled into their new roles.

He rubbed the stubble along his chin, pulling his thoughts back to the phone call, his gaze still fixed on her smiling face.

What's going on with you, Meg?

Maybe she wasn't sure how to help Piper, or she was lonely.

Or was it Jon?

His breath caught. Of course. It had to be Jon.

The blast had brought back the memories for him. It had to have done the same to her. A pang of jealousy tugged at him from deep inside his chest. He fisted his hand, pressing it to his forehead before slamming it down on his desk.

Don't be ridiculous, Charlie. That's not fair to her.

The reprimand in his head did little good. It made sense for her to miss Jon. It was only natural, normal. She'd been Mrs. Haas for five years when he'd died. It had only been that long since.

Jon had been her first love, her first…everything. Charlie

had accepted that, hadn't he? He'd known it with that first date, hell, that first time he'd shown up on her doorstep so long after the funeral. He'd told himself he had just been a guy tracking down an old friend.

But he couldn't deny he'd always hoped for something more, even with all the times he'd confessed to coveting his best friend's wife. He'd been forgiven for that, so why did he feel so much like David killing Uriah so he could have Bathsheba?

A curse echoed in his head.

That was absurd. He wasn't responsible for Jon's death. And he hadn't exactly rejoiced when Meg was suddenly available, no longer off-limits.

That's why he'd run, after all. The PCS had been a convenient excuse for avoiding her, giving him the out he needed to skip town so soon after the funeral.

Legitimate excuse or not, he could have called her, could have kept in touch better. But he hadn't trusted himself to be there for her. He'd left, run. Like Jonah running away from God. But he hadn't been able to outrun his feelings for her any more than Jonah had been able to outrun the Lord.

Charlie collapsed into his chair, a pain rising in his throat as the guilt edged out the jealousy, one awful emotion being exchanged for another.

He'd justified his actions for so long, telling himself she hadn't needed him. She'd been strong when Jon died—stronger than anyone he'd known. Had he imagined it to appease his conscience? Had it been a mask? Had he been so eager to believe she didn't need him that he'd failed to see her struggling?

No.

He pushed to his feet again, pacing.

Not possible.

She had insisted she was fine at the funeral, and there had

been no reason to doubt her words. She'd seemed peaceful, calm. Not in an overdone way, like she was covering it up.

And then, years later, she'd told him everything, had explained it to him in her cute, rambling way, how she'd felt such inexplicable peace after the funeral, a peace that could have only come from God.

Maybe that peace simply hadn't manifested yet for her this time. He rolled his eyes at himself. Of course it hadn't. Her words—or lack thereof—had been far from peaceful.

What if that peace doesn't come again?

He stopped mid-pace. Another curse escaped his lips. What had he told Woods? *"Peace doesn't always come in the way we expect, and it doesn't always come this side of Heaven."* He searched the room for nothing in particular, his eyes darting from corner to corner as his mind raced.

If she didn't remember that, didn't hold onto that truth, it could be worse than his absurd jealousy.

Lord, keep her. Keep her steadfast in Your Word.

He couldn't call her. She'd be asleep, and Lord knew she needed the rest. His prayer would have to do. He had to trust in that.

Meg threw the covers back in a huff, kicking them off to rescue her feet from the sweltering heat. She had gotten no rest after that call with Charlie.

The night had brought with it memories of soldiers on her porch, a flag-draped coffin, and Charlie sitting next to her at the funeral. For hours she had stared at the ceiling, fighting the fatigue as she feared what she'd see when she closed her eyes.

But eventually the exhaustion had won, and she had drifted off to sleep only to be woken by her own screams.

The notification. The funeral. The loneliness. She'd relived all of it in painful detail.

She buried her face in the pillow and screamed again. Why'd Jon have to die on her, leaving her alone? He should be here.

But Charlie…

You are an awful wife. A horrible person.

The words hissed in her head.

She wanted Charlie home too, of course. She missed both men, longed for both of them. But what did that make her? Was this normal? Did all gold star wives go through this?

Her muffled pain turned into uncontrollable sobs.

Screw normal. Everyone experienced grief and healing in different ways. She had to deal with it however she could. With so little control over the emotions tossing about inside, she let the anger take hold, mixing with her own guilt, and shouted her silent prayers at God.

Why? Why am I reliving this agony? You healed me before. You gave me peace. And now this? What the hell?

She'd gotten past all this, moved on. She reached down and pulled the blankets back over her, ignoring the sticky heat from the sheet, which clung to her as she curled up, knees to her chest, chin tucked.

The heat enveloped her, smothering her—a mirror of the storm raging inside that tossed her among waves of guilt and anger, loneliness and grief.

She waited, her breathing shallow and rushed, desperate.

Where's your answer, God? Where's your steadfast love now?

No answer.

No relief, no freedom from the grip of her pain.

The accusatory words of the enemy streamed in from all sides.

Charlie would be angry if he knew.

Your first marriage ended.

You're breaking the sixth commandment. How dare you long for another man?

What would your mother say? What would your pastor say?

With a growl, she sat up, once again flinging the blankets aside. She threw her pillow across the room, but it landed with a barely audible *thump* instead of an impressive shattering of a lamp or something.

She growled again, her fists tightening. Like damaging property would make this easier. What was she, crazy?

Maybe. She certainly felt crazy.

Pulling Charlie's pillow close, she breathed in deeply, but the smell of him was distant, fading. She tossed it back down and rested her head on it, then pulled her legs back up to her chest again, her thumb sneaking its way into the comfort of his wedding band around her neck.

She waited. For God. For peace. For some answer that didn't make it all worse. But the night crept on, and with each ticking hour, the lies echoed inside, chipping away at her resolve, edging out little by little the truth she knew.

Charlie. Jon. Charlie. What would he think if he knew?

Guilt overpowered her, beating her down with wave after crushing wave.

But he had to expect it. Right? It wasn't as if a husband died and his wife forgot about him. But it wasn't fair to Charlie. *Let Jon go! Push him aside!* Charlie, only Charlie.

Could she? How could a person do that?

What did Charlie expect of her? How hard it must have been for Charlie all those years ago, to know a piece of her heart would always belong to another man, a ghost.

Had he anticipated they'd fall in love? Had he hoped they'd get married? He'd never said, and she'd never asked, but looking back, it made sense.

He'd been PCSed soon after the funeral, so she hadn't held it against him that he'd left town. But she'd never understood why he'd stayed away. No phone calls. No emails. She had assumed he'd moved on with his life, since the one thing tying them together was gone.

Yet he'd come back, and she'd fallen in love with him. She loved Charlie, the man who could make her laugh with a single look, whose touch sent fire across her skin, whose kiss could send her both flying into the heavens and melting onto the floor.

He deserved all her love. All of her. She'd tried to give that to him. She thought she'd succeeded.

Charlie's question hung in the air, his voice carrying such hope and longing. She had wanted to turn and accept with excitement, to tell him how she had been praying for this, how nothing would give her more joy than to be his wife.

But she froze, held back by her past—by Jon—unable to throw herself fully into a life with him.

She stayed snuggled against his side, heart pounding and tears welling up as his words echoed the same question she had been asked years earlier by someone else.

She had never imagined loving again, never been able to wrap her mind around or accept the possibility that she could give her heart to anyone new.

In her head she saw Jon down on one knee on her front porch, the sun's morning light shining on the ring and in his eyes.

But Jon was gone. Her finger was bare. Her heart had moved on—or had started to. She had loved and lost. And now she loved again.

Thank you, Lord, for your healing and your mercy, *she prayed.* Thank you for this man who loves my broken heart.

She turned to face Charlie. Charlie, with those grey eyes full of worry and fear instead of the usual confidence and humor.

She whispered, "Yes." A simple word. A promise breathed out.

As he slipped the simple ring on her finger, signifying to the world she was his, she longed for the assurance that she could move on, leave Jon in her past, and believe that Charlie truly was her future.

The phone buzzed beside her feet, buried somewhere in the mess of blankets. Meg blinked, scraping her lids across the surface of her eyes, bone-dry and aching from staring blankly at nothing in her dim room for so long. She'd been replaying scene after scene of her and Charlie, as if she could edge out the memory of Jon somehow.

Another buzz sent her hands fishing through the fabric. It had to be Charlie calling. No one else would call this early.

She found it but nearly dropped it as she fumbled to find the *answer* button.

"Hello?" She wanted her voice to be strong and confident, to show him she was all right, but it wouldn't comply. She winced. With a final twist of his ring around her thumb, she let it fall back against her chest and pulled her legs up, wrapping her arms around them.

"Hey, babe." Charlie sighed, his relief noticeable. "How are you?"

Time to be honest, Meg. Or as honest as she could be. "Not good. I just miss you so much." It wasn't a complete lie, but a lump caught in her throat all the same. Tears welled up, and her heart ached.

"I miss you too." Something in his voice sounded different. It was more than your basic grief or worry. But what? Maybe she really was crazy and was projecting her own messed up issues onto him. "When does Piper get back from Dover? Do you know?"

His question caught her off-guard. She'd been so wrapped up in herself that she'd very nearly forgotten about her friend. That wasn't like her, but then again, this whole situation had flipped everything on its head and changed her life—changed her—so unexpectedly.

"She got back this weekend, I think. They had the funeral last week in Kansas. Still feel bad I wasn't able to make it on such short notice. I should have tried harder." Meg dropped her eyes to her lap as if his gaze was there in the room to be avoided.

"You can only do so much, babe. I'm sure she understands. We should add her to the prayer list at church."

Her cheeks warmed. She'd meant to do that yesterday when she was there but had completely forgotten. "I'll be sure to get an email to Nicole in the church office. Or maybe I'll call her after breakfast."

"I'm sure it could wait until Sunday."

She swallowed hard. It was still a week away, but she'd already decided not to go. Though she told herself she wanted to be there for Piper, to spend the time serving her neighbor, she knew it was her way of justifying her avoidance of God's Word.

Charlie wouldn't understand. He'd never had to sit in that pew alone under the weight of everyone's questioning stares. He'd never dealt with the crushing weight of doubt. He wouldn't, couldn't, understand.

But she needed him. Shutting him out wouldn't do their marriage any good, especially with the miles between them and the secrets she was keeping inside.

She whispered, not sure he would even hear her, "I wasn't planning to go."

Silence.

She continued. "Piper…" No, he would see through that excuse. She knew the importance of the Divine Service. She'd learned it in her catechism classes at Jon's church. But she couldn't go. Not yet.

She needed his help, needed his guidance. "I'm struggling, hon. I don't know…" She couldn't finish the sentence.

A deep breath sounded on the other end. "God's with you, Meg. He knows how you're suffering. It's only been a week. Be patient. He'll see you through this."

She wanted to believe him, wanted to have that solid faith she heard in her husband's voice. "I just don't…I don't feel Him anymore. I've prayed. I've prayed so much. It feels like He's gone, like He's not listening anymore. I feel…abandoned."

She couldn't keep the tears at bay any longer, and they poured down her cheeks. She hated admitting all of this to him, yet she found some relief in knowing she had someone to help with the burden—even if he was on the other side of the world.

Charlie stayed silent. Before he could offer anything though, she choked out the words, "I want to believe, Charlie. I do. I want to trust Him, but I can't. I feel so alone."

The silence stretched out, becoming unbearable until she offered a silent, screaming prayer to God.

Give him the words to help me, Lord! Isn't that how this works? You give him the words I need? Words that will help me? Please! I'm begging you!

"Meg," he said with a mix of hesitation and hope, "what does God tell us? He says He will bring good out of tragedy. And we will face tragedy. He tells us He gives us peace not as the world does. So it may not look like you expect. In the end, the promise of that peace isn't necessarily for this temporal life. Our peace is in Christ, not in our heart."

"I know all of that is supposed to help me, to strengthen my faith, but what if I'm broken? He gave me peace before when…" She couldn't say Jon's name. Not now. "Why would God withhold that same peace now when I desperately need it?"

"Perhaps He wants you to trust in His word and not in your

feelings." His voice was gentle and loving, yet her jaw still stiffened in response.

"I know I'm not supposed to trust my feelings, Charlie. I know that! But it's too damn hard to ignore the pain. I just want to feel better! Now!" She growled at him, her tears dried by the bitterness beginning to brew.

He breathed into the phone but didn't say anything.

"What if it's all an f-ing lie, Charlie?" She slammed her fist against the table, her teeth clenching as she spoke. "What if He's not real and the scriptures are wrong? What if we really are alone with no hope, no peace, no savior?"

What if you're not real, God? What then?

Meg's words slammed into Charlie, knocking the breath out of him. His mind went blank. He had nothing to offer. No words. He wasn't a pastor. He didn't have the endless amount of biblical knowledge to know what to say in this moment.

He felt useless. Helpless. Unable to console his own wife.

Lord, help me! I don't know what to say!

He shouted at God, desperate to help his wife despite the distance between them. Her sobbing continued, and his heart ached with the desire to reach out, to hold her, to comfort her.

God, please! Help her!

"Meg." He inched forward, unsure how to proceed without pushing her further toward the edge. "Pastor Feld can help. Going to church would be best, but if you do nothing else, call Pastor. Please."

He couldn't decipher the sigh that came through the phone. Had he chosen the right words, or had he annoyed her again? She was in a delicate place, a dangerous place in her faith, and he wasn't sure what tactic to take when talking to her.

He needed to fix this, or at least try. That was his job, right? His duty?

Her tears had eased long enough for her to answer him. "You're right. I know you're right. I'll try to call him this afternoon."

It was all he could ask for, and he hoped it was enough. God had created faith in this woman once, and Charlie had no doubt the Spirit could work to heal that faith now.

But when?

16

Meg watched the sun's rays from the kitchen window behind her reflect off her coffee. Her phone lay beside her mug, silent.

She checked her watch.

She'd have to leave soon. A touch to the phone showed no missed calls, no new emails, nothing.

She couldn't blame him for not calling. Last night's conversation hadn't gone as planned. It'd started fine, but fine always turned to crap these days.

Meg cringed, replaying the way she had growled at him. One minute she'd been laughing, trying so hard to wear that mask, and then he had said something that set her off. She couldn't even remember what it'd been, why she'd lost it.

It wasn't like her, this anger. Or at least, it was not like her to not be able to bite it back, keep it hidden.

What if he didn't love her anymore, now that her angry side had shown itself? He would abandon her, like God had seemed to...like Jon had.

Jon. He wouldn't leave her alone. Every night brought images of him, the nightmares now replaced with happier dreams of life with him.

Each morning she had to force her eyes open, push herself to leave Jon and the dreams behind. Even a fake dreamworld with a dead husband seemed better than this cold reality of loneliness and bitterness, fights and tears.

Maybe Charlie knew. Maybe that's why he hadn't called.

He should call. No matter what, he should call her. She had no way of reaching him, completely at his mercy, and he was keeping her from talking to him.

With a growl through clenched teeth, she swept her hand across the table, sending the phone to the floor with a crash. She punched to her feet, grabbed her purse, and stormed out of the house.

Down the driveway and through the trees she drove to town, her eyes not focusing on anything as she passed. With each mile the questions continued.

Did he know? Had he guessed?

The guilt tightened around her throat like a noose. What would he think?

You know what he'd think.

The voice echoed within.

No! He would understand. He always understands!

But the voice dug in, refusing to ease up.

Would he really understand why his wife is here dreaming of another man while he's off risking his life for his country?

She crumpled under the words, falling against the steering wheel, only then realizing that she had arrived. She felt the tremors begin in her chest. She couldn't do this.

She had to. But she couldn't. She couldn't face all the stares, all the questions.

They won't understand.

That damn voice in her head wouldn't leave her be. Charlie had urged her, pleaded with her to at least call Pastor, and she'd failed to do even that. She'd made it this far, but now that she was here, sitting in the parking lot and staring at the cross atop the simple building, all her nerve washed away.

She willed her hand to move to the door handle. If she could take that first step out of the car, she could make it.

She could sit in the back, head down, hear God's Word and receive the Sacrament, and leave before anyone talked to her.

She could wait until after the sharing of the peace and sneak in right before corporate confession. She could.

You haven't checked on Piper in a couple days. Go serve your neighbor. God will understand.

It was wrong—despising the preaching of God's Word, running away from it instead of toward it—but all her resolve was disappearing.

God would understand. God would forgive her.

She was helping a friend, after all, being a good sister in Christ.

She turned the key and headed toward Piper's house, ignoring the smile and wave from Annie Feld, who stood at the door, wrestling the kids on their way into church.

Meg settled onto the couch and flashed a smile to Piper as she accepted the cup of coffee.

"Why aren't you at church, lady?" Piper asked, taking a seat beside her.

Meg hadn't expected this to be the first question out of her friend's mouth. She had no answer other than a shrug.

"I've never known you to skip church before. Didn't Charlie have to call in help to force you to stay home last year when you had the flu?"

"I..." Meg started, but her mind blanked. "Well, why aren't *you* at church?"

Her friend raised an eyebrow at her. "Our service doesn't

start until ten, remember? You want to come with me? You're more than welcome."

The thought of attending her friend's nondenominational church across town didn't feel right either, like she'd be cheating on her church family, betraying them.

"No thanks. I planned to listen to the sermon from home." She cringed. She had no intention of doing anything of the sort. First skipping church, now lying. What was next?

"Okay. Suit yourself. Don't say I didn't offer though!" Her friend's cheeriness gnawed at Meg.

She'd lost a husband who would never meet his baby—his son—and here she was acting as though nothing had changed, cracking jokes and making light conversation as if everything was fine with the world.

It's not fair!

Meg spent every night wrestling with her past, plagued with doubt over her faith, feeling her marriage failing with each tense conversation, and her friend sat here, belly swollen with life and a smile on her face.

Joy. Peace. Meg wanted those for herself.

God, why? Are you even there? Why am I suffering when Piper's not?

No answer. What did she expect, some whisper on a breeze? No, she knew that was not how it worked, not how God spoke to her, if He was even real at all.

Don't say that! You don't believe that.

"How are you doing, Meg? Really?" Piper's concern seemed genuine enough, and Meg forced herself to see past her own jealousy to answer.

"Not good." She looked down into her mug, wishing she could disappear into the abyss, drown herself in coffee.

That would be a weird way to go. Very Lutheran of you.

She chuckled at her own morbid joke. When she looked up,

she found Piper eying her, likely wondering why her friend was laughing after admitting she was struggling.

"Is it Jon?"

She blinked. Her eyes darted to the far corner of the room. Of course her friend would go there when her husband hadn't...when he couldn't.

She should tell Piper, confide in her. It was what friends did —trusted, listened, consoled. But that meant saying the words aloud, giving them life. It would make them too real.

She'll see you for the ugly harlot you are.

No, Meg couldn't tell her. But she also couldn't keep lying.

"Yeah, I guess. A lot of bad memories." *And good ones.*

"Aw, friend." Piper's hand reached out and grabbed hers. "That's to be expected, I think. I'd think you were weird if this didn't bring back all of that...well, you know what I mean."

Meg's chin lifted until her gaze met Piper's—patient, calm, peaceful.

She snapped her eyes shut and pulled her hand away, crossing her arms over her chest. Her lips quivered no matter how hard she pushed them together. She wouldn't cry. Not here.

It's not fair. Not. Fair.

Piper expected her to be a mess when it was Piper's husband who'd just died? Where were Piper's tears, unshowered hair, messy house, and worn face?

Not that she wanted her friend to be miserable. She wasn't a complete monster. But was it too much to ask that she be granted some of that healing too?

It apparently was.

Meg reached a hand up to her neck, keeping her eyes focused on the cup in her lap. "Can I ask you something?"

"Anything. You know that."

She gulped and bit her lip, hearing the ineloquent words forming in her mind. She didn't care how they sounded though. "How are you so damn peaceful? You lost your husband, and you seem fine."

Piper's expression softened. She laid her hand on her belly and lifted a shoulder in a half-shrug. "I don't know. I thought I'd be a wreck forever, you know? And you saw how I was the first couple weeks—"

"But you aren't now. It's been barely a month, and you're..." She waved a hand in the air, gesturing wildly at her friend.

"I know I'm supposed to be the grieving widow, the woman who can't get out of bed, can't stop crying. What does it say about me that I'm not? That I'm happy, joyful even? You think I don't see the looks at church when I'm smiling instead of sobbing?"

Those looks. Meg knew them well. She'd ignored them, endured them, for that first year after Jon died.

She leaned closer to Piper. "How? How are you so..."

"At peace?"

Meg nodded, but she knew the answer. Or she thought she did. She thought she'd known when it had been her in that position, the recipient of some divine gift.

Piper pointed to the ceiling. "I've got no other explanation. I prayed. He answered."

Meg looked down at her lap. Her friend's answer stung. She'd prayed too, and...nothing. The opposite of nothing actually. She'd gotten salt in her wounds instead of the salve she needed.

"I hate not being the model widow everyone expects of me, Meg, but who am I to complain about God's gift of peace? Like I could tell him, 'No thanks, I'll pass'?"

Meg couldn't face her and instead let her gaze trace the rim of the mug. Her mind flitted between thoughts. She could tell Piper that the worry over grieving properly was normal, that the sense you were on display for all to judge took years to go away.

But she had nothing but that black circle in her hands, her gaze going round and round.

"How was it for you when Jon died?"

Piper had never asked her this outright. No one had, not even Charlie. A couple of months ago, she would have given the same answer Piper had. But now, all she had was doubt.

"Similar, I think. I remember knowing everything would be okay, though I didn't know how. The crying, the mourning, it just stopped." She looked up to see Piper nodding.

"And now?" Piper leaned her head forward, her expression warm, urging Meg to open up, even a little.

Meg tore her gaze away, pushing it out the window where the snow still danced on the wind. "I feel like he died all over again."

And this time, God's not here.

Charlie leaned against his desk, his fingers massaging his forehead as they had during every phone call lately. "You didn't go, did you?" He tried to keep his voice calm, but his irritation seeped through.

"No. I didn't. Couldn't," Meg said quietly and timidly but with a sharpness tinging the edge of each word.

"Why haven't you talked to Pastor yet? What are you so afraid of?"

"Look, Charlie." The sharpness swooped in, taking over her voice. "I don't know what to say to him, okay?"

"You could at least answer the phone when he calls you."

A sharp gasp came from her end. "You...you told him to call me?"

"No! I told him I was worried about you. He said he'd called a few times but you never answered or called back."

Her breathing came out ragged. "You're conspiring behind my back? What the hell, Charlie?"

Not again. He ran a hand over his face, dragging his chin down as he stretched out his jaw. His hand fisted and released. He forced himself to calm, needing to bring the conversation back down to a civilized level.

"Not conspiring, babe. I'm trying to help. You can't work through this doubt alone. And I can't seem to help you from over here."

He cringed. How many times had he recycled the same words, always hoping for a different outcome? Wasn't that the definition of stupidity?

"I know! I want to feel better, I do, but I can't seem to escape this…" She trailed off.

He groaned, not caring if she heard or if she was hurt. He couldn't keep repeating himself, saying the same things with the hope that someday they'd suddenly click for her.

Something had to give. She needed a push.

"Have you even tried, Meg? It doesn't seem like you have."

He immediately regretted it, but he couldn't back down now. His gentle urging, his patience during the past weeks, hadn't done any good. At this point, he'd try nearly anything to get her back to God's Word.

"Have you at least been reading scripture? Praying? Anything?" He pushed further, his body tensing, ready for the tirade she'd unleash on him.

But her tone shifted, softened. "I try, Charlie. I do. But the words…they feel…empty. I read them, but it's like God's not there anymore."

Tears sat just under the surface of her voice, and Charlie released the breath he hadn't realized he'd been holding. This wasn't the silly, carefree wife he'd left at home, but it wasn't the angry and annoyed woman he'd known for the last few weeks either.

This Meg sounded so...broken.

The urge to hold her and comfort her and tell her it was all okay came strongly, and he cursed his having to be over here when his place was beside her.

He tried to match her quieter tone. "Just keep trying. Keep reading. Please, don't give up."

Please! He begged God to work some miracle in his wife's heart, to have something he said finally fix this for her.

But her words spewed through the phone, the brokenness replaced by vitriol. "Damn it, Charlie! I'm trying the best I can, okay? There's a whole lot of crap going on in my head that you don't know about."

"Because you won't tell me, Meg!" Desperation drove him to speak his mind, the thoughts he'd been wrestling with for weeks but had been unable to say to her. "You won't let me in. We go round and round in these endless spats about the same junk. This isn't like you to shut me out. I can't keep wondering what's going on—"

"You want to know what's going on?"

He took a deep breath. A curse echoed in his head. "Yes, Meg. Yes!"

"I'm crazy. That's it. I'm plain crazy."

"No, you're not. You are not crazy. You're struggling a bit. That's all."

She huffed into the phone. "No, Charlie. You don't *get* it. I miss you. I miss you like crazy, and it sucks to not have you here, home. And I hate it..." She paused long enough to take a quick breath. "And I miss Jon. And I don't want to! I don't want to be dreaming of him, wanting him, when I know he's gone and I'm yours. All yours. Why can't I let him go?"

Charlie's mind whirled. He'd been so focused on helping her spiritually that he'd failed to see something else might be wrong. Or maybe he hadn't wanted to see it.

Listening to his wife sob into the phone, that stab of jealousy slammed into him again. He'd gotten over that, moved past the juvenile worry, but here it was again—stronger, sharper.

His wife was dreaming of Jon, another man. Like Jon was any other man. How could he have been so stupid to think she'd be able to give her whole heart to him when half of it was buried in Arlington with his best friend?

"I hate myself, Charlie!" Her words cut through his selfish thoughts. "And this pain? This guilt? It's too much on top of all the doubt. I'm mad! Mad at God for leaving me, for taking you away, for killing Jon. I'm angry. And I don't know how to fix it! I don't know how to get through this!"

She broke down, her tears taking over. His heart sank into his gut as the helplessness returned. Minutes passed. He listened to her whimpers, unsure how to help her.

Praying seemed futile. All the prayers he'd offered to God, begging for His help, had done no good. She had lost so much, and being angry with her, being jealous of Jon, felt wrong.

Because it is *wrong, dumbass! Stop it! You're being an idiot.*

But the torrent of emotion gripped his heart, spreading a wave of tension through his limbs. After so many years wishing she was his instead of his buddy's, the old sin wouldn't release its grasp on him so easily.

He dropped his head to his fisted hand, his knuckles white.

"I'm sorry, Charlie," she whispered through the tears.

He ran his hand through his hair and closed his eyes, but he had no words to offer her. He should tell her it was okay, that he understood, that it was fine. But he couldn't.

"I love you," she muttered. She sounded desperate, like she needed him to say something, anything. But he needed time to process and to think.

He managed to choke out an "I love you too," but it felt empty and flat. "I'll call you later, okay?" He clenched his eyes shut harder. He was abandoning her again, right after she'd laid her heart at his feet.

"Yeah. I'll talk to you later," she said, even calmer now, as if finally getting this off her chest had removed the anger and released her from the burden.

Now it was his burden. At least she understood the value of space and time to process. For all her faults, he loved her so.

Lord, I don't deserve this woman. I really don't.

Charlie stared ahead, his gaze settling on his feet, which were propped up on his desk, and the TV beyond that. But his focus remained blurred, disrupted by the conversation replaying in his head.

He didn't know how to handle this turmoil. A firefight or incoming mortars, those he could handle. But no amount of combat training could have prepared him for his wife screaming at him over the phone.

It never got easier.

"You okay?" The voice startled him. He looked up to see Murphy and Baker standing in his doorway, confused looks on their faces.

"Yeah, of course," he said. "Why?"

"Well, for starters, you've been sitting there on the menu screen for the last"—Murphy looked to Baker—"what's it been, fifteen minutes?"

"Or longer." Baker shrugged.

"And second, you look awful."

"It's true. Murphy's mom wouldn't even go near you in the shape you're in." Baker pointed a thumb in Murphy's direction.

"She'd pick him over you though," Murphy said.

Baker shrugged. "Probably for the best. She couldn't handle all of this anyway."

Murphy rolled his eyes.

At least their bickering was back to normal.

"We were actually going to hang out in Murphy's and shoot something if you want to join us," Baker said.

"Nah." Charlie tossed the controller onto his desk and pulled his feet to the floor. "I'm good. I think I might get a workout in."

Murphy eyed him. "So I guess you'd just been working up the nerve to stand up when we interrupted you then, huh?"

He had no witty remark or sharp comeback for that one, but he didn't need it, as Baker spoke first. "Dude, don't be such a jerk." He turned back to Charlie. "Come on. Shoot some zombies. Clear your mind."

"Yeah, dude. C'mon. One round. It'll be good for you," Murphy said. "Well, you know, it won't help all that, but..." He motioned to Charlie's disheveled appearance.

"Think I'll pass this time. Thanks though." Charlie nodded to them, reaching for his tennis shoes, sure to keep up the ruse of wanting exercise.

"Suit yourself," Murphy said and headed out into the hallway, Baker following him.

Once they left, Charlie dropped his forehead against the plywood door. He'd have to be more careful in the future. He couldn't risk the guys thinking he was losing it or doubting if he could be trusted in a pinch.

He might be failing his wife, but he wouldn't fail his team.

Charlie wrung his hands around the phone. He shouldn't call—not this early—but the nagging voice wouldn't shut up, wouldn't quiet. He'd spent the whole day distracted, his tasks taking three times longer than they should have, his brain refusing to let go of the images of Meg with Jon.

He needed help...and quick. If he couldn't manage the menial tasks around camp with this, there'd be no way he could function properly on the next mission.

He lifted a hand to his neck in an effort to ease the stress that plagued him. Before he could reconsider and chicken out, he dialed, checking the number on the scrap of paper lying on his cot.

It rang once, twice.

"Hello?" The voice was groggy and gruff but familiar.

Charlie dropped his head to his hand and closed his eyes. Maybe he should have waited an hour or two. But he'd already woken the guy up. "Pastor? I'm sorry to call you so early."

No answer.

"It's me. Charlie."

"Hi, Charlie." There was a pause and then a stifled yawn. "How are you?"

"To be honest...I could be better." That was an understatement.

"What's on your mind?" The patient voice of his pastor shouldn't have surprised him, but after all the tense calls with Meg, he'd almost expected the guy to blow up at him or make a snarky comment about the time.

"It's Meg." He cringed, hearing her earlier accusations bouncing around in his head. He wasn't conspiring or betraying her. He was simply trying to help.

"How is she?"

"Bad." Another understatement. Words were not his friends today apparently. "I don't know how else to put it. It's getting worse."

A sigh—concern mixed with fatigue—came over the line. "I feared as much when I still hadn't seen her."

"There's more," Charlie said, but the words stalled. It'd been hard enough to hear Meg say it. Now he'd have to say it aloud. He swallowed, forcing his pride back down. "She's dreaming of Jon, her first husband." He paused again. "She misses him."

"I see."

Charlie closed his eyes at the flash of a memory of him and Meg sitting across from Pastor in his office when they'd first become members. Meg had offered only the basics, and Charlie hadn't felt it his place to push her to say much more beyond that.

Only later, over a scotch and a cigar, had he talked with his pastor—more as a friend than a pastor—about his past feelings, explaining the numerous times he'd gone to private confession regarding Meg...and Jon.

At least Charlie didn't need to rehash all the history. He couldn't handle explaining it all again, especially now.

"And how are you handling that, Charlie?"

Before he could think, the words spilled out. "I hate it. It hurts. I'm pissed off and...jealous." He winced at the word, hearing how insane, immature, and stupid it was.

Pastor spoke, his tone compassionate but firm. "And is that justified?"

Charlie sighed. "I know it's not, but I can't shut it out. Just keeps creeping back up. Every time I think I've silenced it, I get another image of them together, and then I'm angry again. She's my wife! What man wants to know his wife is longing for another guy?" His words came out fast, breathless. It wasn't his style—more like Meg really—but if he didn't push through, he might lose his nerve to talk about it.

"She's your wife, yes." Charlie had expected a pause, for his pastor to take time to formulate his response, but the words came nearly as quickly as his own had and with matching intensity. "As such, she needs your love, your support. Not jealousy and anger. The enemy's throwing your old sin in your face right now, drudging up the coveting."

Charlie swallowed, letting the reprimand sink in.

"But you're forgiven, Charlie. Christ has forgiven you of those past sins. Don't let the devil drag them back up to accuse you."

Charlie rested his hand against his mouth, not sure what to say or how to answer. He knew the words to be true, but still, something was missing.

Pastor continued: "She lost her husband. You lost your best friend. You'll both have to deal with that, figure out how to nurture your marriage knowing Jon will always be a part of your history, a part of both of you. If you let jealousy and anger take over? Your marriage is going to struggle more. Don't let it be another weight to drag you both down."

"But what do I do? How do I stop it?" Charlie shook his head. It seemed impossible, the nagging voice in his head too loud.

"There's a quote," Pastor said, "from Martin Luther. Can't remember the source right now, but he says, 'When the devil throws your sin in your face and declares you deserve death and hell, tell him this: I admit I deserve death and hell, what of it? For I know One who suffered and made satisfaction on my behalf. His name is Jesus Christ, Son of God, and where He is, there I shall be also!'"

Charlie released the breath he'd been holding and quickly drew in another. He could do this. He could tell the devil to shove it, declare the name of Christ crucified for him. The familiar words of scripture rushed in: *Armor of God. Extinguish the flaming darts of the evil one.*

Charlie had what he needed. He had God's Word. He had Christ. And he had his pastor to help along the way.

"Thanks, Pastor."

"Anytime, Charlie." A yawn, albeit muffled, sounded through the phone. "I mean it. Anytime."

17

THE GLOW of the laptop screen lit up Charlie's room as he waited. Meg's email had promised she'd log on when she got home from dinner with Piper. He checked his watch again and then the clock on the screen.

He shook his head. He should have insisted on chatting earlier. He'd be late to the mission briefing if she didn't show up soon.

`You there?`

The instant message popped up. His shoulders dropped, but his heart raced on ahead. This would either go really well or horribly wrong. He wasn't sure which.

He clicked open the video chat, and his own face looked back at him, the digital ring coming over the speakers.

The screen shifted, moving his face to the corner of the screen, replacing it with hers. He beamed at her. How had he forgotten how beautiful she was?

Because you're an idiot.

"Hey." She smiled back at him, though it was timid, shy. Her eyes fell, looking away.

"Hi, babe. You look great." He'd pictured her with her hair

up in a crazy nest, wearing his old sweatshirt, but she looked...amazing.

A blush spread across her cheeks as she lifted her face. "Piper insisted we not look like hobos when we went out."

He chuckled. "Probably a good idea. You don't want to scare people."

"At least she let me pick the place."

"Pub?"

"How'd you know?" She flashed him an easy smile, her head dropping to one side.

"Lucky guess."

Her lips pursed. "Too bad they changed the menu. Got rid of my usual."

"Without checking with you first?"

"I know!" Her hands flew into the air. He'd missed this—this ease in the conversation. "I gave Matt an earful though."

He laughed again. "I bet that went over well."

"He said he'd talk to the manager, see if they could figure out a way to still make it for me. You know, like that secret menu some places have. Piper gave me crap about it though. Told me to suck it up and learn to branch out or something."

"And how'd you handle that?"

"I stuck my tongue out at her." She shrugged at him, her face defiant. He'd seen the same look on little Lydia Feld, he was sure.

"Very mature of you, babe. How's Piper doing anyway?"

"Good. Better than you'd guess."

Charlie caught the subtle twitch in his wife's eyes, the way they narrowed slightly at her own words.

"Yeah? How so?"

"She seems...normal? Like nothing's happened. Like she didn't just lose her husband. It's...bizarre."

"Huh." He raised a hand to his lips, trying to find something to say.

"I get it though. I was the same way after..." She looked down, her fingers fiddling with her necklace.

"After Jon." It wasn't a question.

She didn't look up, but he could see her eyes twitch and her jaw tighten.

"It's okay, babe. Really. I'm sorry I lost it the other day. It wasn't fair to you."

Her eyes met his, tears forming at the corners, a quiver settling into her bottom lip. "I'm sorry too. I don't know what's going on with me. I hate it."

She looked so fragile, like one wrong word or look could shatter her into a million pieces. She'd been broken once before, and God had healed her, pulled her back together—and in record time. He could do it again, couldn't He?

Help her, Lord. Please! I can't be there for her, but you can. You are! Show her that!

He pleaded silently, begging.

"I tried to go to church."

His glance snapped back to her, but she was still staring at the dining room table in front of her, avoiding him. At least she was talking and not yelling...yet.

"And?"

"I ran away. Went to see Piper instead."

"She's lucky to have you, Meg. Even if she doesn't seem like she needs a friend. I'm glad she has you." He paused, not sure if he should keep going. The conversation was going well. Could he risk diverting it, screwing it up?

He had to.

"But you need to be at church."

"I know." Her words held no anger, no irritation. No nothing. They were just empty, like the void in her eyes when she finally met his gaze. The greens and golds seemed dimmer, muted by the doubt and the stress.

"Maybe it would help to find someone to drive you?"

"Like an accountability partner?"

"Yeah, maybe. I don't know. Trying to think of something." He ran a hand over his forehead, as if he could somehow will solutions to form if he tried hard enough.

"Maybe." She paused, her lips scrunched to one side as she thought. "Annie might be willing, but she's got all the kids."

"There's always Mrs. Goetz." He raised his eyebrow at her.

She cringed and gave a small laugh. "Oh, man. You know, I love that lady, but…making that drive with her might not give me much incentive to go."

"What about Piper?" It was a long shot. They shared the same faith, sure, but their churches had enough differences to make it uncomfortable for both.

He expected her to light up at the suggestion, even if only a little, but her solemn expression had returned. His eyes trailed over her face, searching for some sign of what gnawed at her, when the realization hit him, sending a lump into his throat.

Piper was doing well—thriving, even—but Meg…

Lord, help her.

He dropped his chin with the prayer, but Meg's words interrupted, cold, distant.

"I should really get to bed."

A swear shot across his mind. He glanced at the time and cringed. "Oh, man, me too. I mean…well, you know what I mean."

She didn't look at him, but he could see her jaw begin to shake. She needed him, and he was out of time.

"I love you, babe." He waited for her to repeat it, but she simply raised her eyes to his, tears brimming. She raised a fist to her mouth before uncurling her fingers in a wave.

His heart lurched. She was breaking, right in front of his eyes, and he could do nothing.

He opened his mouth to say something, but the screen went black, the computer beeping with the disconnection.

Out of time. The mission needed him now.

Focus. Get your head in the game. God's got her.

Let go and let Him care for her.

Please, God. Please do.

Meg wrapped the blankets tighter around her body, one over her legs, another over her shoulders, her breath coming out in a feathery mist. Maybe being on the front porch in February wasn't the best idea, but she needed a change…or something.

Fingering the delicate pages, she hesitated, fighting the temptation to open to a random page, as if the book were some fortune cookie that could mystically give her the answers she sought. Doubt or not, if God's Word and everything she'd learned about it were true, she wouldn't risk misusing it.

Faith comes from hearing, and hearing through the Word of Christ.

The familiar verse filled her head, seemed to spread through her limbs.

But hearing what?

If only there was a specific verse that could restore her faith to where it had been and put everything back into place.

Panic coursed through her, tensing her limbs until they ached. To have her faith restored, she would have had to have faith to begin with. What if the faith she'd been resting on for the last ten years hadn't been real?

Had she been faking it this whole time? Is that why she was struggling with this doubt when Charlie wasn't and when Jon never had?

They'd been Christians their whole lives, baptized as babies, raised in the church, and taught God's Word early and often, but Meg had not. Her parents had baptized her and her sister when they were young, but only because that was what people did. It was the socially proper thing to do for kids.

She'd gotten nothing afterward—no guidance, no encouragement, no church except on the rare occasions a friend had invited her along. It wasn't something her family did.

A bruised reed He will not break, a faintly burning wick He will not quench...

That was her: bruised, faintly burning. If she had no faith, if her faith had never been real, she wouldn't be this afraid of losing it. Would she? So why did she feel so broken, her faith being quenched by everything going on around her?

There's a psalm for that.

Charlie's favorite saying came to mind, his go-to for when prayers wouldn't form and words failed. She opened to the Psalms, flipping through the text, searching for one to match her anger with God. It existed. She knew. If she could find it.

Why, O Lord, do you stand far away?
Why do you hide yourself in times of trouble?
Arise, O Lord, O God, lift up your hand;
Forget not the afflicted.

She flipped a few pages forward and continued reading.

Do not forsake me, O Lord!
O my God, be not far from me!
Make haste to help me,
O Lord, my salvation!

How many times had she prayed similar words these last weeks with no answer, no response, just deafening silence? She went back a few verses.

But for you, O Lord, do I wait;

It is you, O Lord my God, who will answer.
For I am ready to fall,
And my pain is ever before me.

Meg closed her eyes, urging the words on the page to take root, to do something, anything to save her failing faith. Shaking, she lifted her hand to her lips. She read the words, prayed them, and screamed them in her head, but the voice that responded wasn't the one she wanted or needed.

God's gone.

Just like Charlie.

Just like Jon.

You're on your own, Meg.

She slammed the Bible shut and dropped it beside her on the porch swing. Fisting a hand, she took a final breath of the pines and winter air before unraveling her legs and pushing to stand. She needed to move, to clear her head, to get away from that damn voice.

Leaving the blankets behind in a jumbled pile, she rushed inside. Where had she left her running shoes? At least the last snows had melted enough that a run wouldn't be too miserable.

She searched the house, but the voice wouldn't let up.

You couldn't find God in His Word. What makes you think a run will help?

Give up. Let go.

You'll feel better.

How easy it would be to surrender to that voice in her head.

Faith was hard, too hard. She'd spent her whole childhood looking down on Christians around her, chalking them up to being stupid sheep. She had always assumed they had denied reason and taken the easy road, following some guy who'd been dead for nearly two thousand years.

How naive she'd been.

This road wasn't easy. Far from it. It caused irreparable

damage to old relationships, creating chasms between them that couldn't be crossed.

How quickly you surrendered your own reason for a word—a promise—that has failed you now.

She shook her head, her teeth clenched, fighting against the thought. She couldn't believe it. This faith was worth fighting for. The cost of giving up on it—even if that brought temporary relief now—was too great.

She'd lose Charlie, wouldn't she? Would he stay with her if she abandoned their shared faith, walked away from the church and from God?

And then if it were true, if all of it were true, letting that faith be shipwrecked against these rocks would mean an eternity of pain far worse than any she endured now.

No, she needed to fight.

But how?

She barely knew what order the books of the Bible were in. All these words, and she had no idea where to turn.

That wasn't entirely true. Pastor Feld was there. His whole job was to teach her, guide her, watch over her soul.

She found her phone on the kitchen table. With shaky fingers she scrolled to his number and stopped. Her hand hovered over the "Call" button, her finger shaking.

What will he think of you, Meg?

He'll see right through you, know you're a fraud, not a true believer.

The words were wrong, she knew. And yet, they were loud enough to keep her from taking that step.

What's a pastor anyway?

Just a man.

Doesn't God say, "Cursed is the man who trusts in man and makes flesh his strength"?

You can do this on your own.

She dropped her phone back onto the table with a curse. The doorbell rang, and her heart fell.

Charlie inched the Humvee forward, keeping his eyes locked on the truck ahead of him as they crept along the narrow path that passed for a road in this area. A scattering of trees dotted the otherwise desolate terrain.

At least the mission had been a short one, a quick trip to the closest village whose elders were more willing than most to meet with the Americans and their Afghan counterparts. But Charlie hadn't been able to shake that last image of Meg, even when the local kids had swarmed around them with hopes of candy and small gifts.

One kid had flashed him a bright smile when he'd handed over the one thing he had to offer: a pack of strawberry Pop-Tarts. But it'd brought little joy to his worried mind. He could make one Afghan kid's day, but he couldn't help his wife. What was he even doing there? His wife needed him, and he was over here handing out processed sugar and pens.

Boom!

"What was that?" Baker shouted, snapping Charlie out of his thoughts.

"I don't know!" Dust flew up in front of their vehicle, but Charlie couldn't tell where the enemy was firing from. He scanned the horizon but couldn't see anything.

Tat-ta-tat-ta-tat. Boom!

Rounds seemed to come from every side.

"Where's it at? Where's it at?" Baker screamed.

"Contact from two o'clock!" Murphy shouted, swinging the 240 into position, sending rounds toward the ridge three hundred meters away.

Tat-ta-tat-ta-tat-ta-tat.

Murphy called, "We got PKM fire!"

Boom!

"And RPGs!"

Charlie turned to Baker beside him in the passenger seat, keeping their vehicle moving. They needed to get out of this kill zone. And quick. "Where are they? Can you see them?"

Baker let out a string of curses. "No. I've got nothing. Murphy, where are they?"

Crack!

"Two o'clock. Two! They're right on top of that ridge!" He screamed at the enemy while continuing to fire, taunting them to come get him.

"Holy…!" Murphy screamed again.

"What is it? What?"

SHOOOOM...BOOM!

"RPG barely missed my head!"

"God, I hate this place," Baker said, spitting out the words. "We need to move! Get us out of here!"

Tat-ta-tat-ta-tat-ta-tat. Crack! Boom! Boom!

More RPGs hit. Everywhere. One after the other. How many were out there?

Charlie stared at the truck ahead of him. He couldn't speak.

Boom! Crack! Tat-ta-tat-ta-tat-ta-tat.

The incoming rounds mixed with the sounds of his team returning fire. He blanked.

Get it together, man! Focus!

Tat-ta-tat-ta-tat.

Charlie froze. The Humvees in front of him moved, but he couldn't.

"Winters! What the…?!" Baker cursed. "Move! Forward!"

Charlie still didn't move. His vision blanked, and his hands gripped the steering wheel, but his body was unwilling to respond to get them moving again.

"Get 'em, Murphy!" Baker yelled again.

"Whooooo!" Murphy called. "Yeah!"

But Charlie didn't hear it.

The hit landed on his shoulder, but on his right. Not the side he expected, and not from a round but from a fist. He turned to find Baker glaring at him, looking ready to knock some sense into him with his rifle if needed. He snapped his gaze back to the trucks ahead of them, farther away now, and he lowered his foot onto the gas pedal.

He cursed under his breath, trying to ignore the way his buddy eyed him.

Get home to her. Just get home to Meg.

Meg stole a glance out the front window, her heart pounding as she imagined the sight of uniformed soldiers on her porch. There was no way she'd let herself be caught unawares by them in the future. Seeing the minivan in her driveway relaxed the fear away, but a new wave of anxiety took hold, and she placed a hand on her chest to quell it.

She pulled back from the window. Maybe Annie hadn't spotted her. She'd stay quiet, pretend to not hear the doorbell. She could have been in the shower when her friend stopped by. Completely legitimate reason for not answering. Poor timing, that was all.

The doorbell sounded again.

Annie wouldn't give up that easily. *The curse of having good friends who care about you.* Meg cringed. She should be thankful for her church family, but all she wanted to do was be left alone to deal with her mess on her own.

Because that's going so well for you, isn't it?

There was another ring from the door, followed by gentle knocking.

"Meg?" Annie's sweet voice sounded from the porch. "Meg? Are you there?"

She couldn't hide, not from her friend, her pastor's wife. But she couldn't bear to lay her burden on her either. She'd spent years perfecting the art of protecting her heart behind the guise of thinking more of others, and it had worked for this long. It would work still.

Pulling the door open, she forced a slight smile to her lips. "Annie! This is a sweet surprise! Come in?" She motioned for Annie to step inside, praying she would buy that everything was okay.

"Thanks." Annie stepped inside, her gaze never leaving Meg's face, searching. What was she seeing? Meg couldn't be sure.

"Sorry I didn't hear the doorbell. I was…catching a nap. Sleep has been hard these days." It was only a half lie. That was okay, right? Sleep had been difficult.

"Oh."

Annie smiled—a sweet, understanding smile that must have come from years of being the pastor's wife. "I'm sorry I woke you. I won't stay long. I promise."

"Have time for coffee?"

What was she doing? She didn't want Annie to stay, and here she was offering a mug. She didn't even have any freshly brewed.

"No thank you. I've already had my two cups for the morning."

Meg sighed. Crisis averted. She led Annie to the living room and proffered a seat on the sofa. "At least sit down then? Those kids probably keep you on your toes so much. I'm sure you're exhausted."

"You have no idea." Annie smiled again and sat on the edge of the cushion, placing her purse on the coffee table. She reached in and pulled out a sheet of paper, handing it to Meg. "Lydia wanted you to have this."

Meg stared down at the mess of colors woven together. Chaos. A beautiful mess. "I love it." At least that wasn't a lie.

"Our recent trip to the art museum introduced her to modern art, and now she's all about the '*abstrack*.'"

Meg stifled a chuckle. That girl. How she loved that sweet and silly girl. "Tell her thank you for me?"

Annie breathed deeply and held Meg's gaze. "I'd hoped you'd tell her yourself. On Sunday?"

There it was. She was trapped, no escape, the walls closing in. Her friend's stare bore down on her. She should have ignored the door and stayed hidden.

Why couldn't they leave her alone? Meg was growing weary with all the messages from Pastor Feld urging her to come back to church, asking her if she was all right. Then she had Charlie pressuring her, pushing her to go. Now Annie?

No one understood. As lonely as she was at home, the pew was worse. Even with a hundred of her sisters and brothers around her, she could never escape the nagging feeling that she didn't belong, that God's Word of forgiveness was for everyone except her.

She'd been hiding things from Charlie, burdening everyone around her, lying to those closest to her, and harboring jealousy toward a friend who had the promise of a baby she would never have. How could God forgive all of that? And how could she dare stand before Him and ask Him to?

Then there was the gossip, the stares, the questions. She hated that she let them get to her, let others' opinions of her rattle her so much. But she couldn't bear the thought of having to explain why she'd been absent for so long—and then resist the temptation to lie to each person who inquired. Or snap at them.

No. She couldn't do it. Wouldn't. But how could she tell Annie that? Especially to her face?

"You can sit in the back, Meg. The kids and I will sit with you. You're not alone." Annie urged her with a gentleness she hadn't expected. She should be yelling at her, rebuking her for despising God's Word so blatantly.

Isn't that how reproof and correction were to happen? With a firm and heavy hand? That's how her mom had disciplined. And discipline was what she needed now, not understanding and compassion.

But maybe the way her parents had raised her wasn't the best example.

"Thanks, Annie. I would like that." It was true. She'd like to have a friend to help her through this, but she couldn't make any promises. "I'll try."

18

Charlie ran the towel over his hair, still damp from the shower, and stepped into the hallway as he headed toward his room. He kept his gaze forward while passing Carter's old door but stopped short at the sound of his name.

"Winters is cracked, dude," Murphy said from Baker's room, not bothering to keep his voice down even with the door standing wide open.

"Give the man a break," Baker said. "Think he's having issues with the wife."

They knew. Of course they knew. It wasn't like their screaming matches over the past weeks had taken place in a vacuum. There was no place for secrets here unless you kept them inside your own head.

Like Woods.

He cringed and listened for more.

"Whatever it is, he's losing it. Big time."

"You can't blame him though, can ya? I mean, it's hard when life back home falls apart."

They had been falling apart, but it was getting better, wasn't it? They'd met a hill and conquered it. *But she's still struggling. And you're still distracted.*

"But he's still Winters. Whether he's laughing or not, he's still a badass who gets the job done."

"I don't know about that," Murphy said. "You saw him on that last trip. He completely froze!"

"He got us out of there, didn't he?"

"Yeah. Eventually. But not without you snapping him out of it. What if it gets worse? Can we trust him not to lose it on this next mission? Or the next one? The one after that? We've still got months left, and I want to know he's got it together enough that I don't end up like Woods."

Murphy's words slammed him in the gut, pushing bile up to his throat. He'd let them down, lost their trust. Cupping a hand over his mouth, his jaw fell open, stretching out the tension that had collected. His mind whirred, his eyes darting along the floor of the hallway.

I don't need to listen to this.

He wanted to leave, but pride kept him rooted to the spot. His other hand gripped around the towel until his arm shook.

Baker remained silent, and Murphy spoke again. "You've seen how this colonel plans missions! It's like he's trying to get us killed with the routes he's choosing, the villages he's pushing to visit. Charlie needs to get his head back in the game, or—"

"He will," Baker said, cutting him off. "He'll be fine. When it matters, he'll be ready."

Murphy nearly lost it. "Like it didn't matter this last time? I almost lost my *head*!"

"But you didn't." Baker paused. "He'll be fine," he said again, sharp and short.

"I sure hope you're right, man."

Charlie retreated across the hallway, keeping his steps quiet so they wouldn't know he'd heard. He shut his door. Their words echoed in his head as he leaned back against the wall, his gaze falling on Meg's picture by his desk.

I hope he's right too.

Meg skipped across the living room and picked up the remote from the coffee table, turning up the volume of the music until it filled the house. The pulsing beat of the music had her gliding along the wooden floor, her arms wide as she danced. The pure joy of the movement caused tears to rise.

You cry at everything these days.

At least these were happy tears. She couldn't understand, let alone explain it, but the shift was palpable. The doubt was still there ready to burst forth if she let it.

But she wouldn't, not today.

She had a plan. Even if she couldn't feel God's peace at home with her Bible, she would get back to church. She would find Him there for sure.

And she wasn't alone. She had Annie to help her out and sit beside her and give her the accountability she needed.

And she had Charlie.

A smile spread wide. He'd laugh if he saw her now, twirling and spinning like a little kid. He'd laugh until he grabbed her hand and spun her into his arms to kiss her.

Her tears welled up again.

Kisses. What did those even feel like? How was it you could kiss someone for years and in a matter of months forget the feel of their lips on yours? Time was a thief. Distance a murderer.

The song ended, a slower one taking its place, and she turned it down just enough to keep the silence at bay. Her phone buzzed at her—a calendar reminder.

CHAT WITH CHARLIE

Her feet couldn't move quickly enough to the kitchen table and the waiting computer, and she nearly knocked over her chair as she flew into it. Wiggling her fingers over the mouse, she clicked her way to the video chat and waited, a giddy smile glued to her face.

The incoming call alert sounded for only a second before she answered, and his face filled the screen. His hair was in need of a cut, and he hadn't shaved yet that morning, leaving the slight hint of his beard.

"Hi!" She beamed at him, tears threatening to surface again at the sight of him. *Seriously? Crying again? It's only been a few days since you saw him!*

Charlie laughed. "Well you seem better, babe." Light danced across his eyes, playing up their slate-blue hues. Forget drowning in coffee; she wanted to drown in him. A much better way to go if she had the option.

"I feel better. Or at least I'm starting to." She shrugged. A new wave of strength coursed through her, as if new blood ran through her veins, cleansed of all the toxins that had poisoned her lately.

"All you need is a start."

"At this point, I'm ready to celebrate any step in the right direction, no matter how small. Baby steps, right?"

"Maybe I should send this back to you." Charlie held up the crying baby mask, and a snort escaped her. How had it only been a couple of months since she'd sent that to him?

"Nah, I'm good. You might still need it over there." She drew in a sharp breath, and warmth flushed her face as she remembered the last time he had used it to prank his buddies. Buddies who were now gone. "Crap. I didn't mean to..."

He held up his hand and shook his head. "It's okay. I know what you meant. The guys could probably use a good laugh right now."

"How are they?"

"So-so. On the plus side, Murphy and Baker aren't constantly bickering anymore. So that's something."

"And how are you?"

"Same, I guess." A sadness swept through his eyes, like clouds passing over the shoreline.

"You're not constantly bickering with yourself anymore?" She flashed him a goofy smile, needing to see that sadness replaced by his usual humor and joy.

When he offered nothing more than a small curve at the corner of his mouth, she forced her expression into a frown and pouted. She would get him to laugh somehow, even if she had to resort to Three-Stooges-style antics.

"I've missed this, Meg." The smile didn't quite reach his eyes, but the sadness in them had faded. She'd count it as a win.

"Me too. So…how's the winter lull going?" The transition didn't come out quite as she had planned, but she should have known there was no way to make discussion of combat casual. Still, maybe her lighthearted tone would show him she was still the same ol' awkward Meg.

"Okay. I guess."

It was a lie, of course, but a lie she had both expected and accepted. Despite all advice to the contrary, she'd spent every morning since he'd left perusing the news for everything happening in Afghanistan. This year had been different. There had been more engagements with the enemy—far more than was typical for the season—with more and more stories of fratricide committed by the Afghan National Security Forces against the troops there to train them.

She waited for him to say more, but he remained silent, watching her, his eyes sweeping across her features. Even with the delays and blips in the image on the screen, the way he gazed at her sent a thrill through her heart. She'd never expected any man to be willing to pick up the pieces of her wounded heart, but here he was.

He loved her, and she was his. Entirely and forever.

A knocking sounded from the speakers, and Charlie turned to the door. Meg couldn't hear what was said, but Charlie nodded to the visitor. "Yeah, I'll be right there."

When he turned back to her, she made her expression as understanding as she could muster, not wanting him to see how yet another goodbye stung. "I gotta go, babe."

"No problem. I'll talk to you later?"

"Yeah." He tried to smile, but it died halfway through. "I love you."

"Love you too. Bye." She closed the laptop, still pondering what he might not be telling her—what he couldn't tell her—when a text flashed across her phone.

WATER BROKE, HOSPITAL NOW!!!

She scrambled to her feet and froze. It wasn't time yet, was it? Piper still had three weeks. Didn't the baby know he was supposed to stay in there?

She shook her head. Babies came when they came, and this baby was on his way.

Closing his computer, Charlie dropped his face into his hands and ran them up over his head. This wasn't exactly the first time he'd had to omit the truth from a conversation. The job required it. Meg understood.

But this wasn't merely a matter of OPSEC. This was a different code, more like guidelines than rules surrounding marital life during deployment. Even if doing this was for her own good, he hated not being totally honest with her.

He had spent months trying to help her, urging her to open

up to him, knowing it was risky. And now he couldn't—wouldn't—reciprocate.

He couldn't tell her how he was doing, how he was losing it, how he was distracted on the job, letting down his team. That would crush her. Even if she seemed better now, who knew what that would do to her?

No, it was better this way. Better that she not know why he was upset. She didn't need that guilt.

And neither do you. Fix it. Now.

He glanced at the door, remembering he'd told Baker he'd be right there. Good thing they never expected him to be punctual. Pushing back his chair, he started for the door, but not before picking up the baby mask.

Cracking the door open, he poked his head, looking one way, then the other. Seeing no one, he pulled back into his room to slip the mask over his head. In two strides he was at Baker's door across the hallway. He knocked, keeping his head an inch away from it.

The door pulled open, and Murphy leapt back. "Gah! What the *hell*?" He fisted a hand as Charlie pulled the mask off, laughing. "I hate that thing. Seriously, I'm going to burn it."

Charlie leaned back to toss it across the hallway to his own room before entering. Baker was lying on his cot, legs crossed at the ankles, arms behind his head. Murphy returned to his seat at the desk, still shaking his head and muttering something Charlie couldn't hear. He shut the door behind him and leaned against it, hands in his pockets. This looked casual, right?

"What's up?" He nodded to Murphy, his eyes darting over to Baker, who didn't budge as he watched him. What was this, some sort of interrogation? Maybe an intervention.

"Dude! You could have been killed. That's what's up!" Murphy offered him an energy drink, as if it were perfectly normal to proffer caffeine when discussing death.

Charlie nodded and caught the can that was tossed to him. "What're you talking about?" he asked, popping the can open and taking a long sip.

"You didn't hear the alarms? We had mortar fire several times last night." Murphy shot a glance to Baker, as if this presented new evidence for Charlie's compromised mental state.

"Yeah. No. I don't remember that at all." Charlie shrugged. "Why didn't you come get me?"

Baker sat up and propped his elbows on his knees, his eyes boring into Charlie's. "We did! Murphy banged on your door and screamed at you!"

"Yeah! I even insulted your mom. And nothin'."

He smirked. "Huh. That's weird. Did they hit anything this time?"

"Nothing but dirt," Baker said.

"So they're improving." Charlie laughed.

Baker yawned and ran a hand through his hair. "Know what they say: Even a blind squirrel likes nuts."

"What?" Charlie narrowed his eyes at his buddy. "Nobody says that."

"Well, it's still true."

Charlie shook his head and smiled.

"Still..." Baker caught his eye. "Next time might be their lucky day when they land one right on top of you..."

Charlie opened his mouth to speak, keeping his eyes locked on Baker, but Murphy spoke first. "Don't even!"

"What?" Charlie let his chin drop and his eyes go wide with innocence.

"Like Murphy's mom," Murphy said, imitating Charlie's voice. *That's an awful impression of me.* Maybe he had milked this joke for too long, but the look on his buddy's face was priceless. *Worth it.*

"Hey, you said it, not me!"

Murphy huffed and threw an empty can at Charlie's head, but it missed by a good foot. Baker and Charlie swapped amused glances. At least Baker had stopped eying him like he was going to snap at any second.

"Don't you need to be calling that woman of yours?" Murphy scowled and sunk back into his chair, folding his arms across his chest. "I think it's been five minutes since the last time you talked."

Charlie glanced down at his watch. "Nope. Been a good two hours since I talked to your mom." He looked up in time to see a book coming at him, this time set on hitting its target. He ducked. "I'm actually gonna go grab a quick bite before our mission brief."

"Later!" Baker said, ignoring Murphy, who still sulked at the desk.

Charlie waved and stepped through the door, but before it closed, Baker spoke. "Told you he was fine."

As the hospital elevator door crept open, Meg huffed at it for taking its sweet time. It wasn't until after she was buzzed into labor and delivery that the smells and sounds of the hospital fell into her stomach, turning it over…and then over again.

I'm going to be sick.

The sharpness of the alcohol cleanser punched her in the nose, and she took a step back—her shoes squeaking against the freshly cleaned tile—as if it were an enemy that warranted retreat. The starkness of the fluorescent lights, the one above her flickering and buzzing, forced her eyes shut.

The nurses would think she'd escaped from the mental health ward, with the confused and pained look she felt distorting her features. But the L&D staff was too busy to be bothered with her. Thanks be to God, indeed.

She forced her feet to take her farther into the unit, but each step remained heavy, weighed down by the pain. She'd shoved it aside so long ago. Why was it bubbling up now, ignoring her pleas to go away? She'd gotten over this, hadn't she? She'd dealt with it.

If you call ignoring it and forcing it to the bowels of your consciousness "dealing with it."

The piercing wail of a newborn nearby snapped her out of her painful stupor. She'd deal with this later. Had to. For Piper. She straightened and hurried to the nurses station. The nurse smiled at her, eyes weary from a too-long shift, and directed her to Room 415.

She braced herself for the sounds of labor, fisting her hands one last time before knocking on the door.

"Come in." Piper's voice was calm.

Pushing the door open, Meg leaned her head in first, as if afraid to commit to being there.

Piper laughed. "I said 'come in,' silly woman."

Warmth spread across her cheeks as she pushed into the room, taking her time to close the door. She needed the extra seconds to calm her nerves, which seemed to have revved back up into panic mode at the sight of the hospital bed.

Her legs tensed, itching to carry her out the door and back to the Jeep. A weight dropped on her chest, a million tingling legs crawling across her sternum as the anxiety set in. She crossed her arms over her midsection, hoping Piper wouldn't notice how her hands shook.

She half-smiled. "Hey, mama." Piper would see through her, but she had to at least make an effort.

In the dim light, Meg took in the small hospital room. There were no machines tracking contractions, no pained look on her friend's face, no nurses running to and fro talking about centimeters and asking about pain.

Piper chuckled. "Yeah. You missed it."

"I...what?" Meg's eyes darted around the room.

"You missed it, silly." She nodded to the bassinet in the corner of the room that held a tiny bundle wrapped tight, the rise and fall of its chest—his chest—visible within the swaddle even from across the room.

"What? How? I got here as fast as I could."

"So did he." Another chuckle mixed with the easy smile on Piper's face. "I barely made it into the L&D room before he decided to make his entrance."

"That's so..." She didn't have a word for it. Labor was supposed to be long, painful, and drawn out—especially first labors.

"Expected," Piper said, finishing her thought.

"What?"

"My mom—this was her normal with us kids. I had a suspicion I'd be the same way."

"I'm sorry I missed it." She wasn't. Not really.

"Don't lie." Piper smiled again.

She looked amazing. Tired, sure, but relaxed and blissful. Of course Piper would rock everything, including a fast labor. Piper could do anything. If only Meg could have half of the gumption her friend possessed.

Piper eased herself out of the bed and lumbered over to the bassinet. Picking up her son, she angled his swaddled body so Meg could see his face.

"I want you to meet Logan Aaron Woods."

Meg's breath caught. *His precious face.*

"He's beautiful, Piper. Looks so much like his daddy."

"Who would not have wanted to be called beautiful, you know. Wanna hold him?"

Meg hesitated, but the instinct inside her to cradle the baby won over the pain. She nodded and held out her arms.

Rocking, bouncing, patting—it felt so natural, so perfect.

His mouth wiggled, and his brow furrowed, as if moved by some dream he was having behind those closed eyes.

Meg's chest tightened, and her stomach churned. The pain was coming, and she couldn't stop it this time. It rose, fast and hard, choking her before breaking free. She didn't want to cry, not here, not when her friend was so happy.

But there was no shoving this aside anymore, no controlling it.

She gazed down at this perfect blessing, and her tears overflowed, streaming down her cheeks. She wanted a baby, but she'd never have one.

"You did the right thing, Meg."

The words stung, a combination of salt and lemon juice on her fresh wounds. She didn't respond. Couldn't.

"I know it didn't go the way it should have."

Why couldn't her mom stop talking...for once?

"It will be okay. The baby deserved..."

Deserved what exactly? To be killed? Ripped from his mother? Discarded like garbage?

"The baby needed a mom and a dad, and you couldn't provide that, honey."

Her mom was crazy—out of her mind crazy. And Meg had let that crazy rule over her.

Meg wanted to curl up into herself, to disappear into the sheets of the bed, but the incisions in her abdomen wouldn't allow it. Her mom had promised it would be a quick and easy fix to the problem, insisting it was the responsible decision.

But her mom couldn't have known it'd go all wrong, that the doctor would make a mistake, a mistake that would cost her everything.

She laid a hand on her belly where her womb should have been.

No husband. No children. No future. Sterile and broken at only eighteen.

Her sobbing drowned out the sound of her mom's attempts to console her. Her mom had stolen everything from her. She'd never forgive her. Or herself.

19

CHARLIE LEANED against the Humvee beside Baker. Neither man talked as they watched the kids in the small village run around the corner of a simple mud building, pass the parked convoy, and head back around another building.

They seemed happy, as if they hadn't witnessed the atrocities of war for most of their lives.

Murphy walked up and flicked the ash from his cigarette, adjusting the rifle across his chest slightly. "Weren't we supposed to be leaving soon?"

"Five minutes ago, I think," Baker answered him. His eye flashed to the cigarette hanging out of Murphy's mouth. "I thought you said you were going to quit."

Murphy shrugged. "Changed my mind."

"You should quit. They're gonna kill you," Baker said. Charlie kept his eyes on the village while he listened, stifling a laugh behind his gloved hand.

"Yes, dear," Murphy said, taking a long drag before flicking the butt away and grinding it into the ground with his boot.

To their left, a middle-aged Afghan man approached.

Charlie tightened his grip on his M4 but otherwise didn't move. The man didn't appear to be a threat, simply walking along the path through the village, his gaze avoiding the soldiers.

Charlie turned at the sound of laughter as the children rounded the building yet again. Most of the kids saw the man and veered off, sure to stay out of his way, but one kid, a boy of about seven, had been laughing so hard that he didn't notice until it was too late, and he ran headlong into the man.

Charlie straightened, his muscles twitching as he watched the man yank the kid around by the arm. He sent his other hand flying across the kid's cheek, unleashing an angry blast of words Charlie couldn't understand.

He didn't need to either. Without thinking, Charlie was running, his rifle lifted and aimed at the man.

"Stop! Back off!" he screamed at the Afghan, the muzzle of his rifle mere inches from the man's face. "Leave him alone! Stop!"

The man might not speak English, but he understood the firearm. He raised his arms, but his eyes flashed at Charlie. He didn't say anything, but his mouth twitched, his eyes darting between Charlie, the rifle, and the kid, who stood wide-eyed at the standoff for a second before running off and holding his hand to his face.

Baker rushed up beside him. "Charlie, cool it. What are you doing?"

But Charlie kept his rifle lifted, ready. "He shouldn't treat the kid that way."

"I know, but you can't lose it like this. It's their culture, not ours." Baker lifted a hand to Charlie's shoulder and pulled him back, but he resisted, his jaw clenched. "Stand down, Charlie! Before you get us killed."

Charlie blinked. Once, twice. His buddy was right.

He'd lost it. Again. Endangered them. This Afghan wasn't

going to hurt them, not armed with only his hands. But the danger wasn't always immediate.

"Go on. Move," Charlie said to the villager, waving him off to the right with his rifle before lowering it.

He turned to see Murphy standing there with his mouth hanging open. No one else was around. Maybe no one would find out his mistake.

Not likely.

He could only hope the repercussions wouldn't be too severe once the man complained to the village elders.

He nudged past Murphy, with Baker on his heels, and turned to resume his position beside the Humvee as if nothing had happened.

"I'm ready to go," Charlie said, ignoring how Murphy looked at him.

The past stalked Meg as she hurried through the halls. It was biding its time until she was alone, away from prying eyes.

I shouldn't have lied to Piper. What kind of woman ran away from a friend? And under the guise of meeting her pastor, no less. But the fresh air that greeted her outside the hospital's double doors soothed her guilt. She was free—from the hospital, from Piper, from the baby.

She shut the Jeep door behind her and slumped against the steering wheel, letting the memories crush her with feelings she had locked away, forgotten.

But she'd never forgotten, had she?

Her baby, killed and torn from her, haunted her from the shadows of her mind. All these years of ignoring it, of finding ways to function and keep living…little good they did now. The dam had given way, and she could do nothing but wait for it to bury her.

Like my baby.

She fisted her hand and slammed it into the hard leather of the dash. She'd been forgiven for this. She had. She heard that forgiveness every week at church.

Or she had before she'd stopped going.

Why do I keep screwing up? God, what is wrong with me?

Charlie. She needed him. He'd hold her and love her and tell her it was all okay, remind her of Christ's forgiveness and grace for her.

But you murdered your baby, Meg.

That voice snaked its accusations into her ear. She tried to shake it off, tossing her hair as if she could bat it away as a horse shoos a fly.

What will Charlie think? Because of you he'll never be a father.

She stared up at the brick wall of the hospital. *How could you be so selfish?* To accept his hand, to marry him, and to sentence him to carrying this cross of barrenness. What had she done?

This was her cross to bear, her consequence for her sin, and she had wrapped it around him with her vows.

Sure, he knew. She had told him she had needed an emergency hysterectomy, but she had never said why, never told him it'd been her fault, her choice.

He had never pushed her for answers. That wasn't his way. He was always so patient, more patient than she deserved.

You don't deserve him.

She clamped her eyes shut, rocking back and forth from the tension squeezing her chest until she couldn't breathe. She deserved the pain, the loneliness. She'd already condemned him to a childless future. She couldn't burden him with the truth too.

This was her penance. Hers alone.

"How was your week?" Charlie wedged the cell phone between his shoulder and his ear, relaxing back onto his bed and crossing his legs at the ankles. The team had made it back to camp without incident, and so far it appeared his mistake hadn't made it up to command…yet.

But he wasn't going to let anything disrupt their first conversation in days.

She answered with her own question. "All right?"

"You're not sure if it was all right? Did Mrs. Goetz stop by again and gift you some gently used dental floss?"

No giggle came from her end. He frowned into his free hand, the tension mounting in his chest. "What happened, babe?"

"I was at the hospital…"

He sat up, as if there was anything he could do to help. "What? Are you okay? Is Piper okay? Is the baby—"

She cut in. "The baby's fine. He decided to come early. Perfectly healthy. Named him Logan Aaron."

His eyes darted around his room. Something was off here. *Duh, genius. She's obviously upset. Give the award to Captain Obvious!*

Squaring his shoulders, he softened his tone. "You doing okay?"

After a pause, she said, "I'm fine." Her words fell flat, dead. It was the sort of answer you'd expect from a coworker in the break room, not your wife—the woman who trusted you to love her forever and stand by her through all the messes of life.

They'd finally gotten back to some semblance of normal—comfortable, happy. *Let it slide, man. Let her be.*

"I wish I was there." He cringed. Why were words so hard? They never quite fit or felt right.

"I don't want you to worry. I'll be okay."

He ignored the shakiness in her voice that showed her

words to be a lie. Could he pull this off? Did he dare make light of the situation? This could backfire. Big time.

"I thought you said you were fine." He held his breath, waiting to see if she would play along and relax or if she'd retreat further into herself. Or worse. He couldn't handle another out-and-out fight with her.

"Ha-ha, Charlie." There it was—the slight hint of a smile in her tone. "I am fine. And I *will* be okay. They aren't mutually exclusive, you know."

"Well, I'm glad to hear it regardless. Let me know if there's anything I can do to help? Okay? I can have Mrs. Goetz over there in a hurry if you want…"

"Please, no. Anything but that!" She giggled.

"You know that wasn't that funny, right?"

"I don't know what you're talking about. I'm quite hilarious."

He cleared his throat, deepening his voice into the most serious tone he could muster. "Oh, no. This isn't good."

"What? What do you mean?"

The lightness was gone, a switch flipped, replacing it with—what? That couldn't be panic, could it? Had he touched a nerve somehow?

Don't be an idiot. He must have imagined it. There was no way she could have taken the obvious joke as a serious comment on her well-being.

"Your psychosis appears to be worsening."

"Oh, shut up." She'd been holding her breath. But that didn't make sense. He shook his head. *Leave it, man.*

"As you wish."

If something was up—if it was important enough—she'd tell him. Wouldn't she?

Meg glanced down at the red dress she'd chosen for this morning and frowned. Charlie was right. Her psychosis was worsening. She had lost her mind. She'd never blend in.

She looked around the parking lot. Too many cars. Too many people ambling in. She was out of time. She made a mental note to start stashing an extra set of clothes in the car just in case. Something beige or grey. But even that wasn't likely to keep the vultures from descending.

They're not vultures. How could you say that?

She rolled her eyes at her conscience. Fine. They weren't vultures, but that didn't erase the discomfort at having to stand there exposed, wounded meat begging to be picked over.

That's not fair, and you know it. They're only worried about you.

True or not, it held no comfort. The loneliness brewed in her chest, and she bristled. *I don't want them. I want Charlie.* She gritted her teeth.

This would be so much easier with him here—or Jon. Except Jon would have felt equally as uncomfortable, uneasy with all the attention and the questions. No. It was Charlie's confidence she needed now, his ability to see the good in people no matter how they tried to annoy him.

But she didn't have it. She just had her and her cranky self. Even if she could pull off the happy smile and sweet facade she'd perfected, that wouldn't stop the inner cursing and murdering of her neighbors in her head.

God, forgive me. I hate my neighbor! I don't want to, but I do!

She filled her lungs, praying the air somehow carried the strength and courage she needed to face this. *Please help me!* Conflict burned in her chest, half of her pushing her to get over herself and go inside and the other begging her to protect herself from the emotional stress that awaited her in there.

She wrung her fingers, her nerves fraying until her hands shook so much that she had to grip the steering wheel to quiet them. It shouldn't be this hard to move, but all she could manage was to drop her head onto the steering wheel.

Tap. Tap. Tap.

She jolted upright, smoothing her hair down with both hands, hoping she didn't look as disheveled as she felt. She looked up to see Annie smiling at her, David propped on her hip. A head of blonde curls popped up from below her window.

"BOO!"

Meg smiled to herself and then feigned surprise, opening her mouth wide in horror and raising her hands in fear.

"Gotchoo!" Lydia shouted through the window, her curls bouncing as she hopped around her mom.

Stepping out of the car, Meg bent down to Lydia's height. "You sure did! I've never been so scared in my whole life!"

"Liar." Lydia stopped hopping to put her hands on her hips. "I'm scary, but I'm not that scary. I'm only five."

Meg nodded, pulling her lips into a serious line. "You're right. You'll be much scarier once you're six, I bet."

Lydia darted off past Matthew toward the building, shouting a "race ya!" over her shoulder that Meg wasn't sure was meant for her, for Lydia's big brother, or for anyone within earshot who would accept the challenge.

Meg straightened, and Annie placed an arm over her shoulder. "Don't worry, we'll sit in the back. It'll be okay."

Looking down at her feet, Meg let Annie and David guide her inside. *Lord, please let her be right.*

Meg walked through the crowd, longing to sink into the floor. The church narthex was still full of folks mulling about, and all eyes fell on her. The red dress. The pastor's wife. What was she thinking? She might as well have donned a giant chicken costume.

At least then you'd be behind a mask though.

The vultures descended upon her with their stares and their

questions—their judgment still peeking around the facade of care and compassion.

Where have you been? We've missed you! How are you doing? And Charlie, how is he? It's so nice to see you.

The words flew at her. Before Meg could cower beneath them, Annie raised a protective wing and shooed them away. She changed subjects with grace, pulling each attacker's attention with such flawless execution that they showed no sign their efforts had been thwarted, their questions unanswered.

Meg ducked into the pew, and despite several deep breaths, her muscles remained tense. They had made it to the back corner, but this was as bad a choice as the bold dress she smoothed over her lap. After so many years of sitting near the front, she had forgotten the number of people who called these back seats home on Sundays.

Annie had directed them to the middle of the pew. Why? What was she thinking? With Lydia on one side and that young couple—she still didn't know their names—on her other, her heart sped, her breathing quickened. Trapped.

She wasn't ready. She couldn't be here. There were too many people, too many eyes. Even from the back of the sanctuary she could feel them.

Meg fumbled with the hymnal, trying to find the setting for the service, marking the first hymn. But no amount of fidgeting could quiet the voice whispering from the corner of her mind.

You don't belong here. His forgiveness? It's not for you.

Her throat tightened. She tried to swallow air, but it caught. She gripped the padded seat. Eyes clenched tightly shut, she struggled to remain still. Assuming the fetal position here, now, would certainly bring more unwanted attention.

Shut up shut up shut up shut up.

But the voice continued.

You think this is your family? If they knew what you did...

A hand grabbed hers. Lydia was pulling her to her feet. "C'mon, Mrs. Winters! It's time to shake hands and share peace!"

Meg cursed in her head. The greetings. The hands. The smiles. The glares.

How could she share God's peace with these people when she had none of it inside her? How could she utter the words "God's peace" when she was barely convinced it existed at all?

But here was her chance. Lydia had abandoned her, snaking through the flock of bodies to find her daddy near the front and shake his hand. The too-sweet couple at the end had left the exit unguarded, having crossed the aisle to greet their back-pew neighbors. Meg, purse in hand and head down, slithered out of the pew and through the doors, not risking a look back to see if Annie noticed.

Back safely in the Jeep, she slumped against the seat in defeat. Charlie, Annie, Pastor Feld—they'd be so disappointed. She'd let them down, succumbed to that voice and run.

And yet, she was free. She'd escaped the clutches of those scavengers whose guise of caring and love had failed. She'd seen through their lies. They wouldn't get her. Not today.

20

MEG PICKED her way carefully up the steps to the small front porch, watching her feet so as not to slip on the few icy patches remaining from the latest spring storm. Crossing her arms tightly over the ache in her chest, she dug her fingers into the red knit of her dress. Two more steps and she'd be at the front door, but her feet rooted themselves on that top step, refusing to go farther.

Her gaze darted to the door, the window, and back to her feet. The tightness in her chest gripped harder, sending a lump into her throat.

She hadn't intended to come here, but home, with all its bits and pieces of Charlie strewn about, would have been worse. This seemed the better option—a distraction from her guilt and shame.

A baby's cry came from the other side of the door, sending a hard punch to her gut. How had she forgotten about the baby? Her arms wrapped tighter around herself, as if she could protect herself from guilt and grief.

She spun around on a toe, but before she could retreat down the stairs to the Jeep, the door opened.

"Meg? What are you doing here?" Piper's sounded so happy, so put together. Maybe it was contagious. One could hope.

Meg turned back to the door, fighting not to look down at the baby cradled in her friend's arms. Instead her gaze locked onto Piper's for a mere second before darting off to the right and circling back to her feet.

"Lady, you look awful." Piper opened the door further. "Come inside."

Her feet seemed rooted to the porch, protesting against the invitation, protecting her from whatever she might face inside the house. *Come on. It's Piper.*

And the baby.

It's not the baby's fault! Go in before she thinks you're crazy for just standing here.

Raising a hand to her lips, her thumbnail wedged between her teeth, she crept across the threshold.

"Rough morning?" Piper clicked the door shut.

Meg pulled her hand away from her mouth and gestured to her mascara-stained cheeks. "You mean this isn't how a smoky eye is supposed to look?" She meant it to be casual, funny. But the tears she'd finally calmed back in the Jeep gave away her true feelings.

Piper still laughed. "I don't…think so? But I could be wrong." A whimper came from the blanket in Piper's arms, and Meg fixed her gaze on a fresh cobweb in the top left corner of the living room.

"I was just about to change him," Piper said. "Grab yourself some coffee in the kitchen."

As Piper glided down the hallway, Meg plodded into the kitchen and stole a glance at her reflection in the microwave. She frowned. It was worse than she'd thought. The black of her mascara had smudged below each eye and dripped into trails where her tears had blazed down her face.

Grabbing the mugs with one hand, Meg wiped away the

evidence of her breakdown with the other. *What's the point though?* Even if she could remove the black marks from her skin, her eyes would still be red and puffy, swollen from the sobs she'd failed to contain on the drive over. *Piper knows I'm a mess anyway. No point in pretending.*

She pulled a stool out from the counter and sat as Piper returned with the baby, freshly-changed and no longer swaddled. Today was a day for stupid decisions, it seemed.

First the dress, then the back pew, and now this. Like some piece of her subconscious was orchestrating a maniacal plan to force her to stop running and deal with her issues.

"Want to hold him?" Piper lifted her eyebrows, smiling.

"I—I don't know." She fidgeted in her seat, but Piper was already lowering the baby into her arms.

"Yes you do. Here, put your arms out. No, like this." Piper pulled her arms back and retreated to the opposite side of the kitchen, ignoring Meg's pleading look.

Meg's breath caught, choked by the lump that had returned without warning. He was so tiny, so fragile, yet so much bigger than he had been a couple of weeks ago.

"You're acting like you've never held a baby before, silly." Piper chuckled and picked up her coffee. "You're not going to break him, you know."

I've broken others.

But that was so long ago, and this wasn't the first baby she'd held since... How many times had she held David Feld at church without panic? Yet here, with this baby, a miniature version of his father, she wanted to throw up and sob in the corner.

As she stared down at the little one in her arms, she marveled at his tiny fingers clutching the blanket and his mouth twitching as if at any moment he would part his lips and tell her it would all be okay. He blinked and looked up at her, his eyes pools of dark chocolate that pulled her in, drowning her in their rich and bittersweet depths.

There was the answer. This little boy—like her baby—would never know his father. He'd never know where he'd come from, where he'd gotten his quiet demeanor or his double-cowlick or his penchant for sarcasm.

The loss. That's what tied her pain to little Logan. That's what knotted her stomach and ripped a new chasm in her heart at the very sight of him.

But at least Logan is alive.

"What's going on with you, Meg?" Piper's voice cut through her trance.

She blinked, breaking the hold of Logan's eyes. "It's nothing."

"You're an awful liar. Is Charlie on a mission or something?" Piper leaned her hips against the counter and took a long sip of coffee. She cradled the mug in both hands, her fingers criss-crossing over the gold letters—*"Jesus saves."*

Meg dropped her gaze, careful not to look back at the baby in her arms. "Not at the moment. I'm—I'm not ready to talk about it."

"Well, when you are ready, I'll be here, living the glamorous life of nursing every two hours and changing diapers every five minutes. Sore nipples and diaper blowouts. It's the life, I tell ya."

Meg pulled her eyes up to Piper's. "But it's worth it, right?"

"He's my own little piece of Aaron." Piper's expression felt off, her smile forced. *That's not actually a yes either.* Perhaps it was a product of the exhaustion and fatigue that came with motherhood. Piper was still herself. Tired but happy. Peaceful.

But the questions wouldn't stop poking around in her head. Meg knew she'd regret it if she didn't ask. "And you're sure you're doing okay? With everything?"

Piper's smile widened. "I'm good, friend. Really. A little

tired is all." Meg searched her friend's face, looking for any of her own sadness and stress reflected there.

Finding none, she relaxed, glancing down at Logan.

At least one of us is okay.

The evening sun fell fast, bathing the front of the house in a rich golden hue, as Piper, itchy fingers curled around the edge of the door, watched Meg glide down the steps with another "later" thrown over her shoulder. She offered a smile her friend couldn't see, not finding the strength to push words past the tightness in her throat.

Piper retreated back into the house, not waiting to see Meg get into the Jeep or to give one last wave as the vehicle backed out of the driveway. She swung the door closed. The lock snapped into place, and with it, Piper's smile vanished. Her shoulders slumped as the weight of her performance crashed to the floor.

I should move to Hollywood, become an actress. The thought held no humor, and her eyes fell to her hand still resting on the door. But she didn't see it or the ring still sitting on her finger. She didn't see anything except the wavy ripples of her tears.

Logan let out a cry from the bassinet in the corner of the room and then another one. Her head fell, hard, straining the back of her neck as her chin fell to her chest.

He can't be hungry, can he? I just fed him.

She spun around. Another cry had her feet ready to go to him, but she forced them to remain in place. Her eyes flashed to the source of the cries, where a tiny hand flailed in the air before disappearing again behind the white edge of his bed.

Maybe he's dirty? Wet?

She backed away from his cries and his arms reaching for her, wishing she could cry herself, wail her frustration at the world. Piper wedged herself between the door and the wall, hiding without actually leaving. She wasn't a terrible mother. She was heeding all the advice. He was in a safe place. This way she wouldn't hurt him.

Let him cry. Crying won't hurt him.

You might.

His unanswered cries intensified. She clenched her eyes shut, squeezing them until pain radiated across her temples, but the sight of his little face, red with fear and desperation, haunted her from behind her closed lids. His wails grew hoarse, strained, as he called to her.

Her hands flew up to her head, clamping down against her ears as her legs crumpled beneath her, her back sliding against the corner. Hinges scraped against her ribs as she collapsed, reminding her she was still alive, like it or not.

Piper pulled her knees up, hugging them with her elbows as she rocked, hands still over her ears. She hummed no particular tune, just enough noise in her head to drown out the sound of her baby.

Her hums gave way to screams, though silent and contained.

Be quiet. Please. Please be quiet!

She couldn't do this. She couldn't cut it. She'd hurt him.

Why did you give him to me, God? I can't give him what he needs! He'd be better off without me.

She caved in on herself, wishing her tears could dissolve the floor beneath her, create a dark chasm to swallow her whole.

Please, God. I don't want him. I don't want him.

I don't.

Meg hugged a knee to her chest, holding her wine glass close as she watched Charlie on the screen, his eyes lighting up as he recalled his latest strike of comedic genius. She glanced up to the window beyond the computer, watching the last of the sun's rays beaming from behind the clouds that settled along the horizon as she listened to the end of his story.

She took a sip of her wine and smirked at him. "You're still giving Murphy crap about his mom? The guy is going to stab you in your sleep or something."

He backed away from the camera and relaxed into his chair. "He'd like to think he could take me. But he can handle it. It was one joke."

"Uh-huh. Right. One on top of all the others before that."

His lips pursed as he nodded. "Touché."

"And Baker? What are you doing to get him to kill you off?" Meg laughed. It wasn't funny, not even by her low standards, but the conversation needed to stay in this safe area.

"That reminds me," Charlie said. He leaned on his desk, a hand cradling his chin as his fingers tapped against his lips. "I need to give him crap for...something. But I haven't found the right ammo yet."

"Well, I hope you find that something soon. You're running out of time to execute any diabolical schemes."

His hand dropped. He clicked his tongue at her as he shook his head. "Oh, Meg. Sweet, innocent, naive Meg. There's always time for diabolical schemes."

She chuckled. She needed this—his wit, that cute smile. But it wouldn't last.

She dropped her gaze and took another sip, long and deep, downing most of the glass. She couldn't keep up the ruse much longer. Eventually he'd ask how church had gone and how Piper and the baby were doing. The conversation would turn, and she'd have to either confess or lie.

She was so tired of lying to him, but she couldn't dump everything on him.

Not when he has evil plans to forge against Baker.

She laughed to herself.

"What's so funny?"

Her face jerked up to see him eyeing her, his brow raised. *Busted.* She needed to think, and fast, but her head swam in the wine, slowing her search for the right response. Or any response.

She lifted her shoulder in a slow shrug, buying time as the words fumbled their way together in her head. "Oh, just picturing you in your B-hut hatching up plans, like it's your evil lair." She smiled. Or at least she thought she smiled. She couldn't quite see her expression in the thumbnail image at the corner of the screen.

His hand lifted back to his chin, and his tongue clicked again as he thought. "Hmm. It would be so much easier to devise my plans if I had a minion of my own."

"Like a monkey on a motorcycle!"

"Exactly. I need to find that monkey—and the guy whose bike he was on."

She watched his eyes drift around his room, as if he was indeed hatching up a plan to locate the monkey and its owner. Her mind failed her, clouded by the alcohol.

The weather was always a safe bet, right? But then he might realize she was keeping something from him. The Bible study? That was laughable. She hadn't touched hers since Christmas, and it was too dangerously close to the subject of church.

Charlie cleared his throat, snapping her back to the screen. He leaned forward, his gaze and his tone softening. "So how was church this morning?"

His question slammed into her. She blanked, eyes stuck on his face without seeing him. This must be what deer felt like when they saw a car. Trapped. Caught. Like in the pew.

But she'd escaped that. She could escape this too.

"Fine. I guess?" He didn't have to know she'd only been

there for five minutes, hadn't even made it through the opening hymn or even *to* the opening hymn.

"Did you make it through the whole service?"

How did he know? Had Pastor Feld ratted her out, told him how she'd turned tail and ran? She couldn't bear any more lies. The truth, or some of the truth, was the only way.

"No." She bit her lip and lowered her eyes, letting her gaze swim in the straw-hued liquid in her glass, waiting for his reprimand.

But his words came soft and concerned, with none of the sharpness she deserved. "How far did you make it?"

Keeping her eyes lowered, she gulped down her shame and muttered, "Sharing of the peace."

He laughed.

She looked up at him, her lips pulling back into a thin line as she tried to read his expression. This wasn't funny. It was sad.

"I'm sorry, babe. It's not funny." Yet he was still laughing. "But it kind of is."

He should be yelling at her, pleading with her to try harder, to do better. She furrowed her brow, pushing her way through the fogginess in her head, searching for something to say. Anything really.

But his reaction had thrown her for another loop, sending her spinning through thought after thought, unable to grasp onto anything that floated by.

"Well," he said, "you can always try again next week. Maybe make it through the first verse of the hymn?"

Don't ask. Don't bring it up.

"Where's the lecture?" she said, not taking her own advice.

"You want a lecture? I mean, I didn't have one prepared, but I bet I could come up with something on the fly." The jesting in his voice and in his eyes only irritated her more. This was serious, and he was making a joke out of it.

Dropping her leg to the floor, she backed away from the screen and pulled her glass up to her shoulder. She glared.

"I don't see why it's suddenly no big deal."

His shoulders fell, and he leaned back again, his hand sweeping over his mouth. When he spoke again, his tone had shifted, the humor gone.

"I've been really hard on you the last couple months, and it hadn't helped." His eyes bored into her own until she looked away. "I made it worse. Thought I'd try this tactic instead, give you support instead of pressure."

The irritation bubbled under her skin, and she peeked up at him from under her brows. The words came out low, almost in a growl. "I don't *need* you to be easy on me…"

"Woah. Wait, excuse me?" He leaned back in his chair, hands lifted.

"I…" She cowered but kept her eyes on his, forcing herself not to look away. God's Word was for reproof, correction, wasn't it? As much as she didn't want his correction, she knew she needed it, needed to be held accountable. And here he was acting as if she wasn't breaking God's commandments by avoiding church week after week.

"No, Meg." His eyes dug deeper into hers until she had to look away, break that connection before he saw all she had been hiding, protecting him from. His words came out sharper than she expected.

"For weeks you've been biting my head off anytime I tried to help, accusing me of trying to *fix* you. And now? Now I get chewed out for backing off? For being understanding? Letting you work through this at your own pace? What do you want from me?"

In the corner of her eye she saw his hands fly up with his questions.

He was right. He couldn't possibly know how to handle her constant shifts, especially when she'd kept him in the dark on so much. But she had no response, no idea what she wanted or needed from him. Maybe there was no way he could act, nothing he could say that wouldn't set her off. She swallowed and bit her lip.

He spoke again, more quietly but with the same hard edge. "This isn't only about God, is it? What aren't you telling me?"

Her chest caved in on itself. Her breathing became shallow. He was perceptive, but she'd hidden this so well. There was no way he had discovered her shame, her sin.

Her mouth went dry, and she reached for the bottle from beside her computer. With a shaky hand she filled the glass again, avoiding his questioning eyes. She took a long sip.

"How much have you had to drink, Meg?" His tone had eased.

She shrugged. "Don't worry about it. I'm fine."

"What's going on? What are you hiding?"

"What? What do you mean?" She had intended the words to sound strong—defensive—to show him he hadn't rightly guessed she'd been hiding something. But her voice betrayed her.

She sounded meek, guilty.

"Is it…another guy?" His voice cracked.

"What?" She pulled her chin back, straightening to glare at him. She had secrets, but that? How dare he accuse her of sleeping around! "Why would you think that? That's not—no!"

"Then what is it?" He relaxed only slightly. "Babe. We've been married more than two years. Friends for five times that. You think I don't know when something's bothering you?"

He paused, but she had no words, no answer. She took another sip.

"I've waited. Tried to be patient. Told myself you'd tell me in your own time. But you haven't."

Meg clamped her mouth shut and fought the tightening in her chest, her secret crushing her as the anxiety ramped up.

She shook her head, not caring that he saw every movement, every wince.

She couldn't tell him. Not yet. Not ever. He didn't need this burden, especially when he was over there with a job to do.

She couldn't lift her eyes to his. Couldn't respond. Could only listen as he spoke. "I love you. So much. I know you have a past, old wounds that haven't healed. I've respected that, let you have your space..."

She waited for the "but," bracing herself. For what, she didn't know.

His voice remained quiet, but that sharpness crept back in with each word. "But, babe, I don't know how to do this if you won't trust me. I don't know how you expect me to be your *husband,* to protect and serve and love you when I have no clue what's haunting you."

"I..." She opened her mouth to say something, anything. But she snapped it shut.

His eyes lowered, his fingers touching the spot where his wedding band should have been. "If you won't talk to me, at least listen to me. Go talk to Pastor Feld." He paused to swallow before lifting his eyes to meet hers. "Private confession could help. Maybe. It helped me when..."

Confession. Absolution.

"I can't do this, Meg."

What did he mean? Her eyes widened, searching his. Her heart raced. What was he saying?

"I need you to trust me! Let me be your husband! Please!" His lips tightened and released, quivering. Something flashed in his eyes. Panic? Anger? She couldn't read it, not that it mattered. This wasn't good either way.

"I..." she started again. "I don't know..." She shrugged, her shoulders rounding to protect herself. "I don't know how—"

His words cut her off. She looked up in time to see his eyes

—wet with tears—narrow at her as he spoke through clenched teeth.

"I really can't do this anymore, Meg. I can't."

"Then don't," she snapped before she could stop herself.

"Goodbye, Meg."

The image went black.

Call disconnected.

What had just happened? What had she done?

21

THE COFFEE POT BEEPED, cutting through the silence and startling Meg as she sat at the kitchen table, hands wringing in her lap. She blinked, the blank email coming into focus, mocking her.

Her stomach knotted. The pressure on her chest increased. This wasn't the first time Charlie had skipped his regular phone call, but…

What had that goodbye meant? There had to have been some hint in his tone, some way she could know if things were as bad as she feared. Would he really leave her? He couldn't, right? His faith—their faith—made divorce unthinkable.

But he wasn't perfect. He was just a man, and she'd pushed him so far with her silence. Had it been too far?

Meg lifted her fingers back to the keyboard. She needed to say something, tell him what was going on. She could open up. Let him in.

She pushed the keys with careful thought, as if he could read her words in real time.

Charlie, I'm not sure…

No. That was awful. She punched the backspace key until

the screen was empty again. She couldn't drop this on him in an email. What was she thinking?

But what other choice did she have? She couldn't exactly call him. She was at his mercy—if he had any left for her.

She closed the browser window, finger tapping against the mouse. There had to be some way to reach out to him, even if she couldn't tell him everything. She shouldn't have closed the browser. The blank email would have been better than the happy couple staring back at her.

They had been happy once, and not because they'd been on a beach in the Caribbean. How had so much gone so wrong so quickly? The tightness crept up into her throat. Those smiles—that joy—could they ever get that back, or had she thrown it all away?

The image shifted, the sunshine and sand fading into an overcast sky overlooking a stately bridge and majestic city. Prague. The Charles Bridge.

That was it. She still couldn't believe he had good memories of that day, a day that had tainted her own memories of the entire vacation. She clicked the browser back open and attached the image to the email.

She didn't need words. She needed to remind him of what they'd had, who they were.

Once she clicked "send" she fell back into the chair. She couldn't relax. It'd be hours before she'd know if it had worked, if he'd forgive her, and if they could heal.

The silence in the house seemed to grow as she sat. *Maybe a run would help.* But a glance outside at the storm clouds brewing over the treetops said otherwise. There was no point in risking getting stuck in a downpour. That would be worse than this silence.

There was one place that wouldn't be silent, where she wouldn't be lonely and she could be her old awkward self. *Plus, when your marriage is falling apart and your life is a wreck, where else do you turn?*

She grabbed her phone and tapped out a message to Piper.

`On my way over. Make sure you're decent!`

The half-hour drive to Piper's house in town went by quickly with her thoughts flitting by as fast as the trees and landscape out her window. Charlie would get the email. He'd remember. He'd forgive her. All would be right again in the world.

The sky unleashed its first drops of rain as Meg ducked under the small roof of Piper's porch. In two steps she was at the door and knocking.

She waited. No answer. She pulled her phone out. Maybe Piper had tried to text her back, tell her she was out running errands. But there were no messages.

Meg glanced around the neighborhood. It was slowly coming to life as folks left for work and kids headed off to school. She turned back to the door, checking her watch. Piper should be up. She knocked again, more loudly.

Pressing her ear to the door, she listened for footsteps, hoping none of the neighbors would call the cops on her for being a creepy stalker.

Nothing. Wait, was the baby crying? He was. That couldn't be good.

No, everything was probably fine. Piper was likely in the shower. Moms had to shower too, right?

Still, Piper would understand if Meg let herself in, especially with Logan crying. She dug her keys out of her purse and fumbled through the set, trying to guess which would open this door. She should have labeled them.

Logan's cries grew louder, more desperate.

The first key failed. She tried another. Success!

Opening the door a few inches, she poked her head inside. "Piper? You there?"

There was no answer except the pained cries from the bassinet in the corner of the living room. She rushed to him and picked him up, holding him to her chest as she bounced and made shushing noises into his ear. "It's okay. I've got you. It's all right."

Even she didn't believe her words. The shower wasn't running. There was no fan or white noise to cover up Logan's cries. Piper should have heard him.

Walking from room to room, Meg continued to bounce him, thankful to feel him settling against her, his cries turning into whimpers.

"Let's find your mama, okay? Piper? Where are you?"

Down the hallway she crept, not wanting to startle her friend if she was napping. The last thing she needed was to be mistaken for an intruder and shot, especially while holding the baby.

She called again, "Piper? You here?" Of course she was here. What mom would leave her baby alone?

The master bedroom at the end of the hall loomed ahead of her, its door closed. Piper was probably catching a nap with earplugs and hadn't heard, but Meg's stomach tightened as she turned the knob.

"Piper?"

Her eyes took a moment to adjust to the darkness in the room, the drawn curtain shutting out all of the bright morning light. The bedside table was a mess. An empty bottle of wine teetered at a slight angle, one side lifted by a pile of used tissues. Beside it, the corkscrew still had the cork attached. Where was the wine glass?

Two pill bottles lay open on their sides. Empty. Meg reached a hand out to check the labels, her body moving as if pushing through thick mud. Piper wasn't on any medication, was she?

She stopped. Her gaze darted to the bed and her friend's hand dangling over the side.

Meg couldn't move. Couldn't think.

Fight or flight? I apparently freeze.

She should do CPR. Maybe? But she couldn't while she was holding the baby. She shook her head, her heart racing and her mind refusing to focus.

Do something!

She fumbled for the phone in her back pocket and punched in the number while continuing to bounce Logan. She had no idea what she would say, but dispatch would help. They would ask the right questions. She would find the answers.

She would help her friend.

Charlie stopped short beside the B-hut, his running shoes kicking the dust up around his ankles. He'd planned to go farther, to run longer, but the storm clouds were gathering quickly overhead, and the last thing he wanted the night before a three-day mission was to be soaked to the bone by the cold spring rains.

He should get inside before the sky opened up, but voices around the corner made him pause. The sharp banter of Baker and Murphy was distinct, but the other three voices remained faceless. He knew their faces—even their names—but he couldn't seem to pair them with the correct voices.

The new guys had arrived mere weeks after the blast, settling into his buddies' emptied rooms, and while Murphy and Baker had welcomed them into the team without hesitation, Charlie couldn't seem to breach the wall he'd put up.

He'd intended to fix that and get to know them for the past month. He'd even made some progress, cracking jokes and learning some basic facts about each—one was a twin, the other a newlywed, another a teacher—but every time the conversation got too serious, turning to home life or marriage concerns, he'd bolt, making some excuse to get away.

He couldn't invest too much of himself in anyone new—not yet, and especially not with everything happening with Meg.

He looked up to the sky again. A run in the rain might be better than enduring small talk and pretending to be friendly.

Don't be an idiot. Go.

A bolt of lightning flashed in the distance to his right, the crack of thunder following a few seconds later. At least the storm would give him an excuse not to linger outside with them.

As he rounded the corner, cigarette smoke invaded his nose. Murphy still hadn't quit. Maybe tomorrow he would, or maybe Baker had given up nagging him.

"Hey, man," Baker said with a nod.

"What's up?" Charlie asked, hoping he sounded casual and not too eager to get through them and back to his room.

The twin took a long drag from his cigarette and answered through the smoke, "Not much. You?"

"Just finishing up a run."

"You know the showers are over there, right?" the teacher asked, flicking ash into the dust.

"Yeah, well, Murphy's mom likes me sweaty." Charlie raised his brow. It was an awful joke, something Carter would have probably said. His gut tensed as he suppressed a grimace.

Murphy huffed out a single laugh. "Too bad for you my mom's not here."

"You mean too bad for her." Charlie moved around the guys and bounded up the steps in two easy strides. He was inside with the door shut behind him before Murphy could deliver a comeback or the guys could try to reel him into mindless chatter.

Back in his room, the sight of Meg's pictures and all the

letters and packages she'd sent slammed into him. He drew his breath in and held it.

What was he doing? Had he really given Meg an ultimatum? Would he actually leave her?

The laptop on the desk was still open, though its screen was black. Her email had arrived, but he'd ignored it. She wasn't going to open up to him in an email, and he couldn't bear any more of her excuses.

Kicking off his shoes, he tossed them into the middle of the small room and dropped facedown onto his cot, his arms cradling his head. He faced the wall, his gaze landing on her picture still tacked up to the plywood.

His chest tightened. Of course he loved her. That would never change. But was love really enough when there wasn't trust? How could a marriage survive when one kept secrets?

The rain started, hammering against the roof and the walls. Voices and laughter rushed into the hallway as the guys took shelter from the storm.

Charlie clenched his teeth, like he could push away the noise and the world if he squeezed hard enough.

Clear your head. That's the only way you'll get through this.

But how? The old him would have been able to tuck each problem away into its own little box in his head, only letting them out as he needed to deal with them. But he couldn't seem to tame all the wild things on his mind. They wouldn't be contained, couldn't be controlled.

He rolled over onto his back, his hands covering his face. A growl rumbled in the back of his throat.

Seriously. Take care of this, before you get someone hurt!

The upcoming mission depended on that. He wouldn't get these guys killed—not even the guys whose names he could barely remember.

Your marriage may be falling apart, but you will not fail these guys.

With fisted hands against his forehead, he stared hard at the plywood ceiling, listening to the rain turn into a loud and steady hum as he prayed.

By the grace of God, I will not fail them.

The smell of stale coffee and sanitizer filled the hallway as Meg pushed the stroller. Logan had fallen asleep after their third trek down this stretch of tile. The sunlight pouring in through the expanse of windows along the lobby seemed out of place for the situation, reflecting the joy that had vanished the night before.

Having spent the evening trying to sleep in a stiff chair in a room kept far too cold, she trudged along, her feet unable—unwilling—to move faster. Not that she had anywhere to go. Charlie hadn't called that morning, not that she had expected him to. But she had hoped.

Piper's mom had changed her flights—having originally booked them close to Logan's due date—but wouldn't be arriving for a couple more hours. Meg just had to keep the little guy alive until then.

The doctors had said Piper would be fine once everything was out of her system. Since she'd denied wanting to harm herself or Logan, they had agreed to discharge her—waiving the mandatory psych hold—only after Meg had assured them she and Piper's mom would be her support system and ensure she would follow up with her doctor.

But what kind of support can you be? You didn't even notice this time! How did you not know?

Inching forward, forcing one foot in front of the other, she faced each nagging question and chiding thought. She had no answers, only guilt.

Her best friend had attempted suicide. Meg knew this no

matter what Piper had told the doctors about her intentions. And she'd been so self-centered, so worried about her own problems and pain, that she'd failed to see another's depression right in front of her.

Replaying the past weeks' visits with Piper, she could see the signs—the way Piper couldn't quite look at her baby, the way she passed him off to anyone and everyone who was around, always finding some excuse or reason not to have him in her arms.

No, it's easy to miss. You can't beat yourself up over this.

It did no good though. Hindsight might be twenty-twenty, but that didn't make it easier to stomach her failure—a failure that had almost killed someone.

She was failing Charlie too. Her chest heaved, and her legs tensed, as if the ground beneath her feet was crumbling around her. Nope. It was just her marriage falling apart. Every step she took to try and move on from the past—to get past everything —caused more of her foundation to fall away.

The space between her and Charlie was widening. Each missed opportunity to tell him, each refusal to tell him, pulled them farther apart.

Maybe that was for the best.

"Mrs. Winters?" The nurse stood several feet away, eying Meg as if she might also be in need of some psychiatric care herself.

"Yes?"

"Ms. Woods is awake now. And asking for you."

Rushing to follow the nurse, her thoughts raced. She was desperate to get her bearings so she wouldn't sound like a crazy person. She rounded the corner, maneuvering the stroller through the doorway, and her breath hitched, expecting to see her friend's lifeless body hanging on by a mere thread. Would she ever shake that image? Doubtful.

Piper lay in bed, blankets pulled neatly up to her chest,

hands clasped yet tense. Her hair, her face, everything seemed to be in place, normal. No wonder Meg had missed the signs. Her friend was a master. She should take notes.

"How is he?" Piper's gaze fell to the stroller but darted back down to her hands.

"He's okay. Sleeping. Finally."

Silence settled between them, descending on the room like a heavy cloud, thick and ominous. If any room needed to have sunshine pouring in, it was this one, and she cursed the designers of the building for their oversight.

"I'm sorry." Piper's voice pierced the silence, though it was barely over a whisper.

Settling into the chair in the corner—her chair—Meg pushed herself to relax, but the notion was laughable. Maybe she was a comedian after all.

"It's okay." It was far from okay, though, and she tried again. "I mean…it's fine. You're fine. It's all okay now."

A curse echoed in her head. Where was God now when all she had were words and those were eluding her?

Meg leaned forward, resting her elbows on her knees, hands clasped as she forced her gaze up. "What happened?"

"I…" Piper wouldn't meet Meg's eyes. "I couldn't do it anymore."

"It's only been two weeks. You've been a mom for two whole weeks, and you gave up?" Anger rose within her, and she couldn't stop it from escaping.

"I know, right? It's…depressing."

"Why didn't you tell me? I could have helped!"

Piper's chin lifted, her expression a mix of sorrow, fatigue, and despair. "I didn't want to let you down."

"Me? How would you—"

"You…were hurting so much. I could see it. Hell, I'm sure everyone saw it. You're not a very good actor, lady."

Meg rolled her eyes. How could she be joking right now when less than twenty-four hours ago she'd been dying?

Piper continued: "I saw the hope you had when you saw how well I was handling everything."

"You saw that as hope? I was a hot mess, wondering why God loved you more than me, why He'd give you peace and deny me!"

"There was hope under it all, whether you knew it or not. Hope that peace was still possible."

Meg scoffed. She didn't buy it. There had been no hope in her. Only jealousy. Envy. Such ugliness.

"I needed to be that strong woman, you know? The perfect friend. The perfect mom," Piper said. "I couldn't bear to have anyone know I was none of those."

Meg's fury rose. "Well, you sure picked a hell of a way to tell us the truth."

"I wasn't trying to kill myself, you know." Her voice was barely over a whisper. How could she not have intended it? She'd downed an entire bottle of wine and who knew how many pills of what Meg still didn't know. The doctors had rattled off names Meg couldn't remember, let alone pronounce.

"But why didn't you trust me? We're best friends. Did you really think I was so self-absorbed I couldn't share the burden?"

Share the burden. She was one to talk. Like Piper, she'd been trying to hide everything to protect those around her. The parallels were eerie but not surprising. There had to be a link, some common thread, between her friend's postpartum depression and her own post-abortion trauma.

Different. Yet similar.

Her friend had needed help, someone to talk to, someone to take her to get counseling and care. Meg needed that too. But after so many years of guarding her heart and locking this pain away, could she give it a voice? If she hadn't been able to with Jon, how could she now with Charlie?

The sun had been up for nearly an hour, creeping over the Afghan mountains, but the muggy air wouldn't start to warm for at least a few more hours. Thank God for body armor to help keep warm. Having thrown his gear into the Humvee, Charlie walked back to the hood to retrieve his water. The bottle was gone.

Damn Afghans.

Anything left unguarded seemed to disappear in this camp, the local security forces taking whatever they found, even though they simply had to ask to get their own. He clenched a fist and spun around, running straight into Baker, who threw his hands up.

"Woah, man. I'm a friendly." Baker laughed, but Charlie's mouth remained tight, his eyes blazing.

Baker backed away, but his expression softened. "You okay?"

"Yeah."

"Right. And Murphy isn't a pain in my ass." He rolled his eyes.

Charlie dropped his shoulders with a sigh. "It's nothin'. Really."

"Okay. Okay. Whatever you say." Baker spit into the dust. "But don't let that nothin' get into your head too much today. We need you with us. All of you."

Charlie watched Baker head to the other side of the truck to load up. His buddy was right. He needed his head clear, but he was at a loss on how to achieve that.

Others managed this, to be both soldier and husband.

Fathers too. What was broken in him that made it so difficult? His ability to compartmentalize had abandoned him.

Meg's email flashed in his mind. No text, just a picture—the two of them on the Charles Bridge in Prague. The subject line was: "Remember." He shook his head. He'd been wrong on that bridge. They couldn't survive everything.

He slid into the driver's seat and heard Murphy climbing into the back. His head appeared over Charlie's shoulder.

"No letter to send this morning? No phone call to make?"

Shut the hell up.

He kept the thought to himself, pushing himself to do whatever he needed to get through the day, the mission, and the rest of the damn deployment. "Nah. I already called your mom, so..."

Murphy groaned, a curse slipping out under his breath as he retreated up into the turret.

"You walked right into that one," Baker said, slamming his door shut.

Out of habit, Charlie moved to place Meg's picture and the psalm on the dash, but he stopped. Her smile wouldn't help, not today. He needed to focus, and all he saw in her eyes were the excuses she made and the secrets she kept.

He slipped her picture back into his pocket and started the engine, ignoring Baker's eyes on him.

Get it out of your head. Do the job. Get through the mission.

Baker continued to stare, and Charlie steeled himself. He could do this.

"Let's get going. Sooner we leave, sooner we get home," Baker said, shifting his gaze to the gate ahead of them.

Charlie relaxed. "And the sooner I can chat with Murphy's mom."

Murphy groaned into the comms over Baker's laughter as they followed the convoy outside the wire.

Meg trudged through the dining room, removing her boots as she went and leaving them in a muddy, wet pile in the middle of the floor. She shoved a chair out of the way, sending it banging into the edge of the table. What was another dent?

She needed coffee. Yes, coffee would help. Beer would be better.

She shook her head. No. Charlie had been right, even if he hadn't said it directly. He hadn't needed to. She'd been drinking too much.

You don't want to go down that path, Meg. You know how that ends up.

Opening the cabinet, she searched for her favorite mug, the black one with Katie Luther's portrait, but it wasn't there. A swear crossed her mind as she glanced over to the sink, which was overflowing with dishes she'd been meaning to clean for the past week. The mug was in there, trapped.

Meg settled for a plain white mug, its insides showing the faint stains from years of coffee and spoons being dragged along its walls. She reached for the carafe and cursed again. It was empty.

Her fingers tightened around the handle. *Don't do it. Don't slam it down.* Broken glass wouldn't help anybody. It certainly wouldn't make getting coffee any easier or quicker.

There's always the coffee shop in town.

She cringed. The last thing she wanted to deal with was people, and even a drive-thru required some interaction.

With sharp movements she went to work brewing the coffee, banging cabinets closed and slamming the coffee maker shut before punching the brew button as hard as she could. As if any of this would help ease the bitterness.

Resting her hands on the counter, she pressed her fingers hard against the granite. *Brew faster, damn it.*

Why are you getting angry at the coffee pot? It's working as fast as it can. Be patient.

She drew in a breath and pushed it past her chest and into her belly, hoping to calm her nerves. They wouldn't listen. Charlie hadn't called. Piper was in the hospital. Life was royally screwed up.

God? You said you'd never leave me, so why does it feel like you have?

No answer. There was never an answer. Prayers never brought comfort or healing. What was the point?

The coffee pot was still gurgling and churning when she pulled the carafe out and filled the mug. She lifted it to her face, breathing in the rich aroma. She'd made it too strong this time. Strong was good though. Maybe it could strengthen her.

She blew over the edge of the cup and was preparing herself for that first scalding sip when the doorbell rang.

Meg froze. Her mind jumped from one tragic thought to another. Charlie was dead. Piper had hurt herself again. The baby… It could be anything.

She waited. Maybe if she didn't answer, whatever tragedy was knocking on her door would go away, cease to exist.

The doorbell rang again, longer this time and followed by a knock.

Slamming the mug down and ignoring the resulting splash of coffee across the counter, she glided to the window and pulled the curtain back enough to reveal the SUV parked behind her Jeep.

Oh, no. Not again.

Meg pulled a breath in and held it. 1…2…3…4… *You can do this.* She exhaled. 5…6…7…8… *She's trying to help.* She inhaled one more time. 9…10… Exhaled. *Be nice.*

With a quick glance in the mirror to ensure she looked semi-put together, she opened the door with a half-smile—as much as her face could afford. The old woman, with her bright purple scarf hanging loosely around her neck and down the front of her coat, stood on her porch holding a bright red quilted paisley-print casserole cover, presumably with a casserole inside.

"Mrs. Goetz, what are you doing here?" She should have softened the words, but she lacked the energy to care how the old bird took it.

"Elizabeth. Call me Elizabeth," the woman corrected, pushing a smile across her thin lips.

"Sorry, Mrs. Goetz. Just how I was raised." It wasn't, but the old lady didn't need to know that. Meg straightened and lifted her chin. She was being rude, and it felt good. Charlie would have chided her, urged her to settle down, but he wasn't here.

Mrs. Goetz shifted her weight and lifted the casserole dish. "I know you've had a rough go of it lately, and I saw you slip out of church the other day as if you had somewhere more important to be."

Meg fisted a hand at the sharpness in the woman's tone.

"We thought you could use a hand maybe. Or at least a meal." Of course. A meal. Because Meg wasn't capable of preparing food herself.

She's only trying to be nice. Why are you getting so mad?

"Thank you," Meg said, but she didn't move, neither accepting the casserole nor inviting the lady in.

Mrs. Goetz dropped her gaze, shifting her eyes along the floor before lifting them up and over Meg's shoulder, no doubt seeing the mess of clothes on the couch and the pile of dishes and mail on the end table. Meg moved to block her view until the woman's eyes met her own.

"Here." Mrs. Goetz lifted the casserole, pushing it closer to Meg. "It's not much, just my famous chicken enchiladas, but…I hope it helps."

Meg took the casserole. "Thank you again." She should say more, express more gratitude or invite the woman inside for some coffee, but her mouth clamped shut, unwilling to say more than necessary.

"Okay then. Well, I will get going. You can bring me the carrier and dish at church this weekend. Okay?"

"Sure." The word came out short and sharp. Meg's jaw clenched.

You're being ridiculous, like a bratty kid.

But she couldn't find the strength to be kind. She was too tired to hold the mask in place any longer. It had fallen away, revealing the rude and disrespectful person underneath.

Without another word, Mrs. Goetz turned and ambled down the steps, across the path, and into her car. Meg didn't bother to watch her drive off. With a slam of the door, she rushed to put the casserole—carrier and all—into the fridge.

She turned back to the counter, itching for the coffee she'd made and abandoned, but the sight of her kitchen stopped her.

Dishes were piled high. Envelopes and receipts littered every flat surface that wasn't already occupied by crumbs, smeared butter, or spilled coffee. Her arms tensed until they shook, her fists tight.

She'd let life get away from her. She didn't even have kids to worry about, and she couldn't keep her house in order. No wonder God had denied her children. She was unworthy, incapable. A failure undeserving of motherhood.

You don't believe that.

Don't I?

She leaned back against the fridge, her body dragging the magnets down with her as she slid to the floor. Hugging her knees to her chin, she pressed her fists against her mouth, eyes clenched to keep the tears from pouring out.

God, I could really use you right now. Even more than a beer or coffee. Please. Come back.

22

Piper shifted, watching the morning light pour in across her legs from the window beside her. Sunshine was good for one's health, and she certainly needed whatever healing she could get.

The loose floorboard in the hallway creaked under light footsteps. The bedroom door opened, and Meg peeked her head in. Piper looked up, raising a brow at her friend.

Meg approached with two cups of coffee and offered one—the smaller one—to Piper.

"Thanks," Piper said, cradling the cup in her hands and taking a shallow sip. Not too hot. Not too cold. Perfect.

"Your mom took Logan to the park," Meg said. "I hope she knows he's too little to really *play* at the park."

"You really don't have to stay." Piper dropped her gaze, letting her eyes skirt across the floor before turning to the scene outside the window. Trees were starting to bud, and the crab apples and dogwoods would be in bloom before long. Such promise and hope on display, a sign that life kept going.

"I'm here. You're stuck with me."

Piper turned toward her, but there was no humor in her friend's face, despite her words. "You still mad at me?"

Meg pulled the ottoman up and clasped her hands in her lap. "I was never mad…"

"Could've fooled me." Piper locked eyes with Meg for a second before pulling her gaze back to the mug in her hand.

"Okay, maybe a little mad. But at myself more than anything."

"So this is a case of 'it's not you, it's me'?" The corners of Piper's lips curled up, but she continued to stare into her lap.

"I guess you could say that. I should have known. I should have noticed."

Piper dropped her head to one side and glanced at her friend, who was rubbing a hand between her neck and her shoulder as if she could ease away the tension in the room as easily as from a sore muscle.

"I don't know if there was any way for you to know. I didn't even know."

Meg stiffened, her head pulling back slightly.

Piper traced the rim of the mug with her finger as she spoke. "I know it sounds crazy—no pun intended—but I thought I could handle it. I'd read about baby blues. Figured that was all it was, that it would go away on its own after a couple weeks."

"Didn't your doctor tell you what to look out for?"

"Yeah, of course, but… You know, I did call their office last week. I couldn't stop crying. He wouldn't stop crying. I called them to find out what to do, but I had to leave a message with the nurses line. By the time they called me back, it had passed."

"And they didn't want you to come in?" Meg's forehead creased.

Piper shrugged. "No. They asked me if I was wanting to hurt myself or the baby. I said no, because at that moment I didn't—and I really hadn't wanted to. I must have sounded too okay when they called, because they told me they'd see me at my six-week checkup."

Meg's mouth dropped open. "What the heck?"

"Well, I guess I showed them." Piper laughed and stole a glance at Meg.

"It's not funny, Piper! There's nothing funny about this at all."

Piper held Meg's stare. Her lip was on the verge of quivering as she spoke. "If I don't laugh—if I don't try to see humor somewhere—I might not survive this."

Meg's expression went blank, as if Piper had been speaking a foreign language.

"So, enough about me…" Piper said, and Meg groaned. "You ever work through your own baggage?"

Meg shifted, moved a leg underneath her, and then removed it again. She clasped her hands but then released them.

Piper laughed again. "I take that as a no?"

"Not yet, no."

"What are you waiting for exactly?" Piper's eyes narrowed, and Meg shrunk back into her chair.

"I thought I could handle it on my own?" She looked past Piper, probably focused on the budding trees in the yard.

"Where have I heard that before? Oh, right."

"I don't know how. I haven't talked about this with anyone. Not you, not my pastor, not Jon."

"And not Charlie."

Meg looked down in her lap, her voice barely over a whisper. "No. Not even Charlie."

"How's he handling that?"

"About as well as I am, I think."

"So, he's running away?"

Meg shrunk further into herself, dropping her head into her hands. She sighed. "Maybe? I don't know. He hasn't called in days. We had a fight, and I didn't handle it well. I pushed him away, and the last thing he said was 'goodbye.'"

"People do tend to say that before they hang up, you know." A joke might backfire, but maybe Meg needed some humor too, in order to survive.

"But it wasn't the standard *see ya later* type of goodbye." Meg pulled her chin up, the tears brimming along the edges of her eyes.

"Meg." Piper set her mug on the windowsill and pulled Meg's hands into her own. "God gave you Charlie. Trust that."

"But what if God's not—real?" She choked on her sobs, her eyes clenched shut.

"Oh, hon." Piper pulled her closer and wrapped her arms around Meg's shoulders. Hadn't it only been a few months earlier that Meg had been the one offering comfort?

Meg relaxed. "I don't feel Him anymore. Not in His Word. Not in my prayers. I feel so lost. So abandoned. Alone."

Piper said nothing as she held Meg, rocking her as she would her baby.

"Why did He let Jon die? Was it punishment for my…"

Piper interrupted, pulling back so she could look Meg in the eyes. "No. No, it's not punishment for anything you've done. I think you know that too. You know God's Word. Remember Job? Bad things happen. Life is hard. Life in faith especially. That doesn't mean God's abandoned us. He promises us peace, but not on our terms or in our time."

"But I want it now!" Meg cringed.

Piper stifled a chuckle, pushing back a joke. God probably wasn't encouraging childish pouting when He spoke of a child-like faith.

"I know you do. I want you to have it now too. But maybe you have more to learn here?"

Meg sat back.

"You need to talk to Charlie, hon."

"But what if it's too late? What if it doesn't help?"

Piper laid a hand on Meg's knee, hoping her friend could hear the love in her words. "Trust the Lord, Meg. He's put Charlie in your life. Give him the chance to be your husband."

Charlie rubbed the exhaustion from his eyes as he maneuvered the Humvee into the village. Second day. Second village. Hopefully the mission would continue as the first day had: quiet, uneventful.

While the officers met with the village elders, seeking to make connections and build relationships with the locals, Charlie and the other enlisted guys waited, manning the radio and trying to ignore the incessant demands from the Afghans wanting this, that, and everything in-between.

"Hey, man, my turn on watch," Murphy said.

Charlie shifted his weight under the body armor but didn't say anything. He walked away, ignoring Murphy's laughter behind him, not sure what the guy had said. He didn't care.

Near the far edge of the small village, he settled onto a rock overlooking the expanse of hills and brush stretching before him. He loved this job—or at least he used to. God knew this wasn't what he wanted to be doing, driving a truck when his training made him capable of so much more.

Why the hell am I here?

He threw the words high above him but kept his eyes forward, scanning the area. A movement in his periphery snapped his head to the left.

A bird.

It was good to be a bit jumpy—no, aware. Jumpy led to stupid accidents.

Boots in the sand and dirt sounded behind him, but he didn't turn.

"Remind you of home?" Baker said as he came up beside him.

"What?"

He gestured to the view with his M4. "This. Doesn't it remind you of home?"

Charlie shrugged. He wished it were Woods here. He'd always known when Charlie needed quiet…and when he didn't.

"I could go for a decent burger though. And a beer."

The small talk grated on Charlie. Maybe if he didn't respond, the guy would walk away and leave him alone.

"A good IPA or a Belgian tripel. Hell, at this point I might even go for a Bud Light without complaint."

Charlie kept his eyes forward, thankful his buddy couldn't see them rolling with irritation behind his shades.

"Dude…"

If Baker said one more thing about beer or home or food or the weather, Charlie was going to lose it. He clenched his teeth and gripped his rifle tighter, feeling his resolve melting away in the Afghan air, his patience thinning.

"…it's going to be okay."

Charlie turned. "What?"

Baker didn't look at him, eying the area around them instead.

"It's going to be okay," he repeated. "Whatever's going on back home, I mean. Don't sweat it."

The guy had no idea. He didn't know what he was talking about.

"I assume it has to do with your wife?"

Okay, maybe he did know. "How'd you guess?"

"Been there. Only one thing that distracts a soldier quite like this—women."

Charlie cleared his throat. It wasn't that he had anything to say, but he couldn't bear the silence.

"Jen cheated on me last time." Baker's voice fell flat, matter-of-fact.

"I'm sorry." He meant it to be genuine, but he had no idea if he'd pulled it off or not.

"Not looking for sympathy. Just sayin'. I found out about it a couple months before getting home. Called her up, and the dude answered the phone."

Charlie looked at his buddy. "But aren't you guys still married?"

"Yeah. That's my point. It sucked. Worst situation a man can face, maybe, knowing his wife is betraying him while he's halfway around the world. Planned to leave her or make her pay. But, I dunno. Couldn't do it. Counseling helped. Point is, it turned out okay."

So it had worked out for Baker. Didn't mean it would for Charlie.

Still, maybe the guy had wisdom to share. "How'd you get through the last months of the deployment?"

"I used it. All that energy I had being pissed about the mess at home? I channeled it. It's all you can do. Otherwise it eats you up, distracts you, and gets people hurt—or worse."

It was one thing to channel anger, but Charlie had more than anger flowing through him. How did you use doubt to your advantage? How could the crippling sense of failure help him serve his team?

"I..." he started but wasn't sure where his mind was trying to take him.

"I know," Baker said. "Easier said than done. I don't know what she did to you..."

Charlie cringed. Even with the pain he felt, he bristled at the sound of someone else blaming Meg, accusing her of intentionally hurting him.

"...and I don't want to know. My advice? Don't decide the future of your marriage here. This place messes with your head. All you have to decide right now is whether you're going to let it cripple you."

"Cripple" seemed an adequate description. Meg needed him. And what had he done? He'd pushed her. Failed. He'd backed off. Failed again. He'd prayed. And that had failed too. Or at least it hadn't worked yet.

"I can see I helped." Baker laughed and turned back to the village. "Looks like they're wrappin' up. See ya back in the truck."

With a nod, Charlie stood and stretched his back, working the kinks from between his shoulders. Baker was right. These hills were like home but with the bonus of angry locals trying to kill them.

Whatever was haunting his wife wasn't about him. It was keeping her from church, separating her from God and His Word. And here he was nursing his own bruised ego, pissed off that she couldn't open up to him, taking it personally that she wouldn't be honest.

Baker might have been right about a lot of things, but Charlie had already made up his mind. This war had cost them so much already. He wasn't going to let it take his marriage too.

Whatever it took, he was all in.

The heavy spring rain pounded against the windshield, poking holes in Meg's resolve with each drop against the glass. She swallowed. How long had she been avoiding this? Ten years? At least.

The cross looming ahead of her—blurred by the evening thunderstorm—felt ominous. There was hope there. Some part of her still knew that. It was why she was here.

Charlie still hadn't called, and it took every ounce of her

strength not to assume the worst. He was only angry, frustrated, but he was okay. He'd be okay. They'd be okay.

In a way, she was glad he hadn't called. A blessing in disguise. She needed to talk to him and trust him, but not yet. A small piece of her remained cloaked in shame and regret so thick that she wasn't sure she could climb out from under it, even with Charlie there to help.

But she didn't need to tell him yet in order to trust him. She could listen to him and take his advice. Finally.

The parking lot was empty save her car and Pastor Feld's truck. He wasn't expecting her. She should have called. But all her attempts to dial his number had ended with her chickening out. She figured the worst case was she'd sit here until he left to go home. She could leave it to him to initiate the conversation.

As much as the anxiety crawled across her chest, she felt a strength pushing up from underneath it. She'd spent too long letting this sin control her. Even from the darkest corners of her mind, where she thought she'd hidden it well enough, she now recognized that it had been bearing down on her secretly, tainting everything she touched. It had held that power over her for too long.

Christ had forgiven her, hadn't He? But she needed to hear it—not simply the echo in her own head.

Maybe it won't work. It might not bring peace.

She shook her head at the thought. Whether it brought her any comfort and peace or not, she owed it to Charlie to honor his advice to do this and seek out her pastor.

Her resolve strengthened, and she reached for the door handle, pushing the Jeep's door open into the rain. Despite the heavy, large drops falling all around her, she walked steadily to the church.

She reached the door and pulled. It didn't budge. Locked. She peered in through the window but only saw darkness. The light in Pastor Feld's office was dark. Where was he?

Her heart crashed to her feet, and she could almost hear it splash in the puddles of water on the sidewalk. As she turned to head back to her Jeep, she heard the door open.

"Meg? Come in! Let's get you out of the rain." Pastor Feld reached a hand out to her while holding the door with the other.

As she looked at the kind face of her pastor, she wondered why she'd been so scared to face him. All her fears vanished as she took in the warmth of both his smile and the heat inside the building. She hadn't realized how chilled she'd gotten walking through the cold rain.

"What can I do for you?" he asked.

She cleared her throat and swallowed hard. Her eyes wanted to fall to her feet, but she forced them to make contact with his. "I know you're busy, and it's Friday night, and you want to get home. But—I could use private confession..."

"And absolution." His lips pulled back, his expression understanding and gracious—none of the disdain she'd feared. "Of course, Meg. Let's head down to the sanctuary."

Kneeling at the chancel railing, Meg wrung her hands over the hymnal in front of her.

This was it. All those years that she had encouraged others, including Charlie, to seek out the comfort of private confession and absolution slammed into her. Fear had always kept her from doing it herself, but it was time.

Time to face the past.

She kept her gaze down, focusing on the words under her hands, thankful she had a starting place and wouldn't need to come up with what to say. Not that she'd have to say anything more than the words on this page. Pastor Feld had assured her she was free to recite the printed text of confession, but she would have the chance to speak her own as well.

She heard her pastor exit the vestry and waited for him to sit in the chair on the other side of the railing.

She swallowed. She'd memorized the first line of the rite, so she could close her eyes, but her voice cracked, her nerves stealing the confidence she'd hoped for.

Pastor Feld didn't seem to notice or mind.

She opened her eyes. The written words came into focus, and she read. She made it through the provided text with ease, or as much ease as she could, but the anticipation of the next step brought the tears near the surface.

She took a deep breath, steadying herself. *You can do this!*

"In particular, I confess before you that I…" Did she have the words? She'd rehearsed them in her head on the drive over, but now they vanished.

Lord, give me the words! Give me the strength to utter them before You!

Her voice returned, and though it broke around the tears she could no longer hold back, the words came out clear and strong, determined.

"I killed my baby. More than ten years ago, I had my own child killed. I had gotten pregnant from a one-night stand. Didn't know the father. Still don't know his name. I never told anyone except my mom. I let her pressure me into doing it, let her convince me it was for the best. But I—I murdered my baby, and I can never take that back or fix it or make it right."

She sighed, her shoulder falling an inch before the tension returned. The hardest part might be over, but she wasn't done yet.

"And I haven't loved my husband as I should."

It seemed so trite compared to her first confession, but she continued.

"I haven't trusted Charlie to guide me and to love me. I've pushed him away, kept him at a safe distance, and now I don't know if he'll forgive me. I'm afraid it's too late to fix it. I've broken his trust, betrayed him. And I've put him in danger. I've distracted him because I refused to listen and get help when he urged me to."

Her voice trailed off. She searched the threads in the carpet before her, as if she could find more sins to confess buried within the tight weave.

Don't search for sins. Confession is meant to be comforting, not torture.

She lowered her eyes to her hands and the text beneath them and read the final sentence. "For all this I am sorry and… and pray for grace. I want to do better."

Pastor Feld's clear voice answered her. "God be merciful to thee and strengthen thy faith."

She whispered, "Amen."

"Do you believe my forgiveness is God's forgiveness?"

"Yes." Her voice found strength again, and she drew in another breath.

"As you believe, so be it done for you." Pastor stood and placed his hand on her head with such gentleness that she wondered why she had been avoiding this for so long.

His voice cut through her thoughts: "In the stead and by the command of my Lord Jesus Christ, I forgive you all of your sins in the name of the Father and of the Son and of the Holy Spirit. Go in peace."

He made the sign of the cross over her, and she whispered her amen.

Pastor Feld said quietly, "You're welcome to stay, Meg, as long as you need."

She nodded, keeping her eyes on the wood of the altar floor as Pastor backed away to return to the vestry.

Meg thumbed through the hymnal to the Psalms, sure of the one she wanted to read and pray.

Blessed is the one whose transgression is forgiven,
whose sin is covered.

Blessed is the man against whom the Lord counts no iniquity,
and in whose spirit there is no deceit.
For when I kept silent, my bones wasted away
through my groaning all day long.
For day and night your hand was heavy upon me;
my strength was dried up as by the heat of summer.
I acknowledged my sin to you,
and I did not cover my iniquity;
I said, "I will confess my transgressions to the Lord,"
and you forgave the iniquity of my sin.

She raised her eyes to the crucifix above the altar and took in the image of her Lord and God on the cross, taking her place, paying the price for her sins.

The doubt had plagued her, told her He wasn't real and hadn't forgiven her. But here she had heard the words of God's forgiveness spoken to her, and her alone, in response to her sins no longer hidden in shame and guilt.

She was free.

Thanks be to God.

23

The Humvee bounded down the dirt road, following the two in front. The team was quiet now, the tension stifling. Something about this return back to Camp Foster had them all on edge. Charlie felt it, assumed the others did too, but he couldn't pinpoint why. From the corner of his eye he saw Meg's picture on the dash, her smile shining back at him. His reason to get home. They were coming up on an area known for being dangerous. The last several convoys had all been hit here, yet command didn't seem to worry or care.

Returning to Camp Foster meant returning through a handful of small villages. Each one posed a potential threat, but this had been their normal with each mission.

The tension eased in the first village with the steady flow of children approaching the convoy. Baker eased, made jokes with some of the kids, and tossed them some candy his wife had sent him in her last care package. The kids loved this. It was why they swarmed the trucks, looking for a handout.

"Am I the only one who always expects one of those kids to be strapped with explosives and used by the Taliban?" Murphy said.

"Well, if I hadn't thought about it before, I sure as hell will now," Baker said, tossing another piece of candy to the last of the kids before they ran off back to the village center, bartering with each other over the goods they'd gotten.

Charlie kept his eyes on the road ahead, watching the trucks in front of him pass the last of the low mud walls. The normalcy of the last village had calmed their nerves, but he didn't want to let his guard down yet. They still had another fifty kilometers to go before they'd be back at camp, where he could finally get some decent sleep and call Meg.

Baker kept his eyes scanning to the front and right as they creeped past the open fields. "I don't like this," he said.

"What? What d'ya see?" Charlie asked, trying to see where Baker was looking, but the guy's eyes weren't focusing on anything in particular.

"Nothing—yet. Just a feeling."

"So paranoid, man," Murphy said.

"Whatever. Just keep your eyes open and your hand on that 240."

"Roger that, Jack. I'll never let go."

Baker groaned, and Charlie burst out laughing. Poor Baker would never escape that.

Before Charlie's laugh had died down, a *crack* cut through the air—an AK-47 round from the east, on the passenger side.

"D'ya see it? Where'd it come from?" Baker called to Murphy.

"That low wall. Three o'clock." He racked back the M240 Bravo and let loose on the target.

Tat-ta-tat-ta-tat-tat-tat.

The convoy continued to move, and Charlie focused on staying with the truck in front of them. Losing contact with truck two would mean certain death—or capture and then death.

The rev of a smaller engine coming up on his left pulled his attention to the side mirror. A motorcycle was approaching, fast. Two Taliban with AKs ready.

"Murphy. Eight o'clock!" he called.

Murphy let out a loud curse and swung the machine gun around, but he narrowly missed them.

Crack. Crack, crack.

The AK rounds hit the side of the Humvee, but the armor did its job and protected the men inside. Before Murphy could get a shot off on them, the motorcycle had veered off and was headed through the field to the west.

"Those shoot-and-scoot bastards. I swear," Baker said, returning his attention back to his own window. They'd managed to get past that without incident, but the Taliban were experts at running off and regrouping farther down the road.

This wasn't over yet.

He stole a glance again down to Meg's picture. God wasn't going to make it easy to get back to her, was He? God's will be done though.

Hope His will includes keeping me alive.

Meg guided the Jeep down the driveway and onto the gravel road, the overcast skies making it seem earlier than it was, as if the sun hadn't been up for several hours already. The rain, having poured all night, seemed almost to be running low on water as it quieted to a soft drizzle against the windshield.

Despite the chill in the spring air, she had the window down, and she kept her speed low to limit the wind streaming into the car. The smell of the pines wrapped around her. She'd never tire of this scent. It made the long drive to town worth it.

She dropped her gaze to the phone in her lap. Charlie

would have snagged it, reminding her of the dangers of texting and driving. But he wasn't here. He still hadn't called.

He was probably on a mission, but then wouldn't he have told her that was the case? Maybe he had, and she couldn't remember. The week had been a bit hectic, so she had a decent excuse for forgetting.

Lord, keep him safe. Wherever he is.

She could live with him not forgiving her, could even bear him leaving her if that's what he chose. But if he didn't come home at all?

She shook her head to push the thought away.

The Jeep pulled up beside the curb in front of Piper's house. Thank God for muscle memory or she'd never make it anywhere with all these thoughts and worries distracting her.

The door opened before Meg had reached the top step. She ignored the discomfort of knowing someone had watched her arrive and walk up the sidewalk. It wasn't creepy. It was flattering. Maybe.

Piper shot her a half-smile. "Hey, lady. You're late."

"No, I'm not. Am I?" She looked at her watch as she stepped inside. "It's not even nine yet."

Piper shut the door behind her. "Except you said you'd be here at eight."

Meg's mouth dropped open, her eyes flitting around the room. Had she said eight? She pulled her mouth down into an embarrassed frown. "Oops."

Piper let out a single snort. "I guess it's true. Couples do start to resemble each other after so many years."

The words stung, and Meg recoiled.

"Oh, crap. Sorry." Piper shifted her weight and grimaced. "He still hasn't called?"

Meg shook her head. "Do you have coffee?"

"Well, that's a dumb question." Piper ambled down the hall, motioning with a nod for Meg to follow.

Settling onto a stool, Meg propped her elbows on the counter and rested her chin against her fists. "Where's Logan?"

"Out with my mom. She took him to the grocery. Said something about needing more than coffee alone to survive."

"Crazy woman." Meg chuckled as she accepted the mug from Piper, the words *"Jesus Saves"* staring back at her from the white ceramic. Indeed He did.

"I know, right?" Piper rested her hips against the sink and cradled her own mug in her hands, her fingers covering up most of the light-blue letters. But Meg didn't need to see the words to read them.

A friend loves at all times.

She'd given Piper that mug as a gift the first Christmas they'd spent together as friends. After so many years of feeling alone, like she'd never have that elusive best friend everyone always posted about on social media, she'd met Piper. They were an unlikely pair, so much like Charlie and Aaron.

How was Charlie handling everything? In all the turmoil of the past month, had she really forgotten to check in on him, to ask him how he was doing, to really be there for him?

The ache settled in her chest. All this time, she'd been so selfish, so wrapped up in her own past. And now she might have missed her chance to make it right.

No, he would at least give her the opportunity. She just needed to not screw it up.

"Yo, lady. Did you hear me?" Piper's face leaned toward the counter to push its way into Meg's line of sight.

"Huh? What?" Meg blinked, her gaze locking with Piper's.

Piper laughed. "I asked if Charlie had called, but you were apparently off in la-la land."

"Oh, crap. Yeah. I mean, no. He hasn't."

"So still no chance to talk?"

"No. I sent him an email."

Piper pulled her chin back. "You can't do that in an email…"

"I know. I didn't actually write anything…"

"Don't tell me you sent risqué pictures of yourself. I'm sure they have people checking their emails and stuff. You don't want some private somewhere gawking over those." Piper shuddered and laughed.

"No! What? Of course not. It was a picture of a bridge."

Piper wrinkled her nose as she raised a brow. "A bridge?"

Meg groaned. "Yeah, a special bridge. Whatever. It means something to him—to us."

"I hope so, because otherwise that's plain weird."

Meg took a long sip from the mug, the coffee having cooled down enough to make it drinkable without scalding her tongue. "I hope he still cares." She lowered her eyes to the counter. Her lip started to quiver.

"He does, Meg. You know he does."

"But what if he leaves me? What if I've completely screwed it up?" The tears were rising quickly, and she hated it. Her friend had just been in the hospital for a possible suicide attempt, and here she was crying about her own problems. She glanced across at Piper, her eyes falling to the mug, reading it again.

A friend loves at all times.

Piper's hand reached for hers and held tight. "Hon, have a little faith. Pray."

Meg drew in a deep breath, pulling her gaze back to the coffee in front of her. "Would you pray with me?"

"Of course, friend. You want a pre-written one? Or can I wing it?"

She raised her chin and gave the best half-smile she could muster. "Either way works."

Piper closed her eyes, and Meg did the same, wondering how the unscripted prayer would sound.

"Our soul waits for the Lord," Piper said.

Meg looked up at the familiar words of the psalm, but Piper's eyes remained closed as she spoke.

"He is our help and our shield. For our heart is glad in Him, because we trust in His holy name."

She bowed her head again, reciting the prayer silently as her friend spoke the words.

"Let Your steadfast love, O Lord, be upon us, even as we hope in You."

Meg squeezed Piper's hand as they spoke the amen in unison.

God had given her such a friend, a better friend than she deserved. He would certainly see her through whatever lay ahead.

Charlie's shoulders ached under the tension that filled the Humvee. The last stretch of road had been quiet, but it had left a cloud hanging over the convoy. The other boot was going to drop. And right on them most likely.

"I don't like this," Baker said.

"You don't have to like it," Charlie said. "You just have to survive it."

Please, Lord, let us survive this.

The low mud walls of a compound greeted them as they approached the next small village. The contrast to the previous one they'd passed through was palpable, the stillness tightening the knots in Charlie's stomach. Stillness in a village was never a good sign.

The lack of children, livestock, women... He'd been on enough of these missions to know it never meant good things.

Baker let out a low curse beside him, no doubt having the same reaction to what they were driving into.

The convoy crawled through the village. Low buildings and mud walls lined the narrow strip of road.

"See anything?" Charlie asked.

"Negative," Murphy said.

"I don't like it," Baker repeated. He gripped his M4, ready to roll if they got stopped and needed to dismount.

Charlie wanted to pray. All he had was a string of expletives and swears, but he was sure God would understand his language given the situation. He kept the truck moving, not breaking contact with the Humvees ahead.

Baker's attention snapped from building to building, searching for any sign of movement in the alleys or on the rooftops.

What were they waiting for? There was no doubt the Taliban had been operating here. At this time of day, there should have been kids everywhere. But nothing. A ghost town. Full of ghosts aiming to kill them.

As they passed the last of the low buildings, maneuvering their vehicles out into the open, the tension in his gut worsened.

That was too easy. I don't like this.

BOOM!

The ground shook under his feet. The sound rattled every bone in his body. Time slowed. The convoy stopped.

Images rushed through his mind. IEDs did enough damage to vehicles and bodies, but that hadn't been an IED. Too big.

"What the hell!" Murphy screamed, letting out a string of curses.

"Anti-tank mine," Baker said, his voice calm. Was this really the guy who'd completely lost it a couple of months ago? Tragedy changed everyone in different ways though.

"Yeah, no kidding," Murphy said. "Who'd they hit?"

"I don't know," Charlie said. He tried to listen to the radio chatter, but it was a mess of confusion.

Murphy let out another curse, likely scanning the area, moving the machine gun in search of an enemy to unleash his anger on.

"Who's hit? Do we even know who hit that mine?" Murphy asked again. "Was it ours?"

"Negative," Charlie said as he listened to the radio.

"Did they say goats?" Baker asked.

"They've recruited goats now?" Murphy asked.

"I don't know if the goat planned to be a martyr, dumbass," Baker said.

Murphy ignored the insult. "He's really screwed us now though."

Baker looked at Charlie. "We've gotta get out of here."

Baker keyed the mic. "Trojan 1, this is Trojan 3. Are we moving or what? Over?"

"Trojan 3, Trojan 1. Negative. Negative. Sit tight. Secondary IEDs and mines ahead."

This isn't good at all.

Crack, crack, crack.

AK rounds seemed to come from all sides. How they hadn't gotten hit yet he didn't know. The enemy had set up a crossfire ambush, with their fighters planted behind the low compound walls some one hundred fifty to two hundred meters from either side of the road.

Kschumm-BOOM!

The unmistakable sound of an RPG had come from Charlie's left, but it had missed its target, hitting near his front wheel. It sent a cloud of dust and sand into the air, blocking his view. Chaos and confusion swirled around him, keeping him from hearing the words streaming over the comms.

I don't like it. We need to move.

But there was nowhere to go.

The M240 machine gun fire from Murphy in the turret

added to the combat symphony, mixing with the shouts among his team.

"Where are they? Where are they?" Baker asked.

"Gah! They're everywhere," Murphy said and cursed again. "I'm out."

"We're sitting ducks here," Baker said, turning to Charlie while Murphy reloaded.

"We need to move," Charlie said. He tried to listen to the radio chatter, but with Murphy done reloading and firing again, he couldn't make out much.

Then some good news came through. He turned to Baker. "QRF's coming."

"ETA?" Baker asked.

"One hour. Maybe more?"

Murphy yelled a curse as the 240 jammed. He got it cleared and reset and swung it around.

Tat-ta-tat-tat-tat-ta-tat-tat.

Another curse came from the turret, but this time in celebration. "He's down."

"What was that?" Baker said.

"RPG. Behind us. Down now, though."

Despite the small victory, the incoming fire wouldn't let up. They were stuck. Baker had been right. Sitting ducks.

"There! There! Up there on the wall!" Baker yelled to Murphy.

"What? Where?"

Baker let out a curse. "Swing around. Two o'clock. Two. They're right there on that wall!"

Boom!

Another RPG hit behind them.

"We need to move!" Murphy said between bursts.

"I'm moving!" Charlie said as he crept the Humvee a few feet forward, inching toward the vehicle in front of them, but their convoy wasn't going anywhere, not with the threat of secondary explosives in their way.

Crack, crack, crack.

Tat-tat-tat-ta-tat-tat-tat-ta-tat.

Crack.

Boom!

Murphy's machine gun fire joined the sounds of the incoming rounds. The sound, coming from all sides—even from beneath as the ground shook from the RPG impacts—had Charlie's head twisted and jumbled. He squeezed his eyes shut to recalibrate.

Get it together, man. They need you to keep it together.

When he looked up, he saw little but dust and sand filling the air, the faint outline of mud walls to their left and right.

"We're pinned down," Baker said, stealing a look at Charlie as the enemy fire continued to rain down on them.

Charlie gritted his teeth, fisting his hands around the steering wheel. He shouldn't be here, stuck in a Humvee, unable to do anything except listen and wait.

I need to get out of here.

"Where the hell is the QRF?" Baker asked. Murphy continued firing, alternating sides to keep the enemy surrounding them at bay.

"Hell if I know," Charlie said. From the corner of his eye he saw the all-too-familiar sight of smoke as an RPG was fired. This time it hit more than dirt and sand, slamming into the lead truck.

They had sat too long.

The radio chatter became a jumbled mess of calls for the medic, reporting of the wounded, and strings of expletives.

"Take him out!" Baker yelled to Murphy.

"I'm trying!"

Charlie gripped the steering wheel, his eyes locked on the truck in front of him. The medic—the teacher—had dismounted from truck two and was running ahead to check on the wounded. *Lord, help him!*

Help us!

Amid the chaos of gunfire, RPG blasts, and the throaty rumble of his own Humvee, Charlie heard something else. He turned to look behind them as another handful of Humvees approached truck four. *Finally.*

"QRF's here," he said to Baker.

His eyes fell to Meg's picture on his dash. Support was here. He would make it home. He'd be there for her, as he had promised Haas years ago.

With all his gear organized on his rack, Charlie assessed the contents of his pack to ensure he hadn't forgotten anything vital. His mind had been so lost on the task at hand that he hadn't noticed his buddy walk in. Looking up to grab some more tourniquets, he jumped at the sight of Haas.

"Holy—Gah!—What the hell? Don't you know not to sneak up on an armed man?" Charlie tried to save face.

"With your reflexes, I'm lucky to be alive." Haas laughed, but his smile soon faded. He rubbed his neck and jaw with his hand, stretching his head to the side, his face wincing.

"Not sleep well?"

"Not at all. Can't wait to get home to a real bed." Haas dropped his hand but continued to struggle against the ache in his neck.

Charlie raised an eyebrow at him. "And a real woman?"

"You know it. Just a few more weeks."

Haas sighed and looked down at the mess of gear between them. Picking up a pack of gauze, he spoke, his voice cracking.

"So, this is awkward, but..."

"Of course I'll go out with you, dude." Charlie laughed. "Not sure how we'll break it to Meg though."

He looked down again, shaking his head as he finished packing his gear.

Haas let out a chuckle, but it sounded half-hearted. "I hate asking you this, man, because..." He cursed under his breath, and Charlie looked up at him.

"What is it?"

"I don't want to burden you, but I don't know who else—"

"It's not a burden. Whatever it is." He paused, his brow raising again and a smirk appearing on his lips. "Unless you're asking me to do your mom. She's a nice lady and all, but not really my type."

Haas laughed again. "Nah, my mom's too good for you." He paused. "It's about Meg."

"What about her?" He'd spent so many years repenting for coveting her, but he'd never told Haas about the sin he carried in his heart. Did he know? Had he suspected? Charlie's heart raced, and he strained to keep his face calm.

"We're all friends, right?" Haas asked, but he didn't wait for an answer. "If anything happens to me tomorrow..."

"What? No. Don't even think about that."

"How can I not? There's something...I don't know. Bad feeling. Gut feeling. Whatever. I need to make sure that..." His voice trailed off, and his shoulders slumped as his eyes fell to the pictures along the wall.

Charlie followed his gaze to the picture of the three of them—him, Haas, and Meg—laughing at some long-lost joke.

"She's strong. You know that. I know that. But if I don't come home, she's going to need you."

Charlie raised his hands and backed away slightly. "You're not asking me to bang your wife, are you? Because that's a little creepy and weird."

Haas shook his head and chuckled again. Charlie sighed, glad his buddy appreciated his sense of humor and his need to lighten the direst of moods.

"Of course not. But—don't ditch her. It's hard enough to bear the

thought that I might not make it home to her. But she can't be alone. Her family... You know they aren't close. They won't know how to help her. Just...be there for her?"

"You got it, man. No problem. And...when we do get home, we still on for our date?" he asked, gesturing between the two of them.

Haas threw the gauze at Charlie's face. "Hell no. I've got a hotter date waiting for me."

"Incoming!"

Murphy's shout cut through Charlie's memory. He looked to his right.

Horror shot across Baker's face, snapping Charlie's head back to his left, just in time to see the RPG heading straight for him.

He had no time to think or pray before it hit.

He didn't even hear the boom of the impact.

Meg pulled the collar of her jacket up as she stepped out onto the porch. The rain had picked back up again, and she'd stupidly left her umbrella back in the Jeep.

"We still on for dinner tomorrow? My place?" Piper asked, her hand resting on the door.

She nodded. "Yeah. I'll be here. Do I need to bring anything?"

"Only you. I think my mom's got the fridge pretty well stocked now. We could survive the zombie apocalypse even."

"Let's hope that doesn't happen. Not sure I can take any more drama this year."

"And it's only March."

"Don't remind me." Meg gave Piper a final nod before turning back to the steps. "Later!"

Meg sped the whole drive home. It was still too early for Charlie to call, but she didn't want to risk missing him if he did. Plus, she needed the time to settle her thoughts and form her words before then. If she was going to tell him everything, she didn't want it to come out a jumbled, awkward mess.

The trees sped by as she pulled up the driveway, her mind sorting through all she planned to tell him. An apology had to be first, of course. But then what? Should she go right into telling him about the baby and the abortion?

She cut the engine and grabbed her purse. Opening the door, she stepped out into the rain—not bothering with the umbrella for the short distance to the door. It was only then that she saw the unfamiliar car parked in the grass beside the driveway. How had she missed seeing that when she drove up?

Noting the government plates, her eyes flashed to the front porch.

Two men waited, standing tall and formal, and Meg dropped to the ground, her knees hitting the gravel hard.

24

MEG'S HAND trembled against the soft fabric of the worn sweatshirt as she tucked the sleeves in, taking care to line up the edges of the shirt as she folded it and placed it in the bottom of the suitcase. One down. How much more to go?

Lord, help me.

Her flight didn't leave for a few hours, but the need to get this over with had taken hold. Darting to and from the closet, she retrieved tennis shoes, shirts, jeans, and a simple black dress. Where were her heels? In the back of the closet maybe. There, tucked behind an old pair of jeans she hadn't fit into since college.

She rushed back to the bed and threw the shoes with the rest of the clothes. Smoothing down her hair, she looked down at the T-shirt and jeans she'd chosen for the trip—the same ones she'd worn when he'd left. Was it appropriate attire? She couldn't remember what she'd worn the last time the military had flown her somewhere.

What would everyone think, seeing her in a faded brown T-shirt and skinny jeans, her sneakers well past their prime? Would people see a young woman in her late twenties, full of youth and life, or would that be overshadowed by the weariness she carried inside from too many years of pain and strife?

She touched her hand to the crucifix hanging at her chest and repeated her prayer again, this time adding a fervent plea.

Don't leave me.

The doorbell rang, and she glanced down at her watch. How was she late? Piper was right, she was turning into Charlie. *If nothing else, at least that piece of him will live on.*

Throwing the remaining items into the suitcase—her toiletries, a couple of books, and her phone charger—she zipped it shut with a whispered swear. She pulled the bag off the bed and rushed down the hallway as fast as she could with the luggage pressing against her thigh, forcing her to lean far to the left to counter its weight.

The door creaked open. Piper stepped into the entryway and stopped. She stifled a chuckle, her gaze dropping to the bag and back to Meg's face. "Sure you didn't forget anything?"

Meg ignored her. "Logan with your mom?" she asked, not slowing down as she dropped the suitcase at Piper's feet and grabbed her purse off the couch and her jacket off the end table.

"Yeah. I figured a screaming, colicky baby was the last thing you needed today."

Meg shrugged. "Thanks for taking me though. It means a lot."

Piper picked up the suitcase, cringing slightly as she heaved it up and over the threshold. It fell with a thud against the porch before toppling over onto its bloated front. "Hon, you saved my life—literally. Driving you to the airport is the least I can do."

As they drove through the trees, Meg's eyes focused on the span of greens and browns streaming by. Piper flipped on the radio, filling the silence with songs so they wouldn't have to speak.

Thanks be to God for good friends.

The rest of the morning blurred like the trees on the drive. The hugs and tears. The goodbyes. The promises to call when she landed. She tried to catch a nap in the terminal, but her eyes refused to close. Through the floor-to-ceiling window she looked past the runway, the planes, and the airport personnel to the grass beyond, which sloped up the gentle hills along the horizon.

The grass looked soft, but looks were deceiving. It was probably that sharp, prickly grass that caught against your skin and pushed you to put your shoes back on. But that sharpness? Sometimes it was a blessed reminder you were alive, that you could still feel something, that the numbness inside was temporary.

That's how it had been five years ago.

Meg threw her shoes off and slid her toes into the grass. Who cared if anyone thought it inappropriate behavior for a grieving widow? She could do what she wanted, and in that moment, as the pastor spoke over Jon's body, she needed her feet out of her heels.

She couldn't move otherwise. Couldn't stand. Couldn't look up. She could only move her toes among the green blades still wet with the morning dew.

The shots rang through her body. Her muscles tensed, and her heart ached with each echoing boom, hammering home that he was gone.

She half-expected to feel Jon grabbing her hand, to squeeze it as he had so many other times. She half-expected to look to her left and see him staring straight ahead with respect and honor for the dead.

But he didn't. He didn't hold her hand, because he was the one receiving the respect and honor this morning. Never again would she lean into his shoulder or breathe in the woody smell of his cologne.

She turned to her right instead and saw his best friend, Charlie. In his dress uniform he looked regal, refined. He had been there with Jon in his final moments. What pain and memories must be haunting him. Did he stay up at night as she did, wishing Jon were still here and not in the ground?

She should reach for him, grab his hand, thank him for being here, tell him it would be okay.

But her hand stayed frozen, gripping the stars and stripes of the folded flag as she moved her toes in the grass.

She pulled her eyes away from the window as the call came over the speaker. Her flight was boarding. It would all be over soon.

The bad food on the flight was improved only slightly by the strong drink she hoped would calm the tingling in her chest. At least the old guy beside her wasn't the chatty sort. Having forgotten her headphones in her haste, she was defenseless against any extroverted folks she might meet along the way.

Thankful to have gotten a seat near the front, she disembarked soon after arriving at the gate and pushed her way through the crowd toward the baggage claim.

With her bag dragging behind her, she found her driver easily, her name typed neatly on the placard.

Keep moving.

The driver flashed her a soft smile, the wrinkles of his face crinkling around his eyes as he reached for her bag and placed it gently into the trunk. He opened the rear door for her, and she climbed in, hands wringing in her lap.

Her mind—weary from the lack of sleep and the rising stress—couldn't recall the name of her destination, but the driver didn't need her assistance. He'd probably driven this route many times before.

She watched the city creep by, her eyes widening and her breath catching at the sheer beauty in every brick and tree. When they pulled up to the unassuming building, she breathed deeply, willing the tension out of her muscles so she could find the strength to stand and make this walk.

The driver opened her door and motioned for her to exit. Her foot hit the pavement harder than she intended, sending the shock through her and causing the tension to return.

Another breath. Another step.

Keep moving.

Her body gave in and let her push through. With each inch forward, she prayed, her hand gripping the crucifix and his wedding band over her heart.

Lord, have mercy.

The door opened before her, and a wave of heat hit her face, breathing warmth and life into her tired body, chilled by the unusually cool spring temperatures. Her pace quickened, but she stopped short. The luggage—it was still with the driver.

I should turn around.

But her feet wouldn't comply, instead carrying her forward. The driver would know what to do.

The young man at the doorway caught her gaze, his uniform as crisp as his posture. "Mrs. Winters?"

Her tears had eluded her until that moment, but at the sound of her name—his name—they flowed down her cheeks. She nodded, her voice caught on the lump in her throat as she brushed the tears away with her fingers.

"Right this way, ma'am."

He turned and led her through the door.

Meg turned the corner, and the sunlight streaming through the window hit her eyes. She blinked, adjusting to the brightness, searching the room.

Peering out the window, he sat, his outline sharp against the cream-colored walls. Though the light bounced off the dust in the air, clouding her vision, keeping her from seeing each detail of his face, she knew him. Charlie. Her Charlie.

Charlie lifted his head, cringing at the pain in his left leg. The meds were wearing off, but he didn't care. She was here.

Meg flew across the room and fell onto the floor beside him, her knees hitting the ground as her body slammed into his chair.

"Ow!" The sound escaped his lips, his hand reflexively dropping to his leg, though it found nothing but air. Air and pain.

Her eyes darted to his leg and back to his face. Her forehead pinched together, and she grimaced. "Sorry!"

He met her gaze and lifted his brow. His lips curved into a smile. Did she notice how skinny he had gotten or how ragged and worn he had become? Did she still see the man she'd married? The man who had promised to love her forever?

"You have nothing to apologize for, babe." Charlie reached for her, cradling her face with a light and tender touch. It had been so long, but he didn't want to scare her. He'd changed so much. Maybe she wouldn't love him now that he wasn't whole anymore.

With caution and care, she moved toward him, as if testing each movement to avoid hurting him again.

His eyes closed, tears forming behind his lids. Before he could open them again, she was holding his head in her hands and pressing her lips against his. All the months of loneliness, separation, and fear melted with their kiss.

"I'm so glad you're home," she said, her voice choking on her tears.

"Well, I'm not home yet."

"You know what I mean." Meg sighed. "At least you haven't lost your sense of humor."

"Nope. Just my leg." He pulled his mouth into a slight grin, but Meg froze, her eyes narrowing. *Maybe it was too soon to joke about it.* He grabbed her hands and held them in his lap.

"I'm still me, Meg. Hilarious…"

"Good-lookin'," she interrupted. He wouldn't argue.

"...and still always running late."

"Not this time. You actually arrived early for once."

"Not quite. With all the surgeries and rehab I'll probably get out of here after the rest of the team makes it back. Go figure."

Silence—that familiar comfortable silence—filled the space between them as he caressed the back of her hands with a thumb. Meg pulled back and looked up, her gaze tracing his face. She swallowed hard and drew in a breath. "I wanted to tell you—"

Charlie raised his hand to her cheek, his voice softer now. "No, you don't need to. I shouldn't... have given you an ultimatum. It wasn't fair."

She dropped her chin to her chest. "I went to confession."

"Yeah?" He ignored the throbbing below his knee. He could request more meds later, when they came to check his vitals for the millionth time.

Meg's chest rose and fell with another breath, but she didn't lift her chin. "I—I got pregnant when I was eighteen."

His mind whirred. Jon had never mentioned anything about a baby. When had she met Jon again? Not until she was nineteen, wasn't it?

"I didn't know the father. One-night stand my freshman year. Not my most shining moment." She sniffed back tears. Her shoulders tensed. Her hand squeezed his. "My mom, she—she convinced me to have an abortion. Told me it was the best thing for the baby. Told me it would make everything better."

She'd held onto that for over ten years. No wonder she never spoke to her mother. His gut tightened around the anger building. "But you said you had a hysterectomy."

"I did. Doctor botched the abortion. It's rare. But it happens. Needed to take everything out."

He pulled her close to him and hugged her head to his chest, running his hand over her hair. "Oh, babe. I'm so sorry."

"I'm sorry too. I should have told you. But I've never told anyone. Not Jon. Not Piper. I was so…"

"You don't need to be ashamed, Meg. We're all sinners. We stumble, and we fail, and—"

"And we're forgiven," she said, finishing his sentence, her shoulders settling as she relaxed.

Charlie kissed her head and breathed in the scent of her shampoo, faint but still there even after the hours of travel.

"We're okay?" Her voice came out in a whisper.

"Of course. Nothing can undo us. We can overcome anything."

Meg sat up, releasing her fingers from his. She pulled the necklace out from under her shirt, undid the clasp, and pulled it down into her lap. When she lifted her hands again, she reached for his.

"Anything and everything," she said, sliding the wedding band back onto his finger.

EPILOGUE

"BABE? We're going to be late!" Charlie called down the hallway.

"Coming! Do you have the keys?" Meg rounded the corner out of their bedroom, head down as she wrapped her watch around her wrist and ran straight into Charlie's chest.

"Woah there, killer. Trying to take out my other leg?" He laughed and gave her side a squeeze with his hand.

"Like I could do that kind of damage," she said with a smirk.

"You never know."

Her eyes grew wide, and her mouth gaped. "Are you calling me fat?"

"Well…" He took a step back and gave the length of her body a once-over. "Not in so many words."

With a roll of her eyes and a laugh, she went to smack him, but he was too quick for her, catching her around the midsection and lifting her off the ground.

"We're going to be late, Charlie!" she said between laughs as he tickled her.

"Well, if we're going to be late anyway…" He flashed her a

devilish smile and nodded his head back toward their bedroom.

She groaned, but she smiled at him. "You're awful."

"Awfully hot, you mean," he said.

"C'mon. We've got church. I'm not missing church because you want to get lucky."

"What?" He gave her his best innocent look.

"And after church we have Logan's birthday party. We promised Piper we'd show up early to help her set up."

"You mean you promised you'd help set up."

Charlie followed Meg to the door, but the ringing phone in her purse stopped her short. A peculiar look came across her face as she read the screen.

"What? Who is it?" Charlie asked. "Don't they know we're going to be late for church?"

Meg glanced up at him. "It's my sister."

Why was Quinn calling? When was the last time Meg had talked to her sister? Or even mentioned her? As Meg answered the call, Charlie pushed back the desire to point out how she'd shut him down because of church, which they would now definitely be late to anyway because of Quinn.

"Hello? Quinn? What's going on?" Meg paced in the entryway, her thumbnail sliding between her teeth as she spoke.

Charlie waited, trying to get some clue from Meg's face as to the nature of the call, but her expression remained blank.

He looked down at his watch and then at the prosthetic that had replaced his left leg. He'd passed all the boards and evaluations and had been cleared by his unit to return to service. Next weekend would be his first drill. Was he ready? Could he go back to duty?

Meg cleared her throat. "Charlie?" She had her phone pressed against the palm of her hand.

"Yeah? What's up?"

"It's Mom." Meg bit her lip, as if she were biting back the fear and dread and worry he read on her face. "She needs help."

Charlie pulled her close. He didn't need to know what was happening. All he knew was Meg needed him, and that was all that mattered.

"Then we'll help her, Meg. Whatever it is. We can face it, together."

PLEASE LEAVE A REVIEW

If you enjoyed this book, please consider leaving a review.

Reviews help bring my books to the attention of other readers who might love them, too.

Thanks!

VIP MEMBERSHIP

If you want to keep up with Meg and Charlie, consider joining my VIP club!

VIPs receive exclusive content and fun freebies.

It's free to sign up, and you can opt out any time.

Join my VIP Club today at
http://vanessarasanen.com

GLOSSARY OF ACRONYMS

AGR – Active Guard Reserve
APO – Army & Air Force Post Office
DEERS – Defense Enrollment Reporting System
DFAS – Defense Finance and Accounting Service
FOB – Forward Operating Base
FRG – Family Readiness Group
IED – Improvised Explosive Device
JAG – Judge Advocate General's Corps
LES – Leave and Earnings Statement
MOS – Military Occupational Specialty
OPSEC – Operational Security
PCS – Permanent Change of Station
PKM – General-purpose machine gun used by insurgents in Afghanistan
POA – Power of Attorney
PX – Post Exchange
QRF – Quick Reactionary Force
RPG – Rocket-Propelled Grenade

OTHER BOOKS BY VANESSA RASANEN

Hearts On Guard
Let Them Fall (coming soon)

More information available at
http://vanessarasanen.com

ACKNOWLEDGMENTS

Writing is so often a lonely pursuit. We lock the door, don headphones, drown out the world, and dive into a story all our own. We get lost in the lives of our characters—their joys and their trials.

But this dream is not achieved in a vacuum. It takes the love and support of so many, and to these folks, I offer my gratitude.

To my husband, Joel, who watched me start and stop this novel so many times over the years and encouraged me to see it through. Hon, you are my rock. Without you I would not be able to write, let alone write anything even remotely funny. Thank you for all the hours you listened to me ramble on and on. Thank you for enduring my countless questions about the military and healthcare. Thank you for believing in me and loving me more than I deserve.

To my children. When I started this book there were only two of you, and now? I can barely keep up with you four. Thank you for the hugs and the giggles and the brainstorming of ideas. You put up with my combination of mom-brain and writer-brain so well, and I hope you know how much I love you.

To Pastor Scheer and Pastor Baikie who keep us rooted in God's Word, who serve us daily, and who watch over our souls with diligence. Thanks be to God for the gift of steadfast pastors like you both. We are so blessed to have you in our lives both as our pastors and as our friends.

To my friend and fellow army wife, Janice. I don't know how many times I asked you questions about your experience, and every time you showed me grace and patience. Thank you for your insight, for your honesty, and for your husband's service.

To my amazing team of early readers. Thank you thank you thank you. Kandyce, Sara, Courtney, Mary, Elizabeth, Beth, Elisabeth, Shanna, Amanda, Sarah, Nora, Kris, Rachel, Katherine, and Jen. The feedback you provided was priceless.

To my editor, Emily, who cared about this story as much as I did and helped make it shine. Thank you for asking so many questions and helping me polish it over and over again. You are amazing.

To my designer, Suzie. You did more than just design a gorgeous cover for my book. You mentored me and answered my random questions about publishing. That certainly wasn't part of our design contract, but I'm forever grateful.

To my fellow writing friends—Holly, Noelle, Lauren, Katie, and so many more. I am thankful to be sharing this experience with such wonderful and talented writers.

To all the military families. Thank you to those who leave their families behind to serve wherever called in whatever capacity. Thank you to those on the home front who keep everything running smoothly while your loved one is gone. It is a difficult life to be sure. But you are not alone.

We are never alone.

ABOUT THE AUTHOR

Vanessa is an Army wife and a mother of four, living on little sleep and loads of coffee on the plains of Wyoming.

http://vanessarasanen.com

CPSIA information can be obtained
at www.ICGtesting.com
Printed in the USA
FSHW022124220719
60287FS